"WONDER WHAT ALTERNATIVE UNIVERSE THEY'VE SHANGHAIED US INTO THIS TIME?"

As Rod looked around, frowning, a ululating cry slashed through the air and thirty purple-skinned fur-kilted men rose up out of the tall grass a hundred yards away.

Rod and Gwen stared.

A spear arced through the air, to bury its head in the earth half a meter from Rod's feet.

Rod snapped out of his daze. "Wherever we are, we ain't welcome. Run, dear!"

Ace Science Fiction Books by Christopher Stasheff

A WIZARD IN BEDLAM

The Warlock Series

ESCAPE VELOCITY
THE WARLOCK IN SPITE OF HIMSELF
KING KOBOLD REVIVED
THE WARLOCK UNLOCKED
THE WARLOCK ENRAGED
THE WARLOCK WANDERING

THE WARLOCK IS MISSING
(*coming in September 1986*)

THE WARLOCK WANDERING

Christopher Stasheff

ACE SCIENCE FICTION BOOKS
NEW YORK

This book is an Ace Science Fiction original edition,
and has never been previously published.

THE WARLOCK WANDERING

An Ace Science Fiction Book/published by arrangement with
the author

PRINTING HISTORY
Ace Science Fiction edition/May 1986

All rights reserved.
Copyright © 1986 by Christopher Stasheff.
Cover art by Stephen Hickman.
This book may not be reproduced in whole or in part,
by mimeograph or any other means, without permission.
For information address: The Berkley Publishing Group,
200 Madison Avenue, New York, New York 10016.

ISBN: 0-441-87361-8

Ace Science Fiction Books are published by The Berkley Publishing Group,
200 Madison Avenue, New York, New York 10016.
PRINTED IN THE UNITED STATES OF AMERICA

CONTENTS

PART I
WOLMAR

"NAY, PAPA! I AM too old to need one to guide and ward me!"

Rod shook his head. "When you're fifteen, maybe—*may*be. But even then, you won't be old enough to take care of an eight-year-old little brother—nor a ten-year-old, for that matter. Not to mention a thirteen-year-old sister."

"I am ten already!" The little girl jammed her fists on her hips and glared up at him with a jutting chin.

Rod turned to her, suppressing a smile, but Gwen was already chiding gently. "Mayhap when thou art fourteen years aged, my sweet, and thy brother Magnus is sixteen, I'll dare leave the others in thy charge. Yet now . . ." She turned to Big Brother. ". . . thou art but twelve."

"'Tis a worthy age," Magnus declared. "Assuredly might I care for myself." He turned back to Rod. "Many another boy of my age doth already aid his father in plowing, and . . ."

"Other boys your age are pages, and taking squire lessons from the local knight." Rod nodded. "But in both cases, please notice the presence of an adult—and those boys *aren't* taking care of little brothers and sisters!"

"Enough of such chatter!" A foot and a half of elf stepped up beside Rod's knee, arms akimbo, frowning up at the four children. "Be still and heed me, or 'twill be much the worse for thee!"

Rod had a fleeting vision of coming home to four little frogs in nightshirts and nightcaps. The children fell silent. Glowering and truculent, but silent. Even though the smallest of them was twice Puck's size, they all knew that the elf's idea of fun could be more devastating than their parents' notion of punishment.

"Thy parents do wish to take an evening to themselves," the Puck rumbled, "to think of naught but one another's company. The coming-together that this allows them is as much to thy benefit as to theirs—and well thou knowest that they could not thus rejoice in one another's company, an they were continually concerned over what mishaps might befall thee. Yet my biding with thee will allow them assurance sufficient to ease their minds from care, for the space of an evening."

By this time, four sets of eyes were cast toward the ground. Cordelia was drawing imaginary circles with her toe. Rod didn't say anything, but he eyed the elf with renewed respect.

"Bid them good night, then," Puck commanded, "and assure them thou wilt cheerfully bide in my care till they return."

Reluctantly, and with ill grace, the children came up, one by one, for a quick peck on the cheek and a perfunctory hug, for Cordelia and Gregory, and a manly handshake, for Magnus and Geoffrey (but with a peck on the cheek for Mama).

"Go thy ways, now," Puck said to Rod and Gwen, "and concern thyselves not with the fates of thy children. I warrant their safety, though a full score of knights ride against them—for a legion of elves shall defend!"

"Not to mention that you, yourself, could easily confound a dozen." Rod bowed in acknowledgement. "I thank you, Puck."

"Bless thee, Robin." Gwen hid a smile.

Puck winced. "I prithee, lady! Be mindful of my sensibilities!"

"'Tis myself who doth bless thee," Gwen assured him. "I did not invoke any Other. Yet do I thank thee, too, Sprite."

"'Tis ever my pleasure." Puck doffed his cap with a

flourish, and bowed. "Ever, when the lady's so beauteous. Go thy ways, now, free of care—and hasten, ere the gloaming surrenders to Night!"

They followed his advice. Rod closed the door behind them, and they walked five steps down the path, counting under their breaths. Then, "Six," Rod said, and, "seven . . ."

On cue, four small faces filled the window behind them, with cries of "God e'en!" "Good night, Mama!" "Well betide thee!"

Rod grinned, and Gwen answered with a pursed smile. They waved, then turned and strode off down the path.

"We're lucky," Rod reminded her.

"Indeed." Gwen sighed. "But 'twill be pleasant to have some few hours to ourselves once more."

They wandered into the twilit forest, with his arm about her, she with a dreamy, contented smile, he just contented.

"And wither wilt thou carry me away, my lord?" she murmured.

Rod smiled down at her. "I ran into a little old lady who was trying to haul some firewood home on her back—and having very rough going, stumbling and cursing, and needing to put it down every ten feet or so. So I let her ride Fess, and I carried the wood as far as the crossroads where her son was going to meet her. She thanked me a lot and, favor for favor, took me on a short detour and showed me a little glade with a beautiful mini-pond." He heaved a sigh. "I swear I never knew there was something so pretty, so close to home—except, of course, the ones who are in it."

She looked up at him, amused; but he saw the dreaminess behind the smile, and shook a finger at her. "Now, don't you dare try to tell me it's just like the days when we were courting! We only got to know each other in the middle of a minor civil war."

"Aye; yet did I bethink me of the days thereafter."

"Right after the war, we got married."

She snuggled her head up against his chest. "'Tis what I did mind me of."

Rod stared at her for a moment. Then he smiled, and rested his cheek against her head.

Suddenly the woodland path opened out. The branches swung away, and they found themselves gazing at a perfect pool, its waters like a gem. Terraced rocks came down to its edge, festooned with flowers. Branches arched over it like a sheltering dome.

Gwen drew in a breath. "Oh, 'tis beautiful!"

Then she saw the unicorn.

It stepped out of the shadows at the edge of the pond to lower its dainty muzzle to the still water, drinking.

Rod held his breath, but even under the spell of the moment, his mind automatically registered the fact that the water must be extremely pure, if a unicorn was willing to drink it.

Then the silver beast lifted its head, to look directly at them.

Gwen gasped in wonder. Then, slowly, she moved around the pool, entranced.

Rod followed right behind her, scarcely daring to breathe.

As Gwen drew close, the unicorn stepped back. Gwen hesitated.

"Sorry, dear," Rod murmured.

"I will never regret," she answered softly. "But, my lord, there is not only wariness in those eyes—there is imploring. Could it need our aid?"

"Sought us out, you mean?" Rod frowned—then stiffened, as alarm bells went off in the back of his mind. "Gwen—even on Gramarye, unicorns don't exist..."

Gwen shook her head. "Be mindful of witch-moss, my lord. On Gramarye, aught that an old aunt may imagine the whiles she doth tell a tale, can come into being, an she be a witch unknowing."

But Rod didn't answer. He was gazing about him with every sense open, alert for the slightest thing out of place, his awareness widening to encompass the whole of the glen, the patterns of light that the sunset painted on the shrubbery, the rustling of leaves, the whisper of leather, and the slight chink of metal behind him . . .

He whirled about, sword whipping out; the pike smashed past his shoulder and into the ground. "Look out!" he cried, but even as Gwen turned, another cudgel cracked into her skull. She crumpled, and Rod howled with rage, full berserker madness. The glade about him seemed to darken with the hue of blood. He bellowed as he leaped forward, chopping with a sword that burst into flame. His opponent leaped back, eyes alight and wary, but without fear.

His buddies closed in from three sides. Rod knew there was one behind him, too, and he let a glance of his rage dart backward. Flame burst, and somebody screamed. Rod parried a blow from the center man while he glared at the thug to his left. The man slammed back against a tree and slumped to the ground, but the man to his right stepped in, and swung down hard. A crack echoed through Rod's head, filling the world with pain. Through the red mist, he felt himself swaying. He swung his arm with the movement, slashing, and the thug fell back with a howl, a red line beginning to widen across his cheek. But Rod had forgotten his back; rope hissed and burned across his neck, and yanked his feet out from under him. A soft body plummeted against him, knocking the breath out of him. Then they were dragging, bumping, over rough ground, and he realized, dazed, that the body was Gwen. He howled and slashed at the net around them, but his sword caught in the ropes. He tugged at it in fury, hearing somebody call, "We have them! Now—heave! Two meters more!"

Rod struggled frantically to get his feet under him. Whatever lay at the end of those two meters, he wasn't going to like.

Then, through the mesh, he saw it—a jury-rigged thing of telescoping legs, framing a triangular arch that showed only a blaze of sunlight, harsh on his eyes. He recognized the transdimensional gate that had taken himself and his family to the alternate universe of Tir Chlis, and he bellowed in rage and panic, channeling every ounce of it at the gadget. . . .

He was an instant too late. The net cut into his back, heaved up, and shot through, just as the contraption behind him burst into flame.

Sickened, he struggled against the ropes, got his feet under him, and surged up to stand. He thrashed the net off him, and whirled about, wild-eyed.

In every direction, as far as he could see, grassland swept away to the horizon. The air was filled with the fragrance of growth, and the sunshine enveloped him with warmth. It wasn't very far up—which was easy to tell, because the land was flat as a chessboard. He turned, staring, amazed at the silence, all the more vivid for the few faint bird-calls and the murmurings of insects. The land rolled up behind the net, up and up to a high ridge. Everywhere, everywhere was grass, waist-high.

It wasn't Gramarye.

Rod glared about him, powerless to do anything about it. They'd been very neatly caught, he and his wife. . . .

Fury transformed into horror. The ambush had been admirably planned; they'd knocked Gwen out in the first few moments. But how far out? He dropped to one knee, clawing the net away from her, cradling her head in the crook of an elbow, patting her face, caressing it, slapping very gently. "Gwen! Come to! Wake up—please! Are you there? Wake up!" He poised his mouth in front of her lips, felt for breath, and relaxed with a sigh. She was alive. Everything else was secondary—she was alive!

Belatedly, he remembered his psi powers—not surprising, since he'd only had them for a year or two. He stilled, listening closely with his mind—and heard her dream. He smiled, insinuating himself into it, asking her to wake, to speak to him—and she did.

"Nay, I am well now," she murmured. "'Twas but a moment's discomfort. . . ."

"A little more than that, I think." Gently, Rod probed the side of her head. She was still; then, suddenly, she gasped. Rod nodded. "Goose egg already—well, a robin's—but it'll *be* a goose egg."

She reached up to touch the spot tenderly, then winced. "What did hap, my lord? I mind me thou didst turn, with a war-cry . . ."

"A gang of thugs jumped us. They knocked you out on the first swing—and they had me outnumbered. Caught us up in a net, and dragged us through a dimensional gate."

She smiled. "A net? Nay, I must needs think they did find thy skill too great for them."

"Why, thank you." Rod smiled down at her. "Of course, there's also the possibility they were under orders not to kill us—and fighting is more difficult when you have to knock somebody out, but not kill him."

Gwen frowned. "Why dost thou think they abjured slaying?"

"Because they used cudgels, not pikes. But, when they couldn't take us alive, they settled for kidnapping us out of our own time and place." Rod frowned, looking around. "Which means there should be somebody around, waiting for a second try."

"Aye, my lord. If they wished us alive, they must needs have had strong reason." She gazed up at him. "What is this 'dimensional gate' of which thou didst speak? I catch, from thy mind, memories of Tir Chlis."

Rod nodded. "Same type. But how'd they know where to waylay us? That gate had to be set up ahead of time."

"The crone," Gwen murmured.

Rod smacked his forehead with the heel of his hand. "Of course! The whole thing was a setup! She didn't really need my help . . . she was a Futurian agent!"

"They knew thou wouldst not refuse to assist one in need."

Rod nodded. "So good old helpful me gave an old lady a hand, and she bit it! Told me right where to go—and set up her trap." He shook his head. "Remind me not to do anyone any favors."

"I would never wish that," Gwen said firmly. "Yet in future, let us beware of all gifts."

"Yeah—we'll open them under water." Rod looked around, frowning. "Wonder what alternate universe they've shanghaied us into *this* time?"

A ululating cry slashed through the air, and thirty purple-skinned fur-kilted men rose up out of the tall grass a hundred yards away.

Rod and Gwen stared.

A spear arced through the air, to bury its head in the earth half a meter from Rod's feet.

Rod snapped out of his daze. "Wherever we are, we ain't welcome. Run, dear!"

They whirled and charged, Gwen gathering up her skirts. "Our abductors could at the least have sent a broomstick!"

"Yes, very careless of them." But Rod chewed at the inside of his lip. "Still, maybe you had the right idea there, dear. Let's try it and see. Ready?" He slipped an arm around her. "Up we go!"

They leaped into the air. Rod put all his attention into staying up; the natives became secondary, dim and distant. They rose up a good twenty feet.

"Turn," Gwen suggested.

Rod banked, worrying about the "why" later. Until he got good at this game, he'd have to let Gwen do the steering.

She had novel ideas. They swooped back toward the natives like avenging furies.

The savages screeched to a halt, partly from surprise, mostly from alarm. Good little victims weren't supposed to attack.

"Attempt a war-cry," Gwen advised.

Rod grinned, and let out a whoop that would have shamed all the rebels in Dixie.

That was a mistake; it gave the savages something familiar. They snapped out of their shock and closed ranks in front of the flying Gallowglasses.

"Wrong tactic," Rod decided. "Hold tight." He thought *up* hard, and soared way high over the savages' heads, thoroughly out of bowshot. Then they swung down.

"Wherefore so low, my lord?" Gwen asked.

"Just in case I run out of lift."

Gwen blanched. "If we are going to strike the earth, my lord, I would prefer not to fly so swiftly."

"Don't worry, babe, I can stop on a dime. Of course, it doesn't do the dime much good. . . ."

The ground rose up beneath them. They rose with it, too, of course—and the whooping barbarians were growing smaller very quickly, behind them. Up, and over the rise—and the savages disappeared below the curve of the ridge.

"Surely they must be the half of a mile behind us, now, my lord," Gwen protested. "Will they not have given up by now?"

Rod nodded. "If you say so, darling. I just hope they were listening."

They slowed, and dropped gently to the ground. Gwen smiled as her heels touched earth. "Thou dost progress amazingly in thine use of thy powers, my lord."

"Oh, you know—just practice." But Rod felt a thoroughly irrational glow at her praise. "I must say, though, I'm surprised it didn't put more of a shock into our hunters."

"Aye." Gwen frowned. "What manner of men were they?"

"Oh—just your average barbarians."

"But—they were purple!"

"The human race is amazing in its diversity," Rod said piously. "On the other hand, you never know—the color might wash off in a good rain."

Gwen stared. "Dost'a mean they do paint themselves from head to toe?"

Rod nodded. "Not exactly unknown. In fact, if it weren't for the color, I'd guess we were on the Scottish side of

Hadrian's Wall in a country called Great Britain, about 100 A.D."

"Were there truly such?" she asked, wide-eyed.

"Sure were, dear—check any history book, if you can find one. Painted themselves blue, in fact." Rod frowned. "Of course, that theme has been pretty well pict over by now. . . ."

Clamoring howls drifted down the wind again.

Rod's head snapped up and around.

Over the ridge they came—purple, waving spears, and howling like the Eumenides.

"Time to hit the woad!" Rod caught Gwen around the waist again.

"Not so high this time, an it please thee, my lord."

"Anything to please, my dear." Rod frowned, concentrating. The scenery seemed to dim about him, and they rose just to the tops of the grain.

"Forward," Gwen murmured.

They shot straight ahead, faster than a speeding spear (just in case).

"They may not be much on technology, but they've got Terrans beat all hollow on perverse perseverance."

"'Tis even so. How long can they endure?"

Rod looked back, letting the natives' style percolate through the filters of his concentration. "Let's see—they're doing a lope, not an all-out run. . . . Hey, those guys aren't even trying! Not really."

"Scandalous. How long can they maintain such a pace?"

Rod shrugged. "As long as we can, I'd guess."

"And how long is that, my lord?"

Rod shrugged again. "I just had dinner. Six or seven hours, at least." He looked down at Gwen. "Any particular direction you wanted me to go?"

She shook her head. "All bearings are equal, when thou knowest not thy destination."

Rod nodded. "I can sympathize with that; I was young once, myself."

She glanced up at him. "Thou art not greatly anxious, my lord."

"No, not really. These guys haven't invented anti-aircraft guns yet. . . . How about you? Worried?"

"Nay." She leaned back in his arms with a peaceful sigh.

Vivid skins and violent yells erupted over the horizon in front.

Rod stared. "How'd they get around *there* so quickly?"

"Nay, 'tis a different band. These are stained yellow-green."

"Chartreuse, I think they call it—but you're right." Rod frowned. "I don't feel like attacking again. Shall we?"

Gwen nodded. "Turn, an't please thee, my lord. I have no wish to shed blood."

They banked around in a 180-degree turn—just as their previous pursuers came over the rise behind.

"Turn, and turn again." Rod veered ninety degrees. "Pilot to navigator. Setting course perpendicular to angle of pursuit. To the vector go the broils."

Gwen glanced back. "They do join forces in pursuit of us, my lord."

"Too bad." Rod scowled, "I was hoping they might take time out to fight each other."

"United they ran," Gwen sighed. "Why did we turn to the left, my lord?"

"I'm a liberal."

"Wherefore?"

"Why not? Since I don't know where I'm going . . . Say, what's that coming over the rise ahead?"

"More savages," Gwen answered.

"That's a good reason for a turn to the right." Rod veered through a U-turn. "What color of paint were these boys wearing, dear?"

"Orange, my lord."

Rod shuddered. "What a color scheme! Y' know, if any more of them show up in front of us, we're going to be boxed in."

"I prithee, do not speak of it my lord."

"Okay, I won't. I'll just get ready to climb. You *sure* you can't fly?"

Gwen shook her head. "Without a broomstick, I cannot."

"Union rules," Rod sighed.

A spear arced over his head and buried itself in the grass ten feet ahead. Rod watched it go by. "Maybe it's just as well you're next to me. With *their* marksmanship, you're better off with the target."

Gwen watched another spear arc overhead—by a good twenty feet. "I think they do not regard us highly as enemies, my lord. Certes, they cannot have sent picked troops to fight us."

"Everyone here is a Pict troop. Would you mind a little more speed, dear?"

"Certes, I would welcome it." Gwen glanced behind her. "The air is clear of spears, my lord."

"Okay, *now!*" Rod thought hard, and they shot ahead through the grass as though the ghost of Caracatus were hot on their heels. The yells diminished behind them, very quickly. But they boosted to howling level.

"Well, we're out of the trap," Rod sighed, "unless something comes up over the next rise."

They swung up and over the rise—and saw a clear, straight plane sheering across the horizon.

"A wall!" Gwen cried.

"It can't be!" Rod stared. Then he frowned. "How close can parallel universes get? Gwen, I'm taking care of the flying chores; *you* do a little mind-reading and see what language the people behind that Wall are speaking."

Gwen's eyes lost focus for a moment, then cleared. "They do speak our tongue, my lord."

Rod's frown deepened. "Odd . . . but the Roman conquerers weren't the only ones to build walls. There were the Chinese—and, come to think of it, several of the planets in the Terran Sphere, during their frontiering days . . ."

"I think I ken thy meaning. . . ."

"I'll explain it when we're not being chased. See anything resembling a gate?"

"Yonder, my lord." Gwen pointed. "Timbers."

A dark rectangle in the stone, lintel and leaves.

"Yeah, that. That's where we head for. Wonder what this place is like?"

"We shall discover that directly," Gwen murmured.

The gate zoomed up at them.

"Pretend you're running." Rod started pumping his legs like a veteran miler. Gwen gathered up her skirts and tripped merrily along beside him.

Rod dropped the flying power and dug in his heels, plowing to a stop right at the gate, and hammered on the huge oaken leaves with his fist. "Hey! Help! Open up! Let us in! 'Fear! Fire! Foes!' Especially the 'Foes' part!"

He stopped and listened. Silence, total silence—except for the howling behind them, which was showing a definite Doppler shift—the approaching kind.

Rod stepped back and scanned the top of the wall. "Something's wrong here. I don't see any sentries."

Gwen frowned, her eyes losing focus. "They are there, my lord. Yet they feel great caution."

"Why? Just because they've never seen us before, and this whole thing could be a ploy to con them into opening their front door." He cocked his head to the side. "Come to think of it, I suppose I *do* look a little like Ulysses. . . ."

"Mayhap, my lord, but canst thou not convince them of our honesty?"

"How about the direct approach?" Rod wound up a leg and slammed a kick at the middle of the doors. "Hey! We're being chased by wild Indians! Open up in there! Let the cavalry out!"

"Cease your pounding, you panicking prat!" bellowed a voice overhead.

Rod stepped back and looked up.

A scowling, fleshy man in a loose shirt, with an unshaven jaw, and a surly hangover glowered down at them. He pressed a hand to his head. "There, that's better. You were splitting me head open." And he disappeared again. "Good idea!" Rod yelled. "Come back here and let us in—or I *will* split it open, and not just by yelling!"

"You'll have to wait till we finish the hand," the voice growled faintly from above. Several other voices snarled agreement.

"But . . . but . . . but . . ." Rod gave up and turned his attention to his wife. "What kind of an outfit *is* this?"

"We are accompanied, my lord," Gwen murmured.

Rod whirled and looked behind him.

A long line of multi-colored men was drawn up at the skyline, leaning on their spears, watching.

With a gnashing groan, the gate opened. The man who had spoken from the wall above stood in the opening, grinning. "Full house," he announced."My pot."

"It's considerable." Rod eyed the man's midriff. He looked on up to a rum-blossom nose beside a livid scar, topped with a black thatch. The shirt was white, or had been. The belt underscored the midriff, holding up green uniform pants which were tucked into black boots (in crying need of a shine).

"Well," he growled, "don't just stand there gawking. Come in, if your need's so frantic."

"Oh, yes." Rod shut his mouth and stepped through the gateway, his arm carefully around Gwen.

The slob's eyes lit at the sight of her, but he waved a hand in signal to someone on top of the wall anyway. The gate started to swing shut, and the man waved at the savages just before it closed. A great oaken bar, about of a size to fit the huge iron brackets on the inside of the gate, lay on the ground nearby, but the slob ignored it. He turned back toward them, and caught sight of Gwen again. Interest gleamed feebly through the hangover, and he looked her up and down. Gwen flushed, and glared at him.

Rod cleared his throat loudly.

The slob looked up at him and saw the glare. The hangover struggled with lust, and lost. The slob grumbled, by way of a face-saver, "Where'd you get the fancy clothes?"

"Where'd you get the booze?" Rod countered.

Caution flickered in the man's eyes, and they turned opaque.

"Well, ye're in," he grunted, and turned away.

Rod stared. "Hey, wait a minute!"

The slob stopped, threw a despairing glance to the heavens, and turned back. "What now?"

"Where are we supposed to go?"

"Wherever you want to," the slob grunted, turning away.

Rod stood a moment, gaping.

He shrugged and turned back to Gwen. "Might as well follow him, I suppose."

"We might, indeed," she agreed, and they turned to climb the long, sloping ramp that led to the ramparts.

As he climbed the ramp, he noticed that it was poured plasticrete. So was the Wall. Weathered, and buttressed with props here and there, but plasticrete nonetheless. "Well, so much for the Romans," he muttered.

"My lord?"

"This stuff is plasticrete," he explained. "It wasn't even invented until about 2040 A.D. So we can't be in Roman Britain—that was a good sixteen hundred years earlier."

"I have no knowledge of this." Gwen frowned. "'Tis for thee to say. In what world would we be, then?"

Rod rubbed his chin, looking around him. "We might—just might—be in our own universe, Gwen. No, not Gramarye, of course—another world, circling another sun." He looked down at her. "It couldn't be Terra, of course."

"What is 'Terra'?"

For a moment, Rod was galvanized. That a Terran human should not even know the name of the planet that gave birth to her species . . . ! But he caught himself, remembering that Gramarye had never exactly been strong on history. In fact, its inhabitants didn't even know there were any worlds other than their own.

"Terra is the world your ancestors came from, dear—the planet that all human beings ultimately came from. It's the home world of our kind."

Gwen was silent for a moment, digesting that.

As she did, they came out onto the top of the Wall. The ramparts stretched away before them, dwindling into the distance, a concrete channel cutting four feet down into the plasticrete.

A group of men knelt and squatted around a fire near the top of the ramp. Like the slob, they wore white shirts, green trousers, and black boots—but most of them had green jackets, too, fastened up to the throat. Their sleeves held insignia—or patches of lighter color, where the emblems had been. *Uniforms,* Rod realized, and right after that, *They're soldiers!*

Gwen's eyes widened; she was listening to his thoughts.

They didn't seem to be very well-disciplined soldiers, though. Either that, or there wasn't any war going at the moment. Rod heard the rustle of cards and the click of chips.

The soldiers looked up, saw Gwen, and looked harder.

She smiled, politely but firmly.

Something like a hungry purr arose from the soldiers. The nearest, a sergeant, rose to his feet. He straightened up to eight inches taller than Rod, and about four inches wider, three-quarters muscle, the rest fat. He had an ugly face and a leering grin, and a possessive manner as he stepped towards Gwen.

Rod raised a hand, palm out. It jarred against the man's chest, jolting him to a stop. He looked down at Rod's arm in surprise. He pushed against it tentatively a few times, then said in disbelief, "It holds!" He gave Rod a nod of approval. "You're well enough muscled for such a small fellow, ain't you?"

"Why, thank you." Irony in Rod's smile. "Now, just step back to the game, why don't you?"

The other soldiers watched, buzzard-eyed.

The sergeant grinned wickedly and shook his head."Bear ye not too rawly, lad." He took in Rod's doublet and hose. "A juggler, belike, or a clown. Well, learn then, lad, that women be property common on the Wall."

He turned away to Gwen, batting Rod's arm out of the way.

It didn't bat.

Rod tightened his hold on the man's jacket. "Now, just go on back to the game, Sergeant. Be a good fellow."

"Poor manners for a guest," the slob growled from the sidelines.

"Poorer manners for a host," Rod retorted, "trying to rape a guest's . . ."

"Rape??!!?" The big soldier stared.

He threw back his head, roaring laughter, then doubled over, clutching his belly. "A woman on the Wall, needing rape!"

"They couldn't," the slob explained. "They come, oh, quite willingly, yes."

Rod lifted and shoved; the big soldier staggered back a few steps, still laughing. Rod stepped back, too, relaxing into a crouch. "This one," he said grimly, "doesn't."

The soldier quit laughing abruptly, and sobered into a narrow-eyed glare.

"Teach him manners, Thaler," the slob growled.

My lord, Gwen's thoughts said in Rod's head, *there are loose stones on the ground nearby. I might . . .*

No! Rod thought back. *You want to start a witch-hunt? The natives could handle seeing us fly—their culture still believes in magic. But these boys are civilized! They have to kill things they don't understand!* Aloud, he said, "You can pick up the pieces with the first-aid kit."

Thaler's eyes crinkled with amusement. He laughed once, twice, chuckled, roared laughter, and fell to the ground, doubled over, clutching his belly, howling mirth . . .

. . . and shot up like a spring, still laughing, his head crashing up under Rod's jaw.

Rod fell back against the ramparts.

Thaler waded in, fists hammering.

Rod swiveled his head around under the man's fists and dived to the side, flipping over onto his back.

Thaler snarled, and came after him.

Rod shoved hard, his whole body lashing out in a kick that should have caught Thaler under the jaw, heel to chin.

But Thaler ducked under the blow, then leaned back, lashing out with the side of his foot at Rod's chin. Rod sidestepped, hooked his heel behind Thaler's calf, jerked, and saw the edge of Thaler's hand swinging straight at the bridge of his nose.

Rod managed to duck enough for the chop to crack across his forehead instead, and went reeling back stunned, not only by the blow, but also by a horrifying realization: Thaler's chop was the first half of a two-blow series that ended in:

Death.

They really didn't like strangers here.

Thaler's hand slammed down again, in a chop that would have crushed Rod's larynx; but he rolled to the side at the last second, and Thaler's hand cracked into the plasticrete. He howled with pain, and Rod rolled up into a crouch, punching at the solar plexus with stiffened fingers. But Thaler saw the blow coming, and rolled back just enough to take most of the impact out of it. What was left was enough to stiffen him with agony for a moment—and the moment was all Rod needed.

He followed the punch with a series of quick blows that Thaler just barely managed to block, retreating as quickly as he could. Rod got just a touch too confident, let his right foot lead just a little too far—and Thaler's knee snaked around Rod's, and a fist the size of a corned-beef brisket slammed into Rod's ear.

The sky reeled, and the plasticrete struck under him, hard; but he tucked his chin in, and his head didn't hit *too* hard.

As the world circled past, he noticed the sole of Thaler's boot coming down. He grabbed the foot, twisted, and threw. Thaler hopped back, howling and flailing for balance.

Rod gathered himself into a ball, rolled to his feet, and saw the same damn foot coming at his face again.

Now, Thaler didn't look as though he were apt to win any IQ prizes, but he did look very experienced—so he couldn't be dumb enough to try the same trick a second time, when it hadn't worked once already. So Rod caught at the foot, but stayed alert for a trick—and sure enough, there came the fist, swinging down at the back of Rod's neck.

Rod let go of the foot, took a half step forward, and straightened up hard, both fists over his head.

They caught Thaler right under the jaw.

Thaler swayed, glassy-eyed.

Rod stepped back and swung a haymaker uppercut.

Thaler's head snapped back, and his feet snapped up, and his whole body slammed down flat on the plasticrete.

Rod stood, panting, a little wild-eyed, looking around him, woozy, head splitting with pain, but alert for anyone else to start swinging.

But they stayed where they sat, glowering up at Gwen, and nursing their jaws.

Rod looked up at her, incredulous.

Gwen glared about her in indignation. *They have no sense of honor, my lord! They would seek to molest me whiles thou didst defend me!*

In spite of his aches, Rod couldn't help grinning. He pitied any man who had tried to lay a hand on his sweet wife. "What did you do to them?"

"Only a slap for each, my lord."

A slap with its force multiplied by telekinesis, Rod guessed. He was surprised none of the men were heading for the hospital.

"Most excellently done," said a cool, amused voice.

Rod looked up, startled.

A tall, slender young man leaned against the outer wall. His uniform was crisply pressed, and he wore a cap with a polished black visor. His sleeves were bare of insignia, but his shoulder boards were decorated with tiny brass razors.

Obviously an officer.

He turned his head, inclining it toward the slob. "Sergeant."

"Sir." Incredibly, the slob came to attention.

"You are out of uniform, and what you do have is more fatigued than fatigues. And your personal grooming doesn't exist."

"Yes, sir." Then, defiantly, "At least I'm here."

"Indeed you are—so you've only a dozen demerits, not fifty."

The slob winced. "Sir! That's me whole next paycheck!"

"Are you paid so little? My, my. But courage, old chap—a little extra spit and polish can win it back for you, over the next few months." He turned away, and stepped up to nudge Thaler with a boot-toe and a smile. "Poor chap. But what can you expect, really?"

At last, the officer turned to Rod. "You're really quite skilled, you know."

Rod shrugged. "Just a little special training. Your, ah, discipline, is rather, shall we say, remarkable."

The officer shrugged. "It's actually not bad at all, when you consider that our Wolmar was a prison planet, up 'til nine years ago. Nearly everyone here is a convict of one sort or another."

Rod stood stiff with shock, partly at discovering all these soldiers were criminals, and partly from the name of the planet. He didn't know that much about it, but he remembered it from his history books. After all, he was an agent for the Society for the Conversion of Extra-Terrestrial Nascent Totalitarianisms, and before they'd sent him out searching for Terran-colonized planets whose governments were shaping up to become totalitarian, they'd told him a little about all the colonies that had been out of touch while PEST ruled the Terran Sphere. Wolmar had been one of them—one of the furthest from Terra. And it had stayed a prison until PEST cut it off from contact, and supply.

Which meant they were in their own universe, after all, but five hundred years before either of them had been born.

Gwen had been listening to his thoughts, of course. She stepped closer to him, clinging to his arm. He was glad; he needed the contact. Suddenly, their cozy little cottage seemed much, much farther away, and the wind of loneliness blew about their souls.

Thaler rolled over with a groan, opening his eyes to a painful squint. The officer looked down at him, shaking his head and clucking his tongue. "Intolerable, sergeant! Two unarmed civilians, seeking our protection—and what do their rescuers do? Attack them!"

Thaler sat up with a groan. "He wasn't unarmed, Lieutenant."

The lieutenant glanced at Rod's sword and rolled his eyes up. "That oversized toothpick? Don't be ridiculous, man! Report to your quarters until your hearing!"

Thaler blanched, but he managed to keep looking belligerent as he struggled to his feet and turned to go. As he passed by, he gave Rod a quick glare of hatred. Rod watched his retreating back, deciding that he always wanted to know when Thaler was around.

He turned back to the lieutenant, relaxing a little. Thaler's resentment was what he'd have expected from any sergeant talking to a fuzz-cheeked lieutenant—but this lieutenant wasn't extremely young anymore, and he bore himself with the self-confidence that can only come with experience. There was something about him, the way he held himself, that said he didn't need to rely on military rank to enforce his orders.

"My apologies, Sir and Madam." He bowed courteously to Rod, and a bit more courteously to Gwen. "I beg you to pardon that outburst. Please be assured of your welcome, regardless of what you have witnessed here."

"Why, thank you." Rod inclined his head in return, wondering why the lieutenant hadn't stopped the fight. Maybe because it didn't look as though anyone was apt to be killed.

"Thou art most considerate." Gwen dropped a small curtsy.

The lieutenant's eye held a gleam, but he buried it quickly. Rod gave him points for self-discipline—and wondered if it was really from self. "May I have your names, sir and madam?"

"Rodney Gallowglass." He was tempted to use his real name, "d'Armand," but decided against it. He caught Gwen's hand. "And this is my wife, Gwendylon."

Gwen looked up at him in surprise, and he heard her unspoken thought: *Wherefore didst thou not use thy title?*

Other countries, other customs, he answered silently. *People like this are as likely to resent a lord as to honor him.*

"Lieutenant Corrigan, at your service." The young officer clicked his heels and bobbed his head. "Now, Citizen Gallowglass, I would appreciate your explaining to me the presence of our honored antagonists." He nodded toward the outside of the main gate. Rod looked down, and saw a crowd of Wolmen, chanting the same word over and over again. With a shock, Rod realized it was, "Justice! Justice! Justice! Justice!"

"Not that they're unwelcome, you understand," Stuart explained, "but I would like to know the issue I'm going to be discussing."

"I'm afraid I don't really know," Rod confessed. "We were just standing there in the middle of the plain, minding our own business, when they came up over the ridge and started chasing us."

"Ah." The Lieutenant nodded. "A simple question of remuneration, no doubt. If you'll excuse me, I'll go discuss the issue with them." He bowed slightly with a click of the heels, and turned away.

Gwen's voice sounded in Rod's mind: *Is he noble, then?*

No, Rod answered. *I don't think anyone here is. But*

someone has to do the jobs that the lords would do, if they were here—and he's been given that kind of authority. About as much as a knight.

By what right did he claim it?

Training, Rod answered, *knowledge and intelligence. Sometimes even experience.*

The great gates swung open, and the young officer stepped out to confront the wild savages.

He crossed both arms, fingertips touching his shoulders, and bowed slightly. One of the yellow-green men stepped forward, and returned the gesture.

"I think it's a salute," Rod muttered.

The lieutenant's words carried clearly. "I greet you, Scouting-Master."

The Scouting-Master returned the salute. "Have-um sun-filled day, Lieutenant."

"The sentiments are appreciated." The lieutenant's voice switched into crispness. "But though I am honored by your presence, I also wonder at it. For how long have noble warriors been attacking civilians?"

"Them not so civil. Them flew!"

"As I would, if I saw your valiant warriors pursuing me. Why did they?"

The Scouting-Master grinned, and his warriors chuckled. "Not for real. Just good fun."

"Fun!" Gwen gasped.

"Well, be fair." Rod shrugged. "It was, kinda, wasn't it?"

"Indeed?" The lieutenant's voice had become distinctly chilly.

The Scouting-Master's grin widened. "We could see-um was couple greenhorns. Why not have good time with-um?"

The lieutenant gave a wintry smile. "No harm intended, eh?"

"None." The Scouting-Master frowned. "But them have no business outside Wall! Them not traders!"

"A point well-taken, I must admit. Still, I cannot help

but think your mode of contact was something less than honorable."

The natives scowled, muttering to one another, but the Scouting-Master only shrugged. "Could've done much worse, within-um rights. Could Shacklar gainsay?"

The lieutenant was silent a moment, then heaved a sigh. "The General-Governor would say that no lasting harm was done, so no hard feelings should last."

Rod frowned. 'General-Governor?' Didn't they have that the wrong way around?

"Even so." The Scouting-Master's forefinger stabbed upward, and his smile vanished. "Agreements hold. Me file-um complaint—formal! For trespassing!"

The lieutenant stood still for a moment, then sighed, pulled out a pad and began writing. "If you must. However, these two are civilians. That will necessitate a meeting with the General-Governor."

"Sound great." The Scouting-Master grinned. "Him always serve good coffee." He turned to his warriors, making shooing motions. "Go patrol again!"

"Boring," one of the warriors grumbled.

"Want-um soldiers stamp-um all over planet?" the Scouting-Master snapped. "Besides—good for-um! Build-um character!"

The warrior sighed, and the troops turned away. The Scouting-Master turned back, a grin spreading over his face again. "We go see Shacklar now, hm?"

The lieutenant ushered them into a thirty-by-thirty office with large windows (outside, Rod had noticed steel shutters), a desk at one end, and several padded armchairs at the other. All the furniture had a rough-and-ready look about it, as though it had been built out of local materials by an amateur carpenter. But it was made out of real wood. Rod thought that implied status, until he remembered that wood was cheaper than plastic on a frontier world. The floor was polished wood, too, most of it covered by a plaid carpet, woven of orange, purple, chartreuse, and magenta fibers. Rod winced.

The man who sat behind the desk seemed out of place. He was in full uniform, bent over paperwork, but was surprisingly young to be top kick; he couldn't have been much more than forty. He was lean, lanky, brown-haired, and the face that looked up at them as they came in was mild and quizzical, with a gentle smile. There was some indefinable air of sophistication about him, though, that made him seem incongruous with his rough surroundings.

He is a lord, Gwen thought.

She just might be right, Rod realized. Maybe a younger son of a younger son?

"General Shacklar," the lieutenant informed them, "the Governor."

Well. That explained the inverted title.

The General rose with a smile of welcome, and came around his desk toward them. The lieutenant snapped to attention and saluted. The General returned his salute and stopped in front of the native, crossing his arms and bowing. "May your day be sun-filled, Scouting-Master."

"And yours," the native grinned. "Coffee?"

"Of course! Lieutenant, will you serve, please?" But, as the young officer turned away, the General stopped him with an upheld palm. "A moment—introductions?"

"Certainly, sir." The lieutenant turned back to them. "Master Rod Gallowglass and his lady, Gwendylon."

"Charmed." The General took Gwen's hand and bowed. She smiled, pleased.

The lieutenant stepped away toward the coffeepot.

"I don't remember your arrival." The General gave Rod a keen glance.

Rod had a notion this man knew every single person who arrived on his planet—especially if he was, well, basically, warden. Of a planet-wide prison. And Rod and Gwen weren't exactly inconspicuous. "We were, uh, stranded, General. Landed out in the middle of the plains. No way to get back home."

Shacklar frowned. "I don't recall any report of a distress signal."

"We couldn't transmit." So far, Rod hadn't really told any lies. He hoped it would last.

It did. Shacklar gave him the keen glance again; he was definitely aware of the holes in the explanation; but he wasn't about to push them. "My sympathies. Just this morning, was it?"

"Soon after dawn," Gwen explained. "We had scarcely collected ourselves when these . . ."

She hesitated, and Shacklar supplied, "Wolmen. That's what they call themselves. Their ancestors were counterculture romantics, who fled Terra to live the life of the Noble Savage. They invented their own version of aboriginal culture, based largely on novels and screenplays."

Well. That explained some of the more bizarre aspects.

"I take it they discovered you almost immediately, and began to chase you?"

"Aye. We did fly from them."

Rod stiffened. Did she have to be so literal?

Yes, she did, now that he thought of it. When the Wolman talked about them flying, now, Schacklar would assume he was speaking metaphorically. Very clever, his lady. He glowed with pride.

Fortunately, the General didn't notice. He shook his head sadly. "Most unfortunate! My deepest regrets. But really, you see, by the terms of our agreement with the Wolmen, no colonist is supposed to be outside the Wall unless he's on official or commercial business, so you can understand why they would react in so precipitous a manner. And, truly, they did no harm—only enforced their rights under our treaty."

"Aye, that is easily understood." Gwen shrugged. "I cannot truly blame them."

"Most excellent." Shacklar beamed. "Now, if you'll excuse me, I must hear what the Scouting-Master wishes to say."

He turned away. Gwen turned to Rod, speaking softly. "Doth he say that these people but play at being savages, my lord?"

"No—but their ancestors did, so now they're stuck with it. But I get the feeling there was a real war when the Terran government decided to use this planet for a prison. Apparently they didn't consult the Wolmen first—and they resented it. Forcibly." He shrugged. "Can you blame them?"

The General had turned now, facing them again. "The Scouting-Master understands your predicament, but nonetheless charges you with trespassing." He sighed. "Actually, he's shown a considerable amount of forbearance in this matter. He could have taken any number of more or less lethal measures against you, rather than merely herding you to the Wall, as he did."

Herding?

Gwen, did you know we were being herded?

Nay—yet now, I can see it clearly enough.

The General frowned, concerned. "What's the matter, old man? Hadn't you guessed you were being driven?"

"As a matter of fact, I hadn't." Rod found himself smiling back in spite of himself. "Uh, ah—General, please convey my apologies and great thanks to the Scouting-Master."

"Oh, you may convey them yourself, in just a moment! But, ah—" Shacklar looked down at the carpet, rubbing the tip of his nose with a forefinger. "I wouldn't truly recommend it. A simple apology and expression of thanks—no, the Scouting-Master would take it as a sign of weakness."

"Oh." Rod pursed his lips. "I see. Exactly what form should the apology take?"

"Precisely, Master Gallowglass." The General smiled warmly. "It's always a pleasure to deal with a man who understands the true nature of diplomacy!"

"Does he want his diplomacy in gold, or Terran bills?"

"Gold would be pleasant, but I'm sure I.D.E. kwaher bills will suffice." The General smiled sadly. "However, I'm afraid P.E.S.T. bills would not be acceptable; the Wolmen don't have much faith in them."

"I understand." Rod smiled. "Primitive cultures tend to be conservative."

"Indeed." The keen glance again. "Well! In this case, the apology should consist of, ah . . ." Shacklar slipped a small leather-bound pad out of his pocket and flipped it open. ". . . five hundred kwahers."

Rod stared. "Five . . . hundred . . ."

Is the amount so great, my lord?

Not unless you don't have it. How are you at turning lead into gold, dear?

A sudden, faraway look came into Gwen's eyes.

The General was watching them carefully, but with his gentle smile. "I take it you find yourselves temporarily embarrassed?" The General smiled. "We can certainly arrange a temporary, interest-free loan, Master Gallowglass. There is a Bank of Wolmar, and it's solvent at the moment."

"Oh, no! Money's never a problem with us. Uh—*is* it, Gwen?" Rod reached into the purse that hung at his belt. It held only a few Gramarye coins. The silver in them would be perfectly negotiable, but it might be a little difficult to explain Tuan's and Catharine's portraits.

"Nay, money was never our care," Gwen agreed, giving him a sidelong glance. "Indeed, it hath been so long since I have seen it, that I *quite forget the look of it!*"

Rod froze.

He swallowed, hugely. Of course, Gwen couldn't know what I.D.E. bills looked like; she had never seen any money but Gramarye's.

Come to think of it, Rod didn't know what they looked like, either. The I.D.E. government had fallen five hundred years before he was born. "On second thought, General, I think I will take you up on that offer. Could you let me have, say, a twenty-kwaher bill for, oh, about two minutes?"

The General frowned, but reached for his wallet. "At least the interest won't be prohibitive." He passed Rod the bill.

"Thanks very." Rod handed it to Gwen. "Yes, money. That's money, dear."

Gwen stared, thunderstruck. *"Paper,* my lord? *This* is money?"

"Uh, *yes,* dear." Gwen had never seen anything but coins, of course, medieval cultures having a rather elemental view of economics. "That's money. Here, anyway." Rod forced a grin. "Uh, sorry, General. We're not used to, ah, using cash, you know how it is."

"Credit cards." The General nodded with understanding. Rod would've hated to shatter his illusions.

"Now, I just had some, right here." Rod fumbled in the purse again; it was still mostly empty.

"My lord," Gwen murmured, "I cannot . . ."

"That's okay, dear, just try." Rod patted her hand. "Never know just how much you can do, until you give it a try . . . I *know* . . . I had . . ." Rod dug in the purse as though it were a ten-mile pit, a bead of cold sweat trickling down his brow.

Something rustled.

His fingers touched paper. Lots of paper.

He drew it out slowly, with a grin of relief. "There we are, General, twenty-five twenty-kwaher bills." He plucked the original from Gwen's numbed fingers. "Oh, and the one you loaned us, of course."

The General's eyes widened slightly, but he accepted the cash without comment.

"I don't like to carry large denominations," Rod explained.

"But I thought you said . . ." Shacklar clamped his lips shut. "No, really. Not my affair at all . . ." He gave Rod the keen glance again. "Don't you find it troublesome to carry so many bills about?"

"Well, yes," Rod admitted, "but there wasn't time to have them changed."

The General squared the bills into a neat stack. "I take it you left home in a bit of a hurry."

"You might say that, yes."

The General turned to step over to the lieutenant and the Scouting-Master, who broke out in an ear-to-ear grin and hurried over to seize Rod's hand, pumping it. "Glad you one of the good guys!"

"Oh, my pleasure," Rod murmured. "Thanks for understanding."

"Sure, sure! Come outside Wall again, anytime!" The Scouting-Master crossed his arms and bowed, then turned away to the door the lieutenant was holding, licking his thumb and counting the bills. "Nice chasing you!"

"Anytime." Rod waved, feeling slightly numb.

The lieutenant closed the door behind him with relief.

Rod turned back to the General, shaking his head. "Funny how underdeveloped societies always learn the same aspect of our culture first, isn't it?"

"Quite." The General turned away, going back to his desk. "Well! At least *that's* done!"

"Yeah. Nice to have it over with, isn't it?" Rod grabbed Gwen's arm and made for the door. "Thanks for straightening things out for us, General. If there's anything we can ever do for you . . ."

"As a matter of fact," Shacklar murmured, "you *could* answer a few questions. . . ."

Rod's body jerked as his feet stopped and his shoulders tried to keep going. He glared at Gwen.

"We must observe the rules of courtesy, my lord."

"Next time just stop me with a word, okay?" Rod turned back. "Why, sure, General. What kind of questions did you have in mind?"

The General's mouth was pinched at the corners with hidden amusement.

Rod frowned, noticing something he'd missed before. He stepped up to the General's desk, peering at Shacklar's corps insignia. It was the staff of Aesculapius. "You're a doctor!"

"Psychiatrist, actually." The General smiled. "Surely that is an appropriate profession for the chief administrative officer of a former correctional colony?"

"Uh . . . yeah, I guess it is." Rod frowned. "I just wasn't expecting anything so logical."

"I'm not certain it was, in its genesis." Shacklar's smile hardened. "But I do think it's worked out for the best. I've quite a sense of purpose here."

"Yeah, I can see that you would have." Rod straightened, clearing his throat. "Well! About those questions, General . . ."

"Yes, indeed. Would you mind telling me how you came to be shipwrecked on Wolmar?"

"No, not at all." *If I can think of it.*

Shacklar looked up over steepled fingers. "Touch of amnesia?"

"Oh, no, no," Rod said quickly. "Not amnesia, really; it's just that, uh . . ." He took a deep breath and began improvising at top speed. "Uh, I know this is going to sound strange, but, uh . . . we were on our way to a costume ball, aboard a passenger liner from, uh . . ." He tried to remember a ship that had disappeared without a trace, about the end of the I.D.E. era. He could only think of the most famous one, and cursed mentally, then followed it with a quick thought-apology to Gwen. "We were on the, uh, *Alfreda,* outbound from Fido—you know, Beta Canis Minor's fourth planet—on our way to Tuonela, the fifth planet of 61 Cygni . . ."

"But you never attained your destination?"

Rod nodded. After all, the *Alfreda* had left Fido with a remarkable number of famous people aboard, but had never been heard from again. That gave Rod scope for considerable poetic license. "We felt this huge lurch—horrible, I wound up with caviar all over my doublet—and the crew started hollering for all of us to get into suspended-animation pods, and aimed us at random, hoping we'd strike Terran-colonized planets sooner or later."

"Which, fortunately, you did." Shacklar pulled out a pipe and clasped it high on the stem, hiding his mouth; but the corners of his eyes crinkled.

"So here we are," Rod finished. "Our pod landed out in the Wolmen's territory, and . . . uh . . . you . . . don't . . . *believe* me . . ."

"No, I didn't say that at all." The General leaned forward to prop his elbows on his desk.

"But it's the best entertainment you've had all week?"

"All year, in fact." Shacklar smiled warmly. "They don't have tales like that on the 3DT any more."

"Well, if you doubt my word, you can check the records. The *Alfreda* did disappear en route from Beta Canis Minor to 61 Cygni . . ."

"Yes, I remember the incident well; there were so many politicians aboard that it was quite a scandal." Shacklar gave him an amiable smile. "That much, at least, is quite true, I'm certain. As to the rest of it, though . . . Ah, well, I'm not one to press, Master Gallowglass. We rather make a policy of not being too insistent about a man's past, on Wolmar. However, I do appreciate the finer aspects of narrative creativity. I was especially impressed with the piece about the costume ball."

"Oh, yes! She's supposed to be Nell Gwynn, and I'm, uh—Cyrano de Bergerac!"

"And I'm the King of England," Shacklar murmured, fighting a smile. "But as I say, a man's past is his own affair, on Wolmar. No one is here without a reason, and it's generally one that he'd rather weren't known." He shrugged. "Of course, in my own instance, I'm not terribly concerned about secrecy. Ultimately, I'm here because, in addition to being a psychiatrist, I'm also a masochist."

Rod stared, then caught himself. "Oh, really?"

"Yes." Shacklar smiled. "Quite well-adjusted—but it does

create certain problems within the chain of command. Here, though, my men don't seem to care terribly."

Rod nodded, slowly. "I begin to understand why you don't mind staying."

"There *is* some feeling of being appreciated." Shacklar smiled brightly. "But the mild exhibitionism involved in telling you that is part of my disorder, you see. I certainly don't ask that of anyone else."

He leaned forward to glance at his desk readout. "However, I'm keeping you overlong; after so great a time in suspended animation, you must be ravenous. You'll find an excellent tavern just down the street."

"Uh . . . thanks, General." Rod managed a smile. "You've been very helpful."

He turned away to the door, holding it open for Gwen. "If there's anything we can ever do for you, just give us a yell."

"As a matter of fact, there *is* one small thing your lady could do for me, Master Gallowglass."

Rod stopped in mid-stride, a sinking feeling in his belly.

He turned around again. Gwen turned with him, wide-eyed. "And how may I aid you, sir?"

"Slap me," said the General.

Rod set down a small tray, and laid a plate of boiled sausage and buns in front of Gwen, with a tankard of ale to flank it. "Not much, my dear, but I'm afraid that's about the best Cholly's Tavern runs to." He sat down and took a sip of his beer. His eyes widened in surprise. "Not bad, though."

She sipped, carefully. "Indeed, 'tis not! Yet wherefore is't so chill, my lord?"

"Huh?" Rod looked up, surprised. "Oh, uh—they just like it that way, honey. That's all." He leaned back and looked about him, at the unfinished boards and the rough-and-ready chairs and tables. "Sure not what I was planning on when I took you out for an evening alone."

Gwen smiled. "Nay, assuredly 'tis not! Yet—oh, my lord! 'Tis all so new, and marvelous!"

"It is?"

"Indeed." She leaned over the table. "Yet tell me—what mean all these strange manners and artifacts? Why do all wear leggings, even though they have no armor to cover them? What were those odd, bulbous engines each man did wear at his hip, upon the Wall? And wherefore do they not wear them in this place? How do the lights within this inn come to glow? And where are the kegs from which they draw their ale?"

Rod held up a hand. "Hold it, dear. One at a time." He hadn't realized how strange and new the technological world would seem to Gwen—but she did come from a medieval culture, after all. Secretly, he blessed the fate that had brought them to a frontier planet, instead of one of the overly-civilized, total-technology worlds nearer Terra.

How to explain it all to her? He took a deep breath, wondering where to start. "Let's begin with power."

"There's naught so new in that." She shrugged. "Once thou hadst told me there were no nobles, it was truly clear the peasant folk must needs set up orders within their own ranks, even as those Wolmen, who did chase us this morn, have done. Or the wild folk, who do war upon the cities—even as the Beastmen did to our Isle of Gramarye, ten years agone."

The time-lapse hit Rod like a shockwave. "My lord! Was it really ten *years* ago?" He took a shuddering breath. "But of course. We only had one child then, and we have four now—and Magnus is twelve." He studied her face intently. "You don't look any older."

She blushed, lowering her eyes. "'Tis good of thee to say it, my lord—yet I do see the wrinkles, here and there, and the odd strand of gray in mine hair."

"What's odd about it, with *our* four? But they certainly must be rare; I haven't noticed one yet! And as to wrinkles, I've always had my share of those."

"Yet thou art not a woman," Gwen murmured.

"So sweet of you to notice . . . But back to the ins and outs of this world we're on. Government wasn't exactly the kind of 'power' I'd had in mind, dear."

"Indeed?" She looked up, surprised. "Yet assuredly thou didst not speak of magicks!"

"No, no. Definitely not. I was talking about force—the kind that makes things move."

Gwen frowned, not understanding.

Rod took a deep breath. "Look. In Gramarye, there are four kinds of power that can do work for us: muscles, our own or our animals'; wind, which pushes ships and turns windmills; water power, which turns mill wheels; and fire, which heats our houses, boils our water, and cooks our food. And that's about all."

Gwen frowned. "But what of the power of a crossbow, that speeds a bolt to slay a man?"

Rod shook his head. "Just muscle power, stored. When a crossbowman pulls a bowstring, see, he's just transferring power from his arm and shoulder into the springy wood of the bow. But the crossbowman takes several minutes to put that power in, by winding the bowstring back. Then, when he pulls the trigger that releases the string, all that energy is released in one quick burst—and that's what throws the arrow so much harder than an ordinary bow can."

Gwen nodded slowly, following every word. "And 'tis thus, too, that a common archer's bow can throw an arrow so much farther than a man-at-arms can hurl a spear?"

"Why, yes." Rod sat up straighter, surprised at how quickly she had understood. "Of course, the arrow's lighter than the spear, too. That helps."

Gwen frowned. "And 'tis also that the ends of the bow are longer than the spearman's arms, is't not? For I do note that the longer the bow, the farther it doth hurl the arrow."

"Why . . . yes," Rod said, startled. "The longer the lever, the more it multiplies the force—and the two ends of a bow, and a spearman's arm, are all levers."

"And the longer bow can therefore be stiffer, but can still be bent?"

"Uh . . . yeah." Rod felt a faint chill along his back. She was understanding *too* quickly. "And the crossbow is more powerful, because it's so much stiffer."

"But the man who doth shoot it, can bend it by winding." Gwen nodded, seeming almost angry in the intensity of her concentration.

"Right." Rod swallowed heavily. "Well. Uh . . . in this world, there're other sources of power—but the most important one is the kind called 'electricity.' It's like . . ." He groped, trying to find an explanation. "It's invisible, but it flows like water. Only through metals, though. It's . . ." Then inspiration struck. "It's like the force you wield when you make things move with your mind." He waved a hand. "Even though you can't see it, you can feel it, if you touch the wire it's flowing through. Boy, can you feel it!" He frowned. "Though I shouldn't say you can't see it, really. Have you ever looked at a lightning bolt, darling? No, of course you have! What's the matter with me?" He could remember one occasion especially vividly—they had huddled inside a cave, watching the lightning slam the thunder about the skies. And when the storm's fury had thoroughly dazzled them . . . He cleared his throat. "Lightning's electricity—one kind of electricity, anyway."

"Thou dost not say it," she breathed, wide-eyed. "Have these people chained the lightning, then?"

Rod nodded, thrilled (and chilled) by her quickness. "They've figured out how to make it do all sorts of tricks, darling."

Her eyes were huge. "This glow, then, is lightning leashed?"

"That's one way to look at it." Rod nodded slowly. "But they use it for other things, too. Those bulbous things on their hips—they call them 'blasters,' and they use electricity to tickle a ruby into making a sword of light."

Gwen stared, aghast. Rod nodded again. "And there are

other things they can make it do—lots of other things. Think of any job, darling, and the odds are these folk have figured out a way to make electricity do it."

"Caring for others," said the mother, immediately.

Rod sat still for a moment, just staring at her.

Then he smiled, and reached out to take her hand. "Of course. I should have known you'd think of the one thing they can't do. Oh, don't get me wrong—they do have machines that can take care of people's bodies—all their physical needs. Electricity runs machines that can wash clothes, cook food, clean houses. But to give the feeling that somebody cares about you, that another human being is taking care of you?" He shook his head. "No. They might be able to come up with a convincing illusion—but deep inside, everyone knows it's not real. Only people can really care for people. They haven't invented a substitute yet."

She gazed into his eyes for a long moment—and hers were filled with excitement, but warmed with her prime preoccupation—him.

Maybe that was why her eyes were so mesmerizing. They seemed to fill Rod's whole field of view, inviting, craving . . . "I remember the story about the monkey and the python," he said softly.

"In truth?" she murmured.

"Yeah. I just can't figure out which one I am . . ."

A shaggy figure moved into his range of vision, far away. Rod stared, stiffening. "Who's that, who just came in the door?"

Gwen heaved a martyred sigh and turned to look. "The soldier with the thatch of brown hair?" Her eyes widened. "My lord! It cannot be!"

"Why not? We know he's a time traveller—and don't tell me there ain't no such thing, when I *am* one!"

"I would not have dreamed of it. But how doth he come to be here?"

Rod shrugged. "As good a place as any, I expect. After

all, he resigned as Viceroy of Beastland two years ago."

"Aye, though Tuan cried he still had need of him."

"Yeah, that was really fun news for the Viceroy-elect. Too bad it didn't reach *his* ears."

"How could it?" Gwen asked. "He had quite simply disappeared."

The goblin face was scanning the room slowly, a massive frown of its beetling brows. It saw Rod and broke into a grin. Then its owner was hurrying across the room, hand outstretched. "Milord!"

Half the room turned to look, and Rod thought fast to cover. He plastered on a grin of his own and rose to the occasion to grasp the proffered hand. "My lord, Yorick!" he echoed. "It's good to see you!"

The rest of the patrons turned back to their beers with disgruntled mutters—no nobility, just profanity.

Rod slapped Yorick's shoulder and nodded toward a chair. "Sit down! Have a beer! Tell us what you're doing here!"

"Why, thank you! Don't mind if I do." The caveman pulled up a chair. "I'll bet you're surprised to see me here."

Rod sat down slowly to give himself a chance to recover. Then he smiled. "Well, yes, now that you mention it. I mean, this is a good five hundred years *before* you disappeared." He frowned at a sudden thought. "On the other hand, it's about forty thousand years since your whole species died off."

Yorick nodded. "So why not here, as well as there?"

"Aye, wherefore?" Gwen cocked her head to the side. "How does it come that thou'rt in this place?"

"With difficulty," Yorick answered, "quite a bit of it. I mean, when you didn't come back that night, your kids got worried—but Puck managed to get 'em all to bed and to sleep, anyway. When you hadn't shown up by mid-morning, though, even *he* got worried—so he told his boss."

Inwardly, Rod quailed. Brom O'Berin, in addition to being King of the Elves, was also Gwen's father—though nobody knew about it except himself and Rod. If Brom had found out his daughter was missing, it was amazing that he didn't have the whole elfin army in this tavern, instead of one addlepated Neanderthal.

Gwen smiled. "And Brom did order the hue and cry?"

Yorick nodded. "Sent out a scout party of elves. With a hundred or so of the little blighters going at it, they picked up your trail in no time. They tracked you to a little pond, where they found some pretty clear signs of a fight that seemed to end with a couple of bodies being dragged someplace, and just disappearing."

Rod smiled, with sour satisfaction. "Nice to know the Futurian boys hadn't had sense enough to erase their tracks. Overconfidence works wonders."

"No, they did erase 'em." Yorick turned toward Rod. "Straightened up the grass, and everything. Can you blame 'em if they didn't stop to think how good elves are at tracking?"

"Quite unfair," Gwen agreed.

Yorick nodded. "I swear a fly couldn't land on a blade of grass without them being able to tell it."

Rod remembered how insistent Puck was about sipping only from the flowers where the wild bee sucked—after the bee had left, of course. "That's fantastic. But how'd they figure out where we'd disappeared to?"

"The tracks just looked too much like the ones you left the last time you vanished into thin air."

Rod nodded, remembering their involuntary trip to Tir Chlis. "I always keep underestimating Brom. What'd he do about it?"

"Same thing as last time—called me."

Rod frowned. "But you had disappeared, too."

Yorick shrugged. "So he told Korig. You remember him, the big guy with the heavy jaw?"

"Your deputy." Rod nodded. "He knew how to get a hold of you?"

"Oh, you just bet he did! Didn't think I'd leave the poor guy *completely* on his own, did you? I mean, what would happen if SPITE or VETO tried to make trouble in the Neanderthal colony again?"

"The Futurian time-travel departments." Rod nodded, and made a mental note that there was still a time machine in Beastland. One belonging to GRIPE, the democrats' time-travel company—but a time machine nonetheless. Might come in handy, some time. "So Korig called you?"

Yorick nodded. "And I called Doc Angus. Actually, Doc got the message first; I wasn't in at the time. A little problem with King Louis the Bald trying to become a despot."

"What'd you do about it? . . . NO! Strike that! Let's stay with the business at hand."

Yorick shrugged. "Any way you want. So Doc Angus did a little research."

Rod remembered his fleeting glimpse of the white-maned, hawk-nosed, deformed little scientist—the head of GRIPE. "What kind of research?"

"He came, he saw—and he figured you'd been conquered. At least long enough to kidnap you. Of course, you *could* have been dead—but Doc likes to look on the bright side. So he assumed you'd been abducted back into the past."

Rod frowned. "Why not the future? Or an alternate universe?"

"Or even just a matter-transmitter." Yorick shrugged. "All possible, but he checked out the time machine hypothesis first, since that was the easiest for him."

Rod shook his head slowly, staring. "He had eight thousand years of human history to cover, not to mention a good hundred thousand of pre-history—and, for all he knew, a billion years or so before that! How'd he do it?"

Yorick shrugged. "Simple. He just told his agents, all up and down the time-line, to be on the lookout for the two of you—and sure enough, we just happen to have an agent here on Wolmar, and he'd noticed that a pack of Wolmen had chased in a couple of greenhorns in Tudor costumes. So he called for help right away—and as soon as I was done with that French job, Doc sent me to this time-locus. So here I am."

"Whoa." Rod held up a hand. "One problem at a time here. First—here? Wolmar? This insignificant little planet, out in the Marches? Why would Dr. McAran go to the trouble of putting an agent *here?*"

"Because it's pivotal to the rebirth of democracy," Yorick explained. "General Shacklar knows that the only way for anybody to survive on this planet is to get the Wolmen and the colonists working together."

"I'd begun to get an inkling of that." Rod nodded. "Getting two groups of people who're so different to live peacefully—that's an amazing accomplishment."

"Especially considering that they were at each other's throats only about ten years ago."

Rod and Gwen both stared.

Yorick nodded. "Oh yes, milord. It was all-out war, and very bloody, too. It went on for a dozen years before Shacklar came, without the slightest trace of mercy on either side."

"How'd he manage to stop it?"

"Well, he had an advantage." Yorick shrugged. "Both sides were heartily sick of it. All he had to do was find them a good excuse, and they were both ready to stop shooting. Of course, he didn't try to get them to lay down their weapons—that would've been asking too much."

Gwen frowned. "Then this war could begin anew, at a moment's notice."

Yorick nodded. "All that prevents it is the system Shacklar's worked out for resolving disputes."

"Yeah—we kind of had a taste of that earlier today." Rod exchanged glances with Gwen. "It does seem kind of fragile, though."

"Definitely. Shacklar still has a long way to go before

both sides are safe from each other. He's got to weld them together into a single political entity, fully equal, and respecting each other."

"Doth he mean that Wolmen and soldiers both, must have common courts of justice?"

"Well, having them join together in a single judiciary would certainly help." Rod pursed his lips. "But he'd also need some way of making them join in a single legislative body."

Gwen frowned. "What mean these words, milord?"

"That's right, you're a loyal subject of Their Majesties . . . Well, dear, it's possible for people to make their own laws."

"Thou dost not say it!"

"Oh, but I do. Of course, you have to be sure ahead of time that everybody will agree to those laws, or they'll be awfully hard to enforce."

" 'No prince may govern without the consent of the governed,' " Yorick quoted.

Rod threw him a glance of irritation. "Thank you, Nick Machiavelli."

"He wasn't so bad a guy. Just trying to be realistic, that's all."

"Oh? When was the last time you talked to him?"

Yorick opened his mouth to answer.

"NO! I don't want to know!" Rod held up a palm. "Well, dear, the best way to make sure the people won't object to any new laws is to have them choose their own lawmakers."

Gwen just stared at him.

"It's possible," Yorick murmured. "I know it sounds far-fetched, but it's possible."

Gwen turned to him. "Didst thou, then, have to become thus accustomed to such strangeness?"

"Who, me?" The Neanderthal spread his hands. "My people didn't even *have* laws. Everybody just sort of agreed on everything. . . ."

"So, then." Gwen turned back to Rod. "This planet hath no king."

Rod shook his head. "Just General Shacklar, on the colonists' side. I assume the Wolmen have some kind of a leader, too—but I don't think they've decided to get royal about it yet."

"Yet they do govern themselves?"

"Well, that's what Shacklar's working on. But it's been done in other places—quite a few of them. Basically, they choose their own king—but all he gets to do is carry out the lawmakers' decisions. He doesn't even get to judge people charged of crimes, or resolve disputes. There's a system of courts and judges for that."

"So, then." Gwen gazed off into space, and Rod could hear her thoughts—a train of logic tripping over bit by bit in a long chain. "Before it could lead to revolution," she said gently.

"Yes, dear. That's what I'm trying to bring about on Gramarye."

She stared, and he saw understanding come into her eyes. "Thou dost take long enow in the doing of it!"

"Have to." Rod shook his head. "There's no shortcut. It has to develop out of the people themselves, or it won't last. There're a thousand different ways of doing it, one for each society that has developed self-government—because it has to grow, like a tree. It can't be grafted onto a people."

"The grafts never take," Yorick murmured.

"Or they take graft, but that happens in every system when it starts to die. In fact, that's part of what kills it."

"But we're in at the beginning." Yorick grinned. "It can't be corrupted yet, because it hasn't quite begun."

"Amazing how much Shacklar has done, though." Rod turned to the Neanderthal. "How's he going to wield them into one complete political unit?"

"How'd he do *this* much?" Yorick shrugged. "Sorry, Major—I didn't have time for a full briefing; I had to just grab what few facts I could, before I jumped into the time machine. But he *will* manage it, say our boys from up the time-line, if we can fight off the SPITE and VETO agents who're trying to do him in, and his system with him."

Rod stared. The Society for the Prevention of Integration of Telepathic Entities was the Anarchists' time-travel department, as the Vigilant Exterminators of Telepathic Organisms was the Totalitarians'. The two of them were the banes of his existence on Gramarye. "They're after him, too?"

"Sure. Your world isn't the only one that's crucial to the future of democracy, milord."

"But why is Wolmar so important?"

"Mostly because it's one of the few pockets of democracy that's going to keep going all through the PEST centuries; at least it'll keep the idea alive. But also because it's going to be the headquarters for the educational effort."

Rod stared. Then he closed his eyes, gave his head a quick shake, and looked again.

Yorick nodded. "That's why we have to have an agent stationed here—to make sure the SPITE and VETO boys don't get to sabotage Shacklar's system."

"You bet you have to!"

"Yet an there be one of thy folk here," said Gwen, "wherefore can he not care for us?"

"Who said it was a he?"

"Why . . ." Gwen looked at Rod. "I would ha' thought . . ."

Yorick shook his head. "All we ask is that an agent be capable."

"Then thine agent here is female?"

"Now, I didn't say that." Yorick held up a palm. "And I'm not about to, either. The whole point is that our agent has managed to establish a very good cover, and we don't want to blow it. Stop and think about it—can *you* figure out who it is?"

Rod stared at the ape-man for a moment, then shook his

head. "You're right—I can't."

Gwen turned to gaze about them, her eyes losing focus.

"Uh-uh, milady!" Yorick wagged a forefinger at her. "No fair reading minds. It's better for us all if you *don't* know who it is! After all, what you don't know, you can't let slip."

"So they sent in a special agent," Rod said, "you. After all, if *your* cover's blown, it won't be any major tragedy."

"I wasn't planning to use it again, anyway." Yorick nodded.

"Thus thou'rt come in aiding us to return to our home!"

Yorick kept nodding. "Going to try, anyway. I've got a time-beacon with me. All I have to do is push the button, and it'll send a teeny ripple going through the time-stream. When that ripple hits the receiver in Doc Angus' headquarters, he'll know exactly when and where we are, so he'll be able to shoot us all the spare parts for making a time machine. And I'll put them together, press the button—and voilà! You'll be home!"

Rod frowned. "But why can't he just press a button and pick us up? I mean, he shot you here without a time machine to receive you, didn't he?"

"Yeah, but it doesn't work both ways." Yorick shrugged. "Don't ask me why—I'm just the bullet. I don't understand the gun, milord."

"Uh, can the 'milord' business." Rod darted nervous glances around the room. "I don't think they'd understand it here."

"Suits." Yorick shrugged again. "What do you want me to call you?"

"How about, uh—'major?' They'd recognize that, and it's legit; I'm just not in the same army, that's all."

"Any way you want it, Major."

"Thanks." Rod hunched forward, frowning. "Now, about time-travel. Why does it only work one way?"

"I *said* not to ask me that!" Yorick winced. "What do I

know? I'm just a dumb caveman. But I think it's sorta like—well, you can throw a spear, but you can't make it fly back to you. Understand?"

"You can tie a rope to it." Rod remembered reading every other chapter of *Moby Dick*.

"A rope five hundred years long? Gets a little weak in the middle, Major. And five hundred is a short haul, where I come from."

Rod felt an attack of stubbornness coming on. "It should be possible, though."

"Okay, so maybe it is, but Doc Angus just hasn't figured out how to do it yet. And I get the impression that no one ever will."

"Watch out for the absolutes." Rod raised a cautioning finger. "The boys up the time-line might just not have told you yet."

"Possible," Yorick admitted, "but not probable. We're both fighting the same enemies—and if SPITE saw a chance to get the jump on VETO, you can bet they'd leap at it—especially a jump like that! And if the VETO boys thought they could get an edge on SPITE, they'd grab it, too."

"And they would both rejoice to gain advantage over thy GRIPE," Gwen added.

"Oh, you betcha, lady!"

"Well, I guess we all have to take McAran's word for it." Rod pushed back his chair and stood up. "Might as well get moving on it, eh? It's going to be kind of hard, trying to find a place in this colony where we can be alone for a couple of hours."

"Well, more like sixteen, really." Yorick stood up, too. "It takes a little time, getting the components through. Not to mention putting them together." He turned to Gwen. "If you'll excuse us, milady . . ."

"Nay, I will not." Gwen was already coming around the table. "Whither mine husband goeth, I go."

"Oh. Don't think I can take care of myself yet, eh?" Rod grinned. "Or don't you trust me out of your sight?"

"Somewhat of both, mayhap." Gwen tucked her arm through his. "Yet whate'er the cause, thou shalt not leave me. Lead on, Master Yorick."

"Any way you want it, milady." The ape-man laid some IDE bills on the table and turned to the door.

Rod eyed the money with appreciation. "You do come prepared, don't you?"

"Huh?" Yorick turned back and saw where Rod was looking. "Oh! Just the basic survival kit, Major. We have one ready for every time and clime."

Rod turned away to the door with him. "Y' know, it's kind of funny that this outlying planet would still use IDE paper money, even after the government that printed it has died."

"Why? It's not really paper, y' know, it's a very tough plastic. It'll last forever—or a couple of centuries, at least."

"Well, yeah, but it doesn't have any value in itself. It's only as good as the government that printed it."

"Yeah, but it still works just fine, if everybody believes in it—and they do. Helps that it's based on energy—their basic monetary unit was the BTU. So many BTUs equal a kwaher—a kilowatt-hour—and so many kwahers equal a therm. So the money supply only gets increased when there's more energy available within the interplanetary system as a whole."

"Yeah, if the government doesn't rev up the printers!"

"Ah, but the government doesn't exist anymore." Yorick held up a finger. "It can't inflate the currency now."

"Nice bit of irony." Rod smiled. "The IDE's currency is more sound now that the government that made it has disappeared, than it was while that government was alive and kicking."

"Mostly kicking, at least toward the end. I mean, they were even doing everything they could to bump off Cholly, over there, just because he came up with some wild theories."

"Cholly?" Rod turned to stare at the barkeeper. "Mr. Nice

Guy himself? Why would the IDE want to kill *him* off?"

"Well, not the IDE, really—just the LORDS, the majority party that engineered the big coup d'etat, and set up the Proletarian Eclectic State of Terra."

"Before they even came to power?"

Yorick nodded. "And SPITE and VETO are still trying to finish the job. That's one of our agent's main jobs—protecting Cholly and his establishment."

"What's so important about a tavern?"

"Oh, the tavern's just a front. His real establishment is just an idea and a method, with a set of tried-and-true techniques. People who need a reason for living take his method and go out and do the same kind of work, all on their own." Yorick grinned. "Drives PEST crazy. They keep trying to find out how his organization works—who gives the orders, and how they're transmitted—but there isn't any organization! Just ideas . . ."

"Sounds fabulous. What's his *real* work?"

"Mass education—without the masses realizing they're being educated. Cholly is Charles T. Barman, Major."

Rod froze, staring at the cheery tavernkeeper. "That!?! *That* is the man who created the educational system that gave birth to the Decentralized Democratic Tribunal?"

"Yeah, but he's only just now doing the creating, so the DDT's very vulnerable right at this time-locus, five centuries before it'll be born. If anything happens to Cholly, the DDT 'revolution' might never happen. You see why we don't want to compromise our agent here. Don't stare, Major—it makes you conspicuous. Shall we go?"

"Uh—yeah." Rod turned away, feeling numb. "Yeah, sure. Let's go."

"Nar, let's not," rumbled the sergeant.

He wasn't all that big himself, but the troops behind him filled the doorway. Rod stared, shocked—it was the slob from the Wall that morning, Thaler's buddy. But he'd gone through a complete metamorphosis, and maybe even a shower. His uniform was neat and crisp, his cheeks were shaven, and his hair was combed. "Amazing," he murmured.

Behind the bar, Cholly looked up and saw. "Here, now!" he cried, and the whole tavern fell silent. "We'll have no violence in this house!"

"That's up to him," the former slob growled. "Come along to the General nice and peaceablelike, and there won't be no trouble."

Rod frowned. "The General?"

"Aye. You're under arrest."

Rod stood very still. The sergeant grinned.

"Not quite what I had in mind," Yorick muttered.

"Wherefore are we arrested?" Gwen asked.

The sergeant shrugged. "That's for the general to say. Are you coming peaceably, or not?" The glint in his eye said he hoped "not."

Rod sighed and capitulated. "Sure. I always cooperate with the authorities."

"Well, almost always," Yorick muttered.

"Converse with the General was enjoyable," Gwen agreed.

Behind her, most of the soldiers' faces broke into slow, sly grins.

"A woman can't say anything around here without being suspect," Rod sighed. "Of course, they didn't stop to think what kind of a woman would find a masochistic general to be pleasant company."

The grins vanished; the soldiers stared in horror.

Rod nodded, satisfied. "I don't think you'll have any trouble around here, dear. *Now* we can go."

They might have been the dregs of military society, but they marched very nicely—all the way down the street, into the headquarters building. They came to a halt while the sergeant knocked on Shacklar's door, and the receptionist (human—it was a frontier planet; and male—it was a military prison) officially told him he could enter. Then they marched right into the office, and came to a stamping halt in front of Shacklar's desk.

The General looked up from his paperwork and smiled warmly. "Very good, Sergeant." He saluted. "Dismissed."

The ex-slob stared. "But, General . . . these people, they're . . ."

"Very pleasant conversationalists," the General assured him. "I've spoken with them already this morning. I'm sure there won't be any problem—especially with the Chief Chief available." He nodded toward a purple Wolman who stood beside his desk.

The sergeant looked the Wolman up and down, and did not seem assured. "If'n it's all the same to you, sir . . ."

"But I'm afraid it's not." Shacklar's tone was crisp, but polite. "That will be all, Sergeant. I thank you for your concern."

The sergeant and all his troops eyed the Wolman, Rod, and Yorick warily—and Gwen almost with alarm. But the sergeant barked, "About *face!* For'ard harch!" dutifully. The squad pivoted with a multiple stamp, and marched out. The sergeant lingered in the doorway for one more glower, but Shacklar met his gaze, and the man turned and disappeared.

On the other hand, he didn't close the door.

Shacklar ignored it. He turned to the Gallowglasses, beaming. "A pleasure to see you again, Master Gallowglass, Mistress Gallowglass." He turned an inquiring glance to Yorick. "I don't believe I've had the pleasure?"

Rod gestured toward the ape-man. "Oh, this is . . ."

But Yorick cut him off. "Ander Thal, General. But I used to be a comic actor with a two-bit rep company, so they call me . . ."

". . . Yorick," Rod finished. He swallowed. "Uh, General—has it occurred to you that you might be in a rather dangerous position?"

"Outnumbered, you mean? And both of you with weapons?" Shacklar nodded. "I'm aware of it, yes."

"It . . . doesn't bother you."

"Not particularly. I'm trusting to your honor, old boy."

Rod stared. Then he said, just by way of information, "You're a fool, you know."

"I'm aware of that, too." Shacklar smiled up at him.

Yorick locked glances with Rod, and his thoughts were loud. *This man is vital to the future of democracy, Major. If you so much as lay a finger on him . . .* At which point the mental signal deteriorated into some rather gruesome graphics.

Not that Rod needed the urging. He gazed at Shacklar's warm, open countenance, and sighed. "I never kill fools before dinnertime; it's bad for the digestion." Ruefully, he was remembering a few occasions when he'd played the same gambit himself; but it had worked, he *had* gained trust . . .

. . . and it was working again, now.

Shacklar wasn't the only fool in the room, he decided.

A faint smile touched the corners of the General's mouth; he relaxed. "I don't believe you've met this gentleman—Chief Hwun, of the Purple tribe—and acclaimed as Chief of all the Wolman tribes."

"No, I don't believe I've had the pleasure." Rod tried to remember how the salute went—crossed arms, fingers touching the shoulders . . .

Before he could try it, the big Wolman said, "Them do-um it—this man and woman in-um funny clothes."

Rod stared.

Then he said, "Not much on courtesy, is he?"

"Uh—" Yorick glanced about, then at the General. "I know it's none of my business, but . . . what does the Chief think M . . . Mr. Gallowglass did?"

Rod caught the near slip, and gave Yorick points; he'd realized the hazards of having Shacklar think he might be entitled to give Rod orders. "Why, trespassing, of course, on Wolman land." He turned back to Shacklar. "But we cleared that up a couple of hours ago."

"Well, yes—but the Chief's now charging you with an additional transgression."

Rod frowned. "Isn't that 'double jeopardy,' or something?"

"Not at all, since it's a crime you weren't charged with before."

"What crime?"

"Murder."

Rod set a mug of ale down in front of Gwen, then turned back to the bar. "Two of whatever passes for whiskey here. Doubles."

"Done." Cholly thumped two heavy glasses down on the bar, and upended a bottle of vaguely brownish fluid over them. "So he let you loose on your own recognizance?"

"Yeah." Rod shrugged. "We just promised not to kill anybody before dawn tomorrow, and he said, 'Excellent. Why don't you have a look around the town, while you're here?' . . . That's enough!"

"As you will." Cholly waited a second longer, till the brownish fluid was almost up to the rims, then set the bottle down. "Yer trial's tomorrow at sunrise, then?"

"If you can call it that." Rod frowned. "Isn't that a little lenient, for a couple of suspected murderers?"

Cholly nodded. "Even here. I'd guess the General doesn't think you're guilty."

Rod nodded. "Is he hoping we'll escape, or something?"

"Where to?"

"A good point." Rod pursed his lips. "So we're just supposed to relax and enjoy life, huh?"

"That—or find evidence to clear yourselves. Hard to do that inside a cell, yer know."

Rod frowned. "It is, now that you mention it. We were planning to do something of that sort, anyway."

"Well, then." Cholly beamed. "The General knows his man, don't he? Let me know where I can help."

"Thanks. We will." Rod turned back to the table, set one of the glasses down in front of Yorick, sat himself down across from Gwen, and took a hefty swallow. Then he sat very still for a few minutes, waiting till the top of his head settled back on and the room came back into focus. When it did, he exhaled sharply. "*What* do they make *that* out of?"

"Something almost compatible with Terran biochemistry, I'm sure." Yorick looked a little defocused himself.

Rod took a deep breath, then a very cautious sip. He set the glass down gingerly, exhaled carefully, and sat back. "Now!" He looked from Yorick to Gwen and back. "You were both there; you heard everything I did. What was all *that* about?"

Gwen shrugged. "We chanced to be in a position suspect at a time when a man was slain, my lord."

"Yeah, but I highly doubt we were anywhere near this 'Sun-Greeting Place,' or whatever it is. Also, I don't believe in coincidences, especially not when they're so convenient."

Gwen frowned. "In what way dost thou think them opportune?"

"For our enemies."

"I'll drink to that." Yorick lifted his mug, also his glass.

"You'll drink to anything." But Rod clinked glasses with him, anyway. "Here's to the enemy—may he be confounded."

"Whoever he is." Yorick drank, then set his glass down and leaned forward. "But I'll agree with you, Major, somebody's definitely out to get you."

Rod stared. "When did I say that?"

"On our way from the castle," Gwen explained.

"Oh." Rod frowned. "Yeah, I did say something of the sort then, didn't I?"

"Does he get this way often?"

"Off 'n' on," Rod answered; but Gwen assured Yorick, "'Tis only when matters of great moment preoccupy him."

"Oh." Yorick turned back to Rod. "Is that when you get paranoid, too?"

Gwen frowned. "What is the meaning of that word?"

"Suspicious," Rod explained. "He means that I feel as

though everybody's out to get me."

"Oh!" Gwen turned back to Yorick. "Nay; he is always in that condition."

"But this time, he's right."

They turned in surprise; that voice hadn't been one of theirs.

The newcomer was slender, and wore the same uniform as all the other troopers, but she made it look totally feminine. It couldn't have been deliberate: her blond hair was shorter than most of the men's, cropped close and showing her ears; but there was something in its styling, something about the way she held herself, something in the delicacy of her features that made her very clearly female.

"That's a professional opinion," she added. "They're out to get you."

"Who?" Rod demanded; but Yorick said, softly, "What profession?"

"Secret agent," she snapped, "spy." And to Rod, "You should be able to say better than I can. Who'd rather see you dead than alive? Not that it matters much; on this planet, anybody who's getting hassled is my friend."

Rod just stared at her, but Gwen pushed a chair out. "Sit, an it please thee."

The woman sat, scowling. "You've got a funny way of talking."

Rod said, "I hate to be blunt, but—who are you?"

"I'm Chornoi Shershay—and you'd better hear the whole of it. I was a government spy, up until about five years ago."

"Five years." Rod frowned. "That was just about the time of the PEST coup, if I remember . . ." He managed to bite off the sentence just before he said, ". . . my history rightly."

"Yeah." Chornoi nodded. "I was a secret agent for the LORDS party, digging up information for them and helping set up assassinations on some of their more outspoken enemies. I knew I was helping kill people, but I never saw it happen, so it didn't bother me much. I didn't think it would, either." Her face lost expression. "But after the coup, I suddenly found out I was part of the secret police, and the bosses ordered my squad to go hunt down a professor." Her mouth twisted. "He was a gentle old duffer, quiet and humble, and you could see from his house that he and his wife took good care of each other. We yanked him out of bed in the middle of the night, and kicked him out of his house into a darkened floater—and he was terrified, scared stiff but he never blamed us. Not a curse, not a word of anger, just stared at us with those wide, frightened eyes that *knew,* and understood . . ." She shuddered. "So they laid into him harder, of course. Even on the way to HQ, they were working him over. It was cruel, vicious beating until he was out cold. I was lucky—I only had to drive. But I still had to hear it. . . .

"Then we landed on top of Base Building, and I had to help carry him inside. His face was so bloody and swollen that I wouldn't have recognized him. We laid him out on the table, ready for the sadists." Her face worked, then was still. "Oh, they try to pretty it up by calling it 'interrogation,' but it's still just plain torture. They clip electrodes on to them, instead of thumbscrews, but agony is agony. I didn't have to stay and watch it, but I felt soiled and debased anyway, as though I'd been turned into something less than human. They told me I could go back to quarters, but I went straight to the Boss, and told him, I quit.

"He sat back in that plastic-walled office behind his stainless steel desk, and just laughed at me. Then he said, 'You can't quit the Secret Security, Shershay. The only way you go out, is feet-first.' 'It's a deal,' I said, and I slammed out of his office. But I headed for the portal as fast as I could walk. I didn't run—that would have been advertising—but I walked very fast. He was as good as his word, though; I saw a gunman running to intercept me as I came in sight of the main portal. I just kept going while he pulled up and aimed at me, then I jerked to the side at the last second.

He wasted time trying to track me with the gun, then he squeezed off a shot, but the bolt didn't come anywhere near me. I lashed out with a kick, and caught him right under the chin with my heel. His head snapped back, and something made a cracking sound, but I landed on the other side of his body, and I landed running. Right out the door."

She paused for breath, trembling, and Yorick said softly, "How far did you get?"

"About a kilometer. Because there was a courier in a floater, just coming in. I kicked him out at gunpoint and took off—but I just went over the parapet, and down into the city, before they could get an intercepter after me. I was in the Old Town—the part where the streets go this way and that—organic, you know? I ducked in there, and was gone."

"You knew better than to stay there, though," Rod said softly.

"Of course." Chornoi shrugged. "Not that it made much difference. They had the cordon out by dawn, and a SecSec force behind me, tracking. I stepped up to a food-counter, to put down a bowl of soy-meal—and when I came out, they jumped me."

"Hard?" Yorick asked.

Chornoi glared at him. "Very."

She turned to Rod. "But I healed. Oh, I was still bleeding here and there when they hauled me up in front of the judge—that was only a couple of hours later. And, of course, SecSec had six witnesses who swore they'd seen me kill that gunman; they'd never been anywhere near him, of course. I think one of them had watched it on a security monitor, though. Which didn't matter, 'cause they played the recording—and the judge said, 'Re-form her.'"

Gwen frowned, not understanding; but Rod paled. "They were going to wipe your brain and install a new personality?"

Chornoi nodded. "And if I didn't live, what difference

did it make? But I didn't even get that far. They slammed me into the floater, to go to the re-form center—but we never even lifted. There was a courier there, with a document. Seems the whole time I'd been in front of the judge, SecSec had been going to the Secretary-General, convincing him that secret police were military personnel—so they didn't bother re-forming; they just loaded me into a convict barge, and shipped us all out to Wolmar." Her mouth tightened. "It wasn't a pleasant trip. It lasted two weeks, and only three of us convicts were women. The rest of the soldiers tried to take turns on us." She glared at Rod. "But three is just enough to guard each other's backs. After we killed a couple, they held off. They tried to get the ship's brass to tie us down, but they told us they just steered the damn thing and made it go; we convicts were each other's problems." She shivered. "We had to take turns sleeping, but we got here intact."

"And here?" Gwen's eyes were huge.

Chornoi shrugged. "It's a little easier now. Oh, the other two—when they found out how much they could make, once the convicts were getting paychecks again—they set up shop. They own their own houses now, and each of them is richer than any man on the planet."

Gwen was pale now, and her hand trembled as she lifted her glass, then put it down. "Yet thou didst not—how didst thou say it . . ."

"Go into business." Chornoi nodded, eyes glittering. "But I had to fight 'em off every day, at first—two or three in any twenty-four hours, till I got a reputation. Now it's just two or three a week. The ones who survive out here are smart, though—they back off when it starts getting dangerous, so I've never had to kill one."

"Yet do they not come at thee in company?" Gwen whispered.

"That's why I was sitting back there." Chornoi jerked her head toward a table in a back corner. "I can see the door, and the whole room, but nobody can come at me from behind. They haven't tried, though." She took a sip of her ale, but grimaced as though it were bitter. "Gotta say that much for male chauvinism—when there're so few of us, each one is pretty precious. Any one of them might come at me by himself, but he doesn't want any of his mates to see him trying."

"They'd string him up by his toes," Yorick said quietly.

"Probably for target practice." Chornoi shrugged. "Better him than me."

She lifted her mug for a long swallow, then slammed it down. "So, there you have it. I can't walk through this burg without getting razzed, so anybody who's getting hassled, I'm on their side. Especially women." She nodded to Gwen. "And I think I can trust your man, because he's with you—so why would he want me?" Her mouth twisted in self-contempt. "Oh, don't give me that sympathetic look! I know I'm a hot enough item." She turned and glowered at Rod. "Maybe too hot. I want to get off this planet, so badly that I can't think of anything else—and you folks haven't been here before, which means you haven't been sentenced; so you might get to leave. You might be able to spring me."

Rod frowned. "I thought this was a military prison. Shacklar's just the warden. How can he have the authority to let you go?"

"He can do anything he wants—now," Chornoi said, with a mirthless smile. "PEST cut us off four years ago—right after I got here, in fact. They claimed trade to the outlying planets was a losing proposition—*real* losing, trillions of therms' worth. And a prison planet was all loss—it was much cheaper to kill the criminals. So they just stopped trade. The next freighter in brought us the news."

Rod frowned. "How come there was a 'next' freighter? I thought they stopped trade."

"We had a little trade going on our own, with some of the other outlying planets—but we had no more supplies coming in from Terra, no new machinery or spare parts. The good General-Governor made peace with the natives just in time."

"Thou canst sustain thyselves?"

Chornoi nodded. "The Wolmen bring in the food and fiber, and our men do the mining and manufacturing. But the end result is, we're not a prison planet anymore—we're a colony. And Shacklar's the Governor as well as the General, so he can do anything he damn well pleases with us. If he wants to let us go, we can go—but where to?" She waved an arm. "There's nothing out beyond that Wall but grass—and Wolmen."

"He won't let you leave the planet?"

"Oh, sure, if he thinks one of us should be allowed to—and if we can afford it." She shrugged. "He can't give away free spaceships, you know."

Rod exchanged glances with Yorick. "Well, when the time comes, we'll find some way to get the cash."

Yorick nodded. "I think the lady could be useful, Major. Real useful."

"Vacuum your brain," Chornoi snapped. "I offered to help you, not service you."

"Wasn't even thinking of it," Yorick said virtuously. "I meant knowledge-help. I know the basics about this planet, and about PEST . . ."

Chornoi"s mouth twisted. "Who doesn't?"

"Yeah, but, well, uh—about Wolmar. You've been here a few years, you know the lay of the land. It always helps to have a local on your side."

Chornoi shrugged. "I'm as local as they come around here. At least I know who's who, and where the bodies are buried—some of them, anyway. And I've spent time with the Wolmen."

Gwen frowned. "How didst thou come to that?"

"They looked safer than the soldiers—and they were, while I was on probation. But probation with each tribe gave me a year to get my feet under me, and tuck my emotions into place." Chornoi shrugged. "What can I tell you? It worked."

"So," Rod mused, "you're willing to help—if we help you."

"Yeah, if you'll help me get off the planet."

"If we can."

"Well, sure—if you can." Chornoi tossed her head impatiently.

"Of course," Rod mused, "if we do manage to get off this planet, you'll make us a marked crew. I mean, PEST has to have at least one agent here and if you leave, he'll blow the whistle. Then you'll have an assassin hot on your trail before you get past the first light-year."

"I understand that." Chornoi's tone was brittle. "I couldn't blame you if you didn't want to take the chance."

Rod shrugged. "I'm not too worried about it." *Especially since we're planning to leave via time machine.* "After all, there's no danger from assassins as long as we're on Wolmar—and without your help, we might not live to get off the planet."

Chornoi nodded. "I'd say that's true. You said it yourself—that Wolman's murder was too nicely timed. It had to be designed to put you and your wife behind bars—or into an early grave."

"We do have enemies," Rod admitted, "and I think they would be more interested in the 'early grave' option."

"We will rejoice in thine assistance," Gwen assured.

Chornoi gave her a peculiar look, but said, "Thanks, lady." And to Rod, "So what've we got?"

Rod shrugged. "A Purple corpse." He added a bleak smile. "Even though all Purples are present and accounted for."

Yorick spread his hands. "That's about all the information we have. Not exactly what you'd call a lot."

"Nowhere near enough," Chornoi agreed. "We've got to

learn more before we can make any guesses about who really did it."

Yorick leaned back, fingers laced across his belly, thumbs twiddling. "Well, you're the local expert. Tell us—where do we get more information?"

"At the scene of the crime," Chornoi answered.

"Certes, 'tis no great need," Gwen protested. "Thou hast affairs of thine own to be about."

Maybe it was the word "affairs" that made the young private redouble his efforts. "Aw, come on, Ma'am! I'm from Braxa! We used to make our own brooms there, all the time." He gave her a quick grin over his shoulder. "How else'd our mamas keep the houses clean?" He turned back to Gwen's broomstick. "See, it's just this little rope here that's come untied. All it needs is a proper square knot. Now, you just put your finger on it, right there . . ."

Gwen did. Of course, that necessitated bending over, and swaying closer to the young man. He swallowed hard, and gave the knot a jerk that almost broke the cord.

Behind his back, Rod was tossing a loop of rope up to catch around one of the inch-thick spikes that studded the top of the Wall, and beckoning. Chornoi clambered up it, hand over hand, with Yorick right behind her. Rod came last, and tossed the rope over the far side of the Wall. Yorick slipped down first, then Chornoi. Rod glowered down at the young sentry's back, then turned to leap, catch the rope, and glide down. He landed lightly, and Chornoi stared. "How did you do that? Without breaking your arches, I mean."

"Practice," Yorick grunted. "Come on, let's get out of here." He bolted across the open stretch of brightly-lit land, into the shadow of a copse fifty feet away. No alarms went off; the sentry was looking at something else at the moment. Rod held his breath, feeling the jealousy climb up to consume him. Then a whisper and a rustle, and he whirled about to see Gwen gliding in for a landing on her broomstick.

Chornoi turned around, did a double take. "How did *you* get here?"

"I trust that young man will count himself amply repaid for his kindness." Rod snapped.

"Husband, I prithee." Gwen laid a gentle hand on his forearm. "What choice was there? He'd ne'er ha' trusted Demoiselle Chornoi."

"True enough." Rod clipped off the words. "May I congratulate you on a successful flirtation—I mean, diversion. And I'll cut out that kid's liver and lights if I ever bump into him again."

"Truly, husband, 'tis unworthy of thee." Gwen's eyes were large with reproach. "Be mindful that the lad spoke to a Gramarye witch, and, moreover, one who can cast thoughts and feelings. Truly, the lad had no chance."

"In more ways than one," Rod sighed, "and you don't need to mention your powers to explain it. I suppose I don't have any right to be angry with him, do I?"

"Nay, certes," Gwen breathed, swaying close to him. "But we tarry."

"How the hell does she know where to go?" Rod muttered to Yorick. "Okay, so the planet has a moon or two, so we've had light almost all the way, and when the big moon set, she just had us wait twenty minutes till the other one rose. But even with it, I can scarcely see twenty feet in front of me!"

"Well, *I* can see fine." Yorick grinned. "You *Sapiens* have just gone soft, that's all. Too many millennia of lighted streets."

"What's she?" Rod grumbled. "A Neanderthalette?"

Yorick shook his head. "Not a good enough build. Kinda scrawny, y' know? And the face is kinda flat and angular. But I think she's a nice kid underneath it all."

Actually, Rod had been thinking that Chornoi was a classical beauty—or would have been, if her face hadn't been constantly pinched with hostility. And her body was anything but "scrawny." However, he could understand why she wouldn't measure up to the Neanderthal ideal of femininity. The comment on her interior self, though, he doubted. "You must be seeing deeper than I am."

Yorick shrugged. "You *Saps* must be damn near blind."

Rod wondered if he meant that to be interpreted both ways.

"Come on." Yorick stepped up the pace. "We've got some serious catching up to do."

Chornoi strode ahead of them, as briskly as though she hadn't realized she was climbing a thirty-degree slope. Finally she came to a stop, and the men huffed and puffed up beside her, with Gwen silent at Rod's shoulder.

"Here it is." Chornoi waved a hand.

They stood on top of a ridge, oriented roughly east-west. The moonlight showed a plain stretching out for miles about them, unending grassland broken only by the occasional copse and a line of stunted trees that straggled across the prairie, marking a watercourse.

Rod took a deep breath. "Quite a view."

Chornoi nodded. "It's spectacular by sunlight, but I don't think we can wait for that." She pointed. "There's the actual Sun-Greeting Place."

A stone step rose from the ground a few feet in front of them. Thirty feet away, an upright slab bulked large against the night. Chornoi slipped a slender flashlight out of her jacket and aimed it at the boulder. Its beam showed that the top of the standing stone had been flattened from front to back and leveled, then notched, eight deep gouges cut out of the rock. The first, fourth, and eighth were very deep.

"The shamen come up here every morning to greet the sun," Chornoi explained. "They take it in rotation. It's a religious ritual, of course, but it has a very practical purpose, too—every morning, the Shaman of the Day sees how close the sun is coming to one of the big notches. The middle one is the equinox—there're sixteen months here; the two moons revolve eight times a year, and they rule the months in alternation. Figure that the first groove is the winter solstice. The sun starts there, moves down to the middle groove for the vernal equinox, goes on to the eighth groove for the summer solstice, then moves back to the middle groove for the autumnal equinox, and on back to the first one."

"New Year's," Yorick said.

Chornoi nodded. "And it's up to the shaman of the Purple tribe to keep an eye on the sun. When it rises behind the fourth notch, he goes home and tells everybody to start planting. When he sees sunrise through the eighth notch, he tells everybody to celebrate."

"A midsummer night's dream?"

"You could call it that," Chornoi said sourly. "Then the sun starts to swing back, and when it rises behind the fourth notch again, the shaman tells the tribe to get ready for harvest."

"Then back to Midwinter, and the whole thing starts all over again." Yorick knelt by the stone step. "Want to shine that thing down here, Ms.?"

"Why not? But call me 'Chornoi,' all right? We're working together now."

The light gleamed on the rough stone at the base of the slab. Yorick ran a finger across the surface, and stopped at a dark blot.

They all stared, silent for a moment.

Then Yorick's finger went on to trace another drop, and another.

"Blood," Rod said softly.

"I'm not quite equipped to run a chemical analysis," Yorick mused, "but I'd say that was a pretty good bet. Want to scan the area, Ms. Chornoi?"

"Well, that's an improvement, I guess," Chornoi grunted. She moved the circle of light slowly over the area around the stone step. The grass stood about three inches high.

"Nice to find out they keep it mowed," Yorick said, "but that's about all I see."

Rod nodded. "Not the slightest sign of a struggle. Whoever our hatchet man was, he was remarkably neat."

"Damn near inhuman," Yorick agreed.

"Not quite." Chornoi's lips were thin. "Some of my colleagues were extremely efficient. I wasn't too bad, myself."

Yorick looked up. "But the blood on the stone does kind of indicate that the Wolman met the cleaver when he stepped up here to greet the sun."

Rod frowned. "Yeah. So what . . . Oh!"

"Right." Yorick nodded. "Who steps up to the Sun-Greeting Place to greet the sun?"

"A shaman," Chornoi breathed.

"But none of the shamen are missing," Rod pointed out.

"So what?" Yorick shrugged. "None of the *Wolmen* are missing. So why shouldn't it be a shaman who's not missing, instead of just an ordinary warrior?"

"More to the point," Chornoi said softly, "why shouldn't it be Hwun? After all, he's the shaman of the Purple tribe, and they're the ones closest to this place."

"No reason at all, except that Hwun is very much alive. Far too much so, for my liking." Rod frowned. "What is this business about Hwun being the chief chief, when he's also the Purple shaman? I've heard of overlapping directorates, but isn't this a little too obvious?"

"No problem there." Chornoi shook her head. "Wolman government is basic democracy, Major—very basic. They just sit around in a circle and discuss who's going to be leader. And when most of them agree—well, that's who the leader is. Every clan does it that way—and, once they've decided on a leader, they tend to stay with him. So when the clans gather for a tribal meeting, it's the clan headmen who sit down to elect the tribal leader."

Yorick nodded. "Which means that one of the tribal chiefs

is going to be the national chief."

Chornoi frowned at him. "You had experience with this kind of thing?"

"We were Number One. So they held a tribal meeting like that to fight the soldiers better?"

"You *have* been around. But it was a national meeting—all the tribes banded together for an all-out war."

"Makes sense." Yorick agreed. "After all, it was probably the first time in their history that they'd had somebody to fight besides each other."

Gwen shivered. "Must men forever be fighting, then?"

"Sure. How else would we get you ladies to notice us, instead of the other guys?" Yorick turned back to Chornoi. "This wouldn't happen to have been the first time they'd ever banded together for anything, would it?"

Chornoi stared at him, then nodded slowly. "Yeah. Up until the convicts came, they'd always been fighting each other, just the way you said."

Yorick nodded. "Nice of you to help out that way."

"Yes, bringing civilization to the poor savages." Rod's eyes glittered. "I always find unification fascinating."

Something in his voice made Chornoi look up with a scowl. "Don't make any mistake, Major. It was the Wolmen's idea to get together to fight us, not the colonists'. Just a marriage of convenience, that's all."

"And as fragile as such unions usually are, I'm sure—but one which Shacklar and Cholly have steadily been trying to strengthen."

"Oh, that's deliberate enough, sure—and Shacklar definitely likes having a national leader he can deal with. But *they* chose Hwun, not him."

"At a national council?"

Chornoi nodded. "The tribal leaders got together, so of course they chose one of their own number. That's how come Hwun, the Purple chief, wound up being acclaimed chief Wolman chief."

"Makes sense." Rod nodded. "But why'd they elect a

shaman instead of a general—excuse me, 'war-chief?' I mean, how good a tactician is a pholk-physician going to be?"

Chornoi shook her head. "Medicine's only part of it, Major, only a spin-off, really. His main function is spiritual. He's a holy man."

Rod shuddered. "I don't like the sound of that. Religion and politics make a lousy combination."

"But it's very useful when you're trying to keep all the factions of your people together," Chornoi pointed out. "That's Hwun's main job. As to fighting when they went to war, he had four generals, one for each tribe. They took care of the tactics; he just had the final say on strategy."

"Neat." Rod scowled. "In fact, a little too efficient for my liking."

"But his constituents can recall him at any minute," Yorick pointed out.

Chornoi gave him an irritated glare. "That's right, in fact. How'd you know?"

"Y' seen one oral culture, y' seen 'em all," Yorick said. "Not really true, but they do all have certain characteristics in common. Government by consensus is one of 'em, and instant recall is part of that."

"Instant, yes—by the most effective means available. At least, sometimes. In fact, it has occurred to me that we may be looking at an impeachment here."

Yorick shook his head. "You'd know better than I would, but I find it hard to believe. This kind of a society wouldn't understand that kind of sneaky killing. If somebody wanted to challenge the head honcho, he'd just do it. In fact, the more witnesses he had for the fight, the stronger his support would be."

Rod nodded. "That sounds right. Besides, you said it yourself, Chornoi—some of your colleagues are inhumanly efficient. This is such a neat job that it fairly screams 'professional.'"

Slowly, she nodded. "Yeah. Probably well armed, too."

Rod frowned. "But he didn't use a blaster. If he had, there wouldn't have been blood."

Chornoi shook her head. "A pro wouldn't have, Major. This was right at dawn, remember? A blaster bolt would've been seen. It also might have set a fire, and people would have *really* started wondering." She shrugged. "Sometimes the oldest weapons work best."

"Well, one thing's sure, then." Yorick stood up, dusting off his hands. "It wasn't any Wolman who did this killing. I mean, they may be pretty enthusiastic, and I'm sure they're skillful, but when you get right down to it, when it comes to killing people, they're really amateurs." He nodded to Chornoi. "One of the soldiers did this—and one trained for commando work."

"Probably." Chornoi gazed at the dark spatters on the stone. "Don't sell those Wolmen short, though. They've become very competent warriors since they started fighting these convict-soldiers. Very competent—and they've been developing a lot of skill with blasters, ever since Shacklar took over and the truce began."

"I do not understand," Gwen murmured. "Why doth he give Wolmen his weapons, when to keep them to his own men would yield him great advantage?"

Chornoi shrugged. "He seems to think that if it comes to war, the colonists are going to be wiped out, sooner or later. We're so heavily outnumbered that our only *real* hope for survival is peace with the Wolmen."

"And the only way to be sure of that," Rod said stiffly, "is to meld the two cultures into a single, unified society."

Chornoi nodded. "And having all the blasters on the soldiers' side, doesn't exactly help build Wolman confidence."

"Maybe not." Yorick looked around. "I get the feeling we're missing something. There may be evidence of a struggle in the area around here—or some other kind of evidence that we won't find at night."

"True," Rod said judiciously. "With only a flashlight,

we're limited to looking at what we already suspect. We'll have to wait for daylight to get the Big Picture, and any clues we haven't thought of."

"There's a problem with that," Yorick pointed out.

"Aye, my lord," Gwen added. "We must needs be at the Governor's great hall in the morn—e'en by dawn."

Rod shrugged. "So what? We already skipped town, didn't we?"

"Aye, yet they did enlarge us upon our parole."

Chornoi stared. "*What* is she talking about?"

"She means Shacklar only let us go, because we promised to come back in the morning." Rod's mouth tightened at the corners.

"'Twould be dishonorable, an we did not return."

"Well, true, but this isn't Gramarye. Honor isn't quite so important here."

Gwen stared at him, scandalized. More importantly, Rod realized with a sinking feeling in his stomach, he didn't believe it himself anymore. "All right, all right! We'll have to go back to town! Besides—skipping town is one thing, but skipping the planet is entirely another!"

Gwen frowned. "What is a 'planet,' my lord?"

Chornoi just stared at her; but Rod took a deep breath and said, "Well. A planet is a world, darling. It's not flat, you see—it's round, like a ball."

"Assuredly not!" she cried.

Rod shrugged. "Okay, so don't believe me—just take my word for it. I came to Gramarye on a 'shooting star,' remember—and I got to see the planet from way up. *Way* up—and it's round. Oh, believe me, it is round!"

"He's telling you the truth." Chornoi frowned, puzzled. "I've seen planets from space, too, and they're round, all right. Like that." She pointed at the single moon that was still up in the sky. "It's just a very *little* planet. The word means 'wanderer,' see, and you know how the moon wanders; it moves all over the sky."

"Aye." Gwen frowned, trying to absorb the alien concept. “There be others, be there not? Stars that do wander.”

“Right.” Rod nodded. “They’re worlds, too. But most of the stars, the ones that stay put—well, they’re suns, just like the one that gives us light and heat during the daytime.”

“Can they truly be?” Gwen breathed, eyes round. “Nay, surely not! For they be but points of light!”

“That’s because they’re so far away,” Chornoi explained.

“Nay, it could not be.” Gwen turned to her, frowning. “For they would have to be so far distant that . . .” She broke off, her mind reeling as she realized just how far away that would have to be.

Chornoi watched her, nodding slowly. “Yes, ma’am. That’s how far away. So far that it takes their light quite a few years to get here.”

“Yet how can that be?” Gwen asked, looking from Rod to Chornoi and back. “How can light take time to come to a place?”

“Well—it travels,” Rod said. “Believe us, honey—there’s no easy way to prove it. I mean, it has been proven, but it was very hard to do, very complicated. Light travels at 186,282 miles per second. That’s about six trillion miles in a year.” Gwen’s eyes lost focus, and Rod confided, “Don’t try, dear. We can’t really grasp the idea of a distance that huge—not really, not emotionally. But we can be intimidated by trying.” He turned to Chornoi. “The nearest star here—it wouldn’t happen to be visible, would it?”

“Oh, yeah. It’s the third star in the barrel of ‘The Blaster’—one of our homemade constellations.” Chornoi stepped up beside Gwen and pointed. “You see those six stars, forming a rough parallelogram—you know, a rectangle leaning sideways?”

Gwen sighted along her arm. “Aye, I see them.”

“Well, that’s the handgrip. And that line of four stars at a right angle to them? That’s the barrel. The third star in from its end is our nearest neighbor.” Chornoi shrugged. “It doesn’t really have a name—just a number on the star-charts. The soldiers call it ‘The Girl Next Door.’”

"How far away is it?" Rod asked.

"Just under seven light-years."

"Dost mean . . ." Gwen swallowed. ". . . that the star I see now is not truly the star? That 'tis but light that hath left it seven years agone?"

"Right." Rod nodded with vigor. "We're not seeing it as it is, but as it was seven years ago. *Very* right, dear. For all we know, it could be blowing up right now—but we wouldn't find out about it for seven years." Secretly, he was impressed with the quickness of Gwen's understanding.

His wife just stared up into the night sky, lost in the immensity of the concept.

"And planets," Rod murmured, "swing around and around their sun in circles that are just a little bit egg-shaped."

Gwen whirled to stare at him in astonishment. "Nay—for surely the Sun doth go about the Earth! I do see it rise and go across the sky daily!"

Rod shook his head. "It just looks that way. It's the earth that's turning, really." He cranked with a finger. "Around and around, like a spinning top. Stop and think about it—if you're turning around and around, it looks as though Yorick, there, is turning around *you,* when he's really standing still, doesn't it?"

Gwen gazed at Yorick, then slowly began to turn around in place. After two revolutions, she said, "'Tis so." She stopped and looked up at Rod. "Yet merely from looking, how can I tell whether 'tis he that's moving, or I?"

Rod's breath hissed in. He'd known Gwen was intelligent, but he was amazed by the quickness with which her mind darted on to the next question. He stared at her, astounded by her mental leap. Then he smiled weakly. "Well, you have to have other kinds of evidence, too, dear. For example, when we look through telesc . . . uh, *closely* at other planets, we can see their moons going around and around them. That explains why our own moon wanders the way it does—it's really revolving around us. Which makes it a pretty good bet that we're revolving around our sun, especially after we've found out that it's a heck of a lot bigger than any of its planets." He shrugged. "And the bigger it is, the harder it pulls."

She stared at him for a long moment, then said slowly, "And is it for that reason that we will have such great difficulty in leaving this 'planet?'"

Rod caught his breath, staring at her. Then he opened his mouth, breathing in, and finally said, "Yes. The planet pulls things to it, just as the sun pulls the planet toward itself."

"Then why doth the planet not fall into the sun?"

"Because it's going too fast. Like . . ." Inspiration hit. "Like you, when you're trying to catch Geoffrey. He goes flying past, and you grab him, but because he's going so fast, you can't pull him in against you. On the other hand, you're holding on tightly enough so that he can't get away, either, so he just swings around at the end of your arm. Now, imagine that he refuses to stop, and he just goes on swinging around and around you, forever. And it's that same kind of pull, like your pull on him, that attracts things to the planet. Of course, from where we're standing, that 'attracting' looks like 'falling.' We call the force 'gravity.' The planet pulls on the object—like this." He pulled her up against him, and wrapped his arms around her. "And it doesn't want to let the object go."

Gwen smiled, her lids drooping. "Doth the object, then, not also draw the planet?"

"You *do* learn fast, don't you? Yes, the object pulls, too, but its pull is very weak, because it's so small. You and I, now, aren't all that much different in size."

"Nay," she murmured, "we are well matched."

Rod was definitely losing interest in the lecture, but there were people watching. "Now. Your original question was, why is it so hard for the object to get away from the planet?"

She smiled up at him. "Wherefore should it wish to?"

"Can't think of a good reason, myself," Rod admitted,

"but just for the sake of argument, let's assume it does. Go ahead and try."

"An thou dost wish it," she sighed, and pushed against him.

He loosened his arms a little, letting her move away a few inches. "See—you have to be able to push *really* hard to get away from me. And that's how people leave planets—in flying ships that can push really hard against the planet."

"They're called 'spaceships,' by the way," Yorick put in. "Don't let him baby-talk you, milady."

"I would not consider it," Gwen said, with some asperity.

"And the ship," Rod said, "has to push hard enough to go fast enough—that's called 'escape velocity.' And when you're up to escape velocity . . ." He let go, and she stumbled back. ". . . you escape. And that's how you get off the surface of a planet. See?"

"Indeed." She came back, straightening her hair, the gleam of battle in her eye. "Yet could we not build such 'velocity,' my lord? Thou and I, together?"

In spite of himself, Rod took a step back. It took him a second to realize she was talking about telekinesis. "Well . . ."

But Yorick was watching them with growing apprehension. "Uh, Major—milady—don't do anything rash!"

"It would be," Rod admitted. "We might be able to do it if we pooled our forces, darling—but there's another little problem." He coughed delicately and looked up at the stars. "You see, we're not the only thing that the planet's holding to itself. It's also holding the air that we breathe."

She stared, at a loss.

"About twenty miles up . . ." Rod pointed. ". . . you run out of atmosphere. It's just empty space, without any wind, not even a breath of fresh air—or a breath of anything, for that matter. That's why Chornoi said she'd seen a planet *from* space—because there wasn't any air there. Just empty space."

Slowly, Gwen lifted her eyes to the stars again. "So much

blackness between them . . . Yet how can there be 'space,' as thou dost call it, without air to breathe? Is that not the 'space?' "

Rod shook his head. "Air is a substance, too, just like water—only lighter, not as dense. It covers the planet's whole surface, but only because gravity holds it there. The farther you are from a planet, the weaker the pull feels, until it can't even hold air anymore. And when that happens, when you've got space with nothing in it, we call that 'vacuum.' That means there's nothing to breathe, too, of course—so even if we could get out there, honey, we wouldn't last long."

Slowly, Gwen lowered her gaze to him again, but the stars stayed in her eyes. "'Tis wondrous," she breathed. "Nay, I shall trust thee in this, my lord. But I shall trust, also, that together, we may find a way."

Chornoi shook her head in exasperation. "Don't you know better than to put that much trust in a man?"

"Nay." Gwen turned to her with a smile, catching Rod's hand behind her back. "And I trust that I never shall."

It was nice to know that she felt so warm about it, especially since Rod was feeling a chill run down his back and spread out to envelop his rib cage. She had learned it all so quickly! Everything she'd heard, she'd understood instantly, or almost. And every single one of those concepts was totally alien to her culture. He was beginning to dread that she might be smarter than he was. It was one thing for him to understand her culture, but it was entirely another for her to understand his.

"Well, be that all as it may—space, vacuum, and escape," Chornoi grumbled, "but the here-and-now is that we need to look at this place by daylight, and you two have to be back in town before morning."

"I'd say that's pretty clear. It comes down to you or me," Yorick said. "And, if you'll pardon my male chauvinism . . ."

"I won't," Chornoi snapped. "I told you I've spent time among the Wolmen. I'll be safe, believe me, especially since I never made any bones about how much I didn't like the way the colonists did things. The Wolmen heard about it and began to chum up to me—oh, not making passes or anything, don't worry about that; they've got their own ideals of beauty, and I'm not up to their standards."

Rod bit his tongue.

"But they did cultivate me as a possible ally within Shacklar's camp. Not that I ever would've betrayed the soldiers . . ." A shadow crossed Chornoi's face. ". . . I hope. Hope even more that I never have to find out the hard way . . . Anyhow!" She straightened, eyes flashing. "It's enough to guarantee that I'll be safe, till I see you back in town."

"That's kind of odd, as diplomacy goes," Rod said, frowning. "On their part, I mean. That kind of wily statecraft doesn't quite square with the usual concept of the unsophisticated aborigine."

"Shacklar and Cholly have been trying very hard to sophisticate them, thank you," Chornoi snorted. "Cholly's traders are really teachers in disguise."

"Oh!" Rod lifted his head, a few facts suddenly colliding and yielding solutions. "So that's why he doesn't make much money off his pharmaceuticals trade."

Chornoi nodded. "Something like that. His traders keep the prices low and the payments high, so that the Wolmen will keep coming back to talk to them. They've been doing a very good job of giving the Wolmen a modern education—including political science. And they begin it with Machiavelli."

Rod saw Yorick open his mouth, and said quickly, "So they know the realities of technological culture—including back-stabbing."

Chornoi nodded. "And a lot of other things you wouldn't expect them to know. But it has the advantage of letting them take the long view."

"Including being careful to protect a potential ally."

"Yes, as long as the truce holds, and it'll hold at least until your trial is over."

"And thou wilt return ere then?"

Chornoi nodded. "I'll check out this area as soon as it's light. I should be back on the civilized side shortly after dawn. If I'm too late to catch you before the courtroom, I'll drop in there." Her smile hardened. "I'll be back, don't worry. I'll be back. You folks go on now . . . What are you waiting for? Go on, now! Go!"

Slowly, they turned, and began to go down the hillside.

"Dosta truly believe she will be secure?" Gwen asked.

Yorick shrugged. "I dunno—these boys are savages, even though they're synthetic ones. What do you think, Major?"

"I think they're male," Rod answered, "and I think Chornoi knows just how much of a woman she is, regardless of what she said about their standards of beauty."

"There's truth in that," Gwen agreed, "and I doubt not she could lay low any warrior who sought to best her."

"Well, it'd be an even match, at least."

"No, not really," Yorick disagreed. "After all, she *is* a professional."

Gwen turned back for a last look, concern furrowing her brow—and froze, with a gasp.

Yorick and Rod turned back to look.

Chornoi stood at the top of the rise, stripped naked and glowing in the moonlight. As they watched, she scooped her fingers into a flat roundel and rubbed them over her arm. The skin darkened.

"Body-paint," Yorick murmured. "Betcha it's purple, Major."

"And I'll bet we'll find out tomorrow." Rod turned away, shaking his head. "Come on, troops. Somehow, I just became sure she'll be safe."

"As the mercury said to the water, 'Pardon my density.'" Yorick's gaze swiveled from Rod to Gwen and back. "But if we can do it this way, why that charade with the sentry on the way out?"

"Why, for that Chornoi did not know we were witch-folk." Gwen tucked her arm more tightly into Yorick's.

"Yeah—you *know* what we are," Rod reminded him, "but Chornoi probably doesn't even believe in ESP, let alone know we've got it."

"I see." Yorick nodded. "Mustn't shock the poor thing, must we? After all, she might decide she's on the other side."

"Well, her volunteering *was* an enormous stroke of luck..."

"Sure. Now I get it. Oh, I'm quick."

"Indeed thou art, in regard to most matters," Gwen assured him.

"Yeah, we all have our blind spots," Rod agreed. "Now, as one agent to another—do you really think Chornoi will learn anything more than we already found out?"

Yorick shrugged. "Hard to say. I don't *really* think there was any more evidence up there at the murder site, but you never know, do you?"

"True, true." Rod gazed steadily at the top of the wall. "On the other hand, she was pretty obviously planning to interrogate some Wolmen."

"Well, at least Hwun," Yorick qualified. "I mean, he does have to come up to greet the sun tomorrow morning, doesn't he?"

Rod shuddered. "That guy gives me the creeping chillies."

"In truth, he is cold," Gwen agreed.

"Not what you'd expect, in a Gestalt culture," Yorick agreed. "Not quite human, y'know?"

"Look who's talking," Rod grunted.

"Could we hold down on the racial slurs, here?" Yorick had the rare case of using the term correctly. "Besides, even if he is Mr. Fishface, I'll bet Chornoi will get every ounce of information that he's got. I mean, male is male."

"I know what you mean," Rod agreed, "and I don't doubt it for a second. It's just that I don't expect there to be a hell of a lot of information for her to get."

"True, true." Yorick looked towards the Wall. "The really important information is likely to be in there—if we can just figure out where to look for it. Now, let us think, Major, milady—who, besides you two, might have reason to want a Wolman dead?"

"Well, *we* don't have any reason to," Rod snorted. "But the obvious answer is VETO . . . or SPITE."

"Or both of them," Yorick grunted.

"Futurians of some kind. They tried to assassinate Gwen and me and, when we turned out to be a little too lethal, kidnapped us back in time as a second choice."

"Not too bad, either. I mean, without help, your chances of getting back to the future are very slender."

"Nay! Rather, we would surely have returned, sooner or later, to the year from which we left," Gwen objected. "'Tis simply that, when we did, we'd have been five hundred years dead. . . ."

"That is a problem, I think you'll admit. There's a definite limit on how much fun you can have in that condition. But it does bring up the question of why they sent you to this particular here and now."

"Wolmar." Rod frowned. "Right after the PEST coup d'etat." His eyes lost focus as he gazed off into space. "Nice question . . ."

"And, sin that thou didst ask it, I doubt me not an thou hast an answer."

Yorick glanced sideways at Gwen. "Where'd you get *her,* Major?"

"Just lucky, I guess. . . . What was your answer?"

"To make it easy to try another assassination attempt." Yorick grinned. "The early PEST years are ideal for the purpose. The interstellar totalitarian government is brand-new, at its brightest strength, with plenty of agents left over from its coup, but not yet tied down to the central planets as secret police."

Rod nodded, feeling numbed. "Yeah . . . that does kinda stack the odds in their favor. . . . But why one of the frontier planets? Why not Terra?"

"Too hard to cover up a murder attempt." Yorick shook his head. "Too many people."

"Yeah, but would they really care?"

"There is that," Yorick said judiciously. "But a much more practical point is that, with all those people to hide among, it'd be too easy for you to get away. And they know the two of you well enough to realize that you could be very hard to hold on to."

"A point," Rod admitted, "and it is hard for us to just disappear here in the grassland, isn't it?"

"Or even in the town," Yorick agreed, "what there is of it."

"Yet they have already attempted murder," Gwen pointed out, "and failed. Would they not essay summat more subtle?"

"Such as trying to frame us for murder?" Rod nodded. "Yes, I think you've summed it up nicely, dear."

"A nice little death sentence would suit them just fine," Yorick mused, "especially with a bunch of savages to insist on it not being commuted to something humane, such as life imprisonment."

Rod snorted.

"If you say so," Yorick said affably. "But it's the best theory I can come up with. Got any other candidates in mind, Major? Who else might want to create a handy little murder incident?"

Rod glowered, staring at the top of the Wall, thinking it over. Finally he said, "Shacklar."

A sentry paced by, dark against the stars.

They fell silent, staring, eyes locked onto him until he passed, and the curve of the wall hid him from sight.

Rod hissed, "Now!" and closed his eyes, concentrating on the feeling of lightness. He began to drift upward out of the shadow. Gwen matched his pace, rising on her broomstick. They accelerated, moving faster and faster. Yorick swallowed heavily and clamped his jaws shut.

Up, over the wall, and down the other side they glided, Yorick slung between them. His feet jarred against earth, and he let go of them as though their arms were hot metal. He gave himself a shake, heaved a deep breath, and turned to Rod with a bright smile. "Now! Just why did you suspect General Shacklar?"

"Let's talk about it when we're a little further from the Wall." Rod darted an uneasy glance toward the walkway at the top. "Come on, let's go!"

They dashed across fifty yards of open ground, into the shadow of an outbuilding, plowed to a halt, and propped themselves against the shack, chests heaving. "After all," Yorick panted, "this little murder just might bring all Shacklar's last ten years of work crashing down. He's managed to get the two sides almost to the point of joining in a single government. Why would he take a chance on busting it up?"

"To finish the job." Rod grinned.

Yorick and Gwen stared.

"Think it over." Rod felt quite pleased with himself. "Gwen and I have given him the perfect opportunity to hatch his united government. We're totally new, so no one's going to gripe much if we're just handed over to the Wolmen. That would give our friendly natives a heck of a lot more confidence in Shacklar, with the added advantage of having made the Wolmen negotiate with Shacklar as a nation, all banded together. So all the General has to do is make it clear that the Wolmen are just as much involved in deciding this case as the colonists are, and it could be the first action of that unified government he's been trying to develop."

"Very good, so far as it goes." Yorick nodded, lips pursed. "But what if the gamble fails? What happens if you manage to disappear, or if you're so inconsiderate as to prove yourselves innocent, or something? Then he's got a civil war on his hands."

"Not all that civil," Rod said, scowling. "I think he could smooth over a 'Not guilty' verdict, if he had to. He's got the two sides getting along well enough right now. They even need each other a little. Both sides sure want what the other has to offer. All he has to do is find them a convenient excuse for forgetting the whole thing."

"Just a face-saver." Yorick said thoughtfully. "Ever consider diplomacy as a career, Major?"

Rod opened his mouth, but Gwen spoke first. "He hath, and he doth." She looked from Rod to Yorick. "Yet neither of thee doth explain why no Wolman is missing."

Both men stood stock-still."

"Shall I tell thee?" Gwen said, smiling. "It may hap that Shacklar hath had his assassin disguise himself as a Wolman."

"Yeah, it's possible." Rod kept his eyes on Yorick as he nodded. "And, of course, the Futurians could have done that, too."

Yorick returned the nod. "Very possible, Major."

"So, then." Gwen set her fists on her hips and looked from the one to the other. "We have two schemes, either of which may serve. How are we to find out which is true, gentlemen?"

"Or if neither is." Rod shrugged. "We've got to find more information."

"Yeah, we keep coming back to that, don't we?" Yorick rubbed his temple with a forefinger.

"And how wilt thou accomplish this finding, my lord?"

"Go to the place where people talk, of course." Yorick grinned. "Feel like a drink, Major?"

"Very much, but..." Rod exchanged glances with Gwen. "I don't know if it'd be too healthy for us to show up in Cholly's."

Yorick spread his hands. "So it's my job. So what? Do I care? Do I worry about those bloodthirsty soldiers mistaking me for a spy? No! Do I ask for honor? Do I ask for praise?"

"You're asking for it, period! Okay, we're thankful, we're grateful! We'll praise you to the skies! We'll even give you a good reference! What do you think you might hear that's worth repeating?"

Yorick elaborated a shrug. "If I knew, I wouldn't have to socialize. Y' never know—maybe somebody's doing an awful lot of sudden spending. If he is, three guesses where he got the funds? Oh, you can find out all sorts of stuff you weren't expecting!"

Rod pondered. "Might be. But remember, this is all just a guess. For all we know, the Wolman could have committed suicide. Our hypothetical assassin isn't even a rumor."

"Don't worry, I won't give the rumor currency—not so much as a farthing." Yorick flashed him a grin. "I'm off to the pub with the public, Major. See you in the false dawn." He tugged his forelock in Gwen's direction, and turned away to disappear into the night.

"I trust the dawn will be all that is false," Gwen murmured.

"A point," Rod admitted. "What do you say we follow him? Discreetly, of course."

"Assuredly," Gwen agreed. "Who can be so discreet as ourselves?"

Rod proffered his arm. She hooked her hand over his elbow, and they wandered off into the night, following Yorick's mental trail.

"Yet is there not greater hazard here, my lord? We might, after all, sit safe in some shed and listen with our minds."

"No doubt." Rod poked his nose over the windowsill for a quick peek at the inside of Cholly's Tavern. "But I can't resist watching that muscle-bound jester in action. Besides, we're at the back of the building, and in the shadows. Nobody's apt to see us. I mean, they do have indoor plumbing here."

Inside, Yorick was gradually bringing the conversation closer and closer to the politics of the moment.

"Aye, here's to our Wolman brothers!" A corpulent corporal lifted his mug in a toast.

"And our Wolwoman sisters," a PFC agreed.

A trooper shrugged. "*You* have 'em as sisters, if you want. Me, I'd favor closer relations." He won a general, leering laugh, and a middle-aged private called, "Relations is what they'd be, shavetail. These Wolmen don't hold with casual acquaintance. Seducers go quick to the shotgun."

Yorick juggled with it, and lifted his glass. "Well, here's to the distaffs. May they not be disowned by distiffs."

His answer was a chuckle that died a quick death. Soldiers fell silent, glancing at each other. "Don't know much, do yer?" A sergeant snarled.

Yorick frowned at him, and shrugged. "'Last come, first numbed.' So the Wolmen get mad at us. So what?"

"So what, he says!" growled one of the older privates. "Yer wasn't here when the battles was real, chum! Yer didn't have ter go out 'gainst them bloody spears and see yer buddy's bowels ripped out!"

"Yer didn't have an arm chopped off," growled a maimed veteran, "and see the stump a-pumping!"

"Yuh didn't have their devil's yowling clawing at yuh ears, whiles yuh pulled back tuh the Wall with a dozen, where yuh'd gone out with a hundred," growled a grizzled sergeant, "and them spears and arrows poking at yuh from all sides."

"Don't sell them short," a gnarled corporal grated. "Vicious, they is, when they's fighting."

"And they isn't no cowards," another rumbled. "Arrowheads and spears can kill a man as dead as any blaster-bolt, my lad. And y' can't duck 'em, when they come in clouds!"

"How many did we lose?" The grizzled sergeant glared down into his beer. "A dozen a day? Sixty in a week? A hundred?"

"And for years it went on, years and years!" A fortyish

sergeant slammed his tankard down on the bar. "We'll not have those days back—no, not at any cost!"

With a shock, Rod recognized Thaler.

"Well, even I wouldn't go that far," the grizzled sergeant mused. "I can think of some prices I wouldn't pay."

"For all that, so can I," the fortyish one admitted. "But there's plenty of prices well worth it!" He glared around him. "What's two lives, against the thousands that a war would cost? What's two lives, hey?"

The room was silent. Finally, "Aye," grunted the grizzled veteran, "but like as not, they'll squirm out of it at the trial."

"Only if they're innocent," Yorick put in quickly. "Okay, so I haven't known Shacklar as long as you have—but I'd have faith in his justice."

"Innocent or not, who cares?" Thaler turned to glower at Yorick. "If they're freed, the Wolmen will explode and swarm down on us again! And this time, every man jack one of 'em has a blaster!"

A mutter of apprehension ran around the bar. Most men shuddered, and the room was quiet.

For a time. Then a voice said,

"Kill 'em."

Shocked silence.

Then another voice. "Aye."

"Aye, kill 'em!"

"What matter two lives, in place of thousands?"

"Aye! Give the Wolmen their dead bodies in the morning, and they'll go away!"

The grizzled sergeant frowned. "But when Shacklar finds out . . ."

"He won't make no fuss," Thaler said, with a vicious grin. "What's the dead, compared to the living? Nay, Shacklar may be sheet-pale, but he'll say naught."

"But they're innocent!" Yorick protested.

"So're the men who would die in a war!" Thaler snarled. "What's two innocents against a thousand, laddie? Eh?"

"But the trial!" Yorick bleated. "Would *you* want to go without a trial?"

"They're not me," Thaler snarled. "They're not any of us."

That drew a low rumble of agreement.

"But . . ." Yorick stabbed with a finger. "If you sell *them* for peace, what's gonna happen when one of *you* is accused?"

"Oh, my bleedin' heart!" the grizzled sergeant growled.

"What's-a-matter, bucko? You *want* war?" Thaler looked Yorick up and down, as though measuring him for a coffin. "Ayuh, I think that's it. You've never seen a battle, have you, laddie? And you're sick with craving to be blooded."

"The hell I am!" Yorick said quickly. "I saw my share of scrapes before I wound up here—and calling 'em 'police actions' didn't cut the casualty lists!"

"I don't believe a word of it." Thaler slipped off his bar stool and stepped up very close to the Neanderthal, blood in his eye. "You don't have the look of a fighter to me. But you'd be glad enough to see us die in your place."

"Let's go get them," someone growled.

"Aye!" "Aye, get 'em and blast 'em!" "Serve 'em on a platter!" "Aye!"

"You're in it, laddie." Thaler fixed Yorick with a glittering eye. "Come with us now, or we'll know you're against us, and a traitor to the whole of the colony!"

"With you?" Yorick stared.

Then he leaped off his bar stool. "I'll do more than come with you! I saw the two of them scurrying for cover when I was coming in here. You come with me, and I'll show you where to find them!"

Thaler stared, then slowly grinned.

"Let's go!" Yorick shouldered his way through the mob, heading for the door.

Rod and Gwen exchanged one quick, appalled glance, then shot away from the building at top speed.

Where, my lord? Gwen's thoughts sounded inside Rod's head.

Anywhere, Rod answered, looking around frantically. *There!* He pointed to two huge barrels, lying on their sides, empty. *Crouch down!"*

Gwen did, clutching her broom to her, eyes squeezed shut. Rod hefted the barrel up and lowered it gently over her. Then he crouched down beside her, staring at the second barrel, concentrating, blocking out the rest of the world. The barrel lifted slowly, then descended to settle over him. He relaxed and sat back, leaning against its side, but kept his eyes shut, listening with his mind, seeing through the eyes of one of the less-intelligent soldiers back in the middle of the mob.

Yorick exploded out of the tavern with the lynch mob behind him. "Come on! I'll show you the last place I saw them!"

Gwen's thoughts rang in Rod's head: *How could he turn against us so thoroughly, so quickly?*

I don't know, Rod answered grimly, *but I'm considering taking up a new hobby. Say—carving . . .*

The sound of the mob faded, but it still clamored inside their minds. The soldiers ran frantically into the night, then slowed as the first flush of enthusiasm began to wear off. Rod's medium-soldier began to grow resentful—what was he doing, out here in the middle of the night, running nowhere?

Then Yorick's voice crowed, way ahead, "There they go! Quick, after them!"

The soldier's enthusiam leaped up again. Filled with excitement, howling with bloodlust, he ran after his companions. They swerved to the left, dashed down a darkened street, and ran for several minutes. The soldier's breath began to rasp in his lungs, and sullen resentment began again.

Yorick howled, "There! Between those two buildings! I saw 'em run! After 'em, quick!"

Excitement boiled up again, and the soldier leaped after his mates, the thrill of the chase pounding through his veins.

On down the street they ran—and on . . . and on . . . and on . . .

Rod thought at his barrel; it lifted, and he turned to Gwen as her barrel drifted up, then dropped down on its side. They shared a guilty look.

"How could we have doubted him?" Gwen murmured.

"Easy—I never did trust anybody who was always cheerful. But I was wrong—dead wrong."

"Not 'dead,' praise Heaven!"

"But a fool." Rod's mouth tightened. "What's going to happen to me if I keep doubting my real friends?"

"We shall repay him," Gwen assured, "with our safety."

"True," Rod agreed. "That's what he wants most right now. And, come to think of it . . ." He turned toward the tavern with a glint in his eye. "He has bought us a little time here, hasn't he?"

Gwen looked startled, then smiled. "He hath indeed, my lord. Art thou mad as a bantam cock, thus to beard thine enemies?"

Rod nodded. "Not a bad simile, my lady. Y'know, I'm feeling a bit thirsty. Shall we?"

"Certes, an thou dost wish it, my lord." She clasped his arm.

"After all, everyone who's out for our blood has already left, right?"

They turned to face the tavern, threw back their shoulders, and stepped off in unison.

With a jaunty swagger, they sauntered into Cholly's Tavern.

Cholly looked up to see who was coming in, then looked again, wide-eyed.

The half-dozen patrons who were still there looked up, wondering what could startle Cholly—then stared, themselves.

Cholly recovered right away, turning back to mop the

bar. "Well then, now, Master and Missus! What'll be your pleasure?"

"Just a pint." Rod slid onto a bar stool. Gwen slid up beside him, hands folded on the edge of the bar, the very picture of demure innocence. Rod grinned around at the other patrons, and they swallowed heavily, managed feeble grins, and turned back to their drinking.

Cholly set a couple of foaming mugs in front of them, and Rod turned his attention back to the important things in life. He took a long drink, then exhaled with satisfaction. "So! What's the news?"

All of the patrons suddenly became very concerned with their beer and ale.

"Oh," Cholly said affably, "nothing terribly much. The word from the Wall is that the Wolmen're beginning to drift up and pitch camp, just out of blaster range. . . . There're twenty or thirty people out howling fer yer blood. . . . The gin'ral's sent the captains out t' remind people where their battle stations are. . . ."

Rod nodded. "Slow night, huh?"

"Humdrum," Cholly agreed. "I gets rumors all the time."

"Yeah, about those rumors . . ." Rod cocked a forefinger. "Hear anything about Shacklar?"

Cholly looked up, startled. "The gin'ral? What about 'im?"

Rod shrugged. "He seems to be taking the whole thing very calmly, if you ask me."

"We didn't," a young soldier reminded him.

Rod shrugged again. "Whatever. Is he always so cold-blooded about crises?"

"Gin'rally, yes," Cholly said slowly. "I've known him to get excited when he can't find his cat-o'-nine-tails, but nothing else seems to fash him much."

"Cat-o'-nine-tails?" Rod frowned. "I thought you said he outlawed that."

"He did." Cholly fixed him with a level gaze. "But who's

to arrest the General-Governor, hey? *Quis ipsos custodies custodiat,* young man."

"'Who will police the police,' huh?" Rod nodded. "A point."

"He never does anything to anybody else, without a good reason," Cholly supplied helpfully.

"'To anybody else,'" Rod repeated. "Well, I can accept that."

"Yer don't have much choice," a fiftyish ranker snarled.

"He's always fair," Cholly reminded.

"More'n fair," the ranker growled.

"And what he does is always for the greatest good of almost everybody, as Jeremy Bentham used to say."

Rod didn't like the sound of that "almost." "I thought Bentham's line was, 'the greatest good of the greatest number.'"

"Well, that's almost everybody, ain't it?"

"Better than Bentham hoped for, probably," Rod admitted, "but nothing to lose his head over."

As long as there's progress," Cholly sighed.

"That there is," rumbled the grizzled veteran, "with the General. Every year he makes life a little better for everybody."

"Except the Wolmen?"

"The Wolmen, too!" The young soldier looked up in surprise. "I mean, would you believe it? He's actually trying to ease us soldiers into getting along with those savages! Permanently!"

"Why don't I have trouble believing that?" Rod wondered.

"Always a skeptic," Cholly sighed.

Rod turned back to him. "I'll bet this little murder will set his plans back a ways."

Cholly's eyes suddenly clicked into "wariness" mode.

The young soldier said stoutly, "Don't you believe it!" and the grizzled veteran agreed, "He'll find a way to make this work out for the best of all of us."

"Colonists *and* Wolmen?" Rod said, with a lift of one eyebrow.

"Don't you doubt it!" the older man commanded.

"Oh, I don't," Rod said softly, "not one bit."

"Well." The young soldier looked up in surprise. "You're won, then?"

"Totally convinced," Rod confirmed.

The grizzled veteran still glared at him with suspicion, and Cholly just rolled his eyes up, but the young soldier grinned happily. "Well! That's done, then." He set both palms against the edge of the bar and, with a manful push, slid off his bar stool. "For my part, if I don't hit my bunk within the quarter hour, I won't make my sentry duty in the morning. Of course, I'll have a nice, snug berth in the stockade waiting for me."

"Morning?" Rod pricked up his ears. "How early? I mean, it's only . . ." He glanced at the clock over the bar. ". . . twenty-five hundred. . . . *Huh?"*

The young soldier grinned wickedly at Cholly, jerking his head toward Rod. "He *is* new here, isn't he?"

The young always so enjoyed being able to feel superior.

"There're twenty-six hours in a Wolmar day, chum," he advised Rod. "If I get to bed by twenty-five hundred, I'll have plenty of time for my six hours, and still make my five o'clock sentry-go."

Rod shuddered appropriately. "Horrible hours. Say, uh . . . you didn't happen to notice anybody going outside the Wall yesterday morning, did you?"

The young man shook his head, not quite noticing Cholly's frantic signals. "Nobody, except for Sergeant Thaler." He lifted his mug in a toast. "Your health, Cholly."

"Yours, Spar," the bartender sighed.

Spar downed the rest of his beer and turned away to the door, wiping his mouth on his sleeve. He waved, and drifted on out.

Rod turned back to Cholly. "That's strange. Thaler isn't

one of your traders, is he?"

Cholly opened his mouth, but the grizzled corporal was a phoneme ahead. "No. Not that it matters—they usually come in around midday, anyway."

"Oh," Rod said, with total innocence, "they do?"

"Thaler's a valuable noncom," Cholly warned. "Shacklar trusts him down to his boot tops."

"Yes," Rod said softly, "that's what worries me."

"Milord." Gwen laid a hand on his arm. "I bethink me thou hast had ale enow, for this night."

"Hm?" Rod looked up in surprise. He caught the meaning in her gaze, and said, "Oh!" He turned his attention to what was going on outside the tavern for a minute, and heard disgruntled, frustrated, thirsty thoughts—the lynch mob, coming back. "Uh, yeah! Probably. We should be going." He chugged the rest of the mug, set it down. "Put it on my tab, will you?" Then he slipped off the stool, offered Gwen his arm, and turned to stroll out the door. "Thanks for everything," he called back.

Cholly raised a hand in farewell. "Keep the faith."

Rod wondered which one, but decided not to ask. As soon as they were out the door, they leaped to the side, ran around to the back. They crouched down by the window with the bulk of the building between them and the returning lynch mob, ears and minds wide open, listening. Rod had one eye above the windowsill. After a moment, Gwen joined him.

The mob streamed in, breaking up into individual soldiers who began to think as people again. "Ar, what a waste of good drinking time!" "I've had more luck chasing extinct species!" "Reminds me of the last time I went fishing . . ." "Blinkin' witches, that's what they are!" growled a portly private, bellying up to the bar.

"Witches!" Sergeant Thaler sneered. "Nay, ain't nothin' but the natural in this!" He turned to glare at Yorick. "Natural fowl, that is! Led us a merry chase after the wild goose, didn't you?"

"Who, me?" Yorick shook his head violently, all offended innocence."You've got the wrong bird, Sergeant."

"Have I really, now?" Thaler purred, sliding off his bar stool and taking a step toward Yorick.

The Neanderthal laid a hand over his heart. "Never chased a wild goose in my life. Just wait till they fly by, usually. Not bad, with a little orange sauce and a side of peas . . ."

"No more of yer lip!" Thaler snarled. "Y' won't turn us aside with yer jestin' this time!" He wrapped a hand in Yorick's jacket, and jerked his head close. "You're in cahoots with 'em, ain'cha?"

The nearest soldiers looked up, startled. Then they scowled, and an ugly murmur began.

"I saw him in here with 'em this afternoon," a private called.

"Aye, and right chummy he was!"

Thaler slid a knife out of his boot and rested the point against Yorick's belly. "I shave with this, so mind you tell the truth. You're in it with 'em, ain'cha? Up to yer eyebrows. And all you're angling for, is helping them escape."

"Whup! Whoa! Hold it, here!" Yorick waved a hand. "Fair trial! Let's be fair about this!"

"Nay," an older corporal growled. "Where's yer mind? We've been through that, and through! We wants dead murderers, not live suspects!"

"I'm not talking about them—just me!"

"What should you have a trial for?" Thaler snarled. "You're trying to help them get away, and that'll bring a war on us!" He shouted out to the rest of the soldiers, "He's a traitor! A traitor to the colony, and all of us!"

"Aye!" The soldiers began crowding around. "What do you want, all of us dead?"

"Never seen the color of blood, have yuh?"

"Aye! Let's show him his own!"

"Who's got a rope here?"

"Whup! Hold it! I give!" Yorick waved both hands as though he were erasing a blackboard. "I admit it! I'm guilty!

Just back off, boys!" He heaved a sigh. "You caught me. All right. Anything except the rope and the knife. I'll show you where they *really* are."

Outside, Rod and Gwen exchanged appalled glances. Then they dove for the empty barrels again.

"This way!" Yorick bellowed, charging toward the door. The soldiers parted and let him through, taken by surprise.

He leaped out the tavern door, bellowing, "Right on the first try this time! Come on! Catch the witches!"

The mob roared out behind him, baying at full voice. Footsteps thundered right past the two barrels, then faded into the distance.

The barrels glided up. Rod and Gwen uncoiled, and Rod shook his head. "I've got to see this. I've just got to."

"Aye." Glints danced in Gwen's eyes. "How will he turn them this time?"

"I dunno, but he'll find a way." Rod caught her hand. "He's a man of amazing resources. He may not be able to manipulate symbols—but people are another matter entirely. Come on, they're getting away!"

Feather-footed and silent, they fled through the night.

They sighted the mob just as it came into a large, open plaza. Beyond it, the Wall bulked large against the stars.

Yorick plowed to a stop and held up a hand. "Quiet!" he bellowed at the top of his voice. "I hear them coming! Ambush stations, quick!"

All the soldiers froze for an instant, startled. Then they melted away, as sudden as a cloudburst and as silent as the night, disappearing among the low plasticrete buildings around the plaza.

Rod felt a chill spread outward from his spine. *These guys are* good! he thought at Gwen. *We'd better be, too! After all, we wouldn't want them to* really *find us, would we?*

Nay, certes! Gwen melted into the shadows. From the darkness that had swallowed her came a thought: *My lord? Wilt thou come?*

Just a minute. Rod held up a hand. *Why waste the chance? Come on—home in on Sergeant Thaler's thoughts for me!*

Gwen smiled slowly, then beckoned.

They tiptoed away behind the huts and houses, drifting silently as ghosts behind soldiers whose attention was riveted to the main pathway, with the Wall at its end.

They drifted around to the side, then back in, coming up behind the leaders. Rod hefted his knife, pommel first, but Gwen held up a hand to stop him. She scowled, glaring at Sergeant Thaler. The man suddenly jerked stiff, eyes bulging out, throat swelling. Then his eyes rolled up, and he fell back—but he didn't make any noise, because he didn't hit the dirt. Rod caught him, heaved him up over a shoulder, and turned to tiptoe away.

Gwen tapped Yorick on the shoulder. He looked up at her, startled, then grinned. She beckoned, and he drifted out behind her.

The plaza lay still in the moonlight.

After a while, somebody muttered something. Somebody else muttered an answer. Then another muttered, and another, and another. The voices grew louder. Then, one by one, the soldiers began to drift out into the plaza. They looked about them, baffled and angry.

"Where be they?" a corporal growled.

"Another wild goose." A superannuated private turned his head and spat.

"He's had us again," another snarled. Then he called out, "Sergeant! Sergeant Thaler! Sap the bastard!"

They stilled, waiting for the sound of the blow, for Thaler's angry oath—but silence filled the spaces of the night.

"Where's the sergeant?" a private asked.

"I saw him hide over there." A corporal pointed toward the shadow of a low, one-storied building.

They started toward the spot, walking faster and faster.

The back of the building was bare, the space around it empty.

"Not a sign of him!"

"Y' don't mean Thaler would've run out on us!"

"That's right, I don't mean that." A staff sergeant pointed at the dirt. "Look at that sign. There's been a scuffle here, there has."

"He did for him!" the private cried. "That lousy grinning blockhead did for the sergeant!"

"Stove in his skull, likely." The corporal's eyes turned very pale, very hard. "Let's find him."

"Aye! The bloody, grinning ape!"

"Spread out, lads!" the sergeant roared. "Find the bastard, and string him up!"

"What good'll that do?" A private scratched his head.

"A world of good, for my soul," the sergeant snapped. Then a cunning gleam came into his eye, and he grinned. "Besides, one dead body's as good as another, ain't it? We'll just tell the Wolmen they was wrong; we did some clever detectin', and found out *he* killed their bloomin' warrior!"

The private grinned slowly, his eyes lighting with devilish glee.

"There's a sergeant'll get another stripe for brains," called another soldier.

The sergeant grinned wider.

"Y' oughta be a lieutenant, Sergeant!" called a young corporal.

The sergeant shrugged, embarrassed. "Don't make it more than it is, lads." Then he roared, "Let's go find the blighter!"

The soldiers howled and surged after the sergeant as he strode away between two buildings, following a trail that he thought he saw.

"Welcome to the wanted list." Rod slapped Yorick on the shoulder.

"Thanks, Major." Yorick heaved a sigh. "Shame to disappoint those eager beavers out there, though."

Rod nodded, commiserating. "It's hard to find a trail, when your quarry has flown—literally."

"Yeah." Yorick turned to Gwen. "Thanks for the lift, milady."

"'Twas naught." Gwen gave him a warm smile. "Ever shall my broomstick be at thy bidding."

"Uh, thanks, but I don't think I could last through enough flight hours to qualify." Yorick's grin turned a little queasy. "Definitely a vivid experience, though."

"And we're in the one place where they'd really never think to look for us." Rod glanced up as footsteps crossed above his head.

Yorick leaned back against the wall, blowing out a stream of cigar smoke. "Gotta hand it to you, Major. When you go to ground, you do a real job of it."

Rod shrugged. "Comes of long practice." He nudged the unconscious body that lay between them. "What do you think we ought to do with him, Cholly?"

"Be gentle," the tavernkeeper advised. "Fact is, if you've any bloody intentions, you can take 'em right out into the night with yer. I'm keepin' yer down here just 'cause I don't like to see innocent blood shed."

"Thaler is innocent?" Yorick asked, wide-eyed.

"As much as yerself." Cholly eyed him warily.

"I protest." Yorick laid a hand on his breast. "I am innocent! I am pure! I am . . ."

". . . full of it," Cholly finished. "And I've got to be up there behind the bar when that merry mob you've been leading comes in from this latest snipe hunt." He turned to Rod. "How'd ye work that one?"

"I didn't. Ask *him.*" He nodded toward Yorick.

Cholly's gaze swiveled toward the Neanderthal. The caveman spread his hands. "Just gave 'em what they wanted, mine host. After all, isn't that what *you* do?"

"Aye, along with a measure of what they never thought of." He wagged a forefinger. "That's my calling in life, mind—and I've had all the disruption of it I can take for one night. You lie low, and keep quiet, now. If they hear yer down here, there'll be naught I can do to aid yer."

"Oh, we'll be mice," Rod promised.

"With the cat in sight," Yorick agreed.

"Thou'lt hear not so much as a scratch in the baseboard," Gwen reassured him.

Cholly turned to go up the stairs, but stopped to cast a worried glance at Thaler.

"He won't make any noise, either." Rod's smile hardened. "I mean, we wouldn't be so stupid as to take that kind of chance, would we?"

"True," Cholly admitted. "What ever ye aren't, y're canny enough. And try to catch some sleep, for I doubt not ye'll need it."

He shouldn't have said that. As he turned and went up the stairs, Rod felt the sleepies coming on. He yawned, then shook his head and blinked. "Oh, we'll manage somehow. Right?"

"Aye, my lord. Shall I give to thee . . ."

". . . a mild stimulant?" Yorick fished in his pocket and held out a pillbox. "Go ahead, Major. Nothing lethal or addictive, I assure you."

Rod gave the pillbox a jaundiced glance, then sighed, reached out, and popped one into his mouth. "Why not? You could have bumped us off at least four times today—and without laying a hand on either of us, too."

Gwen stared at the caveman, startled.

Yorick shrugged. "I'm on your side, remember? What do I have to do to prove it—give you a deadly illness, so I can nurse you through it?"

"Nay." Gwen smiled, and Rod said, "Not that we mistrust your ministrations, understand—we'd just rather not need them."

Gwen glanced at Thaler. "Yet I beg of thee, do not give this one any lasting malady."

"Oh, of course not!" Rod said, shocked.

"Nothing *lasting*," Yorick agreed. He reached out a boot

toe to prod the unconscious sergeant. "Come on, soldier, up and at 'em. Reveille's about to blow—and so are you." He hefted and shoved, and the sergeant flopped over, limp as a leaky rainsack.

Rod sighed, and looked up at his wife. "When you do it to 'em, honey, you really do it right. Wake him up, will you?"

Gwen's brow furrowed as she gazed at Thaler. His eyelids fluttered, then opened. He looked about him, frowning and blinking, then rolled up onto one elbow, rubbing the back of a hand across his eyes. "How . . . where . . ."

"I called 'ambush stations,'" Yorick reminded him. "I didn't say who was going to be ambushed."

Thaler's head snapped up. He glared at the caveman. "You *are* in cahoots with them!"

"No, just a cellar. And so're you."

"Yeah," Rod said, with a wolfish grin. "You're in this, too, you know."

Thaler darted glances from Rod to Gwen and back. "What're you talking about? How the hell could I be mixed up in this? This is *your . . .*"

His voice trailed off as he saw the look in Rod's eyes. In spite of himself, he inched away—and ran into Yorick's toe. His head snapped up with a wild look, which met Yorick's flinty gaze. The caveman grinned. He had a lot of teeth. "Don't mean to inconvenience you, Sergeant. It's just that you were talking about altering my collar size, and I thought you might appreciate my returning the favor."

"You bastards!" Thaler growled, but his face paled.

There was a slam overhead, and a thundering of feet. Rod scowled up at the ceiling.

"Squire Mob," Gwen informed him. She turned to Thaler. "Thy followers return."

Thaler's face brightened. He took a deep breath—then swallowed hard as he froze, eyes rolling down to look at Yorick's blade, its point resting against his Adam's apple.

"Softly, softly," the Neanderthal crooned. "You wouldn't want your buddies to know you'd been caught like the greenest new chum, would you? Especially caught by the very people you were hunting! Can you imagine the lowliest private being willing to take orders from such a klutz of a sergeant?"

Thaler's eyes turned calculating. He closed his mouth.

"Having second thoughts?" Yorick nodded. "Wise. I always knew you were the prudent sort."

"Always an eye for the main chance, anyway," Rod agreed.

"That's a nice Sergeant." The dagger backed away a little—but only a little. "Now—the Major, here, says he'd like to get to know you better."

"Yes, indeed." Rod stepped a little closer. "It's been very instructive meeting you, Sergeant, but I'd like it a little longer on the information, and shorter on the rhetoric."

"He means he'd like you to answer a few questions," Yorick explained.

"See? *He* understands." Rod nodded at Yorick. "Now—what were you doing at the Sun-Greeting Place yesterday morning?"

"I wouldn't tell you the time of day," Thaler spat, but Rod felt the answer leap into the sergeant's mind. He couldn't spare time for the details, especially since Gwen's gaze was riveted to Thaler, all her attention focused on his thoughts.

Yorick snatched Thaler's wrist, whipped his arm through a half turn, and wrenched it up behind his back. Thaler exploded into mad thrashing, but he couldn't budge the Neanderthal's grip.

"Manners, manners!" Yorick chided. "We must be polite, now. Tell the nice major what he wants to know."

Thaler's eyes bulged, but he clamped his jaw shut, exuding a whining sound.

"Yeah. Let's just be friendly about it all." Rod gazed up at the ceiling, lips pursed. "Now . . . just what were you doing outside the Wall yesterday morning, anyway?"

"Stuff it, sniffer," Thaler growled through clenched teeth.

Rod frowned. Sniffer? Odd term. He'd have to find out what it meant in local slang. "Well, you do kind of wonder, when a sergeant takes off in the middle of the night. I mean, without any sign or explanation, he just trots past the sentry, and heads for the high hills. You can't help wondering: where was he going to? What for? Who told him to?"

Yorick twisted the wrist a little harder, and Thaler's jaw gaped open. But he groaned and panted, "No . . . way . . . tell . . ."

But the answers were there, popping into his mind, one after another, as Rod called for them.

"Yes, I suppose there *is* no way to tell," Rod mused, "but you can't help wondering what the whole reason was. Why, in the middle of the night? Why not just wait until morning?"

Yorick dangled the knife point in front of Thaler's eyes, letting it swing back and forth. The light glinted off the edge. Thaler gazed at it, fascinated, but he still muttered, "Go peddle your product in Hell."

"I don't think it'd keep too well," Rod sighed. "Uh . . . what say, dear?"

Gwen was tugging on his shoulder, thinking, *I have learned all he knows*. Aloud, she said, "There is no point in tormenting him further, my lord."

"You call that torment?" Rod scoffed, and his mind added, *That was just a little stage dressing, dear, to convince him we meant business. Of course, we weren't planning on completing the transaction. If we had . . .*

Spare me, Gwen thought quickly. *But bind him, my lord.*

"Ah, well," Rod sighed, "why waste time on a know-nothing? Roll over and play dead, Sergeant, so we don't have to make it real. Okay?"

Yorick let go of Thaler's arm and began to rub his shoulder solicitously. Thaler knocked his hand away and growled, eyes full of apprehension.

"Don't worry, we're just going to tie you up," Rod explained. "We can do it with you awake, or out cold, it's completely up to you. Come on, now, don't be difficult—roll over on your stomach, there's a good fellow. Hands behind your back . . ."

Thaler glared at him.

Then, suddenly, he surged to his feet, fist cutting up at Rod, who leaned back at the last second, but not far enough. The punch clipped his cheekbone, and he staggered back, hands snapping up to guard automatically. Fury flamed, white-hot, but he managed to direct it toward Thaler, blocking his next punch, leaning aside from the kick, then whirling back like a spring unwinding. Thaler blocked and countered, but Rod had spun inside his guard, slamming a fist into his belly. Thaler bent forward, eyes bulging again, the whining coming out of his nose. Yorick flipped him over and let him fall, face down in the dirt, dropping down with him and pinning a knee across his back, pressing his wrists together and holding them while Rod whipped a rope around them. "Gently, Sergeant," he soothed. "We could have done this the nice way, you know."

"On the other hand," Yorick pointed out, "we could have been much rougher about it, too. I didn't get *my* licks in, Major."

Rod cut another length of rope from the coil on the shelf. "You'd think Cholly would keep some tape around here."

"What for?" Yorick shrugged. "This isn't his ordinary line of work, you know."

"Yeah, you've got a point." Rod reached down for Thaler's ankle. The sergeant slashed a kick at him, but Rod was expecting it now. He leaped aside, caught the ankle as it passed, and bent it on up toward Thaler's buttocks. "Come, come, now! Do you *really* think I'm such an innocent? Haul a little on that other rope, will you, Yorick?"

The Neanderthal yanked Thaler's wrists up toward his

shoulder blades. The sergeant made a whinnying sound, and his legs relaxed. Rod whipped them together with the rope, then ran a length from ankles to wrists, pulled so that Thaler's legs were bent. "Now for those nifty new knots I've been practicing!"

"Change! Innovation! Always gotta go for the new stuff," Yorick grumbled. "You *Sapiens* are all the same! I'll stick to the good old tried-and-true ones, thank you."

Rod sneaked a peek. "If that's your idea of an *old* knot . . ."

"I meant *really* old. You *Sapiens* never even learned 'em! . . . There! All neatly packaged. Roll over, pretty boy!" He flipped Thaler onto his back. "We don't trust you not to yell." He pinched Thaler where he had the most flesh available. The sergeant opened his mouth in a bleat of sheer surprise, and Rod jammed a handkerchief into it. Yorick grabbed Thaler's head and held it still, while Rod wrapped another handkerchief over his mouth and around behind his head, tying it with a square knot. "Sorry you're going to be feeling so dry, especially with all that beer just overhead. But don't worry, somebody's bound to find you, right after breakfast."

Yorick tucked his hands under Thaler's shoulders and nodded to Rod who caught Thaler's knees. They both heaved up and carried the sergeant over under the stairs, where it was nice and dark.

Gwen's thoughts sounded in Rod's head, disappointed: *Didst thou truly need be so rough?*

'Fraid so, dear, Rod thought back. *Didn't you see what his psyche was doing when you woke him up?*

Gwen was silent a moment. Then: *Aye, indeed. The feeling of helplessness, of being totally without defense.*

Rod nodded. *Psychologically, he can handle this much better than your mental knockout, with no visible means. This, he can comprehend; it's ordinary to him. He can deal with it.* He shrugged. *But we had to make it convincing.*

An thou sayest it. Gwen sighed. *Shall I tell thee, then, what his thoughts were?*

That, I'd like to hear. Rod strolled back toward her, beckoning Yorick, and sat down, with the length of the basement between them and Thaler. The Neanderthal settled beside him, and Rod breathed, "Aloud, but softly, so the big guy can hear, but his victim can't."

"What do you mean, *my* victim?" Yorick snorted.

"I kind of got the gist, while we were questioning," Rod went on, "but I missed the details."

"Oh, so *that's* what you were doing!" Yorick grinned. "I wondered why you gave up so easily."

Gwen just stared at him.

"I wasn't kidding, dear," Rod said softly. "We *were* being gentle."

"Relatively," Yorick agreed. "But then, everything is relative, isn't it? According to the anthropologists, I'm even a relative of yours."

"Removed," Rod said quickly. "Several times removed—but not far enough."

"Aw, you're just a stickler about the straight line of descent," Yorick groused.

"Sure." Rod shrugged. "It's mine. We've got a common ancestor—but you guys branched off into a dead end road that fizzled out."

"If you can call a hundred thousand years 'fizzling out,'" Yorick snorted. "As to its being a dead end—well, at least *we* left Terra in good shape, when we ran off."

"Gentlemen!" Gwen held up her hands, one palm toward each mouth. "Will it please thee to hear what our sergeant did outside the Wall, yestermorn?"

"Yeah, that would be nice." Rod turned back to her, all attention. "He never went anywhere *near* the Sun-Greeting Place, did he?"

"Not by a league," Gwen confirmed, "nor a dozen leagues, for all that."

Yorick frowned. "Spare me the suspense. What *was* he doing outside the Wall?"

"He did perform the role of a courier," Gwen explained.

"The General-Governor had sent him to bear word to the Chartreuse tribe." She turned to Rod, frowning. "'Tis an odd name for a color."

"Unchartered territory," Rod agreed. "So what was he telling the Chief?"

"Yeah." Yorick frowned. "Why the hell did he have to go out in the middle of the night?"

"For that," Gwen explained, "the Chartreuse tribe had borrowed a great sum from the General's—'bank,' did he call it?"

"Savings," Rod explained. "Think of embers banked, to be saved through the night, dear."

"'Tis an odd word, yet an odder thought." Gwen turned to him, frowning. "Why do these folk not keep their money themselves? Wherefore must they give it to others to save for them?"

"Too much chance of thieves," Rod explained. "This way, instead of always worrying about robbers, they only have to worry about the banker—and they always know where *he* is."

"Almost always," Yorick qualified.

"Well, true," Rod admitted. "Anyway, it's much more efficient."

"An thou sayest it," Gwen sighed, "though I bethink me I'll comprehend thy 'gravity' sooner than thy banks."

"Just think how the Wolmen feel. So the Chartreuse tribe owes the Bank of Wolmar a lot, huh?"

"Aye, yet they did have the wherewithal to repay stored in the bank. Naetheless, they had sent to ask for the . . ." she scowled ". . . for the . . . 'interest rate?' . . . on the loan, as it did compare with the 'interest rate' they did receive, on their saved money." She frowned. "What is this 'interest rate,' my lord? Doth it denote the degree of attention the Chief doth pay to the Banker?"

Rod had to swallow hard. "I suppose you could say that, dear. What it means, though, is how much the bank is paying the Chartreuse tribe for the use of its money."

Gwen stared. "But why would the bank wish to use money?"

"Same reason any of us would," Yorick sighed.

"To invest, dear," Rod explained, "Say, to buy shares in a captain's trading voyage. He wants to make the voyage right *now,* not in ten years, which is how long it would take him to save up the money by himself."

"Then this bank will make *more* money from the captain?"

"A lot more, and it'll deal with lots of captains, not just one."

Gwen frowned, eyeing him strangely, then sighed. "An thou sayest it. I ken the meaning of the words, but I do not ken the manner of thought that doth produce it."

Rod said "I'm not certain about it, myself."

"Yet wherefore doth the bank pay the Chartreuse for the use of their money, whiles the tribe doth pay the bank for the use of *its* money? It doth but go about and about in a circle, my lord! It maketh no sense!"

"I'm not sure it does to me, either," Rod confessed. "But I think it works this way: if the Wolmen are getting twelve percent—twelve BTUs for every hundred—and are only paying ten percent for the money they've borrowed, they make two percent profit by keeping the money in the bank, instead of using it to pay off their loan."

Gwen stared.

Then she took a deep breath, and said, "Yet the bank thereby doth lose this two percent thou speakest of! Wherefore doth it pay more than it doth receive?"

"I can't make sense of that one, either," Rod confessed. "The only thing I can think of is that Shacklar must run the bank, and that he's willing to take the loss to make the Wolmen dependent on him. After all, if a man has all your money locked up, you're . . . not . . . too . . . apt to make war on him!" He stared, his eyes huge. "My lord! Of course! He's buying them off!"

"Yet, then, if they send to learn of their money's interest, doth it not mean..." Gwen's eyes rounded, too. "Nay, certes! They did seek to recover their money, that they might be free to make war!"

"Without taking a loss on it," Rod said grimly. "Which is plenty of reason for Shacklar to send a courier out in the middle of the night. Just what was the message he carried?"

"That the interest rate was but now increased by five parts in a hundred."

"A five percent hike, on the spur of the moment?" Rod goggled, and Yorick whistled. "This Chartreuse chief knows how to bargain! Nothing like the threat of war to motivate the General into giving them a little extra profit."

"Very sharp," Rod agreed. "What did the Chartreuse tribe send back—a polite 'Yes,' or a withdrawal slip?"

"Sergeant Thaler did bear back word lauding General Shacklar for his honesty, and naught more."

"Which means they left their money on deposit." Rod drew a deep breath. "Y'know, Shacklar's not too bad a horse trader himself. What's five percent against forestalling a war? He may just have had the right idea, trying to bring the Wolmen into the modern world." But he wasn't sure that applied to Gwen.

"Here, then!" Cholly's voice called down the stairwell. "Have a care, mister and missus! Here's one who wants t' talk t' yer!"

Rod looked up, adrenaline thrilling through him.

Chornoi came down the steps, face a bright pink.

Gwen smiled. "Thou dost seem newly scrubbed."

"Of course," Chornoi snapped. "Wouldn't you be?"

"Aw! I thought you looked good in that color," Yorick protested.

Rod relaxed, feeling the adrenaline ebb. "Yeah, it was the real you."

"Oh, stuff it!" she blazed.

Rod stared, taken aback for a moment. "What's the matter? Didn't you *like* being a Wolman?"

"What do *you* think?" she snorted. "It's not easy, being Orange."

Yorick pushed a crate over with his foot. "Sit. Tell us what's happening under the big open skies."

"Do not heed their impudence," Gwen advised. "Truly, within, they rejoice to see thee home and hale."

"They sure hide it well," Chornoi growled.

"Thanks." Rod nodded. "Now, tell us what happened out there."

Chornoi snorted, and dropped down on the crate. "Nothing. Absolutely nothing."

They stared at her for a moment.

Then Rod sighed and leaned back. "We couldn't really expect anything more, anyway. But somebody must have come to the Sun-Greeting Place."

"Oh, he did—and it was Hwun, all right."

"But he smelled a rat?" Then Rod struck the heel of his hand against his forehead. "Of course—what's the matter with me? He knows every member of his tribe by sight! Why didn't I . . ."

"Don't worry, I did." Chornoi's mouth turned down at the corners. "He's a Purple chief, so I was wearing Orange paint. And I staged it well: When he came up in the false dawn there, with the sky just beginning to glow in the east, he found me on my knees, weeping." Her eyes lost focus; she gave a slow, critical nod. "Yeah, I did it well. . . . He just stood there for a few minutes. I pretended I didn't notice. Then he reached down and grabbed my shoulder." She winced. "He grabs *hard!* Talk about a grip of steel . . ."

"I trust he did not hurt thee!" Gwen frowned, concerned.

Chornoi shook her head. "I don't think he meant to, and I suppose he was sympathetic, by his lights. He said, 'Woman. Why you weep?'"

"Wait a minute." Yorick held up a finger. "Didn't he want to know your name?"

Chornoi shook her head. "No need. I was from another

tribe—that was all he needed to know. And that I wasn't trespassing—because I was on sacred ground, which is open to all. So I told him that I was weeping for the man who was killed yesterday morning. And Hwun said, 'But him not of your tribe.'"

"Oh, did he!" Rod lifted his head slowly. "That means the corpse must've still had his body-paint on when Hwun found him."

"Which means Hwun washed it off." Yorick frowned.

"Yeah, to hide the victim's identity." Rod scowled. "Why would he want to do that?"

But Chornoi was shaking her bowed head, waving her hands in front of her, palms out. "No! Hold it! Stop! You're both missing the main point!"

"Which is?" Rod asked.

"That Hwun wants to get all the tribes together, and the dead Wolman could be a very powerful common focus. But it'll work much better for that, if nobody can tell which tribe he came from."

They sat still for a moment. Then Rod nodded slowly. "Yeah . . . that could be . . ."

"More than 'could,'" Chornoi snorted.

"Then he did tell thee thou wert not of the slain man's tribe?" Gwen said.

Chornoi nodded. "So why was I weeping? Well, I had to think fast, I tell you! But I did, and I told him I was weeping for all Wolmen, that I would weep for any, who died at the hands of the Colonists!" She frowned. "I was waiting for him to tell me to stand up, but he never did."

"And for him to warm toward a weeping woman?" Rod said softly.

Chornoi glared at him. "I told you, I don't fit their standards of beauty!"

Rod didn't believe it. "Even so—you were female, and grieving. And you're young enough. You were waiting for something resembling a chivalrous response, weren't you?"

Chornoi held the glare a moment longer. Then her mouth twisted, and she admitted, "Yes, I was. But there wasn't any—not the ghost of a one."

Yorick grinned. "Well, you knew the Wolmen were a bunch of male chauvinists."

"Sure," Rod cut in. "Any primitive culture's going to be patriarchal."

"Not 'any.'" Yorick held up a palm. "But these guys are. Comes from imitating commercial fiction, no doubt." He turned back to Chornoi. "So you stood up anyway, huh?"

She shrugged, irritated. "I was getting a crick in my neck."

"So you stood up," Rod inferred. "Slowly, sinuously, with a few discreet wriggles."

Fury flared in Chornoi's eyes, but she didn't answer.

"It didn't work?" Rod said gently.

The fury faded a bit. Reluctantly, Chornoi inclined her head. "All he did was start reasoning. He pointed out that I shouldn't take it so hard. As a bona fide female, I had more to gain from the colonists than to lose."

Rod scowled. "Was he being sarcastic or something?"

Chornoi shook her head. "No . . . From his tone, he was just stating the facts of the case. As though it was a logical point, you know?"

"These subsistence cultures end up preoccupied with common sense," Yorick said. "So how did you answer that one? After all, there *is* a surplus of Wolman women, with the resulting polygamy." He frowned. "Odd, though—you wouldn't expect a leader to be quite so carefree about one of his people's women going to the men of his enemies."

"Well, that's just where I hit it. I put on the big indignant scene—that no true Wolwoman would want a man all to herself, if that man wouldn't be a Wolman, just a colonist. But Hwun just went on telling me, in that emotionless style of his, that it would make much more sense for me to have one man all to myself, if I could.

Rod frowned. "I thought he was trying to get the Wolmen *out* of association with the colonists."

"So did I. I stepped a little closer, snapping that there would've been plenty of Wolmen to go around, if the colonist soldiers hadn't killed off so many of our men in the war. But Hwun told me that there are always two percent more female children surviving infancy than male. . . . I wonder who does his statistics?"

Yorick shook his head, looking dazzled. "Odd bunch of primitives they've got here."

"Must be Cholly and his educational force." Rod shrugged. "I'm surprised he didn't quote the last IDE census at you."

"No, but he did finally get around to praising my patriotism. Almost as an afterthought. Then he fed me some sort of line about how literate cultures always destroy oral cultures, then swallow them up or kill off their members."

Rod just stared at her for a moment. Then he said, "Not exactly what I usually think of as a call to arms."

"Well, it could have been, if he hadn't sounded like some damn professor!"

Rod wondered at her irritability. Of course, Chornoi was always touchy . . . "So what did he say to comfort you?"

"Nothing." Chornoi turned away in disgust. "All of a sudden, he spun around and ran over to the stone step. And believe me, he can sprint!"

"Primitives stay in good physical shape," Yorick assured her.

"Not *that* good! I swear he could've run a horse race without the horse!" She shook her head, exasperated. "He got there just in time, too. He barely set foot on the stone, and the sun came up."

"Natural sense of timing," Yorick said.

"Which some people don't have." Rod fixed him with a beady eye.

Chornoi shook her head in exasperation. "Talk about a wasted night!"

"Oh, I don't know." Rod pursed his lips. "At least, now we're pretty sure he didn't want anybody to know which tribe the corpse came from. *That's* something."

"Not much," Chornoi snapped, but Gwen smiled with gentle amusement. "Thou shouldst not be so aggrieved, solely for cause that he did not sway to thy charms."

Rod's eyebrows shot up as he turned to look at her.

Chornoi sat very still, paling. Then she heaved a sigh. "All right, so my feminine pride's been hit. How'd you know, Ms.?"

Gwen answered with a shrug of her shoulders. "The lilt of thy voice, the tilt of thine head. Thou art quite knowledgeable in the use of thy womanhood, art thou not?"

"I've gotten pretty good at it," Chornoi admitted, "ever since I found out that the Wolmen have a very stiff code of honor where women are concerned—especially unmarried ones. It was such a welcome relief from my fellow colonists!"

"Also safer?" Rod guessed.

Chornoi nodded, chagrined. "I've always been a favorite with them, and not just because I was disaffected. Maybe they all thought I'd make a nice addition to their lodges, I don't know—but it was nice to be treated like a lady again after all these years. And I got to be pretty good at flirting." She sounded vaguely surprised.

Rod frowned. "But if their code of honor was so stiff that they wouldn't even try to seduce you . . ."

"Oh, I didn't say that!" Chornoi glared icicles at him. "They all did, always, every single one. That was what was so nice about it. I could flirt all I wanted to, then say 'No,' and they'd accept it. Even if they didn't want to, they'd stop right away."

"But this Hwun did not attempt to seduce thee?"

"Not a bit, not the tiniest flirt. Not even a leer, let alone a bedroom eye."

Rod cocked his head to the side. "But it sounded as though he was interested in you."

"Oh, yeah! In who I was, and why I was there, but beyond that . . . Well, he didn't even seem to be aware that I was female!"

Yorick shook his head. "Odd. Definitely odd. Anomalous, in fact. Y' might expect that kind of thing in a civilized culture, but . . ."

"Whoa! Hold it!" Chornoi's palm went up. "What makes you so sure the Wolmen aren't civilized?"

"Because the word means 'citified,'" Yorick answered, irritated. "At least pick *legitimate* nits, will you?"

"Yet wherefore wouldst thou look for such behavior in cities, yet not in the country?" Gwen asked.

"Because it takes a higher degree of technology to build cities than to build temporary villages," Yorick said. "I suppose I really should have said 'highly-technological,' instead of 'civilized.' I mean, can you really call it a 'city' if it's only got a hundred thousand people, and not a single factory?"

"Yes," Rod said, with conviction.

Yorick shrugged. "All right, so we're down to definitions. Me, I think of industrial ugliness as a 'city'—you know, steam engines, power looms, railroads, factories . . ."

"No, I don't know." Rod shook his head. "I didn't study that much archaeology. But I can play straight man—'Why would you expect a man from an industrial civilization to not even notice that a woman was a woman?'"

Yorick frowned. "Well, maybe not 'expect', but at least not be surprised by. In the industrial culture, Major, you make progress by putting each item into its own separate pigeonhole, so you can control it and assemble it with a lot of other things into whatever new gadget you want—and what you do with your tools, you also do with your minds. So the industrial man starts seeing 'emotion' as one aspect of the mind, and 'intellect' as another, and he puts each one into its own separate pigeonhole in his soul, where it can't get in the other's way. So you might not be surprised to find that a leader who was currently dealing with a major problem, might have sex safely pigeonholed out of the way for the time being."

"But to the point where he wouldn't even notice that a woman was a woman?" Chornoi stared, appalled.

"Oh, he'd notice it, all right—but he'd ignore it."

"Even to the point of not responding as a man?"

Yorick shrugged. "What can I tell you? It's possible. But the Wolman culture isn't industrial—it's tribal, with a very basic technology that concentrates on wholeness and individuality. They see everything as weaving together into one great big configuration—and sex as a natural part of life, just like every other part. Feelings and thoughts are naturally interwoven in a culture like that. The one leads to the other, in an endless circle."

Rod pursed his lips. "Are you trying to tell me that Hwun wasn't reacting like a true tribal chieftain?"

Yorick stood still with his mouth open. Then he closed it, disgruntled. "Well, yeah, something like that. Right."

"Well, I'd say you pinned that one right on the donkey. But there's something that really bothers me about that guy's attitude." He scowled off into space, chewing at the thought mentally for a few minutes, then shrugged his shoulders with a sigh. "I can't pin it down."

"Give it time," Yorick advised. "It'll come home."

"Wagging a tale behind it, no doubt."

The door at the top of the stairs slammed, and Rod was on his feet, one hand on his dagger.

"Nay, my lord." Gwen laid a hand on his forearm. "'Tis more likely a friend than an enemy."

Boots appeared on the stairs, marching down, with loose green trousers tucked into them. Then a white apron appeared, tucked over an ample belly; then a barrel chest and bull shoulders, with Cholly's grinning face on top of them, and a huge tray piled high with steaming goodies in his hands. "Thought yer might like a nibble. After all, the sun's almost up."

"And our time with it?" Rod reached out to help lift the tray down.

"Here, now! Away with yer!" Cholly swung the tray up out of his reach. "Can't leave these things t' base amateurs, yer know! Sit down, sit down! The pleasure in a meal is as much in the service as in the cuisine."

Rod put his hands up, palms out. "Innocent, sheriff." He sat down.

"There! That's a bit better." Cholly kicked a crate into the middle of their circle and set the tray down on it, then picked up platters and began to fill them with eggs and sausage, muffins, toast, steak, and fried potatoes. "It's a local bird does these eggs, now, not yer average Terran hen. But she's a good fowl, and takes pride in her work. Lower in cholesterol, too." He set the plate on Yorick's lap. "And I won't tell yer what the steak was in its earlier incarnation. Just relax and enjoy it."

"Good, though," Yorick mumbled around a mouthful.

Rod eyed the sausages warily as they passed him, bound for Chornoi. "What's in the cartridges?"

"Pork." Cholly heaped a platter for him. "Naught but good old pork, Major. Where yer finds human folk, yer finds pigs. And why not?" He passed the plate to Rod and began to load another. "They're tasty, portable, and thrives on yer garbage. So what if they're ornery, and got nasty tempers? Just give 'em some mud, and they'll rest content." He set the plate in front of Gwen and turned to serve Yorick and Chornoi, but found they'd served themselves while he wasn't looking. "Ah, well-a-day!" he sighed, and folded his arms, watching the Gallowglasses dine with enthusiasm. "Eh, it does my old heart good to see the young'uns tuckin' into their tucker like that!"

"Couldn't be more than a few years older than we are," Rod mumbled.

"Don't bet on it, laddie." Cholly wagged a forefinger at him. "I'm all of fifty."

"Why, he is ten years my senior!" Gwen said brightly.

"A positive antique," Rod agreed. "But he cooks well, so we won't hold it against him."

"Have it as you will, it does my heart good to see folk enjoy my food." But Cholly's face puckered into a frown. "Yer surely do seem the carefree pair, don't yer?"

"What?" Rod looked up, surprised. "Oh. Just because we don't seem particularly worried?" He shrugged and turned back to his plate. "We aren't."

"Wherefore ought we be?" Gwen looked up in wide-eyed innocence.

"Well . . ." Cholly coughed delicately into his fist. "There is this little matter of a million or so wild savages who're thirsting fer yer blood."

"He's so clinical with his descriptions, isn't he?"

"Aye, my lord. Dry and bare of emotion."

"It don't worry yer." Cholly tipped his head toward them, eyebrows lifted.

Rod shook his head. "Why should they? We can always escape."

"We do excel at quick disappearing," Gwen confirmed. "'Tis merely a matter of waiting thine opportunity."

Cholly looked astounded. "Then why not escape now?"

Rod shook his head. "Don't want to create an incident."

Gwen nodded. "When we do depart, we'd liefer not leave a war in our wake."

"I mean," Rod explained, "if we don't go to that trial, what's going to happen to Wolman-colonist politics here?"

Cholly was still for a moment, gazing off into space. Then he said, "'Tis a point well-taken—and 'tis good of yer to care. But ought yer not have some concern fer yer-selves?"

"We do," Gwen assured him.

"We meant what we said—if push comes to shove, we

can always disappear, fade into the woodwork. But there would still be the little problem of getting off this planet," Rod explained.

Cholly leaned back on one leg, scratching where his sideburn had been. "Aye. There'd be some difficulty to that. That's why they made the whole *planet* a prison, now that yer mention it. Mind yer, there's a-plenty of places to hide here on Wolmar; there're some patches of mountains that not even the Wolmen would bother to go to, but as would have game enough to support just a man and his wife, and mayhap even a family."

Gwen shook her head and swallowed. "Nay. 'Tis this matter of family, even as thou sayest. I must needs return to them, look thou."

Cholly just gazed at her, brooding, his lower lip thrust out. "Aye, I can understand that. But where be they, Missus?"

Gwen opened her mouth to answer, but Rod said quickly, "On another planet, far away."

"Aren't they all!" Cholly sighed. He set his hands on his hips and stared up at the ceiling beams. "Aye, then, 'tis needful indeed. But I can't give yer any help if y're out to launch, in a manner of speakin'. My men only work dirt-side."

"'S okay." Rod shrugged. "We weren't really expecting anything."

"Yet 'tis good of thee to offer thine aid," Gwen said softly.

Chornoi looked up from her plate and shifted a mouthful of food over into her cheek. "That reminds me, speaking of peuple hiding out in Wolman territory . . ."

Cholly's attention shifted to her, with total intensity. "Say," he commanded.

"Strangers." Chornoi finished chewing and swallowed. "I've spent most of the last month wandering around among the Wolmen . . ."

"That, I know." Cholly said. "And I'll not argue that they're more considerate, and more mannerly than our colonists—and if a lady says 'No,' they'll agree, and not take exception. After all, they've plenty of women on hand. But how did this bring you knowledge of strangers?"

Chornoi shrugged. "It takes one to know one. I'm sure their disguises fooled the Wolmen, but I saw through them—maybe because I was looking from the outside."

"Indeed," Cholly breathed. "And what have these false Wolmen been doing?"

"Nothing much. Claiming a free lunch, and a place in the shade for a few hours, which the Wolmen were glad to supply—that good old primitive code of hospitality. . . ."

"Members of the same tribe, no doubt," Cholly breathed.

"Oh, sure, if they'd come from a different tribe, that would have been a horse of a different color! But being of the same hue, if you follow me, they had the green-carpet treatment. . . ."

"The green carpet being grass?" Rod asked.

"Of course." Chornoi gave him an irritated glance. "So the visitors just sat down, filled up, and discussed the fate of the world."

"For some hours, yer said?"

"Two or three. Then they drifted on. But afterwards I heard the occasional Wolman talking against General Shacklar and us colonists."

"Not exactly what I'd call a positive symptom," Yorick said.

"Nay, certes," Gwen breathed.

"What complaints had they?" Cholly asked. "The Wolmen hailed Shacklar as the voice of reason, right from the start. The only gripes about him came from Terra, and she was only objecting, because our good General-Governor didn't need her!"

"Ever the way with women," Yorick sighed, and Chornoi favored him with her skewerest glance.

"Of course, she hasn't been complaining lately." Cholly noted. "How can she, when she's cut us off?"

Yorick started to answer, but Chornoi snapped, "Can it!"

Rod shrugged. "Okay, so there are a few kvetchers out beyond the Wall. Why let it bother you? There are always a few malcontents."

But Yorick looked doubtful now, and Cholly shook his head. "Malcontents stay in their own villages, but Ms. Chornoi's seen several of 'em wandering about."

Chornoi nodded. "All different tribes, too."

Cholly shook his head again. "That smacks of organization."

"Plus a lot of body-paint," Rod added. "Could be the same agents, just changing their colors each time."

"Like enough." Cholly shook his head. "I'll have to apprise the General of it."

"If you have to." Chornoi was suddenly as tight as a wire. "Just don't tell him who did the noticing, okay?"

"Be easy," Cholly assured her. "I've only to refer to 'my sources,' and he never questions."

"Of course." Chornoi relaxed. "All those traders. What difference would it make which one brought the news?"

"None, to him." Cholly frowned. "Some, to me." He turned to Rod and Gwen. "But I take her point. It's worth talking, fer yerselves."

"Why?" Rod looked up. "Because it gives us a way to have a body, where there isn't a Wolman missing?"

Chornoi shook her head. "That body was a real Wolman."

Rod frowned. "How can they tell? Tattoos?"

"That, and other tribal marks."

Cholly nodded in agreement. "Yer wouldn't notice 'em in the usual course of action. However, fer yerselves, yer might be able to use 'em to win a stay of execution, by demanding that Hwun prove none of his own people was responsible fer the murder, nor that it wasn't committed by no impersonator, neither."

Rod smiled slowly, and Gwen said, "They're as likely to demand that *we* prove there were no false Wolmen had a blade into this, either."

"True," Rod agreed, "but no one could expect us to have evidence about *real* Wolmen, could they?" He grinned at Chornoi. "Thanks, lady. That might win us time."

"I'm not a lady," Chornoi snapped.

Before Rod could say it, they heard the tavern door open upstairs, and a dozen pairs of boots tramped across the floor above their heads.

"Ah!" Cholly looked upward. "Yer escort's come, I dare say."

The troop didn't lead them to Shacklar's office. Instead, it took them to a giant log cabin between the tavern and the administrative compound.

"What is this?" Rod asked the lieutenant. "Town Hall?"

"Close enough," the man growled, and he threw the door open. Rod and Gwen marched in, shoulders square and chins high. Their escort followed.

Rod took a quick look around. Inside, you couldn't have told it was built of logs. The walls were paneled and plastered, and the furniture was so smoothly finished that, at first glance, it looked like plastic.

There was a beautifully finished desk, too, squarely in front of Rod, and at least six feet high. Shacklar would've been dwarfed behind it, if his chair hadn't been so huge and ornate. Real leather upholstery, Rod noted. Well, colonists had to make do with what they could find.

The side desks were just as sumptuous, but a foot shorter. The one at the left had five Wolmen behind it, and the one at the right had five soldiers, each of whom had officer's insignia gleaming on his collar tabs.

Rod scanned the scene and saw the basis for a constitution.

A sergeant stepped out in front of Shacklar's bench, thumped the floor with an oaken pole tipped with chalk, and bellowed, "Order in the court!"

Rod bit back the traditional rejoinder, but Gwen caught his thought, and had to suppress a smile.

"Accused, please present yourselves," Shacklar said quietly.

Rod looked at Gwen. Gwen looked at Rod. They shrugged, and took a joint step forward.

"How do you plead?" Shacklar inquired.

"Guilty, or not guilty?" the sergeant prompted.

"Not guilty," Rod said firmly.

"Proof!" Hwun was on his feet behind the Wolmen's bench. "What proof them show? Must give evidence that them not do murder!"

"Come to that, I don't believe I'd mentioned that a murder had been committed," Shacklar mused. "Horrible oversight. But really, old chap, I must request that if you intend to prosecute the case, you remove yourself from the bench."

Hwun stared at him, then slowly nodded. "It is sensible."

Rod stared in amazement as the Wolman came down from the bench and around in front of it. The move seemed completely at odds with what he knew of the intractable, hostile Wolman chief. Why had he been so quick to agree?

There was a slight stirring at the back of the room, near the outer door. Out of the corner of his eye, Rod noticed Yorick and Chornoi slide in quietly. He bit his lip in vexation—he hadn't wanted them to get pulled in so openly. The soldiers might assume guilt by association.

But it was nice to feel their support.

Hwun strode up to glower at Rod and Gwen. "You say you not guilty. Give proof!"

Rod suddenly realized that he and Hwun were going to determine, right here and now, whether Wolmar's legal code would be basically Napoleonic, or basically English. If it were basically Napoleonic, it would assume that the accused was guilty, and had to prove his innocence, which meant that the rights of the individual wouldn't be the most important element in the constitution about to be born.

"No," Rod said softly. "It's not our job to prove we're innocent. *You* have to prove we're guilty!"

Hwun just stared at him, and his gaze was so cold that

Rod could have sworn it was giving him frostbite.

"That's so."

The Chief Chief spun around to look at the colonists' bench. A slender officer was on his feet. With a shock, Rod recognized the officer who had been so courteous to them on the Wall the morning before.

"Lieutenant Corrigan," Shacklar acknowledged. "On what basis do you state agreement with the accused?"

"Why not?" Corrigan answered, with an easy smile. "Still, it's common sense, sir. We know nothing of these two people, except that a Wolman patrol chased them to us. If anything, that would indicate a Wolman bias against them. No, really, in all fairness, we must ask that some reason be given for believing them guilty of a capital crime."

"The point is well-taken." Shacklar turned to the Wolmen's bench. "Those of us present at the hearing yesterday morning have heard such reasons, but the majority of the individuals making up this court have not. We will hear it stated anew."

Rod breathed a sigh of relief—the English concept had won out. The laws of Wolmar would assume that the accused was innocent, and the state would have to prove his guilt, which meant that the rights of the individual would be the most important element in the embryonic constitution. All of a sudden, the term "founding fathers" gained a whole new meaning.

Shacklar turned back to Corrigan. "However, Lieutenant, I must ask that if you intend to take the part of the accused, you also step down from your bench."

Thereby preserving an equal number on each side, Rod noted, as well as establishing the functions of prosecutor and defense. He hoped Shacklar would be as careful in his judgment as he was in his establishing of precedents.

Corrigan stared blankly for a moment, then heaved a sigh and stepped down to the floor.

Shacklar turned back to Hwun. "Please present your proofs, Chief Chief, your reasons why we should believe these two people murdered a Wolman."

Hwun only stared at him.

Shacklar leaned back in his chair, fingers steepled, totally at ease.

Finally, Hwun said, "They were there."

Rod breathed a sigh of relief. The English concept had triumphed.

"Yester morning," Hwun went on, "them outside Wall. Outside, in middle of plain. Who know where before that?"

"Precisely," Corrigan agreed. "Who *does* know?"

Hwun didn't even acknowledge him. "Wolman found dead. Dead, at Sun-Greeting Place. *Me* found body! Who would kill him? Only colonist!" His finger stabbed out at Rod and Gwen. "Only them outside Wall—no reason! So!" He folded his arms across his chest. "Them kill Wolman."

"Oh, come now!" Corrigan scoffed. "There were traders outside the Wall, too, and Wolmen from other tribes. Even if you assume that no member of his own tribe would kill him..." He spun to the General, stabbing a forefinger. "Which point has not been established, sir!" Then back to Hwun. "Even if, *if,* no member of his own tribe slew him, there's no reason to think a member of another tribe didn't!"

Hwun kept his face turned toward Shacklar. "Wolmen not bloodthirsty."

Shacklar sat very still, and the faces of the other officers froze. Rod could almost hear the laughter they were holding back, and really could hear them thinking, *That's not how it looked!*

"Wolmen not slay other Wolmen!" Hwun thundered.

The officers' faces stayed frozen. *Just what the blinking hell do you think you were doing when we came here—holding community picnics?*

Shacklar managed to sublimate his feelings into a huge sigh, and leaned forward. "Be that as it may... Accused!"

"Uh, yes?" Rod looked up.

"Were you, or your wife, at the Sun-Greeting Place yesterday morning?"

Rod shook his head. "Never saw it till we went to look for evidence last night."

Hwun's head snapped around to stare at Rod, but Shacklar said, "And no one was slain last night." He turned to the panel of Wolman chiefs. "Would any of you happen to know where these two were first sighted?"

"In middle of Horse Plain," answered the Purple chief.

"On foot?" Corrigan asked.

"On foot," the chief confirmed.

"And that's a good ten kilometers from the Sun-Greeting Place. At what time did your warriors sight the accused, Chief?"

The chief shrugged. "Sun not up long."

"Soon after dawn," Corrigan translated. "Was the sun completely above the horizon?"

The chief nodded.

"How far above?"

The chief demonstrated with his hands. "Two fingers' width."

"Two fingers' width, at arm's length." Corrigan held his own fingers out, squinting at them. "Perhaps a half an hour after dawn." He dropped his hand, and was looking at Hwun. "I submit that it would have been rather difficult for the defendants to kill a man at the Sun-Greeting Place, and be in middle of the Horse Plain, ten kilometers away, half an hour later."

Hwun stared for a moment, then said, "Could have killed earlier."

"Indeed, they *could* have," Corrigan countered, "but *did* they? Have you the slightest shred of evidence that indicates they so much as *met* the deceased, let alone slew him?"

Hwun gave him a long, cold stare. Then, turning to his fellow Wolmen with frigid dignity, he drew himself up and stated, "Soldiers stalling." His forefinger jabbed out at Rod and Gwen again. "These two did murder! Plain for all to see!" He turned back to Shacklar. "And all can see soldiers not deal fairly with Wolmen! Oh, with goods, cash, pipeweed, soldiers deal fair—but not life! Then, no soldier deal fairly!"

The other chiefs glared, then began to mutter to one another, darting hostile glances at Shacklar and the officers' panel. The officers stiffened, their faces turning to wood.

"Give!" Hwun thundered, holding out a hand, palm up. "Give these two to Wolmen! Give murderer of brother into our hands, to slay in justice here, now!"

"Justice! Why, you pious prig!" Chornoi was on her feet, raging. "You're not looking for justice; you're looking for a scapegoat! You know damn well that if you can't satisfy your fellow chiefs, they'll kick you out of office! And you can't satisfy them all, if it turns out it was a Wolman who murdered a Wolman! Because if it was, the murderer's tribe will defend him, and the victim's tribe will charge out for revenge! And that'll be the end of your nice little Confederation!"

"Not so!" "Wolman law!" "All tribes heed!" The chiefs were on their feet, shouting.

But Hwun drowned them all out. "Justice! Seek only justice!"

"Justice!" Chornoi sneered, pacing up to him. "How can a tyrant seek justice? Because that's what you really want to be, isn't it? King of all the Wolmen! Tyrant! Dictator! That's all you are—just a power-driven machine!"

Rod stiffened, feeling as though his spine had turned into a hot wire. Facts suddenly connected in his head, and sparked into fusion.

"Machine!" Chornoi spat.

Hwun's hand lashed out so fast it seemed to blur, cracking backhanded against Chornoi's jaw. She shot back, crashing into the colonists' bench.

Rod bellowed, rage erupting as he whirled toward Hwun, which brought him just far enough to the side so that the Chief Chief's fist hissed past his ear. An icicle stabbed Rod as he realized the blow would have killed him. He was fighting for his life!

The hell with fighting fair!

He came out of his crouch in a whirl, knee driving up into Hwun's groin. It struck—

With a hollow crack.

Rod howled as his knee burst into fire.

Everyone in the courtroom stood frozen, galvanized by the sound.

Hwun's hand reached for Rod's throat—but Rod's leg gave way, and crashed to the floor. Hwun's hand clawed through empty air. Fear sizzled through Rod, opening a channel for the scarlet wrath that boiled through him in a raging torrent. Rod focused it on his hand, shoving himself back up onto one knee, concentrating on the hand's edge, willing it into a sword, a battle-ax, slamming out in a chop so fast that no one noticed it had turned into the shiny gray of tungsten steel. It crashed up into Hwun's jaw. The Wolman shot into the air and crashed down to the floor, right in front of the Wolman bench.

Rod knelt, arm falling limp, panting, wild-eyed, amazed and terrified by his own action. *I couldn't have hit him* that *hard!*

Aye, thou couldst.

Rod looked up, and saw the steel of his hand reflected in his wife's eyes.

But Hwun was rolling to his feet...

...and a searing, ruby ray skewered his head.

For a frozen moment, Rod could see the line of light joining the Wolman chieftain to the blaster in the General's hand, seeming as much a part of him as his uniform.

Then the moment thawed, the beam of light winked out, and Hwun crashed to the ground.

The Wolmen stared, appalled.

Then they leaped to their feet, blasters whipping out from under their cloaks. "Blood!" They howled. "Justice!" "Treachery!" *"Kill!"*

But Shacklar vaulted over his bench and landed beside Hwun's body. He yanked off the chief's loincloth. The other

Wolmen howled, outraged—but the howls died, and their eyes bulged as they stared, frozen. For a moment, the room was totally silent.

Then groans welled up from the Wolmen's chests, as they gazed in horror at the smooth curve of a groin without genitals.

Rod shoved himself over to Hwun, whipping out his dagger. He gripped the corpse's hair, and the blade sliced keenly around in a single stroke. Rod peeled back the skin. There was no blood, no fatty tissue—only the bland curve of a beige skull, with four hairline cracks forming a perfect rectangle.

The chiefs still stared, too stunned to move.

Rod jammed the tip of his dagger into one of the cracks and pried. The material resisted for a moment, then the rectangle popped open. Rod stared at a cluster of jewels, gleaming from the darkness inside.

"Molecular circuits, of course," Rod explained. "Each one of those 'jewels' was a computer big enough to run all the utilities for a small city."

He lifted his stein for a swallow, and Cholly asked, "How did you guess he was a robot?"

"Easy," Rod said, with a wry smile. "In fact, I can't understand why I *didn't* figure it out, for so long. I mean, a Wolman had been murdered, right? But no Wolman was missing. Which meant there was one extra Wolman." He spread his hands. "Couldn't be. And we'd met Hwun. He hadn't shown any emotion at all, except anger—but a very cold anger, if you follow me. That's how he was in everything—very cold, very factual. I suppose it was his lousy logic that sidetracked me."

"Yeah." Yorick scratched his head. "How could a computer 'brain' do such sloppy thinking, as to think you two were guilty just because you were outside the Wall that morning?"

"Especially when there were others out, too." Rod held

up a forefinger. "Thaler—and we don't know how many traders."

"Right. So how come Hwun didn't see that suspecting you two, didn't make sense?"

Rod shrugged. "He could only think the way he'd been programmed—'garbage in, garbage out.' But it really should have hit me when Chornoi told us that he didn't show the slightest flicker of response to her flirting, even though every other Wolman she'd met liked flirting so much that it was her guarantee of safety. That *really* should have made Hwun stand out in my mind. And the real clincher is that he broke off conversation with her to run over to the stone step and greet the sun just *before* it rose."

Yorick frowned. "So?"

"How could he have known?" Gwen breathed.

Yorick sat for a moment. Then he lifted his head slowly.

Rod nodded. "His programming included a schedule of sunrises. Yeah, I really should have caught that. But all those factors didn't add up and hit me until Chornoi called him a machine right there in the courtroom—and I realized that explained everything odd about him."

"And that's when yer figured out that the robot committed the murder?" Cholly asked.

Rod nodded again. "Totally possible, if you program it to be an assassin, which is why the laws against doing that are so stiff. But our Futurian buddies don't care too much about laws."

"It's illegal to use blasters to kill people, too," Yorick said, wryly. "But your average murderer can't afford a robot for the job. So how often do you come across a homicidal android?"

"First one *I've* ever seen," Rod said. "Every other robot was programmed to protect life."

"Was't therefore thou didst not look for a murderer to be a . . . 'robot,' didst thou term it?"

Rod sat still, then nodded slowly. "Yeah, darling. That's probably why. Know me pretty well, don't you?" He smiled at Gwen. "And yes, you've got the word right—'robot.' The word means 'worker,' literally. It's a machine made to look like a human being, or to do the work a human being does."

"Yet how was't this 'robot' did so perfectly resemble the true Hwun?"

"Now we come to the real villain." Rod's mouth tightened. "Somebody very obviously planned the whole thing ahead of time . . . carefully, too. Someone—probably one of those fake Wolmen Chornoi mentioned—took a picture of Hwun, then sculpted the robot's face to look exactly like his. And put him where he could be sure the robot would be able to find Hwun alone."

"At the Sun-Greeting Place," Yorick interjected. "Then all he had to do was make sure the robot's programming included the right moves for making a fuss after the murder was over."

"So." Chornoi scowled. "Hwun went up to say his morning prayers—the real Hwun, I mean—and as he turned to face the sun, the robot hit him." She shuddered. "At least it was quick."

Rod nodded. "The robot mutilated the face so nobody'd realize he wasn't the real Hwun. Then it took the body to the closest stream, washed off the paint, and brought it to the nearest tribal village, howling for vengeance. Then it just took Hwun's place and did the best it could to make a huge fuss."

Yorick nodded. "Neatly done."

"Very professional," Chornoi agreed. "So who's the bastard who programmed the robot?"

"I'm afraid we're not to know that," a voice sighed.

They turned, startled, as Shacklar stepped up to their table. "It seems my shot burned out the android's memory, along with its vital functions—and, of course, the program with it."

"Not a huge surprise." Rod nodded. "I mean, the program is the most vital function."

"Precisely." Shacklar laid his hand on a chair. "May I join you?"

"Aye, an't please thee," Gwen said.

Rod cast a stern glance at her.

Shacklar pulled out the chair and sat. "Mind you, I'm not apologizing. The monster had to be stopped, stopped instantly—and there was only one way to do it. We're fortunate that the controlling computer was located in its skull, where I placed my first shot."

"Not just 'fortunate.'" Rod smiled. "You were pretty sure that's where it would be, weren't you?"

Shacklar grinned. "Teleology generally wins out. If we make a machine in our own form, we put the computer in the head, simply because that's where our brains are, even though there's more room in the torso. Which, of course, is where my second shot would have gone."

"But, fortunately, it wasn't needed." Rod smiled. "Mind you, General, I'm glad you did it—very glad, considering it was me the blasted thing was trying to kill."

Shacklar acknowledged his support with a nod and a smile. "But I'm afraid we'll never be able to tell what the program was exactly. And, of course, there will be no means of guessing who programmed it, or why."

Rod shrugged. "We can speculate."

"True." Shacklar's smile intensified. "We can always speculate—but we ought to remember that we're merely conjecturing."

"Naetheless," Gwen reminded them, "*we* are proven innocent."

"Oh, quite true," said the General. "There's absolutely no question of that. And *my* problem, that of pacifying the Wolmen, is nicely solved."

"Yeah." Yorick grinned. "As soon as the Major showed them what was inside Hwun's skull, they didn't have any trouble believing the robot committed the murder."

Shacklar nodded. "And I can turn the 'dead' android over to the Wolmen—which I have done—so that, if they have any doubts at all, they can take it apart themselves, to see that it really is only a machine."

"Which they will do, of course." Cholly came up behind them and reached across shoulders to set new mugs of ale down for everyone. "And just think how much they'll learn about cybernetics!"

"Oh, I did." Shacklar contemplated his mug with a smile. "Moreover, by having 'slain' the android myself, I seem to have become something of a celebrity among the Wolmen."

Yorick grinned. "'Demon-killer,' huh?"

Shacklar nodded.

"Then you've got it all." Rod set his palms down on the table. "Your Wolmar Federation—the prototype for your government of colonists and Wolmen, coming together in two separate bodies to decide a common problem."

Shacklar looked up, surprised. "Very perceptive, really, Mr. Gallowglass. Do you do this sort of thing yourself?"

Rod opened his mouth, but Gwen answered. "He hath occasion for awareness of it. Then he hath guessed aright?"

"Indeed," Shacklar answered. "In fact, I've had the first draft of the Constitution sitting in my files for several years, waiting for the right moment."

"Which we have managed to trigger for you," Rod inferred.

The General nodded. "Copies are currently en route to each of the four Wolman tribes, and the officers and rankers of our Parliament."

"And with your new status," Yorick pointed out, "you don't have to worry too much about whether or not the Wolmen will accept the new Constitution."

Shacklar smiled. "I do seem to have gained an impressive amount of credibility with them, yes."

"He's a demigod," Yorick explained.

"Certainly." Cholly grinned. "It makes the Union all the tighter, to have the whole thing both triggered and solved by somebody who's neither Wolman nor colonist."

Rod inclined his head. "We thank you."

Chornoi glared. "How could *you* know whether or not *she* does?"

Rod just stared, but Gwen said, "Be sure, he doth."

Chornoi rounded on her. "Then how come *you* don't know what *he* thinks?"

"I do." Gwen shrugged. "In this instance, he spoke first."

"I just wish," Rod went on quickly, "that I knew whether or not the nasty who programmed the robot was trying to sabotage the General-Governor's budding republic, or to assassinate Gwen and myself."

"Why not both?" Yorick spread his hands.

Chornoi nodded. "Does it really matter?"

"Well, kind of. If we knew which, we might be able to figure out why."

"A point," the General admitted. "However, I think we'd best stay with the pragmatic aspect of the situation. No matter what their ultimate goal was, old boy, I daresay someone is attempting to kill you."

"I . . . would . . . say that was a reasonable guess." Rod gazed into Gwen's eyes as he nodded slowly.

"Therefore," the General said, "it behooves us to get you off-planet as quickly as possible, before your would-be assassins create an incident that *does* rip Wolmar apart."

Rod looked up, with a sour smile. "To our mutual benefit, eh?"

"Let us say, a point of intersection between our areas of interest."

"Well, no offense, General, but we'd love to leave. Any ideas how to escape from a prison planet?"

"Ah, but we're no longer a prison." Shacklar held up a forefinger. "When the Proletarian Eclectic State of Terra cut us off from the central government, we became an independent entity by default. Of course, I do understand that I have some genuine homicidal maniacs living here, and I wouldn't loose *them* on the galaxy—nor any of my sadomasochists." He shivered, took a deep breath. "Nor any of the truly dedicated thieves. Still, you must understand that we do have some export trade in the raw materials for pharmaceuticals . . ."

"He's talking about pipeweed," Cholly explained.

"Quite. And we've discovered that we can actually make a small profit, trading with other outlying planets."

"Enough to exchange for the few imports you really need?"

Shacklar nodded. "Our main markets are Haskerville and Otranto."

"Otranto?" Rod frowned. "That's a resort planet!" It still had that reputation in Rod's time, five hundred years later. Then his eyes widened. "Oh. *That* kind of pharmaceutical."

"No, not really." Shacklar smiled. "It's simply that a great many ships berth at Otranto, with pleasure-seekers from all over the Terran Sphere. They also carry a bit of cargo, especially if it's low-bulk—so one of the pharmaceutical companies operates a factory there, bringing in raw materials from several of the outlying planets, extracting their essential chemicals, and shipping them on to the central planets for further processing and distribution. Thus we've managed to maintain some trade."

"The rejects have managed to stay civilized in spite of the in-group, eh?" Rod couldn't help smiling.

"If you must put it in the vulgar cant," Shacklar sighed. "In fact, it was one of the freighters that brought us word of the PEST coup."

Rod suddenly realized where the conversation was heading. "There wouldn't happen to be a freighter in port right now, would there?"

Shacklar nodded. "On our moon. You must understand that due to our genesis as a prison planet, it can be quite difficult to go from our spaceport to our moon. In fact, there are some very elaborate security procedures left over from the PEST days, which I've seen no reason to relax. However, since I've no records of any of you three being criminals, I've no reason to detain you."

"And every reason to help us move on, huh?"

"Thou wilt assist us in our travels, then?" Gwen asked.

"I shall be delighted." Shacklar gravely bowed his head.

Rod held his breath, screwed up his courage, and took a chance. "Of course, we couldn't agree to go without our guide."

Yorick looked surprised, then grinned. "Yeah. We think we're gonna need her expertise, no matter where we go."

Shacklar gave Chornoi a long, assessing gaze. Slowly, he nodded. "Given her history, I don't believe she should have been with us to begin with."

Hope flared in Chornoi's eyes.

"I certainly see no reason to detain you further, mademoiselle." Shacklar inclined his head with grave courtesy. "And to be certain no other officials misunderstand, I'll equip you with an official pardon."

Rod sat back with a sigh of relief. "General, your cooperation is amazing." He frowned at a sudden thought. "But there is the little matter of the fare. I'm afraid we don't have enough money for the tickets."

Yorick started to say something, but Shacklar was already gazing off into space and nodding. "I'm certain that could be managed. As I say, we do have something of a trade balance. I believe the Bank of Wolmar will prove willing to advance funds for the next leg of your journey."

"Our greatest thanks." Gwen's eyes sparkled.

The General held his eyes on her for a few moments. He may have been always calm and cool, but he wasn't immune.

Personally, Rod was amazed at just how anxious Shacklar was to be rid of them.

PART II

OTRANTO

Gwen released her shock webbing with a bemused frown. "Why, that was naught! Or, at least, 'twas naught when I liken it to the terror of that devil's ride from the planet to the moon." She turned to Rod, anxiety shadowing her eyes. "Be we truly in the sky, my lord?"

"We be," Rod assured her.

"And that bare, great hall that we came into from the ship—that was truly on the moon? Truly perched upon that circle of light within the nighttime sky?"

"It really was, dear. Of course, that 'circle of light' was actually a ball of rock, five hundred miles thick."

She sank back into her seat, shaking her head. "'Tis wondrous!" Then she looked down at the chair beneath her. "As is this throne! How marvelously soft it is, and how wondrous is this cloth that covers it!" She looked up at Rod. "And they are not for nobility alone?"

"Well, technically, no." Rod frowned. "Though I suppose anyone who can afford space travel has to be as rich as an aristocrat."

"Or a criminal," Yorick added, from across the aisle. "In which case, he doesn't have to pay anything at all."

"Yeah, but the accommodations aren't quite this classy. And he doesn't really want to be going where he's headed, either."

"True," Yorick said judiciously. "Of course, if you're going *away* from prison, you're not too picky about the service."

"This isn't really all that fancy," Rod explained to Gwen.

"This whole room is just a little blip on the side of a great, big freight-carrier, so they can carry passengers if they have to."

"Or get a chance to," Yorick added. "We bring in a lot more money per cubic meter than cargo does."

"That is *somewhat* reassuring." Gwen looked up at Rod. "But explain to me again the nature of this moment of strangeness that we but now suffered, when it seemed that up was down and, for a moment, I had thought we were on the outside of this ship of the skies."

Rod shook his head. "Don't know if I really can, dear. I know the words for it, but I'm not sure what they mean."

"Then say them to me," she urged.

"Okay. The fastest anything can go is the speed of light—about 186,280 miles per second, remember? But the only reason light goes that fast is because it's made of infinitesimal little motes called photons . . ."

"There's nothing to it," Yorick confided.

Rod nodded. "Right. Nothing at all. Photons don't weigh anything, don't have any substance, any 'mass.' If you or I climbed into a spaceship and tried to go faster and faster until we got to the speed of light, our ship would get shorter and shorter, and heavier and heavier, and more and more massive. And the more mass it would have, the more power it would take to make it go faster."

"So there doth come a point at which each mite more of power, doth make so much more 'mass,' that the ship doth go no faster?"

"Right!" Rod beamed at her, delighted again by her quickness of understanding. But a chill passed through his belly—how could she understand so quickly, when her culture didn't give her the necessary background concepts? "Technically, we would be going just a fraction faster; we'd always be getting a tiny bit closer to the speed of light, and a tiny bit more, and a tiny bit more, but we'd never quite reach it."

"I cannot truly understand it," she sighed, sinking back.

"Yet an thou dost say it, my lord, I will credit it."

"Well, that helps a little. But you'll understand it thoroughly soon enough, dear, or I quite mistake you. Then you can decide for yourself whether you believe it or not."

"Yet what is this 'other space' thou, and Yorick and Chornoi, did say we have passed into?"

"Oh." Rod rolled his eyes to the side, pursing his lips for a moment. "Well, you see, dear . . . uh . . . Otranto, the planet we're going to, is about forty-five light-years from Wolmar. The distance that light can travel in a year is about five billion, eight hundred eighty million miles—and forty-five times that is something like 265 trillion. And that's roughly how far it is from Wolmar to Otranto."

She turned her head from side to side, wide-eyed. "'Tis inconceivable."

"Totally. We can't even imagine a distance that great, not really. It's just a string of numbers."

"But we do get the main point," said Yorick, "which is that even if we could go almost as fast as light does, it'd still take us fifty years to get to Otranto."

"And I don't know about you," Chornoi added, "but for myself, I have a lot of better things to do, than just sit around aboard a ship playing checkers for that long a time."

"I assure thee, so have I." Gwen shivered.

"But we can't go any faster," Yorick reminded her. "Not if we want to stay solid. No faster than the speed of light."

"So we go around it," Rod explained.

Gwen squeezed her eyes shut, shaking her head. "I cannot comprehend that."

"Neither can I," Rod admitted. "But there's a gadget in the back of the ship called an 'isomorpher,' and when the pilot turns it on, it makes us isomorphic with H-space. I'm not sure what H-space is, but I gather it's a kind of space that isn't quite part of this universe."

Gwen frowned. "And we are part of that H-space?"

"Well, no, not part of it, really." Rod sat back, staring at the corner of the ceiling, pursing his lips. "Just identified with it—point for point, atom for atom. Which is what we are right now." He looked around at the interior of the cabin.

"But I feel no differently," she cried, "nor doth aught appear transformed!"

"We aren't." Rod shook his head. "We aren't different, at all—relative to this ship, and relative to each other—because we're *all* isomorphic with H-space right now. But when the ship's computer pulls out the pattern for what normal space is like, near Otranto, and when it identifies that pattern, it'll turn off the isomorpher, and we'll go back to being ordinary parts of the regular universe."

"'Tis magic," Gwen said firmly.

"Personally, I agree," Rod sighed, "but the man who explained it to me, assured me it was all perfectly natural, and thoroughly understandable."

"So," said Gwen, "are my witch-powers."

"Only on Gramarye, my dear." Rod squeezed her hand. "And I suppose all this isomorphism and H-space is normal and understandable out here." He turned to Yorick. "I don't suppose it's possible for Dr. McAran to shoot you the pieces of the time machine while we're in this condition, is it?"

Yorick shook his head. "He can't lock onto us, Major. However his time machines work, it ain't through H-space."

"I thought not," Rod sighed, "which is too bad, because this is going to be at least half the trip—two days, at least. But he can do it once we're back into normal space."

"Well, he can try." Yorick frowned. "But that's what I was trying to signal you about back there at Cholly's, when you were talking to the General-Governor. Locking onto a moving object that's any smaller than a planet, is an awfully tricky operation. If Doc Angus misses, the components he's trying to throw at us are lost for good, and time machine parts cost enough to make even *him* wince."

Rod just stared at Yorick for a moment. Then he said, "You're telling me that, even though we have a good day or two between our break out point and Otranto, forty-eight perfectly usable hours without any interruptions, you're *not* going to be able to build us a time machine?"

Yorick shook his head. "Sorry, Major. 'It ain't in the state of the art.'"

"And probably never will be," Rod sighed. "But inside a shed back on Wolmar would have been a moving target, too—and you were so sure you could manage it there!"

"Yeah, but it was a stationary target, relative to the huge mass it was sitting on. It was only the planet that was moving—and all that planetary mass is easy enough to lock onto. Then it's just a matter of aiming at a small target that stays put, relative to the large one." Yorick shrugged. "You know what a planet's gravitational field does to space-time, Major. It makes space curve, so it does most of the focusing for you. All you have to do is lock onto the planet's rotation, and as soon as you have that rate figured out, it's no problem. But here . . ." He spread his hands, a gesture taking in the whole cabin and the vast ship outside it. "I mean, this whole freighter can't be more than half a kilometer long!"

"Well, what do you expect?" Chornoi snapped. "Bush-league planets don't get the big ships, you know."

Yorick ignored her. "Half a kilometer, two kilometers, what difference does it make? That's just a dust-mote on the planetary scale. It just ain't big enough to have enough mass to have any major effect on the curvature of space!" He shook his head, looking doleful. "Sorry, but I can't get you out of this mess while we're in transit."

"Oh, well, I should have known better," Rod sighed. "All right, if we can't get a portable time machine here, we'll just have to find some quiet place on Otranto where we can set one up."

Yorick nodded. "Shouldn't be any problem, Major."

"It shouldn't have been any problem on Wolmar, either." Rod gave Yorick a jaundiced glance. "I don't suppose there'd happen to be a permanent time machine somewhere on Otranto, all ready and waiting, would there?"

Yorick shook his head. "Not that I know of. In fact, the only permanent installation that I know about, at this point in history . . ." He frowned. "Well, I can't say I *know* about it, damn it!"

"Where *is* it?" Rod exploded.

"All right, all right!" Yorick held up both palms, shielding himself. "Not so loud, okay? We're *pretty* sure that the LORDS party, the ones who are running the Proletarian Eclectic State of Terra, had some Futurian help in engineering their coup d'etat—and they've probably stayed in contact, all the way through their regime. I mean, PEST *could* have figured out which planet was going to rebel, when—but it is kind of odd that they just happened to always have a naval squadron right nearby."

"Very odd," Rod agreed. "So you're pretty sure there's a permanent time machine somewhere in PEST headquarters on Terra?"

"Yeah." Yorick gave him a bleak smile. "But good luck getting to it. It belongs to the opposition, and it's guaranteed to be very tightly guarded."

"Well, nothing ventured, nothing gained," Rod sighed. "I always did want to visit humanity's ancestral home, anyway."

"Well, that's great! I mean, you'll love it there, Major, it's . . ." Suddenly the Neanderthal's eyes widened in horror. "My lord! Chornoi! We shouldn't be talking about this with her around!"

"So I thought," Gwen agreed. "The poor lass was overly wearied. I thought it best that she slumber awhile."

Yorick turned around, craning his neck over the back of the seat, and saw Chornoi slumped in her recliner, head rolled to the side, breathing deeply and evenly. "Well, that's a relief! Thank you, Lady Gallowglass! I really gotta keep a better eye on my tongue!" He frowned. "That didn't sound right . . ."

"We catch your meaning," Rod assured him.

"Thou hast yet to tell me of this 'Terra' of thine," Gwen reminded.

"Earth," Rod answered. "The place where your ultimate

ancestors came from—and mine, too, of course. And everybody's. It's the planet where humanity evolved, the only planet where our bodies really feel at home."

"Not anymore, they don't." Yorick shook his head. "The whole place is concrete and steel now." He frowned. "Well, there are a *few* parks . . ."

"Are we to go there, then?"

"We can't. This freighter is going to Otranto. But maybe, there, we can find a ship that's going to Terra."

"Of course, we may not need to," Yorick said. "If we can just find a quiet place for a little while, Doc Angus can shoot me the spare parts I need to make a time machine." He sighed. "Of course, there is another little problem . . ."

Rod felt the familiar cold chill spread over his back. "Oh? *What* problem?"

"The Futurians. I mean, they kidnapped you in the first place. Then they set up an elaborate little plot that had almost everybody on Wolmar cooperating in an attempt to assassinate you."

"Yeah, but that was Wolmar," Rod said. "And the people of this time haven't invented faster-than-light radio yet, so their communication is still limited to couriers riding FTL ships, like this one."

Yorick nodded. "But VETO and SPITE have time machines. So *they* can send a message from Wolmar to Otranto, and get it there the next day." He frowned. "Or the day before, if it comes to that."

Rod stared.

"So it's quite possible, Major, that we might find a reception committee waiting for us."

Rod leaned back, trying to relax. "Give me a little while to get used to the idea."

"Sure." Yorick leaned back, too, and twiddled his thumbs. "You've got time. A couple of days, at least."

"The waiting is driving me crazy," Chornoi growled.

"Anticipay-hay-hay-shun," Yorick sang.

The world twisted inside out.

Then it twisted right-side-out again, leaving Gwen holding her stomach. Rod clapped a hand over his mouth. They both swallowed, hard, then looked across the cabin. Chornoi was a delicate shade of green, and Yorick was gulping air. "Yes," he said finally. "Well—the wonders of modern travel, right?"

Rod nodded. "The price you pay for speed, and all that."

The Neanderthal heaved himself to his feet and waddled down the aisle to the viewscreen. "As long as we're back where there's something to see, let's look at the outside, instead of this saccharine melodrama that nobody's been watching anyway." He punched a button, and a vast vista of unwinking stars replaced the 3DT program.

"Hey!" yelped Chornoi. "How'll I find out whether or not Chuck will stop Allison from marrying Tony, because she's about to have Tommy's baby, but doesn't want Karen to have Tony, even though she really wants to marry Chuck?"

Then she fell silent, awed by the majesty of the panorama before her. The computer had dimmed the brightness of the sun, of course, or they wouldn't have been able to look directly at it, even though it was only a very small disk in the center of the huge screen. Blips that were planets floated around it, brightened and colorized electronically—and the net impression was gorgeous. Gwen caught her breath with delight. "Eh, my lord! Be this truly how a sun and its worlds do appear?"

Rod nodded. "This is the real thing, darling. Of course, if you saw it with your naked eye, the sun would be a lot brighter, and the planets would be lost in its glare. They aren't lined up so neatly that you can count them, but you can ferret 'em out. Let's see—there's one, that little dot near the sun, that's probably a planet. And, yes, there's number two, a little further away, and number three . . ."

"Yet what is that one that doth grow?"

Rod frowned. "Yeah, that is kind of funny."

"Not humorous at all!" Yorick whirled and scuttled back

to his seat. "That swelling dot is growing knobs and fins! Web in, everybody—we're about to be intercepted!"

Rod stared. Then he whipped about to Gwen, but her webbing was still secure from break out. So was his, for that matter.

"What's the trouble?" Chornoi looked around at them, frowning. "So they're intercepting us. They're not going to shoot us down, you know."

"No," Rod grated, "we don't know. They tried to kill us twice already, remember?"

Chornoi stared at the screen, her eyes growing huge.

Gwen frowned up at Rod. "What is it, mine husband?"

"Another ship," Rod explained, "and there's no way to tell who's steering it."

Across the aisle, Yorick looked nervous. "I'm sure the captain is busy trying to find out that very datum."

The glowing dot had swelled into the form of a spaceship, seen head-on. It spat a bolt of light that washed the screen with searing brightness. The ship lurched about them, and somewhere, a huge gong chimed.

"Yoicks!" Yorick bleated. "What a way to answer a hail! Doesn't his radio work?"

Rod felt his stomach sliding over toward his left kidney. "Everybody hold on! Our pilot isn't waiting for a second sentence!"

On the screen, the attacking ship slid up to the upper right-hand corner. Another bolt of energy shot out from it—and off the screen.

"Missed!" Rod squeezed his fist tight. "Way to go, skipper! Zig your zags!"

His stomach dropped back toward his coccyx. Gwen gasped, and Chornoi moaned. On the screen, the attacker veered toward the lower left-hand corner, and the stars wheeled behind it. The sun slipped toward the left, too.

"Be brave, dear." Rod clasped her hand. "It has to end some time." *Hopefully, the right way . . .*

"'Tis not . . . entirely . . . unpleasant," Gwen gasped. "I

shall become accustomed to it, my lord."

"I hope you won't have time..."

The enemy ship fired another bolt that lit up the upper right-hand corner of the screen. The sun-disc drifted off the screen to the left.

"Missed again." Rod nodded. "Have we got a good pilot!"

"Or a good computer," Yorick added. "No human being could react this fast. So just punch the buttons for 'evasive action.'"

Rod glowered at him. "Just had to make a point of it, didn't you?"

Yorick grinned. "What can I tell you? *Homo sapiens* has its limits, too."

"You don't have to be so happy about it, though... Whoa! Hold on!"

The other ship veered into the center of the screen; the sun-disc disappeared entirely.

"What is that maniac doing?" Chornoi gasped.

"Trying to get between the ship and the planet." Rod put out an arm as Gwen leaned over against him—or tried to, but the webbing held her tightly.

"Smart!" Chornoi's eyes glowed. "If he can get close enough to the planet's surface, the bandit won't dare shoot, for fear he'll fry innocent people."

"I... don't... really think that would make him hesitate." Rod scowled. "But he might attract the attention of the local constabulary."

"You mean *I'm* supposed to cheer for the *cops?*" Chornoi asked.

"Why not? You were one..."

On the screen, the pirate spat another bolt. It mushroomed out to fill the screen with glaring whiteness, and the whole cabin sang as though they were inside a piano string. Stars glared through a ragged hole in the ceiling.

"Abandon ship!" Yorick howled. "Or is it the other way around?"

But Rod didn't answer. His eyes lost focus as, frantically,

he concentrated on his psi powers, seeing the passenger blister not as it really was, but as he wanted it to be. In his mind's eye, he saw the little bulge falling away from the main freight ship. He pictured a thin membrane sliding over the open side, where the ship had been.

Yorick looked around, flabbergasted. "Hey! I can still breathe! How come we're not drinking vacuum? How come our blood isn't boiling out our noses, from sheer lack of air pressure?"

Chornoi saw Rod's abstracted gaze. "Major, what are you doing?"

To Rod, her words seemed to come thinly from a great distance. Carefully, he answered, "I'm . . . holding the air . . . in . . . with us."

Chornoi stared. White showed around the irises of her eyes.

"Gwen?"

"Aye, my lord."

"We're . . . falling."

"Our ship was heading toward the planet when the pirate shot our cabin off the freighter's side," Yorick explained, "so *we're* still going toward the planet, too."

Gwen looked from the one to the other. "Is that not where we wish to go?"

"Yeah, but . . . not so fast . . ." Rod answered. "Take us down . . . darling . . . slowly . . ."

Gwen looked about them, and finally thought to look up. She gasped. "But . . . there is no 'down,' my lord. There is only some great bulge above us, a curving wall of blue, with swirls of white!"

"That's . . . Otranto," Rod grated.

"We're not close enough for it to seem like 'down' yet," Yorick explained, "but we're moving toward it, right enough. It's just that we're moving toward what you call 'up,' just now."

Gwen stared. "But how can one fall upward?"

"Gravity," Yorick explained.

Gwen's eyes opened wide. "That's to say that when I toss a ball into the air and it falls, 'tis the earth that pulls it down."

Yorick nodded. "Yeah, that's most of it. Of course, the ball pulls, too."

Gwen smiled. "Though so small a pull, could scarce be more than a wish."

"I suppose that's one way of looking at it." Yorick sucked in one cheek. "The ball *wants* to come down."

"And so . . . do . . . we," Rod grated.

"The closer we get to each other, the planet and us," Yorick explained, "the stronger the pull."

Gwen stared. Then her mouth opened in a silent "O."

Yorick nodded. "So the closer we get to the planet, milady, the faster we're gonna be going."

"Very . . . fast . . . already," Rod reminded him.

"Yeah." Yorick gave a bleak smile. "We're already traveling a thousand miles per second."

"And we will gain speed as we fall?"

Yorick nodded. "Unless you can do something about it."

"Well . . . mayhap I can." Gwen leaned back, gazing thoughtfully up at the bulge of the planet above them.

"Do it . . . soon," Rod begged.

"Uh, yeah." Yorick scratched at his ear. "That's the other thing I forgot to mention, Lady Gallowglass. It's called 'friction.' You know how when you rub your hands together, they start feeling hot?"

Gwen nodded, not taking her eyes off the planet above.

"Well, we're going so fast that just our hull pushing through the *air* can be friction enough to cause a lot of heat," Yorick explained. "Enough to kill us."

"So," Gwen mused, "I must slow us *and* cool us."

Beside her, Rod nodded. "Molecules . . . slow 'em down . . ."

"Thou hast explained that to me oft enow, my lord," Gwen said, with some asperity. "I must own, 'twas thou who didst teach me what my mind did when I did stare at a branch, and made it burst into flame. Nay, I ken the slowing of these 'molecules,' as thou dost term them. And, I think, I can slow our descent enow so that we may land gently." She frowned up at the planet. "Let us begin by putting the world where it doth belong."

Slowly, the huge curve moved off to the side. There was no sensation of movement, but the sun-disc slowly slewed into the center of the hole in the ceiling.

Yorick exhaled sharply. "Yes. Everyday occurrence. Right."

Gwen nodded, satisfied. "*Now* we fall downward."

Across the aisle, Chornoi stared, aghast. "What *are* they?"

"A witch and a warlock," Yorick informed her. "But that's just the local term, where they come from."

"This isn't really magic?" Chornoi said hopefully.

Yorick shook his head. "Just psionics. These are two *very* high-powered espers."

Chornoi sat back, going limp. "I'm glad to hear *that's* all it is."

"Right." Yorick's smile soured. "It's so much less scary when you can give it a name, isn't it?"

"The pirate is gone now," Gwen informed them.

"Huh?" Yorick looked up and saw a clear sky. "Well. Guess once he saw he'd shot off our cabin, he figured we were dead."

"He had every right to," Chornoi said devoutly.

"Well." Yorick laced his fingers across his midriff and settled back into his acceleration couch. "Might as well relax and enjoy the ride."

"It may be rough," Gwen warned.

"'S okay! That's just fine, Lady Gallowglass!" Yorick held up a palm. "No matter how you slice it, it's going to be a hell of a lot better than I thought it was."

Actually, it was rather boring from that point on. Gwen was very good at slowing them down, but she had a lot of speed to kill, so it did take a little while. Every now and then, things did begin to get a little too warm, and Gwen had to frown in deep concentration until they cooled off. Yorick did some exploring, and found a couple of emergency oxygen generators, but even so, Rod was worried that he might have to try to precipitate the carbon out of the carbon dioxide in the air, and he wasn't exactly burning to have black dust all over the glowing brocade of his new doublet.

At one point, Rod said, "Dear . . . the planet . . . is turning . . . under us. Match . . . velocities . . ."

"That means matching the spin of the planet," Yorick explained. "'Velocity' is how fast something's going in any given direction. Just make sure we're moving at the same speed as the world's surface."

"How am I to do that?" Gwen asked.

"Find some landmark," Yorick explained. He glanced at the viewscreen. "Can't do much with that, the power cut off as soon as we broke away from the ship. All we've got is a little emergency power for lights, air, and heat, nothing left over for sight-seeing."

Gwen frowned at the screen, and it burst into life. A landscape reeled across it, blurred by speed, obscured by darkness.

Yorick stared. "How did you do *that?*" Then he squeezed his eyes shut and shook his head. "Never mind—I don't think I want to know. But try to pick out some big landmark, Lady Gallowglass, and slow us down until it stays put in the middle of the screen."

The landscape began to slow. Moonlight outlined ridges that were chains of hills, showing a groove that must have been a valley.

In its center, pricks of light glittered.

"Civilization!" Chornoi cried. "That's gotta be a city! Only people make that kind of light! Quick, Lady Gallowglass, put us down there!"

Gwen concentrated harder on the screen. "I will essay it . . ."

Chornoi leaned over to Yorick. "How come she can talk while she's doing it, and he can't?"

"'Cause she's better at it than he is." Yorick spread his hands. "What can I tell you? She's been practicing since she was born, and he only found out he had power three years ago."

Chornoi reared her head back, looking askance at him. "How come you know so much about them?"

"Friend of the family," Yorick assured her, "and if you met their kids, you'd want to be friendly, too."

"There." Sweat beaded Gwen's brow. "Master Yorick, is that as thou didst wish it?"

"Beautiful," Rod mumbled.

Yorick looked at the screen. It was as rock-still as though someone had hung a map at the front of the cabin. He blinked. "How the hell did you do that? I didn't feel a thing!"

"I slowed us folk as I slowed the vessel."

Yorick stared at her. "Right." He shook himself. "Sure. Inertia—what's that? just a frame of reference, right?"

"Then refer to that frame." Gwen pointed at the screen. "That square of darkness in the center—what is it?"

Yorick leaned forward, squinting. Then he shook his head. "Can't tell yet, Lady Gallowglass. When we're closer, maybe."

The tiny square started growing. It swelled until it filled the screen. Moonlight silvered the dark square, revealing textures.

"Treetops!" Chornoi exclaimed.

Yorick stared. "Did you drop us lower, or did you just make the picture get bigger?"

Chornoi pointed. "See that silver thread straggling kitty-corner across it? Has to be a stream."

"I think it's a park, Lady Gallowglass."

"Then there should be few folk about," Gwen said, with growing excitement. "'Twill make a good landing field."

The park swelled in the screen. They could see individual trees, which moved off to the edges of the screen as they grew.

Gwen concentrated all of her attention on the screen.

The stream grew broader and broader, filling the center of the screen. Then it drifted off to the right and out of the screen entirely.

Chornoi and Yorick stared for a few seconds, holding their breath. The wreck jolted violently, slamming everybody back against their acceleration couches. They all sat still for a few minutes.

Then Gwen spoke, her voice soft in the dimness of the emergency lights. "My apologies. I had not meant to strike with such force."

"Oh, that's fine!" Chornoi held up a palm.

"Wonderful." Yorick nodded, with great enthusiasm. "Believe me, Lady Gallowglass, that's a much softer landing than we were expecting."

"Any landing is just great," Chornoi added.

Yorick loosed his webbing and stood up. "Here, let me give you a hand." He helped Gwen disengage her webbing. She caught his arm as she stood. "Gramercy, Master Yorick."

"Oh, it's nothing. It's . . . Hey! The major! Is he all right?"

Rod was leaning back in his couch, his eyes closed, chest heaving.

"Aye, he is well."

Rod pried an eyelid open. "Yeah." The other eyelid opened, too, and he rolled both eyeballs over toward Yorick. "Just a little tired."

"He did aid me in the moving of the vessel," Gwen explained.

"A little tired." Yorick nodded. "Sure, Major. Uh—before we do anything else—how about a little nap?"

Rod shook his head, loosening his webbing and struggling to his feet. "Haven't got time. We've got to get out of here before dawn."

Yorick reached out to stop him, saying, "No, Major. You're not . . ." But Rod was already past him, tottering toward the hatch.

Yorick shoved himself to his feet with a shrug. "Well,

he's got a point. We landed pretty close to the terminator, as I remember my last glimpse of the viewscreen."

Chornoi hurried after Rod, bleating, "But how do we know the air is even breathable here!"

"Because approximately two million colonists are already breathing it." Yorick swung into step beside her. "And, of course, there's always the hole in our own roof. Nice try, lady, but you're not going to stop him with cobblestones for roadblocks."

Rod threw his weight against the locking lever and shoved. The door swung open, and he went with it. He half fell, half jumped, and felt as though he were dropping through molasses. As his feet touched the ground, Gwen was beside him, holding onto his elbow. "Gently, I prithee, my lord!"

"Why, with you there to cushion my falls? Thanks, though, darling."

Gwen smiled, and shook her head. "Wilt thou not rest, my lord? . . . Nay, 'tis even as thou sayest, we must be gone—yet favor thine own weakness, I prithee!"

Rod smiled gently at her. "You can always float me, if I collapse, dear. After all, I won't be able to float alone. . . ." He looked around. "Hey! Not bad."

One moon was high in the sky, and another just above the horizon. Between them, they gave just enough light to show manicured lawns and sculpted trees all about them. Flowers rustled in formal beds, their petals closed against the night, and a small pond gleamed like a mirror a few hundred yards away.

"Why . . . 'tis beautiful," Gwen breathed, looking about.

Yorick sidled up next to Rod and nudged him with an elbow, pointing toward Chornoi. She was silent, her face strained and eyes haunted, drinking in the lush beauty around her.

Rod looked and nodded. "Yeah. Glad we got her off that prison planet."

"Aye, the poor lass!" Gwen said. "To have so much of beauty, after years of such bleakness. . . ."

"We may have it again, if we don't get out of here." Rod scanned the trees and shrubbery, feeling his fatigue shoved into the background as adrenaline spiked him. "No way to tell which inviting piece of topiary is hiding a vision pickup. Maybe even sound."

Yorick nodded. "Somebody's got to have noticed we dropped in on them."

"Well, then, let's see if we can disappear before they send a welcoming committee." Rod turned away. "See if you can't wake up Chornoi, will you?"

Yorick reached out carefully, touching Chornoi's arm. Her head jerked around, eyes wide, and Yorick stepped back fast, just as a precaution. "I really hate to interrupt your reverie, Ms., but we gotta get going, or we're going to have company."

Chornoi whirled, staring about her, wild-eyed.

"Right." Yorick nodded. "No telling where from. Only that they're on their way."

"We can't be sure of that." Chornoi swung back to him. "But we'd be fools to take the chance. Which way did the Major go?"

Yorick pointed, and Chornoi set off after Rod and Gwen at a pace that made Yorick hustle.

They came out onto cobblestones as dawn was lightening the sky, permeating everything with a dim, sourceless light, punctuated by slivers of late moonlight. It was the time when night had died and day hadn't been born, a time between realities, when nothing is definite and everything is possible—a time of fantasy when anything can happen.

And the landscape was right for it. Mist rose about their knees, and its tendrils wisped up to veil a row of half-timbered houses, their second stories overhanging the street. Shop signs creaked in the breeze. Far away, something barked.

"Why, 'tis like home," Gwen said, wide-eyed.

"Yeah." Rod frowned. "Wonder what's wrong?"

"Why're we talking so softly?" Chornoi whispered.

"Who could be loud in a place like this?" Yorick murmured.

"Besides, we might wake the neighbors." Rod shouldered his fatigue and mustered his resolution. "And we don't want them to see us—just yet."

"Wherefore not?"

"Because they're going to find that capsule that brought us here, and we don't want some idle bystander with a high sense of drama telling the authorities that they saw us near the park this morning."

"I get the point," Yorick said. "Some enthusiastic soul might jump to the conclusion that we came in on that ship."

"But wherefore ought we wish him not to?" Gwen looked from man to man, puzzled. "We *were* aboard it."

"Yeah, dear, but whoever tried to shoot us down thinks we're dead. We wouldn't want to disillusion him, would we?"

"Or her," Chornoi put in.

"But when they find the empty ship, they will know we do live!"

"Yes, but they *won't* know what we look like!"

"Camouflage, Lady Gallowglass," Yorick explained. "Odds are that our attacker doesn't know what we look like, aside from a general description. He'll know we escaped, but nothing more since nobody on Otranto has seen us. But if he can get a detailed description from an eyewitness . . ."

"Hold on!" Chornoi held her hands up like a football referee. "Time out! You're both assuming that pirate was out to get *us!* He *could* have just been after the ship!"

Rod looked at Yorick. Yorick looked at Rod.

"All right, all right! I get the point!" Chornoi snarled, yanking her hands down. "Come on, let's go!" She set off down the street, walking fast.

Rod followed after her. "Can I help it if I'm a cynic?"

"Dost thou wish to?" Gwen murmured.

Four blocks later, Rod came to a sudden halt. "Would you look at that! You'd think a surveyor had drawn a line and a town board had declared a zone."

"Probably did," Chornoi declared.

"There goes the neighborhood," Yorick sighed.

"And the business district begins." Rod agreed.

"But what manner of business isn't?" Gwen wondered.

"Woman's oldest," Chornoi stated.

"Oh, they're not that exclusive." Rod pursed his lips. "I see at least three gambling halls in there, and five saloons."

"And five feelie theaters, three dance parlors, two opium dens, and a pawnshop." Yorick looked up and down the street. "Have I missed anything?"

"Yes. But *they* haven't."

As far as they could see, the street was one mass of blinking, scrambling, writhing holographic displays in garish colors, advertising every form of pleasure conceived by mortal man and woman.

"Wonder what the buildings look like?" Yorick mused.

"Who can tell?" Rod shrugged. "Even if you could see one, you couldn't be sure it was real."

Chornoi nodded. "That about sums up this whole planet, from what I've heard."

"I thought it was a resort."

"It is. And it's amazing what people will resort to, if they can find the money."

"Otranto," Rod said, remembering the planet's reputation, stronger than ever in his own time, five hundred years later. "Isn't their motto, 'It's been a business doing pleasure with you'?"

"No, but it will be," Yorick assured him. He took a deep breath. "Well, folks—we gotta get through it, right?"

"Right." Rod squared his shoulders and stepped manfully in. "Breathe every five steps, friends."

That wasn't as easy as it sounded. The signs weren't just visual—most of them were aural and olfactory, too. And, occasionally, tactile. The company waded through a melange of sounds and smells, their senses assaulted by every glamour in the state of the art. Erotic images gyrated and beckoned, male and female; delectable aromas wafted out to envelop them; images of riches and luxury flashed before their eyes. Holographic hucksters stepped out to entice them, as real as life and twice as pungent. They gritted their teeth and forced themselves to keep going, wading through every distraction they had ever desired.

A sleek, unbelievably handsome young man stepped out of a doorway, muscles rippling underneath his evening clothes, one arm full of long-stemmed roses, the other dangling a diamond necklace. Chornoi swerved after him like a needle to a magnet.

"Hold it, sister." Yorick caught her arm. "Just illusion, remember? Besides, he costs money."

Chornoi shook herself, coming out of her trance with a gasp. "Thanks. They almost got me with that one."

"Close," Yorick agreed. "Courage, lady. You're almost out of it."

"How do you know?" Chornoi wondered.

"I don't—but this kind of thing *can't* go on forever!"

"Optimist," she snorted.

However, the colony was young yet; the cheapside didn't last more than a quarter mile. They came up out of aromas and sensations with huge, rasping gasps, into clear, quiet air.

"I don't think I could have taken much more." Rod sagged against a lamp post.

"And you didn't even have any money." Yorick finally took his hand off his hip pocket and flexed it. "I think I've got cramps."

Cramps in your soul, friend? Does this mortal world pain you, with its plethora of Philistines?"

They looked up, startled.

A monk stood before them—the real, genuine article, in a brown robe and rope belt. No tonsure, though.

"Why, he is quite like those at home," Gwen cried.

"Uh, well, no, not really, dear." Rod scratched the tip of his nose. "Just looks like it."

"Nay! He doth wear the badge! Dost'a not see?"

Gwen pointed, and Rod looked. The robe had a breast pocket, and in it was a small yellow-handled screwdriver. "You're a Cathodean."

The monk bowed his head in greeting. "Brother Joseph Fumble, though my acquaintances generally call me Brother Joey. And yourselves?"

"Gwen and Rod Gallowglass." Rod pointed at his wife. "She's Gwen." He gestured toward the other two. "He's Yorick, and she's Chornoi."

"Pleased to meet you," Brother Joey said, with a small bow. "I don't suppose any of you would be interested in taking up religion?"

"Uhhhh . . ." Rod glanced uncomfortably at Gwen. "We're, ah, pretty well set along that line, thanks. I take it you're a priest?"

"No, but I'm working on it."

Rod eyed the man; he wasn't all *that* young. "But you are a deacon."

"Oh, yes, everything set except final vows." Brother Joey sighed and shook his head. "It's just that I'm not really sure I'm cut out for this sort of thing."

"For what? The priesthood?"

Brother Joey nodded. "I've got the drive, mind you; I've visited nine planets so far, but I've had spectacularly little success as a missionary. Only two converts so far, and they were both religious recidivists." He brightened. "I'm an excellent engineer, though."

"I see the problem," Rod agreed. "But isn't Otranto a rather odd place to be preaching?"

"Apparently it is, but I thought it would be an excellent, ah, 'hunting-ground,' if you follow me. Sort of a virgin wilderness of the spirit. I mean, if there's any planet where people need religion, it's Otranto!"

"Yes, but considering how much money most of them have spent to come here to wallow in pleasure, and how much more the rest are making from giving it to them, it's the last place I'd expect to find people in remorse."

"And, apparently, your expectations are sharper than mine," the monk sighed. "But it seemed such an excellent idea!"

"Yet not all clergymen must needs be missionaries," Gwen said gently. "Mayhap thou wouldst be more suited to a village church."

"Uh, if you two are gonna talk about it . . ." Rod glanced nervously along their back trail. "Would you mind if you keep walking while you do? I admit it'd take a genius of a bloodhound to track us through that aroma heaven back there, but we did kind of stand out, being live people in the vapor-light district at this hour of the morning. I need room."

"Well, you'll find it in this neighborhood, I assure you." Brother Joey fell into step beside them, gesturing about him.

Rod had to agree with him. The houses, if you could call them that, were far apart and far back from the road, each one sitting centered on several acres of ground, with flawless lawns rolling down to the walkway. The nearest was a gloomy old Tudor manor house, but right next to it was a Gothic castle. A rambling Georgian mansion glowered across from it, and the lot after that held a medieval ruin.

"Odd notion of housing developments they have here." Rod frowned, looking about him, and sniffing the air. "Smells like rain."

"It always does, here," Brother Joey assured him, "and it's always overcast, except for the first half-hour after dawn each day. Just enough so that those who like sunrises, can have them."

"They're doing such wonderful things with weather control these days." Rod shook his head in wonder. "But *why?*"

"To make Otranto stand out," Brother Joey explained. "There are only a half-dozen of these pleasure-planets so far, but that's already enough to make the competition strong—after all, there are just so many really wealthy citizens in the Terran Sphere."

Chornoi nodded. "And most of them want to go to Orlando."

"Orlando does seem to have the general tourist trade locked up—'something for everyone,' and all that. I understand they have a separate continent for each amusement theme."

"More like very large islands," Chornoi said, "but there are a lot of them, yes."

Brother Joey nodded. "So the other pleasure-planets have to specialize. They draw only a small percentage of the customers, but that small percentage comes to a billion a year. They attract those customers by doing only one theme, but doing it in all the variations that a whole planet has room for."

"Oh." Rod looked around at the ruined castle and the gloomy manor houses, with the heavy gray sky brooding over it all. "I take it Otranto opted for Gothic romance."

Brother Joey nodded. "They even renamed the planet for the purpose. It used to be Zane's Star IV."

Chornoi said, "They've filled it with haunted houses, gloomy moors, and the most elaborate graveyards ever to bear bodies. The tourists get to live out their fantasies, dressing up in full costume and stalking around their borrowed family mansions, listening for clanking chains or moaning ghosts."

"So," Rod said, "I can expect to see a whole pack of decadent aristocrats haunted by family spectres?"

Chornoi nodded. "And a bevy of penurious governesses, a host of crochety country squires fairly overflowing with *Weltschmerz,* and a veritable zooful of assorted monsters."

"But the biggest attractions, of course," said Brother Joey, "are the dreamhouses."

"Yeah." Chornoi gazed off into space with a dreamy

smile. "You lie down, take a drug that puts you into a trance..."

Rod jerked to a halt, staring in horror. "A zombie-drug?!!?"

"No, no! It just deadens bodily sensations, and heightens suggestibility. A zombie-drug would totally knock out the forebrain, leave the customer without any freedom of choice! And choice plays a big part in it—the customer actually gets to react! Of course, he reacts pretty much in keeping with the plot line, unless he's a real maverick...."

"Plot?" Rod frowned. "I thought he just dreamed!"

"Well, she does, but it's a dream coming out of a computer directly into the customer's brain. Completely prescripted, of course—and the customer plays the hero or heroine. I hear it's the ultimate entertainment—exciting, emotion-stirring, full color, total sound-surround, full range of aromas and tastes—and the full sensation of touch." She shivered. "Bodice-rippers cost extra."

Gwen was staring in disbelief.

"I understand," said Brother Joey, "that it's all considerably more vivid than reality."

"Oh, no!" Rod squeezed his eyes shut. "Why do I suddenly feel sorry for anyone who's been through one of those?"

"Possibly because most of their customers are never able to be satisfied with actual life, after they've been through one such dream. As a result, they constantly crave another dream, and another." Brother Joey shuddered. "Under such circumstances, to claim they're not addictive, just because they don't build physical dependence, is simply weaseling with the meaning of the term."

"Never," Gwen said, with total determination, "shall I ever essay such."

"Oh, but they're not dangerous!" Chornoi cried. "They can't be, or the dreamhouses would lose customers."

Rod shook his head. "Forget about the dream itself. You're

lying there, out cold, for a few hours, right?"

Chornoi shook her head. "Just a few minutes, real time. An hour, at the most."

"An hour?" Yorick turned to her, frowning. "Just how much does this emotional candy cost, anyway?"

"Only a couple of hundred kwahers . . ."

"A couple of *hundred?* For less than an *hour?"*

"That's *real* time," Chornoi protested. "But while you're dreaming, it seems to go on and on for weeks—maybe even months!"

"So you're really paying for weeks of entertainment." Rod nodded, his mouth wry. "But it only costs the house a few minutes' use of its facilities. Talk about high turnover. . . ."

"The overnight vacation," Yorick mused, gazing off into space. "Fun, excitement, and romance, all in an evening's sleep. . . ."

Rod shook himself. "What are we, the dreamhouses' advertising bureau? The fact remains that while your mind is enjoying this total illusion, your body is lying there, totally vulnerable!"

Chornoi nodded. "That's why the dreamhouses guarantee your safety."

"How can they do *that?* I mean, while you're asleep, they could . . ." Rod stared in horror. "My lord! They could just channel indoctrination into your brain, along with the entertainment!"

"No, they couldn't," Chornoi said quickly. "I mean, they could, but it's totally illegal. The laws safeguarding dreamhouse patrons are *very* rigid."

"Rather elaborate, too," Brother Joey agreed.

Rod shrugged. "So? As I believe I pointed out not too long ago, murder is illegal, but people get killed anyway."

"But *these* laws get enforced! Very tightly!"

"So do the laws against murder. It doesn't help the corpse much."

Chornoi's jaw set. "Say what you like—the dreams are

safe. Not even the police are allowed to disturb a dreamer."

"Oh!" Rod smiled brightly. "So a dreamhouse is the perfect hiding-place for a crook on the lam!"

"As long as his money holds out," Yorick qualified.

"The Church used to be able to offer a better deal than that," Brother Joey sighed.

"You can't deny we could use a good place to rest." Chornoi stabbed a finger at Rod.

Rod parried. "And *you* can't deny we're short on cash. In fact, we're going to have trouble scrounging fare to Terra."

"Of course . . ." Yorick pursed his lips. ". . . we *might* be able to persuade the local government to want to get rid of us, really badly, again . . ."

"Not *too* badly," Rod said quickly.

"I must ask your pardon," said tall, dark, and bloodless as he brushed past them and hurried away, muttering to the man beside him, "We will be late for our call."

"Aren't you getting into character a little bit early?" his partner asked.

Chornoi's head swiveled, tracking him. "Wasn't that guy a little long in the tooth?"

"I do get the feeling I've seen him before," Yorick agreed.

"Count *Dracula?*" Rod stared. "And who was that guy with him?"

"The one with the shaggy face?" Yorick asked. "For a minute, I thought he was a relative."

"'Twas a werewolf," Gwen gasped.

"More like one who got stuck halfway." Rod had vivid memories of the werewolf he'd had to fight once. "Didn't you say the customers like to dress up in costumes here?"

"Yeah, but they wouldn't be up *this* early in the morning!"

"Especially if the guy pretending to be the vampire was really going to try to get into character," Yorick agreed. "After all, we might get sunshine any minute now."

"I gotta see where they're going." Rod started after the pair. "Go ahead, call me gullible, but I *gotta* see!"

Gwen and Chornoi exchanged glances, then shrugs. "Wherefore not?" "Can't think of a reason."

"One direction's as good as another when you don't know where you're going," Yorick agreed.

"I'll come along, if you don't mind," Brother Joey said. "After all, I'm not doing much good where I am . . ."

"Who among us is?" Yorick sighed.

They came out into a village square, surrounded by half-timbered shops on three sides, the fourth open to a gloomy castle atop an artificial crag, several hundred yards away. A rough hillside with picturesque, stunted trees led up to its walls.

"Good landscape architect," Rod noted.

"Or set designer." Yorick pointed. "Look."

"My lord, what be these folk?" Gwen asked.

"A group of arcane specialists, dear," Rod answered. "I think they're making a story."

The square was littered with people, most of them in Bavarian peasant costumes, one or two in nineteenth century business suits. Right in among them were people in up-to-date coveralls. Most of them were gathered around a long table fairly groaning with food.

A woman in her early twenties, with a focal headband low on her forehead and her hair tied up in a kerchief, hurried past them. The headband had thickened the air in front of her eyes with twin forcefields, suggesting how she would have looked if she were wearing spectacles, which is what the forcefields were—energy lenses. She carried a computer pad in her left hand. As she passed, she glanced up at them, then jerked to a halt, frowning at Rod and Gwen. "How did the costumer get you into *those* rigs? You're at least three hundred years out of period! Those outfits are Elizabethan, if they're anything. Go back to Wardrobe and tell them you want nineteenth century Bavarian." She turned to Brother Joey, looking him up and down. "You'll do, but if you've seen one monk, you've seen 'em all." Brother Joey started to protest, but she held up a hand. "No, don't tell me—'Monk, he see; monk, he do.' I've heard it already. I don't remember ordering you, though."

"Maybe somebody else . . .?" Yorick suggested, grinning hugely.

The young woman threw up her hands. "Producers! What do they expect production secretaries to do, if they keep bypassing 'em and ordering things on their own? Stroganoff!" and she was off, careening through the crowd.

"Stroganoff?" Yorick looked at the table. "Little odd, for breakfast."

"I think it's somebody's name." Brother Joey pointed at someone. "See the plump fellow she's talking to? The one in the gray flannel coverall?"

Yorick nodded. "Probably giving him what-for, about sending for a monk when the script didn't call for it."

"You're enjoying this," Chornoi accused.

"Why not?" Yorick couldn't stifle a chuckle. "I just love other people's mistakes!"

"Do you get the feeling we've wandered into a 3DT set?" Rod asked Brother Joey.

"Oh, of course," the monk confirmed. "Where else would so many weird people seem so normal?"

"What is a '3DT set'?" Gwen asked.

"An absurdity based on a fantasy derived from a reality that never existed," Rod answered. "The abbreviation stands for 'Three-Dimensional Television'—pictures that look and move like real people, but are absolutely artificial. The folk you see there, use 3DT for telling stories. Well, no," he said, correcting himself instantly, "not *telling*, really—showing. They show a story, as though you were right there, watching it happen."

"Yes, but *this* story is much more interesting." Brother Joey beamed, watching the actors mill about. "I've been watching these people for three or four days now. They're fascinating, they take so much time to do something that seems so simple!"

"Well, if they're making it look simple, they must be

doing it really well." Rod had enough experience trying to run an army, to be sure that managing even a hundred people had to be a minor nightmare.

"My lord," said Gwen, "who are those men with those devices strapped on their shoulders?"

"Camera operators, darling. Those little plastic bulges are 3DT cameras. When they're recording, the men will wear special goggles that sense every movement of their eye muscles, and transmit them to the cameras. Then the cameras will automatically 'look' wherever the men do."

Chornoi frowned. "I thought they made all these 3DT epics on Luna."

Brother Joey looked up in surprise. "Oh, no! Not since the PEST regime took over Terra and cut off the unprofitable planets. The ones that still had trade operating, adapted—quickly, too! And while they were at it, they developed ways of making their own entertainment. You really didn't know about this?"

"I've been out of circulation for a while," Chornoi said, flustered.

"Cloistered, you might say," Rod put in.

Chornoi glared daggers at him, but Brother Joey nodded with full understanding. "Oh, a retreat? Well, let me explain it to you, then. You see, some of these people were nice enough to explain it all to me. Not the young lady in the kerchief and computer tablet, of course—she's always busy, and she never remembers me from one day to the next. But the 'extras' do—the ones who just dress up like peasants and lurk in the background, bystanding."

"They get *paid* for that?"

Brother Joey nodded. "So they always have a great deal of time on their hands, and they're glad to talk."

"But how can the company afford it?" Rod looked around, frowning. "This looks like a pretty expensive operation."

"Oh, yes, it certainly is! So when PEST cut them off, they had to work out ways of cutting costs. The main one seems to be specialization: Each 3DT company works in just one genre, and settles down on whichever pleasure-planet has its kind of settings."

"So this company is making a Gothic epic—a horror story," Rod observed. "But didn't PEST want to keep the resort planets?"

"No. Pleasure costs money, so it isn't profitable."

"For the customers, at least." Rod gave him a dry smile. "Never mind how much money it makes for the sellers."

"PEST doesn't. They're rather puritanical."

"Most dictatorships are, during their early years."

"All PEST could see was the amount of money Terran citizens were spending on those 'foreign' planets, so they cut off trade with the resorts. They reasoned that if the dissolute couldn't go to the pleasure-planets, the money would stay at home."

Rod's smile gained real warmth. "I take it that only drove up the price of transportation?"

"Correct. Which *did* rather hold down the number of people who could come here from Terra."

"Let me guess—most of the ones who do are in the PEST bureaucracy."

"Why, how did you know? You're right, of course—the really wealthy will keep their privileges, no matter who sits on the throne. But it has been hard on the people who live here; they're experiencing some rather lean times."

"But not starving," Rod noted.

Brother Joey shook his head. "No. They're managing, on the handful of Terran patrons, and the few who come in from each of the frontier planets."

"Which makes them a nexus," Rod said softly, "one of the few surviving links between the outlying planets and the shrunken Terran Sphere."

"Yes." Brother Joey looked directly into his eyes. "Some trade survives. Only a trickle, perhaps, but it's there. In both directions."

Yorick grinned. "No wonder our freighter was bound for Otranto."

"The resorts become trade centers." Rod nodded slowly, as understanding dawned. He'd always thought the resort planets of his own time had become Sin Cities to service the merchants. He'd never realized it could have begun the other way.

"And that," Yorick went on, "is why we're here."

"Oh." Brother Joey looked up in surprise. "Did you want to go to Terra?"

Rod opened his mouth, but a short, lean man with white hair and a face with a few wrinkles bawled, "Mirane!"

"Over here, Whitey!" the girl with the computer-pad called back. She dived into the crowd and plowed toward him.

As she came up to him, he said, "About time to roll, isn't it?"

"Eight o'clock," Mirane confirmed. "And all present or accounted for."

"'Accounted for'?" Whitey's eyebrows lifted. "How many are we missing?"

"Only a couple of extras." Mirane touched a few keys on her pad. "A middle-aged peasant and a matron in a babushka."

"Nobody we can't shoot without." Whitey scowled up at the sky. "But we can't start until the clouds cooperate. What is it with that weatherman? He promised us a low overcast, with threatening thunderheads, and all we've got is a high haze!"

"We paid enough for it." Stroganoff, the plump man, joined them, scowling. "Check and find out what happened to it, will you, Mirane?"

The young woman punched buttons on her computer-pad, then pulled a handset from a pouch at her belt and talked into it, frowning at the sky.

The plump man paced. "Hang it, we've got three stars,

five supporting actors, and a hundred extras tied up here! We can't afford to waste time on a weatherman who can't deliver!"

"So sue him." Whitey lounged back against a shopfront, hands in his jacket pockets. "You worry too much, Dave."

"Somebody's got to." Dave pinned him with a glare. "It's okay for you to talk, you're just the director!"

"Also the backer," Whitey reminded him. "It's my money we're wasting. Come off it, Dave, relax."

Dave heaved a sigh. "You make it sound good, Whitey. But blast it, we've got a schedule to keep! If we get behind a little every day, pretty soon we'll need an extra day's shooting—and that'll cost you a couple of therms! Besides, we lose Gawain after the twenty-seventh."

"So what's a leading man?" Whitey shrugged. "We'll just have to make sure we get all his scenes shot before then."

"All right, all right! So make sure of it, will you?"

"Oh, all right." Whitey heaved himself up with a sigh and stepped over to a fiftyish woman behind a complicated-looking console. He talked quietly with her a moment, then turned to call out, "Okay, Gawain, Herman, and Clyde! As long as we're waiting, let's run the first part of the scene, before the mob jumps the vampire."

"Where I throw the handkerchief?" asked a little man in a dark blue robe and pointed cap sprinkled with signs of the zodiac.

Whitey nodded. "Let's take it back a bit, to where Gawain has just come out of the inn and seen Herman waiting for him across the plaza."

"Right." A blond young man in a tweed suit stepped up beside Whitey. "I just woke up and found out breakfast wasn't even made yet, right?"

"That's it, Gawain. And a nice young guy like Dr. Vailin wouldn't even dream of waking somebody up just to get him a cup of coffee."

"So I'm stepping out into the false dawn to let the chill wake me up."

Whitey nodded again. "That's right. You enter from camera left, take a deep breath, look around, and see Count Dracula."

"Over there." The young man pointed at the vampire—and frowned. "Aw, come on, Herman! You had all night with that script!"

"Just making sure, lad." The vampire closed the cover on a small computer-pad and handed it to a coveralled brunette. He turned back toward Gawain and straightened his collar. "Now, then: 'It is pleasant, is it not? The air of my Transylvania.'"

"The approach of dawn clears the air," Gawain agreed. "But aren't you becoming careless, my lord? The first rays of the rising sun will touch you quite soon."

"What is existence without risk?" the vampire asked. "Only a dull, endless round of absurdity. Still, I do not hazard greatly; I have yet a little time."

"Thirteen and a half minutes," snapped the little man in the blue gown.

"Ah, my colleague is always precise," Dracula purred. "You have not been introduced, I believe. Dr. Vailin, allow me to present the esteemed sorcerer, Vaneskin Plochayet."

Gawain gave a slight bow. "Charmed."

"Not yet," the sorcerer chuckled, "not yet."

"Not ever," Gawain's face became stern. "The words of Aristotle will preserve me from your illusions, Master Plochayet."

The little sorcerer cackled, and Dracula sneered, "Surely you do not believe that your puny science can avail against our might, young man! You are not now in your native Germany, so far to the north and west! Nor are you in Italy, the Land of Faith; nor Greece, the Land of Reason! Nay, both are . . ." He broke off, turning to the director. "Damn it, Whitey! Am I supposed to make that sound realistic?"

"Of course not," Whitey retorted, "it's a fantasy. Just make it believable. Come on, come on! 'Greece, the Land of Reason . . .' "

Herman sighed and turned back to Gawain. " 'Nay! Both are my neighbors—and uneasy neighbors they are. For you bide now in Transylvania, home of witchcraft and horror! Southeast of Austria, southwest of Russia we bide, poised between the lands of Reason and the land of feudal darkness, where your Science can have no sway!"

"Not so," Dr. Vailin smiled, almost amused. "Science rules the universe, even this small, forgotten corner—for science is the description of Order, and Order proceeds from the Good. No creature of Evil can stand against its symbol!" He slipped a crucifix from his breast pocket and brandished it. The Count shrieked and cowered, hands raised to ward him from the sight of holiness. But his sorcerer-ally leaped in front of him, hurling something as he shouted an incantation.

It was a silk scarf, and it fluttered to the pavement at his feet.

"Cut!" Whitey bawled, and he turned to the woman behind the console. "Well! That was a majestic flop. What happened, Hilda? The kerchief was supposed to fly across to drape itself over the crucifix!"

Hilda was punching buttons, looking miffed. "Sorry, Whitey. It's the static-charge generator. It was working ten minutes ago, I swear!"

"Don't," Whitey advised, "it's not nice. Get the gremlins out of it, will you?"

"Clouds!" Dave slapped Whitey on the shoulder, pointing at the sky.

Ominous charcoal-colored thunderheads were drifting toward them in full majesty.

Whitey turned to Mirane, beaming. "You got through!"

She nodded. "Just a clerk's foul-up. They promised it'll be nicely ominous within fifteen minutes."

"Awright!" Whitey grinned. "Now we can get to work!" He turned to Hilda. "How soon can you have that static generator fixed?"

Hilda's jaw set. "I'm a special-effects operator, Whitey, not a repairman!"

"Specialists!" Whitey rolled his eyes up. "Preserve me from 'em, Lord—or David. You're closer. Talk to her, will you?" He turned back to Mirane. "What else can we shoot?"

Dave heaved a sigh and rolled over to Hilda. "Don't you know how the gadget works?"

She stared at him for a moment, then blushed and shook her head. "Sorry, Dave. I just push the buttons."

Whitey turned away from Mirane, bawling, "Places for Scene 123!"

Dave stepped up to Mirane. "Where's the nearest electronics tech?"

"They're all kinds of them on this planet," she answered. "Somebody has to keep all those holo effects working. But they're all on salary, Dave, and they've all got regular rounds. I don't think we could get one on less than a day's notice."

"Blast!" Dave scowled. "And I was hoping we could finish up with Clyde and Herman today. Well, no help for it. We'll just have to scratch the scene and pick it up tomorrow."

Mirane punched keys, and frowned at her pad. "Another day of Clyde and Herman will cost you a therm and a half each. And the minimum crew for an extra day is 843 kwahers."

Dave paled. "That'll put us over budget."

"Uh, your pardon, please." Brother Joey stepped up. "I'm afraid I eavesdropped."

"Not hard," Dave grunted. "We haven't exactly been tiptoeing."

"Perhaps I could help." Brother Joey slipped his screwdriver out. "I'm very good with gadgets and gizindigees."

Dave stared a moment, then smiled with tolerant patience. "This isn't exactly a job for a hobbyist, fella."

"I made a living at it," Brother Joey said, poker-faced. "I used to fix holo gear on spaceliners."

Dave really stared now, his lips parting toward a grin.

"But you're not in the union!" Hilda howled.

"He doesn't have to be; we aren't on Luna now." Dave grinned wickedly. "Or anywhere within the Terran Sphere, for that matter—so we don't have unions yet."

"Well, we ought to," Hilda grumbled.

"Why, Hildie?" one of the camera ops said. "If we had, you couldn't've gotten in—or any of us, except Harve, here. He's the only one who had an uncle in the union."

Harve nodded. "Besides, union max was twenty kwahers a day below what they're paying us here."

"Bribery," Hilda snapped. "Lousy union-busters."

"No, victims." Harve grinned wickedly. "There ain't too many of us out here, Hilda. We can call down top money."

"It's right here, I think," Brother Joey called, his head and shoulders inside an access hatch. "The trouble, I mean. A weak chip."

"How canst thou tell?" Gwen knelt beside the hatch, peering in with avid interest.

Rod listened with growing trepidation as Brother Joey explained about test meters. Gwen's infatuation with technology was really beginning to be depressing.

"Paranoid?" Chornoi asked at his shoulder.

"Always," Rod assured her.

"Turn it off, please." Brother Joey pulled himself out of the hatch and looked up at Hilda. "Let it cool down."

Tight-lipped, she stabbed at a button, and the telltale lights died.

Brother Joey stood up, dusting off his hands, and turned to the producer. "That chip quits when it overheats. Just get it to a circuit-doctor, and have him put in a new one."

Dave pressed a hand to his forehead. "You mean we have to scrap the scene, after all?"

"No, of course not. Just have somebody run over to the multi-shop and pick up a freezer. You know, one of the little plug-in sticks for cooling down martinis? I'll frost that chip for you just before you run the scene. That'll get you through the day."

"My savior!" Dave grabbed him by the shoulders.

"No, that's my boss." Brother Joey held up a cautioning forefinger. "But I get paid, you know. In my business, we have to pull our own weight. The chapter house is too far away to send me a salary."

"Union rates plus!" Dave turned to Mirane. "Send a gopher for a freezer, will you?"

"He's on his way."

"That's my girl!" Dave spun away too fast to see Mirane blush. "We just have to wait for this scene, Whitey."

"I was going to, anyway." Whitey surveyed the ersatz peasant mob. "Hey, wait a minute—who put the monk in with the farmers?"

Mirane stepped up beside him, frowning. "He's in costume. And that outfit goes with any period—after 1100 A.D., of course."

"Yeah, but the poor vampire wouldn't stand a chance with a priest in the crowd. Besides, look at that little yellow screwdriver in his pocket. They never had those in nineteenth century Transylvania." He turned to Dave. "Who hired him for this scene?"

Dave opened his mouth, but Brother Joey answered, "Nobody."

Mirane was touching computer keys again. "He's right. I checked off all the extras, and he's not included." She looked up at Rod, frowning. "None of you are."

"Never claimed to be," Rod confirmed.

Dave was frowning. "Uh, come over here a second, would you?"

Rod and Gwen exchanged glances, then stepped over to the producer.

"I hate to seem rude," Dave muttered, "but if you weren't hired for this scene, what're you doing here?"

Rod shrugged. "Just watching."

"Tourists!" Dave heaved a martyred sigh. "How do you keep 'em out? Look, folks, I appreciate your interest, but we can't have you mixing in with the cast. Just too many legal problems."

"Well, that's show biz," Yorick sighed.

"Very short career," Rod agreed.

"'Twas pleasant, whilst it endured," Gwen concurred.

"Um, I don't mean to give you the bum's rush, especially since we just hired your friend, here, below-the-line." Dave nodded toward Brother Joey. "You're welcome to watch, if you want to. Just stand way behind the camera ops, okay?"

"I shall surely watch!" Gwen stepped over to Brother Joey and knelt down to study what he was doing. Apprehension prickled Rod's spine.

"Figure it out?" Whitey asked, stepping up.

"Yeah—and I appointed them guests." Dave waved toward Whitey. "This is the director, folks. His name's Tod Tambourin."

Chornoi stared. So did Rod. Even Yorick looked impressed.

"Yes," Dave sighed, "*the* Tod Tambourin."

"The poet laureate of the Terran Sphere?" Chornoi gasped.

"Not anymore," Whitey assured her. "PEST took the laurels away. They didn't like my verses—decided I favored individualism too much. Horrible, immoral concepts, you know, such as 'freedom' and 'human rights.'"

Chornoi paled. "PEST did *that?*"

"Hey!" Yorick clasped her shoulder. "Don't take it personally. It's not as though *you* did it."

"But I did," she breathed, "I did."

"So did every person who voted extra power to the Executive Secretary," Whitey snorted, "but I'm not about to blame each one of 'em." He shrugged. "Besides, they're paying for it now, anyway. Just a bunch of poor suckers, that's all."

"Yes," Chornoi whispered, "we were."

"Hey, don't let it bog you down! Spend too much time

cursing yourself for what you did yesterday, and you'll hamstring yourself for tomorrow! Besides..." Whitey shrugged. "I never was too comfortable being 'Tod Tambourin,' anyway. Always preferred being 'Whitey the Wino.'"

Chornoi stared. Then she straightened, and her mouth firmed with resolution.

"Well! Always glad to have admirers around." Whitey turned to pump Rod's hand. "What do you think of my show?"

"Uh..." Rod cast a look of appeal to Gwen. "You wrote the script for this epic?"

"Yeah, me." Whitey frowned. "What is it? What don't you like?"

Rod took a deep breath and plunged. "Little on the wordy side, isn't it?"

"Hm." Whitey gazed at him, scowling.

Then he turned to Mirane. "Call Gawain over here, will you? And Clyde and Herman." He gazed off into space, abstracted.

Rod turned to Dave with a word of apology on his lips, but Dave held up a palm. "Shh! He's working."

The actors came up, and Whitey said, "Herman, take it from, 'You are not now in your native Germany,' will you?"

Herman frowned. "'You are not now in your native Germany, so far to the north and west! Nor are you in...'"

"All right, cut!" Whitey chopped down with his hand. "Condense it, Herman. How would your character say it?"

Herman stared at him for a moment, then smiled and said, "'Surely you do not believe that puny science can prevail against *me,* young man!'"

Mirane stared up at him, her finger keying the dictation mode on her keypad.

"'You are in my Transylvania now, not in your native Germany, where logic prevails!'" Herman went on. "'No, you are caught between Faith and Reason to the west, and witchcraft and superstition to the east . . .'"

"That's enough." Whitey chopped crosswise with his hand. "I get the point; I tried to work in too much geography at one blow. Okay, let's try it this way: Uh . . . 'You are trapped here, young man—trapped in Transylvania, trapped between the logic of Germany, to the west, and the superstition of Russia, to the east.'"

"Dracula would keep the '*my* Transylvania,'" Herman said softly.

Whitey nodded. "Right. Yeah, he would." He flashed a glare at Rod. "Always listen to the actors, because they know the characters better than the writer does."

"But the writer *created* those characters!" Chornoi objected.

"But the actor re-creates the character his own way," Whitey corrected her. "If I get an actor to portray my character, it ceases to be just mine anymore. It becomes that actor's character, even more than mine, or the actor will do a lousy job." He turned back to Herman with a grin. "But *I* get the final say."

"Only because you hired the producer," Clyde snorted. "It's immoral, young man—the Executive Producer doing his own directing."

"It's my money, and I'll spend it as I like, old-timer. Now—'You are trapped in Transylvania, *my* Transylvania, the land of superstition . . . no . . . the land of Superstition and Sorcery . . . no, Superstition and Black Magic . . . where Science can have no sway!'"

They went on, overhauling the section of dialogue. When they were done, Mirane reminded, "We were going to shoot the scene with the peasants."

"Of course!" Whitey struck his forehead with the heel of his hand. "How much time have we wasted?"

"Not a second," Dave assured him. "We'll make it all back, because it'll be a better epic. But we should shoot all the day's scenes, Whitey."

"Right! Back to your places!" Whitey spun to the camera ops. "George, you go over by the south wall. Harve, over here, next to me!"

"That's one disadvantage of the writer doing his own directing," Dave confided to Rod. "A separate director could have been shooting a different scene, while he was overhauling this one."

"But how can he?" Chornoi cried. "How can he allow his deathless prose to be violated this way?"

Whitey heard her, and turned back, raising a hand. "Guilty. I hereby confess to writing deathless prose, on occasion—and even immortal verse, now and then. But when I do, I do it alone, with only a split of *vin ordinaire* for company, and I do it for me, myself, only. It's pure self-indulgence, of course—'art for art's sake' really means 'art for the artist's sake.' It's the sheer personal gratification of doing something as well as I can possibly do it, of expressing my feelings, my view of existence, my self—and it's for me, alone. Oh, I don't mind if other people read it, and it's nice if they like it. Sure, I enjoy praise; *I'm* human, too. But that's just a by-product, a side issue." He looked around at the crowd of actors and technicians. "This—this is another matter. It's another thing entirely. This script, I wrote for other people, and I make it with a host of other people. If no one else ever hears it or sees it, it will have failed. Worse, it'll be absurd, without purpose. Without an audience, it's incomplete."

He turned back to Herman and Gawain. "Okay, Mirane'll tidy that up and get hard copies for you. But let's tape it with the script the way it is first, just in case."

The vampire and the hero nodded happily and went back to their places. The little sorcerer followed, grumbling contentedly.

"Places!" Mirane spoke into a ring on her index finger, and her voice boomed out of a loudspeaker. "Quiet on the set."

"Mist," Whitey said quietly.

Fog seemed to grow out of the ground, rising up to obscure Herman and Clyde.

"Lights," Whitey commanded.

High in the air, light suddenly glared from six spots. The two camera operators sauntered out to the side and turned toward the actors. Everyone was silent for a moment, then Harve said, "Balanced."

"Ditto," George called.

Whitey nodded. "Roll."

"Rolling," the camera ops responded.

"Confirm," said a man at a console behind Whitey.

"Action," Whitey called.

The set was quiet a moment longer. Then Gawain came out of the hotel, looked around him with a bemused smile, and inhaled deeply.

"It is pleasant, is it not?" said a sepulchral voice with a heavy accent. "The air of my Transylvania."

The mist thinned, gradually revealing the tall, cloaked figure and the stooped, gnarled silhouette behind him.

"The approach of dawn clears the air," Gawain agreed, and the scene went on.

Whitey stood by, approving, at peace.

Finally, Clyde stepped forward, hurling the silk kerchief. Hilda watched, alert, pushing sliders and twisting a knob, and the kerchief fluttered straight at Gawain, settling over the crucifix. Herman grinned, showing his fangs, but this time everyone froze. Silence enveloped the set again.

Then Whitey sighed, and called, "Cut."

Everyone relaxed, and Herman came striding out of the mist, grinning and chatting with Clyde. Gawain grinned and turned away to have a word with a young lady. Noise swelled up, as everyone started chattering, released from the thralldom of silence.

Whitey turned to Rod with a raised eyebrow. "Little better that time?"

"Uh . . . yeah!" Rod stared, astounded. "It, uh . . . it helps to do it for real, huh?"

"Yeah, it does." Whitey turned and looked around. "But the new dialogue will make it work better." He turned back to Rod with a smile. "It only seems natural if you don't break the spell, you see."

Rod gazed at him for a moment, then said, "No, I don't think I do. You mean the old dialogue might make the audience realize they were just watching a show?"

"It might," Whitey said. "If it stood out for you, it might distract them. Then we might as well have never come to this place. Our work here would have been wasted." He smiled suddenly. "But I don't think the new version will distract anybody. No. It'll hold their attention."

Rod frowned. "Why do you care about that so much? Isn't it enough just to know you did the job right?"

Whitey shook his head. "If the audience is bored, they'll spread the word, and nobody'll buy the cube to view, and if nobody buys a copy, we won't make money. If we don't make money, we can't make any more epics."

"But that's not the main reason."

"No, of course not." Whitey grinned. "Let's get down to basics—if nobody watches it, there was no point in making it."

"*What* point?" Rod demanded. "You've been the top poet of your time! Your place in history is guaranteed, and so is your bankroll, if you can afford to make an epic like this! Why should you sully your reputation by making 3DT epics?"

"Because people need to learn things," Whitey said, "or they'll let themselves fall prey to slavemasters—the way the Terrans actually voted in the PEST regime. And that hurts me, because I want everybody to be free to read what I write. I don't want to take a chance that some censor might lock up my manuscript and not let anyone read it. So I'm going to teach them what they need to know, to insist on staying free."

"With a *horror story?* A Dracula spectacula?" Rod exclaimed.

"You've got it," Whitey affirmed. "Even this, just a

cheap work of entertainment, can do it. What'll they learn? Oh, just a few random bits about Terran geography. After all, most people don't know where Transylvania was, or how the Dracula legend came to be, so we give them just a few facts about that. And along with it, just a touch of the history of Terra's Europe—and the peasants' struggle out of the chains of feudalism. Just a few facts, mind you; just a dozen, in a whole two hours. But if they watch two hours and twelve facts every day of their lives, they can learn enough to yell 'No!' when the next man on horseback comes riding in."

"You're a *teacher!*" Rod exploded. "On the sly! This is covert action! Subversive education!"

"I'll plead guilty again." Whitey grinned. "But I can't claim all the credit. Most of these techniques, I picked up from a cheery old reprobate on a frontier planet."

"Cholly!"

"Oh, you've met him?" Whitey grinned again. "Charles T. Barman, officially."

"I, uh, did hear something of the, uh, sort . . ."

"The rogue educator," Whitey said, "the only professor living who doesn't worry about tenure. Business, maybe, but not tenure. Strog and I spent a year with him out on Wolmar. Quite a chap, that. Couldn't believe how much he taught me—and at my age!" He grinned. "Not that I didn't throw him a curve or two. Dave and I thought up some techniques between us that he'd never dreamed of."

But his words had suddenly moved away from Rod, become remote. He was remembering that Whitey the Wino had been the creative force behind the DDT's mass-education movement. It had culminated in the coup d'etat that eliminated PEST, and brought in the Decentralized Democratic Tribunal of his own times. But the history books hadn't exactly stressed the fact that Whitey the Wino was the same person as the revered, austere poet, Tod Tambourin.

He'd been quiet too long; Whitey's attention had strayed.

He turned away to call the extras, bustling around to set them up in a rough semicircle, facing toward the cameras. A portly man in a tan coverall moved among them, passing out flails and pitchforks.

"And you two lounge out here in the middle for your dialogue." Whitey waved, shooing two actors into place. "Come on, now, hit your marks! You know, ninety degrees to each other! Upstage man sets up the over-the-shoulder! Okay, let's run through the lines."

"I don't know . . . maybe we shouldn't try it," the innkeeper said through his walrus mustache.

"We got to try it," the old farmer answered, testing one of his pitchfork points with a finger. "Ow! Ya, that's sharp enough."

"To do what?" the innkeeper was irritated. "To poke him in his *zitsfleisch?* What good is that going to do with a vampire, hanh?"

"You talk like an old woman," the farmer snorted. "The pitchfork is just to hold him off while we get a rope around him."

"He'll just go to bat," the innkeeper warned.

The farmer shrugged. "So? We'll have Lugorf standing by with his butterfly net. Sooner or later, we slam the stake through his heart."

"And then what?" The innkeeper spread his hands. "So he lies there in his coffin for twenty, thirty years. Sooner or later, some young idiot who's looking for a reputation will go down there and pull out the stake, and where will we be? Right where we are now."

"We've done it before," the farmer maintained, "and we'll do it again."

"Again, and again, and again," the innkeeper moaned. "How many times do we have to go through it?"

"How many times did our ancestors have to?" the farmer growled. "Five hundred years they've been cleaning up his messes!"

"Five hundred years?" The innkeeper frowned. "That was the first of them—back when 'Dracula' was a title, not a name."

"That's right. It meant 'dragon,' didn't it? Shame on them, giving dragons a bad name like that!"

"At least dragons didn't hurt people for the fun of it," the innkeeper agreed. "At least, that's what they *say* about the first one."

"His name was 'Vlad.' They called him 'the Impaler.'"

The innkeeper nodded. "I remember. This mountain country was just a bunch of tiny kingdoms then, wasn't it?"

"Ya. No kingdom bigger than a hundred miles each way, but their rulers called themselves kings." The farmer shook his head. "What a life for our poor ancestors! Trying to scratch a living out of scraps of level ground, whenever they weren't busy dodging whichever petty king had a war going at the moment!"

"Always fighting," the innkeeper grumbled, "always a battle. It wasn't any better the first time they woke him, a hundred years later . . ."

Rod listened, amazed, as the two men gossiped through a three-minute history of the Balkans, as seen through the eyes of a couple of Transylvanian peasants. It was ridiculous, it was asinine—and it was working.

"So stick a stake in his sternum . . . and, at least, we get twenty years of peace," the farmer reminded the innkeeper. "Maybe that doesn't mean much to you, but my cattle start looking pale when there aren't enough gullible people around."

"Where do you think the gullible people stay away from?" the innkeeper retorted. "My inn! Maybe you've got a point. No matter how you bite it, the Count's bad for business."

"So we nail him down again," the farmer sighed, hefting his pitchfork, "and twenty years from now, our sons take their turn. So? You do what you have to do to make a living, right?"

"Right." The innkeeper nodded. "Each generation has to kill its own vampire. You don't stop planting crops just because there's a drought."

"Right," the farmer agreed, "and you don't . . ."

Out of the corner of his eye, Rod saw the arm whirl, saw the pitchfork fly. "Down!" he bellowed, and leaped into a dive at Chornoi. His shoulder slammed into her as she howled in anger. She chopped at him as he tried to untangle himself enough to stand up, then managed to get a one-handed choke hold—and froze, staring at the pitchfork sticking in the ground, its handle still vibrating.

Rod knocked her hand loose, bawling, "Stop him!" He leaped to his feet, whirling toward the mob of extras, just in time to see the ersatz peasant disappear into the crowd. Rod bellowed and leaped after him.

The crowd parted, giving him plenty of room.

It made a nice lane—just in time. At its far end, Rod saw the "peasant" disappearing into an alley.

Gwen caught a broomstick out of the hands of a stunned extra, leaped on it, and shot off after the "peasant."

Hilda stared after her, then gave her head a quick shake and scowled down at her console. "Now, how the hell did I do *that?*"

Rod sped down the lane and into the alley. He was just in time to see the "peasant" disappearing around a corner. Rod kicked into overdrive and pelted after him.

The "peasant" dashed back out. Rod stared, then launched himself into a flying tackle. But the "peasant" saw him coming and jumped forward, and Rod smashed into the pavement with a howl of rage. He landed judo-fashion, but pain seared his side.

"Down!" Gwen cried.

Rod did a good imitation of a pancake, just in time for Gwen to flash by directly above him on the broomstick.

He rolled to his feet, shaking his head, and hobbled after her with a limping run.

A block later, he saw Gwen coming toward him, carrying

her broomstick. "What's the matter?" he called. "Isn't this backwards? I thought *it* was supposed to be carrying *you*."

"I had no wish to scandalize those who live here," she explained.

"Honey, this is the one planet in the whole Terran Sphere where they wouldn't think much of it. They might ask you how you did the effect, though. I take it our man got away?"

Gwen nodded. "There is a town square. From it doth open many streets."

"Here, let me see." Rod limped on past her. The street curved and ended in a plaza, where five narrow, crooked streets fanned out amid tottering houses. The lanes twisted away out of sight.

Rod stood in the center, looking about him and shaking his head. "Right, lady. He could have gone down any one of them."

"Aye," Gwen agreed. "We have lost him."

Rod glowered from one street to another, remembering the pitchfork sticking in the ground. "The bastard almost got Chornoi. Didn't take them long to find us, did it?"

"Peace, husband." Gwen laid a gentle hand on his arm. "The man himself is of no consequence. E'en an thou wert to slay him, a dozen more like to him would spring up."

"Like dragon's teeth," Rod agreed. "The one we need to get is the one who's sending them out. But we don't even know what outfit he works for!"

"Is he not of our old enemies from tomorrow?"

"SPITE or VETO? I'd thought so, but that ersatz extra was after Chornoi, not us."

"Gwen's eyes widened. "Her erstwhile employers?"

"The PEST secret police." Rod nodded. "Probably. I was right when I said we'd be a marked crew if we took her along."

Gwen's hand tightened on his arm. "We cannot desert her."

"No," Rod agreed, "we can't. Besides, we still need a native of this era to guide us. Okay, so we could probably find one who isn't as big a potential liability as Chornoi, but we'd still have GRIPE and/or VETO after us."

"Thou dost but seek to discover reasons," Gwen accused. "When all's said and done, thou'lt not abandon a companion."

"Probably," Rod admitted. "Sometimes I wish I had as high an opinion of me as you do."

Gwen smiled, and slipped her arm through his. "That is my province, my lord. Thou mayest entrust it to me."

"Then I will." Rod smiled down at her. "And try to perform the same function for you."

"Not too well," she murmured, as his face came closer. "'Tis drafty, placed up so high."

"Oh, come down off your pedestal for a moment!" Rod muttered. Then his lips brushed, touched, and claimed hers.

A minute or two later, she murmured, "We must preserve those poor folk from Yorick."

"Yeah," Rod sighed, clasping her hand around his arm as he turned back. "We must save those poor, innocent city folks from our Stone Age country slicker."

As they came back to the shooting site, they heard a voice protesting, "But we weren't really planning it that way. . . ."

"Darn straight you weren't." Whitey's voice was grim. "In fact, this whole elaborate explanation has the definite ring of an ad-lib. Now, what say we try it again—with the truth?"

"If you say so," Yorick sighed, "but you're not going to believe this."

"So what else is new?"

"We are . . . or at least, two of my friends are. They were born about five hundred years from now. And there's an interstellar organization out to get them. It kidnapped them and dumped them back here."

Whitey just stared at him for a moment, then said, "You're right. I don't believe you."

"Then try this," Chornoi snapped. "I used to be a spy

for the LORDS. That's right, I'm one of the ones who got us all into this mess! But after the coup, I realized what an amoral, calloused cadre they were, and tried to quit, so they sent me to Wolmar. Gwen Gallowglass and her husband got me out of there, and I'm trying to guide them to Terra."

Whitey stared at her while the slight remaining amount of color drained out of his albino face. Then he said, "That, I believe." He turned to Stroganoff. "Take over, Dave. I suddenly got hit with a yen for a stroll."

"Sounds good to me, too." Stroganoff was pale as a skid row bum with an air conditioned bar available. He turned to Mirane. "Tell 'em to go home."

"Home?" Mirane yelped. "Are you *crazy?* They each have to be paid for the full day; it's in their contracts!"

"Do it," Whitey said grimly. "It's cheaper than a coffin."

Mirane stared at him for a moment, then threw her computer-pad up in despair. She turned to the cast and crew, stretching out a hand to catch the pad. "Okay, that's it for the day! Strike the setup and go home!"

One or two of the extras cheered, but the principal actors and the technicians stared at her, then scowled and started packing up.

Mirane watched them for a moment, then turned to Whitey. "You run a good company. This is the first time I've ever seen a crew who'd rather finish the shoot than have the day off."

"They're good kids," Whitey agreed, "but I'd rather be shooting with them tomorrow, than having them come to my funeral." He turned to Rod, Gwen, Yorick, Chornoi, and Brother Joey. "I think you'd better come with me."

"I'm not sure whether it's safer with us, or away from us," Stroganoff explained to Mirane.

"Neither am I, but I don't feel safe alone."

Dave nodded. "Let's go, then."

They hurried to catch up with the cortege.

As they came up, Rod was saying, "Why a casino?"

"Safest place," Whitey explained, "except for a dreamhouse. I mean, you're out there in public, where plenty of people are watching you, and the management doesn't want any unpleasant scenes for the patrons."

"I like the dreamhouse idea better." Chornoi had a happy, faraway look.

"So do I," Whitey grunted. "Whether it's a PEST agent who's after you or not, he's on a free planet now, and he has to adhere to local laws. And the dreamhouses are *very* good at keeping unwanted clients out." He turned to Rod. "Stroganoff and I aren't exactly popular with PEST, either."

Dave nodded. "They know about our epics. And they know that education is the dictator's enemy."

"And the easiest way to stop your epics is to stop you?"

"Like a dropped watch." Whitey nodded. "If there's an agent after your friend Chornoi, he might decide to bump us off, too."

Chornoi screeched to a halt. "Bye-bye." She turned away.

"*Come* back here." Yorick put out a hand to catch her, then snatched it back as she whirled, chopping out. "See? I knew I could stop you."

"There's not much point in going off by yourself, Miz," Whitey said. "If there's an assassin on the planet, we're in danger. The only difference in having you with us is that we have some idea of where the bastard is."

Chornoi hesitated.

Stroganoff nodded. "It's easier to duck when you know where the knives are coming from."

"There speaks a true organization man," Yorick muttered.

"But a dreamhouse is out." Whitey started walking again. "There's the little matter of cash; I don't have enough of it."

Stroganoff nodded. "Every penny's tied up in this epic."

"We're a little short ourselves," Rod said.

"When PEST took over Terra," Whitey went on, "they also took over my royalties. Oh, not that they've attached my earnings, or anything, but they're censoring the mail, and they won't let my agent send me a check. So the royalties are there, piling up nicely in a trust fund on Terra, and no doubt they'll do my heirs all kinds of good, five hundred years from now—but that doesn't help much, at the moment."

Rod had a faraway look in his eyes. "You say we're going to a casino?"

"Take your choice." Whitey turned to him with a dry smile. "The planet's lousy with 'em. Every pleasure-planet is." But he frowned at the look in Rod's eye, then suddenly grinned and slapped his thigh. "Of course! If your ecclesiastical friend can fix a static generator, he can gimmick a roulette wheel as easy as pi!"

Brother Joey went pale. "Rig a roulette wheel? My heavens, that would be stealing!"

"So what do you think the house is doing?" Whitey demanded. "Come on, Brother, all we're asking is that you make the machines shave a few percentage points in our favor."

"No." Brother Joey's jaw firmed. "I couldn't possibly do anything so immoral."

"That's right, preserve your integrity," Whitey sighed, "and more power to you, Brother, for sticking to your principles. But that still leaves us without admission to a dreamhouse."

"Oh, not necessarily." Rod was gazing at his wife. "That wasn't exactly what I had in mind, anyway."

Gwen had gained an abstracted, dreamy, fascinated gaze. "'Twould be but a matter of having some whirling wheel come to stop where we wished it to, would it not? Or causing a pair of dice to fall as we chose?"

"That's right, nothing heavy-duty. Think you can handle it, dear?"

"I will be delighted to essay it," Gwen answered, with a smile that made Rod shiver. After all, he knew what she could do when she put her mind to it.

Whitey frowned. "What is she—a telekinetic?"

"Among other things," Yorick muttered.

"Well, *well!*" Whitey offered Gwen his arm. "Allow me to escort you, Ms. Gallowglass!"

"Lady," she corrected.

"Would I be seen with anything else? Where a reporter can see me, anyway. Shall we go?"

They sauntered off toward the nearest casino, with Rod, Chornoi, Yorick and Brother Joey in tow. Dave and Mirane exchanged glances and followed.

"Les jeux sont faits," the croupier pronounced. He wore a satin dressing gown, muttonchop whiskers, and a stuffed raven on his shoulder. At least, Rod thought it was stuffed, but it kept turning its head to regard him with a beady ruby eye. A robot, no doubt, but was its eye really a lens for a surveillance camera?

"Les jeux sont faits," the croupier said again, "the bets are made."

"The die is cast?" Rod suggested.

"Non, monsieur," the croupier said primly. "We play roulette at this table, not hazard."

"Oh! My apologies." Rod bit his lip in consternation; the last thing he wanted was to stand out enough for the croupier to recognize him.

The wheel spun, and Rod gazed at it, fascinated. He had lost most of the 10-therm stake Yorick had given him, before he had begun to get the knack of just how hard to think at the hopping ball. But he'd picked it up, bit by bit, and was now winning seven games out of thirteen. That was enough; he'd made back his stake, and his profits were rising slowly but steadily. On the other hand, he wasn't winning so flagrantly as to attract notice.

Since this was his turn to lose, he glanced around the room, seeking out his companions. They were easy to find in the midst of all these mock werewolves, vampires, ancestral ghosts, and decadent aristocrats. Especially the decadent aristocrats; they seemed to be in fashion this year. Rod couldn't decide whether it was the 'aristocrat' part, or the 'decadent,' that made those disguises so attractive to the tourists.

But Rod's people were dressed in ordinary coveralls or, in Gwen's case, in Renaissance peasant garb. They were definitely conspicuous—and that worried Rod, but there was nothing he could do about it.

They seemed to be doing a good job of keeping a low profile in other ways, though. Whitey had given them a brief lecture on how to win and get away with it. "Lose a lot. But make the odd win bigger than all the little losses, so that you make an overall profit. Don't make any fortunes, though, just a dozen therms or so. When we pool our winnings, we'll have enough to buy safe hiding."

They'd paid attention, and seemed to be doing well. Gwen was just one of many at the craps table; and, if her pile of chips was growing steadily larger than those of the other players, nobody seemed to be taking any particular notice of it. Yorick was building up large stacks of chips at the poker table; Whitey was busy demonstrating that he was a better whist player than the dealer. Stroganoff and Mirane were making a valiant try at contract bridge, but doing their part for the overall image of the group by losing—and Brother Joey was walking around in a daze.

Rod turned back to the table, satisfied—everything was going according to plan.

"Red twenty-one," the dealer called, and Rod stared as a pile of chips slid over in front of him. Then he shrugged, scooped them into his palm, and turned away.

"Monsieur?" the croupier inquired politely.

"I'm going to quit while I'm ahead," Rod explained. "That last win wasn't supposed to happen." And he sauntered away from the table, leaving the croupier staring after him. "Red twenty-one," he murmured, and that reminded him; he ambled over to the blackjack table. He'd always wondered if the casino version was really an honest game, and this was his chance to find out. Who better to play blackjack against the house than a mind reader?

Behind the bar at the far end of the hall, the huge 3DT tank suddenly went black, drawing bleats of protest from the loyal few who'd been watching a particularly obnoxious melodrama. Then it lit up again to show a benign, handsome face three feet high, with steel-gray hair turning white at the temples. "Fellow citizens." The face looked stern. "And you, honored guests. The Government of Otranto has just been notified that four dangerous criminals landed their spacer illegally on the surface of our fair planet, during the darkest hours of last night."

Rod's head snapped up. He stared at the screen, then recovered and turned back to fix his gaze on the blackjack table. Out of the corner of his eye, he noticed that his companions had done the same thing, except for Gwen and Whitey, who were so wrapped up in their games that they didn't seem to have noticed.

"These criminals are convicts, who have escaped from the prison-planet Wolmar," the voice went on. "The High Vampire has just confirmed the report, and believes the criminals are at large on Otranto."

The screen dissolved to a picture of Rod. It was an atrocious likeness, really, obviously a candid, taken while Rod was running somewhere, and he'd never really looked best from his left profile—but he had to admit, with a sinking heart, that it was recognizable.

"This man is their ringleader," the unseen announcer went on, "currently traveling under the name of Gallowglass."

The picture dissolved to a shot of Gwen. Even in a mug shot, she was beautiful.

"These are his accomplices," the announcer went on, "a woman, posing as his wife..."

Rod sneaked a quick peek, and was relieved to see that the other patrons were all staring avidly at their games—well, almost all. And none of the croupiers were looking; his own dealer had a clamped and rigid jaw, but he was staring firmly at the cards. No doubt they'd been warned about such distractions, and about what unscrupulous but light-fingered customers do while a dealer's back was turned.

Chornoi's picture was on the screen. ". . . a young woman," the announcer went on, "no doubt unaware of the company into which she has strayed . . ."

"Twenty-one," the dealer admitted, as he laid a black jack onto the top of Rod's hand.

"Uh—thanks." Rod slid the chips into his purse and stood up. "Think I need a drink."

". . . and a very burly man of particularly repellent aspect," the announcer finished, as a picture of Yorick appeared in the tank. "He even looks like a brute."

"He's talking about you, you know," Rod muttered into Yorick's ear.

"Not a word of truth in it," the caveman said automatically. He looked up. "I don't mean to gripe, Major, but I've got a hell of a hand going, here, and . . . HUH?"

"These convicts are presumed armed, and are highly dangerous." The announcer was back on the screen, gazing somberly out at the customers. "Please, if you are a right-minded citizen who values your personal safety, and the safety of your beloved Otranto—if you see any one or more of these criminals, notify a Public Safety official immediately."

He droned on, but Yorick said grimly, "I think I got the gist of it."

"So does he," Rod pointed out. "In fact, he's got the gist of both of us. Not to mention . . ."

"So don't." Yorick's glance flicked around the room. He sat up a little straighter, and the grim set of his mouth actually seemed to be curving in a slight smile.

"Damn it," Rod hissed, "you're enjoying this!"

"No, but I get a thrill out of it. If I didn't, I'd go into another line of work." Yorick looked up at Rod, his eyes narrowed. "Look, my face was on the screen; they might recognize me. Or you, for that matter—or Chornoi, or Lady Gallowglass. We'll have to depend on our local friends for a way out of this."

Rod looked furtively over his head at Whitey. "Think we can trust him?"

"You know his history as well as I do, Major. And, as they've pointed out, they're in kind of the same class of pickle jar as ourselves."

"So we can trust them—as much as we can trust anybody here." Rod slapped Yorick's shoulder. "You might think about cashing in your chips."

Yorick nodded. "At the end of the play. I don't want to look conspicuous."

This was analogous to a wolf claiming he didn't want to stand out in a flock of sheep, but Rod let it pass. He sauntered over to the whist table where Whitey was holding away, the gleam of battle in his eye. Rod leaned down and murmured, "The party's over."

"You're out of your mind," Whitey snorted. "I'm on a roll."

"The ones who're going to be rolling you, are the neighborhood police. Their local hallucination was just on the screen, identifying me and my three companions as dangerous criminals. He even showed the nice people our pictures."

"I fold." Whitey laid down his cards, raked in his chips, and stood up. The dealer looked up in surprise, but Whitey was already on his way over to the cashier's cage. "You'd better round up your crew. I'll get Dave and Mirane moving."

Rod nodded. "Meet you at the exit." He turned away toward the craps table and sidled up to a comely woman who was staring at the dice in fascination, lower lip caught between her teeth, a damp strand of hair straggling loose at the side of her forehead. "Sorry to interrupt, dear, but I think you'd better wrap it up."

"'Tis what I'm attempting, yet they have so cursedly

much money that I nearly despair of gaining it all."

"Spoken like a true housewife." Rod glanced at the mountain of chips in front of her, then stared in horror. "My lord! They'll never let us out of here with all that!"

"Assuredly thou canst make it to disappear, and appear again where we may find it." Gwen shook the dice in her hand.

"No!" Rod hissed. "Don't you remember what Whitey said? If we win too much, they'll steal it back!"

"Not whiles I've breath in my body!"

"They can fix that. Not that they'll have to; the whole casino just got the message that the four of us are on the lam. Showed everyone our pictures, too."

Gwen froze, paling. "Wherefore did I not hear this message?"

"You were a little preoccupied."

Gwen held still a moment longer, then nodded once. "True."

With her free hand, she shoved about half her pile of chips out. The croupier stared at the mound, astonished. Then Gwen's arm flashed down, and the dice sprang out, bounced up against the board, and fell back onto the baize, two gleaming ivories with single black dots in the center.

The croupier released his breath with a hiss. "Snake eyes!"

"Oh!" Gwen clenched her fists in exasperation. "I've lost!" She stooped to scoop her chips into her apron. "Well, I've wisdom enough to quit while I may."

"Naw, you can get it back. Come on, double or nothing," the croupier urged.

Gwen shook her head with decision. "I thank thee, but I've wanted to try my skill at that little hopping ball within the wheel."

The croupier relaxed, with only a slight smile. "Right, lady. Roulette. Yeah, go ahead." And he smiled, showing fangs.

Gwen hurried away with Rod. "Wherefore did that man

not recognize me from this picture thou sayest all did see?"

"The house personnel were careful not to look. They figured it might be part of a swindle—somebody putting a fake squawk on the tank to distract them, while their partners cleaned up the tables." Rod saw Yorick heading away from the cage, sliding a billfold back inside his tunic. "Just hand your chips to the man inside the wire net, dear. He'll give you bills for them."

"But wherefore is he gaoled?"

"The wire's to keep us out, not to keep him in. When you have your money, go over by the doorway; I'll meet you there. Right now, I have to go pry Chornoi loose." He steered her toward the cage and left her there. Then Rod turned away toward the fourth member of his crew, but saw Yorick bending over, muttering into her ear. She sat very still, then deliberately set about finishing the hand. Rod approved; she wasn't going to look suspicious, no matter how much it hurt. He turned to find Whitey chatting with Mirane, who was growing paler by the syllable, and saw Dave saunter around the perimeter of the room, admiring the wallpaper—no doubt looking for the back door.

Then, across the big room, Brother Joey waved, catching Stroganoff's attention. The monk must have found an "Authorized Personnel Only" door. Rod turned toward Gwen just as she came up beside him, shaking her head as she held up a wad of bills. "I still cannot believe, my lord, that mere ink on paper can have such worth."

"Don't worry, we'll spend it before the rest of them catch on." Rod tucked her hand into the crook of his elbow. "Let's meander on over toward Brother Joey, dear. He seems to have found a bolthole."

Gwen frowned. "Wherefore might we not go out as we came in?"

"What, broke? Oh, you mean the main entrance! No, there is a chance it might be guarded. Besides, you remember the doorman? You know, the one wearing the ghost makeup and the shroud, who looked so bored? Odds are *he* was watching the tank, even if nobody else was. No, I think we'd better settle for what our good Brother has found."

Ten feet from the door, someone behind them gasped and yelled, "That's them! The people who were on the tank! *Stop* them!"

"Somebody would have to be observant!" Rod groaned.

A dozen or so ersatz Rochesters and Janes looked up, staring at them, then nudged their neighbors, nodding toward Rod and Gwen (they were too polite to point). Their neighbors—several score languid Byrons and Wollstonecrofts—looked up and stared. Then they all started grins that turned into hungry leers, and voices began to call, "Who are they?" "Convicts! We just saw their pictures on the tank!" "On the tank?" "Convicts?" "Quick! Don't let them get away!" "Catch them!" "There they go!"

And in two seconds, the crowd of cultured, refined patrons had turned into a howling mob, boiling toward Rod and his companions.

"I might have known," Rod groaned. "Boredom—and we're something to do!"

Gwen hung back. "They could not stand against us, my lord! There cannot be but an hundred of them!"

"That's too many to be sure we won't kill somebody! And besides, while we're mowing them down, they could maul these people who've been trying to help us!"

He could see her hesitate. "I mislike to run from such as these, my lord."

"I know what you mean, but in this case, discretion is definitely the better part of valor. *Fly,* dear!"

Fortunately, Gwen didn't take him literally, but they were at the door almost as quickly as though she had. They jammed in between Chornoi and Mirane, just as Brother Joey slammed into the pressure-plate lettered, "Authorized Personnel Only."

"I never expected to be *that* right!" Rod waved Chornoi through first, then Mirane.

"But I'm not authorized," she protested.

"Yes, you are," said Whitey. "You're one of my personnel, and I'm an author. *Git!*"

Mirane stopped, gazing up at the dreamhouse facade with foreboding. "I don't like it, Whitey."

"I thought it was a little too rococo, myself." Whitey frowned up at the front of the building. "And all those chubby little angels are definitely déclassé. But it's their services we're buying, not their decor."

"You're right; I don't care a fig how it looks. It's just the *idea,* Whitey. I can't stand the thought of being so helpless!"

"Yeah," the old man said grimly, "I know what you mean. But there isn't much choice."

"There isn't really any danger, either!" Chornoi glared daggers at Whitey. "The dreamhouse will guard you as though you were one of their own, Miz—which you will be, in a way."

"Why does that idea make me shudder?"

"Because you think of being absorbed." Stroganoff laid a hand on her shoulder. "It's a fear we all have, from time to time. But in this case, it's foolish. The laws that guard dreamhouse patients are very strict, Mirane, and they're very tightly enforced."

"I'm sorry you got caught up in this," Whitey said, his face hard. "But if PEST actually does try anything against us, they're likely to catch you in the overflow."

"You're worrying about nothing, really!" Chornoi smiled brightly. "And it'll be fun. If only half the things I've heard are true, it'll be more fun than you've ever had."

Mirane still looked doubtful, but she clutched her computer-pad tightly and followed them in.

The thinclad attendant just inside the front door smiled brightly, ran a practiced eye over them, added in the fact that they'd come in a batch, and asked, "Single dream, or group?"

Yorick frowned. "What's a group dream?"

"You'd all be tied into the same computer," the hostess explained, "and you'd share the same dream. Only two of you would be the protagonists, of course, but you'd all be characters in it."

Whitey gave his companions a jaundiced glance. "How does the computer decide who's going to be the hero, and who's going to be the heroine? Chance?"

"No, it matches character to personality type. And it's less expensive, on a per person basis."

"Less expensive?" Mirane pounced. "How does the billing work?"

"For individual dreams, you'd each be charged 937 kwahers," the hostess explained. She ignored Rod's gulp and went on, "that's about 7500 kwahers for all of you. But a group dream only costs 3000 for any number of persons up to thirteen."

"There're eight of us," Mirane muttered to Stroganoff. "The group dream might even leave our fugitives enough cash for passage to Terra."

"Don't worry about us," Rod hissed.

"Thank you, Don Quixote," Whitey snorted. "Don't forget, the faster you're off Otranto, the safer *we* are."

"Why do they say that, everywhere I go?" Rod sighed.

"Speculation later." Whitey nodded to the hostess. "We'll take the group dream, Miz."

She took their money, then took them to a wide, low-ceilinged room with ten couches upholstered in varying degrees of opulence, and invited them to lie down. They did, casting wary glances at the headboards full of electronic gear.

"Hold very still," the hostess cooed. "This won't hurt a bit."

They were each ramrod stiff as she fitted skull caps over their heads. "Nothing penetrates the skull," she assured them. "The electrodes just fit against your scalps and induce the dream through the bone."

That wasn't exactly reassuring, but they submitted with

good grace, and all took their medicine like good boys and girls. It was thick and syrupy, and tasted like pomegranates.

"Now just relax," the hostess soothed, but the drug flowed through their veins so fast that they were very relaxed indeed, before she finished the sentence. Delicious languor enveloped them, and they drifted off into a sleep that was so welcome, it was positively sybaritic.

The young woman glanced about to make sure no one was watching, then quickly stepped into the shadow of a huge old tree and fumbled with something behind her back. "There! Darn bosom-binder keeps coming unfastened!" She stepped back out, with her mammary measurements drastically dwindled. "Golly whillikers, Deviz, it's really unfair to have to put up with so much out in front, when some lucky girls scarcely have any!"

Her Scots terrier looked up at her and yapped in agreement.

The young woman glanced about nervously. "Golly whillikers, Deviz, maybe we shoulda stayed on the street where we live! I don't think I like this gloomy old neighborhood!" She swallowed heavily. "Maybe I wouldn't be so scared if I weren't still a virgin. But all those spooky old houses set back so far from the sidewalk . . . And all those bony old trees, with the brown and sere leaves dropping off and drifting to the ground like the ghosts of sorrows worn out with grieving." She frowned, jogging the side of her head with the heel of her hand. "What's the matter with me? I don't speak like that!"

There was a sudden flurry of yaps, and her head snapped up, just in time to see Deviz go bounding away after a dim and spectral squirrel. "Deviz!" she yelped, and leaped to follow him, the skirts of her jumper billowing in the breeze. "No, Deviz! Not in there!"

But the dog dashed right after the bounding rodent as it leaped through the rusty grillwork of the ancient fence and sprinted up the rotting flagstones of the curving path, all the way up the hill to the gaunt old house that brooded over the scene.

"No, Deviz!" The girl struggled with the rusty gate, then climbed over the fence. Her skirt caught on one of the iron points, but she yanked it loose and leaped down to follow her dog.

She almost caught up with him on the porch, but the door suddenly opened, and the squirrel shot through with Deviz hot on its heels. The girl bolted after them, but skidded to a halt as she saw the lady who stood in the doorway.

"Good afternoon, my dear." She was tall, slender, and pale, with just a touch too much rouge, and glossy black hair that swept down to her shoulders in a straight fall, turned up just a little on the ends. The girl stared, then squeezed her eyes shut, opened them, and looked again. She couldn't be sure, but she thought the woman's eyeteeth were much longer than usual. And very sharply pointed.

"Do come in," the lady purred, stepping back from the doorway.

Dread rose up in the young girl, but her beloved dog was in that house, so she hadn't much choice. With reluctance weighing down her dainty feet, she stepped across the threshold.

Her hostess closed the door with unseemly speed. "My name is L'Age D'or. What is yours?"

"Petty," the girl stammered, "Petty Pure." She stared around her. "Golly! You've got an awful lot of real old things . . . YIKE! One of them *moved!*"

"Why, yes, that's my uncle." L'Age took the arm of the old gnarled man with the yellowed straggling hair and the shiny black suit. "Petty Pure, allow me to introduce Sucar Blutstein."

The old man stared at Petty, his eyes wide and round, his mouth stretched wide in a grin. A drop of moisture dripped from one pointed fang. Petty shuddered.

"Ah, I see you've noticed his dentition." L'Age smiled, revealing her own fangs. "It runs in the family."

"Puh . . . pleased to meet you, I'm sure," Petty stammered.

"And I," Sucar Blutstein chuckled, "and I."

"Keep a lid on it, you old fool," L'Age muttered to him, "or you'll scare her off." Aloud, she said to Petty, "Won't you sit down and make yourself comfortable? I'll ring for tea." She stepped over to the corner to pull on a bell-rope. A moment later, the butler shambled in, and Petty gasped in horror. He was a giant, seven feet at least, and all his clothes were way too small for him. His feet were too large, and his face was seamed with scars and was squarish, with a ragged hairline. His eyelids drooped, and an electrical contact protruded from each side of his neck. He hooted sullenly.

"Tea," L'Age snapped, then beamed at Petty. "Cream or lemon, my dear?"

"Uh . . . cream, if you please. And sugar." Petty scrunched back against the high back of her wing-chair in terror.

"And, um, tomato juice for me," L'Age finished. "And some teacakes, of course. Yes, that will be all, Frank."

The butler growled and shambled from the room.

Petty slowly uncurled. "What . . . what is he?"

"Oh, just some tinkering I did in an idle moment." L'Age waved the issue away. "Now, my dear, tell me about yourself. Have you any family?"

The butler shambled into the kitchen, grunting. Auntie Diluvian, a fat, sweaty old woman in a floor-length gaudy dress, looked up from the pot she was stirring. "She wants what? . . . Tea? Whatever for? . . . Company? A virgin? Oh, yes, I'm sure they welcomed her with open arms—first real food they've seen in years. Been living on that son of hers, she has—and what *he's* been living on, I hate to think. . . . Roderick!"

Uncle Roderick, an aging hunchback, looked up from the tomatoes he was squeezing. "Eh?"

"Run upstairs and drain me two ounces," Auntie Dil called.

"But he already gave today," Uncle Roderick protested.

"It's a special occasion," Auntie Dil snapped. "He'll just have to pump up some more."

"Bleed him white, that's what she'll do," Roderick grumbled, but he picked up a small beaker and trudged up the back stairs.

On the first floor landing, he limped past the sumptuous mistress bedroom and turned into the adjoining chamber. It was spare and Spartan—only a bare wooden floor, blank beige walls, and, in a corner, an old, forgotten, dried-up Christmas tree, its balls cracked and broken, its tinsel sadly tarnished.

In the center of the room stood a dusty old canopied bed, and on it lay a bronzed body, eyelids closed, chest rising and falling gently.

"The poor lad," Uncle Roderick sighed as he hobbled over and sat in the straight chair beside the bed. "The poor lad." He took the young man's unresisting hand, propped it over the edge of the bed, held the beaker under the wrist, and turned the little spigot set into the vein. Dark ruby fluid welled out and into the beaker. When it had risen to the "2 oz." line etched in the glass, Uncle Roderick turned off the little faucet, wiped it with a hanky, and laid the hand gently back on the bed. "There, there," he soothed, even though he knew McChurch couldn't hear him. "There, there."

He stood up with a creak of old bones and a sigh, and turned away to leave, but stopped in the doorway to look back at the incredibly handsome young man, his muscular shoulders and chest bulging up from under the sheets, his eyes closed. Uncle Roderick sighed and shook his head, and shut the door behind him.

As he reached the bottom of the stairs, Sucar Blutstein fairly pounced on him, eyes glittering. "Did you get it? Do you have it?"

"Oh, yes, Master Blutstein," Roderick sighed.

"Oh, bliss! Oh, rapture!" Sucar Blutstein poised clawed fingers, drooling only a little. "Let me see it! Let me taste . . ." He broke off as Roderick held up the beaker, showing the two inches of dark red fluid. Blutstein stared at it, lips writhing back in terror. "Aieeeee!" He squeezed his eyes shut, raising his hands to block out the sight. "Take it away! Take it away!" He staggered off toward the drawing room, shuddering.

"Ah, the poor man," Roderick sighed. "How horrible to be a vampire, but feel your stomach turn at the sight of blood." Shaking his head, he limped on into the kitchen.

"Did you get it?" called Auntie Dil.

"Of course I got it," Roderick grumbled as he hobbled over to his wife. "What was he to do—leap up and fight me off? When he's been in a coma these two years now? The poor lad!"

"Poor lad, my great toenail!" Auntie cried. "Who gave him the blow that first laid him cold, eh? Yourself!"

"Well, yes—but who'd have thought he'd never waken? Besides, what would you have had me do, when his mother and his uncle were stepping in through our front door without so much as a by-your-leave, to tell us this was *their* house now, and we'd have to serve them forevermore, or serve as entrees?"

"So, of course, you smashed your club into the only one who wasn't threatening us!"

"But he was the only one who looked strong enough to do any damage," Roderick protested. He pulled the step-stool over to the doorway and climbed up with two boards and a string.

"And what are you doing now, you old fool? You *know* your traps never work!"

"Well, we must keep trying, mustn't we?" Roderick glared pointedly at her steaming cauldron. "Or do *you* intend to give over stirring up witch's brews?"

Auntie stepped in front of the cauldron as though to

defend it. "What else should I do? I'm a witch, aren't I?"

"No. You're a fortune-teller." Roderick used the one board to prop up the other. "Only an old Gypsy fortune-teller. Which might be why none of your brews ever work. But if you don't deride my traps, I'll say nothing of your potions. What's the secret ingredient *this* time?"

"Silver salts," Auntie Dil snapped. "What's in the bucket?"

"Water." Roderick climbed back up the step stool and hefted a pail up onto his impromptu shelf. "Only water."

"What good will *that* do?"

"Probably none, but I've tried everything else." Roderick tied the string to the bucket handle and led it over to a thumbtack in the door-corner. "Besides, I read a story when I was a boy . . ."

"That was a witch, you idiot, not a vampire!"

"Oh, *that's* why the salts! But doesn't it have to be *pure* silver?"

"Look out!" Auntie Dil cried, but the door crashed open, and Roderick went flying. So did the bucket, but it only flipped over once and clanged down over the head of the monster coming through. He froze for a second in stunned astonishment, then tore the bucket off with a roar.

"Now, now, nephew." Auntie Dil slipped between the giant and Roderick. "I know it's nasty to be drenched like that, Frank, but it was just an accident. He meant it for that old biddy and her uncle."

The monster grumbled and growled, rubbing the contacts in his neck.

"Yes, I know it could have short-circuited you, and I'm sure he's sorry." Auntie Dil turned to glare over her shoulder. "Aren't you, Roderick?"

"Oh, indubitably," Roderick moaned, pulling himself to his feet and rubbing his back.

The monster glowered at him, grumbling something deep in its throat. Then it turned back to Auntie Dil and grunted a question.

"The tomato juice? Yes, it's ready." Auntie Dil poured

the contents of the beaker into a small glass and set it on a tray with the tea service. She took down a shaker and started to sprinkle something into the glass, but Frank caught her hand and shook his head, rumbling negatives.

"Oh, all right, I'll leave out the arsenic," Auntie Dil grumbled. "But we do need some lemon slices. Be a dear and fetch them from the icebox, won't you, Frank?"

The monster turned away, and Auntie Dil whirled to snatch up a pharmacist's bottle. "Now! Just a pinch of the silver nitrate . . ." She stopped suddenly, pressing a hand to her brow. "Nay! Wherefore do I such deeds? 'Tis naught that I would ever consider . . ."

"Yeah, I know what you mean." Roderick squeezed his eyes shut, then opened them again. "I get the feeling that I'm not really Roderick. Some name like that, maybe, but . . ."

"Oh, we all get these feelings from time to time," said a smooth, urbane voice. "Nothing to worry about, really—just a trick our neurons are playing on us, like *déjà vu.*"

"Oh, no!" Roderick recoiled in horror. "It's Old Nick!"

"Not old at all." The suave, debonair devil stroked his goatee. "And not Old Nick, just Old Nick's son. But you can call me 'Buzzabeez.'"

"Well, that's just fine for *you,*" Roderick said, with a truculent frown, "but what do I call *myself?*"

"Roderick," the devil said, with steel in his tone, "and don't you *dare* try to be anything different!" Then he smiled, softening his approach. "I know how it is—you keep having these flashes, snatches of feeling that you're really someone else. Don't let it bother you; it's just a symptom of an internal conflict. I have them myself. You wouldn't believe it, but every now and then I find myself muttering in Church Latin!"

"You're right," Roderick growled, "I don't believe it."

"Whether you believe it or not, you'll do it!" Buzzabeez glared around at the three of them. "I'd like to make one thing perfectly clear: You're under my power, and you'll damned well do as you're told!"

"'Damned' is right," Roderick snorted.

"And that'll be enough out of *you!*" Buzzabeez stabbed a finger at Roderick, and a half-dozen little red dots blossomed on his cheeks and forehead. He howled with pain, bowing away and covering his face with his hands, and Buzzabeez chuckled. "Phantom hornets—gets 'em every time. Don't worry, though; a little vinegar and some ice cubes will get you through it . . . Uh, uh, there!" He whirled to stab a finger at Auntie Dil, who'd been trying to sneak the shaker into the waste basket. "Now," said Buzzabeez, "sprinkle it in!" He moved his finger slowly, and Auntie Dil's hand tracked with it, back to the juice glass, upending the shaker and sprinkling. Buzzabeez nodded, satisfied. "That's a good old girl. Now then, you!" He pointed to Frank. "Take the tray back out to the ladies, right away!"

Frank shuffled over, muttering and groaning, but he picked up the tray and turned toward the door.

"Better," Buzzabeez nodded. "Much better. All right, you just do as you're told from now on. And no more of this subversive individualism, do you hear? Because I'll be watching!" He waved a hand over himself and disappeared. For a moment, the kitchen was filled with the faint sound of distant buzzing; then that faded, too, and Frank went on out the door.

Roderick groaned and finished dabbing his face with little plasters. Then he turned to set the step stool against the doorframe again, and hobbled back up with his two boards and bucket.

"You forgot to refill it," Auntie Dil snapped.

Roderick groaned again, and started back down.

Frank shuffled into the drawing room and set the tray on the little table between L'Age and Petty.

"That'll do," L'Age snapped. "You can go now."

Grumbling, Frank went.

Uncle Sucar leaned forward, smacking his lips.

"Patience, Uncle," L'Age said sternly, "you'll have your refreshment. But our young guest first."

"But of course," Sucar breathed, "of course."

"What a beautiful service," Petty murmured. "Pewter, isn't it?"

"Why, thank you, my dear." L'Age added cream to Petty's cup. "Yes, it is pewter. Silver is so terribly flamboyant, really. . . . There." She handed Petty a fragile china cup and saucer. "Feel free to sip. You'll excuse me if I don't, though."

"She has to drink her tomato juice before it clots," Uncle Sucar explained.

"Oh, of course," Petty agreed, then frowned. "What?"

"Uh, Frank!" L'Age called quickly.

The butler shambled forward, grumbling again.

"My cigarette." L'Age flourished a 100 mm Russian at the end of an immense ebony holder.

Snarling, Frank fumbled out an archaic tinder box and struck flint against steel. The spark fell into a mound of lycopodium, and a gout of flame shot up, out-flaring magnesium.

The light hit the silver salts in the tomato juice and developed a quick portrait—of a muscular form in an upstairs room, in a bed. Petty gazed on the face of Adonis, and gasped. "Um—if you'll excuse me, I think I'll just run upstairs to the power room." She set down her teacup and rose.

"Oh, but we've one down here," L'Age informed her.

"I'm sure the one upstairs is much nicer." Petty tripped away toward the wide, curving staircase beyond the drawing room archway.

"Quickly, Frank! Fetch!" L'Age cried.

Frank roared and whirled about, crashing heavy-footed after Petty. Very heavy-footed, and he had a doubtful look on his face. But Petty glanced back, gasped in horror, and fled.

L'Age, however, felt no compunction. She dashed past the slow-footed Frank and grabbed a lever just inside the hallway. As Petty hit the first step, L'Age hauled on the lever, and the first three stairs fell away as a hidden panel opened. Petty's scream faded away as she dropped into the cellar.

"Down!" L'Age commanded, glaring at Frank and pointing into the hole.

Muttering protest, Frank sat down on the edge of the hole, one foot at a time.

"Faster, monstrosity! Faster!"

Frank grumbled something that sounded like, "Not right."

"Don't you dare preach to me!" L'Age screamed, and slammed a kick into his fundament. Frank bellowed as he dropped into the cellar.

He picked himself up just in time to see Petty pelting madly up the cellar stairs. Frank heaved 1) a sigh, and 2) himself (to his feet). He thudded over to the steps just as Petty reached the top. She pounded on the door, rattling the latch, screaming. Frank waited for her to take a breath, then rumbled, "Turn."

"What?" Petty looked down at her hand, saw it shaking the knob back and forth. "Oh! Yes! Thanks." She turned the knob and burst out into the foyer just as Frank pounded up to the halfway mark.

"*Catch* her, Frank! *Catch* her!" L'Age screamed, but Petty had rounded the turn and was vaulting over the hole in the staircase. "Can't *anybody* around here do something right?" L'Age howled, and yanked on another lever.

With a rumble, the stairs started moving—downward, of course. Petty cried out in frustration and ran harder, but the escalator picked up speed, and she just barely managed to stay in place.

"*Catch* her, Frank! *Catch* her!" L'Age screamed.

Frank plowed his way out of the cellar with a rumble of disgust and veered around the corner to the stairway. He leaped the open trapdoor—and hit the escalator. Even his huge, galumphing strides couldn't make headway, though admittedly, he wasn't trying very hard.

"Incompetents!" L'Age screamed. "All I get in this script are *incompetents!*" She glared up at the ornate brass-armed chandelier that hung over the stairway, then tore open a black panel in the foyer wall. With a snarl, she threw a power key, then thrust her hands into two metallic gloves. Current began to hum through servomotors, and the brass arms of the chandelier curved downward into two huge hands. They swung down on their lengthening chain, groping toward Petty. Suddenly, they plunged and snatched. Petty leaped aside with a scream, and the giant hands closed on empty air. The shock gave Petty a boost, and she made it two more stairs. The giant hands groped after her.

Out in the kitchen, the Scots terrier came bounding up to Roderick, yapping and growling. Roderick frowned down at it. "What's that? What did you say? . . . Logical inconsistencies? What, for example?"

The dog snarled and barked sharply.

"Yes . . ." Roderick nodded, lower lip thrusting out. "Now that you mention it, I had noticed that . . ."

The dog yapped three times and growled.

"Frank couldn't expend all this energy without a recharge, that's true," Roderick agreed. "And it *is* rather odd that a couple of vampires wouldn't have drained Auntie Dil and myself when they commandeered our house . . ."

Deviz yapped frantically, angrily.

"'Wake up?'" Roderick frowned, shaking his head. "What are you talking about? We *are* awake."

The terrier nearly went frantic.

"What do you mean, we're just dreaming?" Roderick shook his head again. "I don't understand."

"Nay, but *I* do!" Auntie Dil cried. She swept out the kitchen door with Deviz at her heels, yapping triumphantly.

Auntie Dil sailed into the foyer, crying, "Frank! Frank! Whoever thou truly art. Thou must waken! Dost'a hear me? Then hearken! Frank, waken!"

"You meddling busybody! What do you think you're *doing?*" L'Age cried.

Frank only grunted and kept running.

"He's a very primitive android," Buzzabeez explained as

he appeared. "He can't take more than one order at a time. But *you* can! Now get back to the kitchen—that's your place!" He stabbed a finger at the swinging door.

"*My* place? Only for that I'm a woman? Nay! For I'll have thee know I'm a lady of power!" Auntie Dil drew back her hand, cupping invisible energy.

"Just my luck—an activist housekeeper," Buzzabeez snorted. "All right, go ahead. *Try* it!"

"Croak and hop!" Auntie Dil cried, throwing a whammy.

Blue sparks coruscated around Buzzabeez. He stood against it, letting the sparks dissipate. Then he advanced on her, seeming to swell and grow taller, and infinitely more menacing.

"But . . . how? Wherefore?" Auntie Dil cried, as she backed through the swinging door into the kitchen.

"Why, because you're only . . ."

The swinging door swung.

"Yeowtch!" cried Buzzabeez, as it slammed into his face. He pushed through, rubbing his nose and glowering at Auntie Dil. "It's because you're only a witch, you old bat!"

"I resent that!" L'Age's voice cried on the other side of the door.

"Only a witch," Buzzabeez snarled again, "and I'm a devil. A full-fledged, high-powered, hundred-percent devil—and much more evil than any mere witch . . ." He suddenly closed his eyes, pressing his hand to his forehead and swaying. "What am I saying? I can't be evil; I mustn't be! I mustn't give in to it . . . No, I must! If I don't enforce some disorder here, who will?" He lowered his hand, glaring at Gwen. "Where was I? . . . Oh, yes." Buzzabeez grinned his most oily. "A devil's more evil than any witch—so I'm much more powerful. That's the hell of it."

But Auntie Dil straightened, glaring in fury. "Nay! Evil's not the source of power—not of my sort of power, at all accounts! For I am no Auntie Diluvian, but Gwendylon Gallowglass, most powerful witch of Gramarye!"

Roderick stiffened, staring. Then he squeezed his eyes

shut, and gave his head a quick shake.

"I am Gwen Gallowglass," the old fortune-teller cried, "and I will not tolerate such deceptions and . . ."

"Be quiet, you fool!" Buzzabeez shrieked. "You'll ruin the whole selection!" And he stretched his hand backward to throw, as a fireball exploded into existence between his fingertips.

"Look out, Gwen!" the old hunchback cried, and he threw himself at her. His shoulder slammed into her a split second before the fireball hissed through the air where she'd been, and she tumbled head over heels into the dumbwaiter.

Roderick hauled 1) himself to his feet, then 2) on the dumbwaiter rope. The compartment lifted up out of sight.

"I'll take that rope!" Buzzabeez snarled, but the bell chimed, and Roderick cried, "Second floor! Linens and bedroom furniture! All out!"

"Out of the way!" Buzzabeez howled. "Let me at that dumbwaiter!"

Roderick slammed the panel shut and whirled around to face the devil, leaning back and folding his arms. "What dumbwaiter?"

"That dumbwaiter you're leaning against!"

Roderick shook his head. "Never was such a thing. Just a figment of your imagination."

"What are you talking about?" Buzzabeez cried. "I saw it with my own eyes!"

"Yes, but can you really believe the evidence of your senses? That might have been a hallucination, you know."

"Ridiculous," the devil scoffed. "Claim that, and next you'll be saying the whole universe is *maya,* illusion."

"Well, isn't it?" Roderick demanded. "At least, if you're a good Hindu."

"But I'm not—I'm a good Catholic!" Buzzabeez went rigid, shocked at his own words. "What am I *saying?"*

"That you're a good Catholic," Roderick answered obligingly.

"Yes, yes! I'm a good Catholic . . . No! I mean, I'm a bad Catholic! No! I mean . . ."

"You mean, *nothing* exists," Roderick prompted.

"That's right! Nothing exists! None of you! You're all just figments of my imagination! This is all just a dream. . . . NO! I can't be saying that!"

"See? Even your words don't exist!" Roderick jabbed a forefinger. "Come to that, even *you* don't exist!"

"What are you saying? Of course I exist!"

"Ah, but how do you *know* you exist?"

"Why, because I think! *Cogito, ergo sum!*" Buzzabeez clapped his hands over his mouth. "Iyuch! Latin!"

"Bite your tongue!" Roderick reproved. "Wash your mouth out!"

"Yes! With brimstone! And hot coals! Even as the angel cleansed the lips of the prophet Isaiah with . . . Oh, hell! Hel-l-l-l-p!" And Buzzabeez fled screaming, and faded into thin air.

"*Thick* air, really." Roderick sniffed, and wrinkled his nose. "Phew! Now I know why religions use incense . . . Well! Back to work." And he limped merrily out into the foyer, where the escalator was still running, with Frank galumphing along after Petty, who was sprinting flat-out for all she was worth, and dodging the claws of the erstwhile chandelier, which still somehow hadn't managed to catch her.

Roderick limped over to the stairway, pulled open a panel underneath it, yanked off his wooden shoe, and shouted, "Down with the bosses!" as he threw it into the gearbox. He slammed the door shut just as something inside cracked like a cannon shot, and the escalator jerked to a halt.

Petty shot on up the stairway and catapulted into the room at the top.

Frank crashed down flat on his face.

Inside the bedroom, Petty slammed the door shut. There was a hasp with a broken safety pin hanging by a thread;

she slapped it shut and jammed the pin through.

Outside, L'Age screamed, "After her, iceberg bait!"

Frank scrambled to his feet and slogged on up the stairs, rumbling curses.

"Break down the door!" L'Age howled. "Get her *out* of there!"

Obediently, Frank hammered at the door with his fist.

The safety pin held.

Petty whirled about and sagged back against the door, gasping for breath, chest heaving.

The light of the oil lamp glowed on Sucar's face. He knelt beside the cot, rubbing McChurch's hand and moaning, "Wake up, wake up! Oh, I know it's no use; I've been trying for years, but if I keep on, maybe someday you'll open your eyes. Wake up, McChurch! Surely your name will protect you. Though I admit, it didn't do you much good when I shoved you in front of me at that crazy little hunchback. Oh, I never dreamed he'd render you insensible! I didn't mean it to happen, and I promise you, I've never tasted a drop. I never really wanted to be a vampire, anyway—but my mother would have her way! It's not really my natural role, you know; it's not my identity, it's not the real me! Not that I've anything against that kind of person, you understand—I just can't stand the sight of blood! At least, not the blood of people I like." He cocked his head. "Now, there's a thought! How about the blood of people I *don't* like? Take L'Age, now—could I acquire a taste for her? Could I lust for some of her blood? How would I feel if I had a chance to drain *her?* Ah, now *that* would be another matter!"

Petty stared at the handsome, muscular, unconscious young man, and gasped in wonder. The extra strain was just a little too much for steel hooks and eyes; with a muted ripping, her bosom expanded, lifting and mushrooming outward with a whoosh of displaced air.

McChurch frowned and turned his head a little, as though listening.

Petty didn't even notice; she was lost in gazing at her ideal of male beauty.

McChurch looked up at her, blinking, frowning. Then the sight of her registered, and he rolled out of bed with his eyes glowing. He was completely naked, and Petty did notice that, but a second later, she was wrapped in his embrace, and wasn't seeing much of anything, because her eyes were closed for her first, and very long, kiss.

In the wall, a panel slammed open, and Auntie Dil jumped out. She ran to McChurch and Petty and began to shake them, crying, "Waken! Thou must needs waken! Dost thou not know thou dost slumber? And this weak and idle theme is no more yielding but a dream!"

"If this is a dream, let me sleep forever," Petty murmured, and went back into the clinch.

"Nay! Now I say *nay!"* Auntie Dil seized McChurch's arm and threw her weight back against it, trying to pull them apart, but McChurch stood like the rock of Gibraltar, as though he'd traded a horizontal coma for a vertical one. "Nay, nay!" Auntie Dil cried, tears in her eyes. "Dosta not know we come dreadfully close to the moment when the monster, Frank, shall come crashing through the door?"

"All right, that's enough of that!" Buzzabeez snapped as he climbed out of the dumbwaiter. "Let go of that body!"

Auntie Dil whirled to face him, arms outspread to protect the couple. "How didst *thou* come to be in that chamber?"

"I materialized there, to make sure your husband wasn't around." Buzzabeez advanced on her with a tiger's tread, glowering. "Now go to the kitchen, where you belong!"

"Go to hell," Auntie Dil retorted, "where *thou* dost belong!"

"Uh-h-h-h-h . . . End of scene!" Buzzabeez waved his hands back in front of his face, then whirled and stabbed a finger at the door. "Next scene!"

The broken safety pin gave way and the door crashed down. Frank stumbled in over it, and L'Age leaped past him, took one look at Petty and McChurch, and sprang at

Petty, shrieking. Her talons dug into Petty's arm as she yanked the girl away from McChurch, and her fangs flashed down at the virgin's fair, unprotected throat.

Her chin jarred against McChurch's arm as he raised it to fend her off. "Please, Mother! I'd rather do it myself." And his head descended down over Petty's again as he folded her back into his embrace.

"Ah, young love!" Roderick sighed, peeking in through the doorway. Then he frowned. "But that seems to remind me of something. I just wish I could remember what. . . ."

"Don't let it bother you," Buzzabeez said quickly, "just a momentary aberration."

Roderick's roving gaze fell on Auntie Dil. He shook his head in wonder. "I know it sounds ridiculous, but I really want to be with that old slattern right now." And he started into the room, just as L'Age howled in rage and frustration, pulling out a dagger and charging at Petty.

Deviz scampered in between her feet.

L'Age tripped and crashed to the floor with a shriek that would have wakened bats.

Roderick, hurrying toward Auntie Dil, bumped into the ancient Christmas tree. It swayed and tottered.

"No!" Buzzabeez cried in anguish. "Catch it!" And he sprang forward, but the tree crashed down onto L'Age. Her head jerked up, eyes staring in agony, mouth gaping for a scream—and froze.

"Well, what do you know," Roderick murmured into the sudden hush, "the tinsel was real silver."

"Food!" Sucar screamed, and he pounced on L'Age with wild joy. "At last! Something I can really sink my teeth into!" He lifted L'Age by the shoulders and reared his head back, fangs springing out as he bared her throat—then froze. Puzzlement clouded his features. "How did I used to do this? It's been so long that I can't remember!"

"Just the way you're doing," Roderick prompted. "Bare her throat, then bite!"

"Don't give him any help!" Buzzabeez clapped a horny

hand over Roderick's mouth, and Roderick recoiled at the stench. "You can't do it," the devil assured Sucar. "Not without condiments."

"Condiments! Of course! *Now* I remember!" Sucar dug in his coat pocket and pulled out a saltshaker with a triumphant flourish. "I always carry it with me, for my tomato juice!"

"No!" Buzzabeez screamed. "Don't you dare touch her with that!"

"Why not?" Roderick asked.

"Because . . . because . . ." Buzzabeez was trembling. "Why, because it isn't in the script!"

"What is a 'script'?" Auntie Dil asked, frowning.

"Only a prediction," Roderick assured her. "Nothing that can't be changed."

"You *can't* change it!" Buzzabeez howled. "It is written!"

"But I don't have to follow it. We *are* the masters of our own actions."

"Heresy!" Buzzabeez screamed.

Deviz yapped up at Roderick.

"What? . . . He's afraid? Yes, I can see that. . . . That means *what?* He shouldn't be? Why? . . . Because if he really had power over us, there wouldn't be any reason for fear? Hm! Good point, that!" Roderick looked up brightly.

Buzzabeez could see his brain working, and shuddered. "I order you not to think! It's immoral! *I'll* do the thinking around here!"

"No you won't," Roderick said reasonably, "you'll just follow a script." He frowned at the devil. "What makes you so tense, anyway?"

"I don't know." Buzzabeez stood rigid, trembling. "I really don't know."

Roderick pursed his lips. "Could it be you really *want* Sucar to use that salt?"

"I prefer saltpeter," Buzzabeez corrected. "After all, I'm a devil."

"Don't worry," Roderick assured him, "I'll figure it out."

"That's what I'm afraid of!"

"What? People doing their own thinking?" Roderick nodded. "Makes sense. You never can tell what'll happen then. Makes life totally unpredictable. And I *am* thinking, now."

Buzzabeez nodded, still trembling. "Becoming pretty willful, too."

"Yes, I am, aren't I?"

"Thou art near to wakening," Auntie Dil advised him.

"Yeah." Roderick frowned. "I just can't remember who I really am."

"Roderick," Buzzabeez said quickly. "Just ordinary old Roderick."

"Close." Roderick nodded. "Close. But maybe just a little too much."

Sucar pressed a hand to his forehead. "Come to think of it . . . I used to be somebody, too. . . ."

"You still are," Buzzabeez snapped.

"No," Roderick contradicted, "right now, he's who *you* want him to be. And doing what you want him to do. We all are—just taking your orders, without resisting much. Between you and the script, you've had all of us just meekly accepting your orders."

"Yes! Wonderful way to live, isn't it? So peaceful! So harmonious!"

"For *you,* maybe. Not for the rest of us."

"But isn't it better this way?" Buzzabeez pleaded.

"NO!" said everybody, all at once—except L'Age, who was frozen, and Petty and McChurch, whose lips weren't free at the moment.

Buzzabeez's face wrinkled with disgust. "What a revolting development!"

"Good idea!" Sucar cried. "Let's have a revolution!"

"Shut up," Buzzabeez snapped.

But Sucar went on. "Myself, I'm beginning to remember that I'm not really me—not Sucar Blutstein, anyway."

"Shut up," Buzzabeez snapped again.

"I was once someone else," Sucar cried, "but somebody did something to me, fed me something, that made me into what I am now!"

"Shut up!" Buzzabeez shouted.

"No, *you* shut up!" Roderick commanded. "Sucar has the floor."

"Who appointed *you* chairman?" Buzzabeez snarled.

"I did, myself!"

"And I impeach Buzzabeez!" Sucar cried. "I move that Buzzabeez be deposed!"

Deviz yapped.

"He says, 'I second the motion,'" Roderick explained. "All in favor?"

"Aye!" shouted Auntie Dil, Roderick, and Sucar. Deviz barked.

"The vote is unanimous," Roderick confirmed, "except for L'Age, who's incapacitated, and McChurch and Petty, who're oblivious. The motion passes, and so does Buzzabeez."

"You can't do this!" Buzzabeez shouted.

"We just did, as I remember."

"And I remember something else!" Sucar cried. "I remember that what whoever-it-was fed me, was only supposed to put me to sleep and make me more amenable to suggestion! But it did more—it made me willing to do whatever this deposed dumbkopf dictated!"

"Watch the pejoratives," Buzzabeez snarled, but Auntie Dil cried, "I too," and Roderick said, "Same here."

Deviz yapped and snarled.

"He says, 'The drug that produces those effects is commonly known as the zombie drug,'" Roderick translated.

"I deny it!" Buzzabeez ranted, waving his hands. "I deny everything! I didn't do it! I didn't give orders for it to be done! Nobody told me..."

"That, I believe." Roderick nodded. "You're probably just another poor zombie like the rest of us—but for some reason, you were much more apt to do what the script said."

"But that means he's the one who's acting as the voice of the script!" Sucar cried.

"Aye," Auntie Dil said, frowning. "I' truth, we know not what this 'script' doth say, save what he doth tell us."

"So," Sucar said, with a bright smile, "if we can just wake up Buzzabeez, we won't have to listen to any nonsense about this 'script' anymore!"

"No!" Buzzabeez was beginning to foam at the mouth. "You can't! That'd destroy any semblance of order! It'll shred sensibility! It'll play dice with the universe!"

"But we'll be able to do as we think right," Roderick said.

"See? Rampant chaos!"

"But we'll all wake up, and quit being zombies," Sucar pointed out.

"Anarchy!"

"Grab him!"

They all pounced on Buzzabeez, who realized what was happening just a second too late to dodge. He thrashed about, howling and trying to break free, but Sucar and Roderick wrestled him to the ground, and Auntie Dil sat on his legs while Roderick pinned his arms and Sucar pulled out his saltshaker.

"You can't do this!" Buzzabeez shouted. "It's immoral! It's unethical! It's against all . . . GACK!"

"Helped that he had his mouth open," Roderick commented.

"I couldn't miss," Sucar agreed.

Buzzabeez swallowed convulsively, and his eyes bulged, staring, his whole body rigid. He began to tremble, and as he shook, he faded away and was gone.

Auntie Dil landed with a thump on her rump, and stared at the empty floor in astonishment. "Forsooth! Wither went he?"

Deviz yapped happily.

"He says, 'Wherever he came from,'" Roderick translated.

"But where is that?" Auntie Dil asked.

"None of us know," Sucar told her. He turned to Roderick. "Do you know where *you* came from?"

Roderick stared up at the ceiling, frowning, then shook his head. "Not quite. I can *almost* remember . . ."

Deviz yapped, barked, and growled.

"He says he does," Roderick explained. "He says, 'I know who I am—I am Notem-Modem 409, a computerized notepad—and I know where I came from. But where did all you zombies come from?'"

Sucar shrugged. "I don't know, to tell the truth."

"Neither do I," Roderick confessed.

"Nor I," Auntie Diluvian said, "yet I do know that we must waken."

"Good point." Roderick held up a finger, then used it to point to L'Age's mouth, frozen open. "Maestro, if you please?"

"Glad to." Sucar turned to sprinkle a little salt into L'Age's mouth. Instantly, she faded away, and they found themselves staring at a very dusty oaken floor.

"Success!" Roderick said, elated. "Now for the hard job. You grab him, Auntie, and I'll grab her."

"I mislike the sound of that, somehow," Auntie Dil said, but she took hold of McChurch's biceps while Roderick caught Petty's shoulder. "Now," he said, "Sucar, you stand ready to sprinkle. All right, now, on the count of three—One! Two! *Three!*"

He and Auntie Dil heaved. With a smacking like a huge suction cup coming unglued, Petty and McChurch peeled apart and stared in total bewilderment, mouths still wide open.

"Gotcha!" Sucar cried, sprinkling salt in each one's mouth.

Startled, they closed their mouths and swallowed with twin gulps, then stared at each other, appalled, as they faded.

Petty gave a mew of distress, reaching out toward the vanishing McChurch, but she faded too, and was gone.

"Success!" Sucar crowed. "Okay, you three—line up! Shoulders back! Stomachs in! Mouths open!"

Roderick and Auntie Dil snapped to attention, side by side, and Deviz sat up on his hind legs next to Auntie Dil. Sucar walked down the line, sprinkling salt on each tongue, and, one by one, they faded. Sucar halted, appalled, as he looked around at the bare, empty room and, for the first time, became aware of the wind's muted moaning around the corners of the huge old house. Left to himself, Sucar sniffed, wiped away a tear of loneliness, and said, "I miss you very much."

Then he tilted his head back, opened his mouth, sprinkled salt on his own tongue, and disappeared.

One by one, the dreamers wakened. They opened their eyes, frowning, squinting against the light, and began to struggle up from their couches.

The hostess stared at them, horrified, then turned and ran from the room, crying, "Get the manager! These patrons just woke up—before the dream ended!"

Rod groaned, and swung his legs over the side of the couch. "I feel as though I've just been hit by a meteor!"

Mirane slid off her sofa blinking, and tried to stand up. Her knees gave way, and she caught at the cushions. Stroganoff leaped off his couch with a cry, but she called, "No, I'm all right. But . . . but thanks, Dave." And she blushed.

Rod frowned, wondering what the red face was about. Then he hauled his mind back to the immediate problem. "Hold on, everybody! Remember, take the helmets off carefully! I don't *think* they could do any harm if we yanked 'em off, but I'd rather not find out the hard way."

Brother Joey lifted his helmet off with caution, then held it out, staring at it and blinking, then pushed it away with revulsion.

Chornoi took hers off with regret. "Well, it was fun while it lasted."

Rod looked up in surprise. "You must have been L'Age d'Or."

A short, stocky man in a business coverall bustled into the room. "All right, what's going on here?"

Rod felt his hackles rise. "Who the hell are you?"

"I'm Roksa, the manager. How the hell did you wake up before the dream was over?"

"Oh, that's easy enough to answer," Brother Joey said. "According to the traditional superstitions, you see, you can break the spell that holds a zombie, by filling his mouth with salt. Of course, you have to sew his lips shut so he can't spit it out, and when he comes out of the spell, he may try to kill you. But after that, he'll go back to where he came from—his grave—as fast as he can."

Roksa frowned. "What's that got to do with you waking up from the dream?"

Brother Joey shrugged. "Dreams are fantasies, so the symbols of superstition work, within the structure of the dream-universe. When our dream selves realized we'd been fed zombie drugs, they sprinkled salt on each other's tongues—and the symbol worked; we went back to where we'd come from—here."

"Zombie drugs?" The manager darted glances from one face to another. "Who said anything about zombie drugs?"

"I did."

They all turned, astonished. The tinny voice was coming from Mirane's couch, where her computer-notepad lay. "I am a Notem-Modem 409, and I have wireless capabilities for connection to larger computers—and for interfacing with the human brain. I have become symbiotic with my operator."

Mirane paled. Her eyes were huge.

Stroganoff clasped her around the shoulders. "Take it easy, kid. I know it's hard to take, but any artist has to develop a feel for her tools."

Mirane snatched up the notepad and clutched it to her.

"Consequently, when my operator entered into the dream-state, I participated in it with her," the notepad went on. "However, being electronic, I was immune to the drug, and was able to realize that the dream was not the safe and pleasant refuge these patrons had anticipated."

"Oh, I don't know about that," Chornoi muttered.

Stroganoff shook his head. "Lousy plot. Not to mention the characterization."

Roksa's head lifted, eyes narrowing. "You don't like my dreams, citizen, you can make your own."

"I just might."

"The zombie drug isn't terribly legal," Rod pointed out. "And there are supposed to be certain guarantees of safety, for patrons experiencing a dream."

Roksa shrugged impatiently. "All right, so I bent a few rules."

"Bent!" Yorick snorted. "How about 'mangled'?"

But Whitey held up a hand. "Hold on, you two. The laws he broke don't really matter."

"Don't *matter?"*

"Not compared to what that dream was doing, all by itself." Whitey faced Roksa squarely, head lowered a little, glowering. "That plot just took it for granted that people should take orders and not think about them. If we'd stayed in it long enough, we'd have waked up conditioned to just accept whatever Authority said, without question, without even a notion of resisting!"

Yorick whistled. "Wow! The ideal brainwashing system—with the victims footing the bill!"

Roksa paled and took a step back. "You can't prove that."

"Oh, I think I could," Whitey said with a shark's grin. "A semiotic analysis of the plot, and a neurological analysis of the choice-alternatives . . . yes, I think I could prove it very thoroughly."

"So what?" Roksa's jaw thrust out a little. "There's nothing illegal about it."

"Only because nobody's thought of it yet. Tell me—do *all* your dreams do that?"

"I don't have to answer that question!"

Yorick grinned and stepped forward, massaging his fist. "Why not?"

"Because of *them!*" Roksa stepped back and yanked the door open. A dozen big, muscular men slouched into the room. Only eight of them carried clubs. The other four carried blasters.

Rod stabbed a finger at the leader. "You're the peasant! The one with the pitchfork!"

The leader gave a mock bow. "Wirlin Eaves, at your service."

"He's too modest," Roksa chuckled. "That's Wirlin Eaves, Ph.D."

"Ph.D.?" Rod frowned. "What're you doing leading a bunch of assassins?"

"I couldn't get a job teaching. Besides, this pays better."

"What's your area," Rod snorted, "political science?"

"Naw." Eaves grinned wickedly. "I'm the real thing—a Ph.D. in *philosophy.*"

Rod stared. "You're a certified philosopher?"

"What's so strange about that?"

"But—you *kill* people!"

"You noticed."

"How can a philosopher justify doing such horrible things?"

"What else is philosophy for, these days?"

"But what kind of reasons could philosophy give you for killing people!"

"The best." Eaves grinned. "It's profitable."

"I thought philosophy was supposed to be ethical."

"Haven't you ever heard of existentialism?" Eaves shrugged. "Besides, it *is* ethical; it's just that you don't agree with this ethic." He turned serious for a moment. "But if you really want to know, before I burn your brains out, I'll tell you. It's a way of exercising power over my subjective universe."

"A solipsist," Rod groaned. "I thought you were supposed to be a philosopher, not a hatchet man. No, one last question!" He held up a hand as Eaves started forward, and the thug stopped."What would have happened if we'd slept through the whole dream?"

"Oh, you would've waked up, same as usual." Eaves shrugged. "You just would've found yourselves surrounded, that's all—and wearing straitjackets."

"But the inmates took over the asylum, eh?"

"Management's about to reassert itself," Eaves informed him. *"Take 'em!"*

He lifted his blaster.

Gwen concentrated all of her attention on the weapon.

Eaves pressed the trigger with an ecstatic grin. Then the grin faded into horrified shock. He pressed the trigger again—and again, and again.

His three sidekicks lifted their blasters and pressed their triggers, too, with the same lack of result.

"What'd you do to them?" Eaves growled.

"You really don't want to know," Rod assured him. "It might upset your philosophical system."

Eaves' eyes narrowed. "All right, we'll do it the old-fashioned way. *Now!"*

He and his men waded in, swinging their blasters as clubs. Their mates fanned out fast around the company and started in with their truncheons.

Whitey shouted and lashed a kick at a thug. The man howled and dropped his club, as Chornoi barked and chopped at another one. He blocked and snapped his club down, but she twisted aside and bounced a chop off another man's neck. As he dropped, she slashed a kick at the first one, ducked under a swing from a third and stabbed him in the solar plexus with a shout, then blocked a swing from the first attacker and followed it with a kick in the chin. He slammed back into the wall, and she spun to a fourth thug.

Yorick was much more conservative. He dodged as an attacker swung a club at him, caught the man's wrist and whipped it around and up behind his back—way up. The thug howled as Yorick twisted the club out of his hand and cracked it down on his skull. Then he shoved the man into an oncoming assassin, grabbed a third by the neck and rammed his head into the wall, then turned back just as the second was picking himself up, and slammed a haymaker into his jaw.

Rod's head was ringing; Eaves had connected. But so had Rod, and the lead thug had dropped his blaster. He circled to Rod's left, guard tight, shaking his head. Rod jabbed at his belly, his head, his belly again, and caught him with a right cross. Eaves staggered back, and Rod followed with a kick that sent him crashing into the wall.

Gwen glared at three other thugs who were crowding back together, trying to fend off a cloud of dream-helmets and fallen clubs that whirled at them. Every now and then, one got through.

Mirane crouched behind Stroganoff, frantically punching keys on her computer-pad. He stood between her and the thugs, arms outstretched to shield her as he watched, dazed and muttering, "I gotta remember this! For my next fight sequence! Gotta remember!"

"*Not* quite!" Rod yanked Roksa and the hostess back into the room and kicked the door shut. He sent the girl spinning over to Chornoi, who advanced on her, eyes steely. The hostess backed against the wall, terrified. Roksa tried to twist to swing at Rod, but Rod had him by the coverall collar at the end of a very long arm, and Roksa's eyes bulged as the collar tightened around his neck. He turned back, quickly—and stared at twelve unconscious men littering the floor of his dream-room.

"Don't take it so hard," Rod soothed. "Only one of them is dead." He raised his voice. "A little careless there, Chornoi."

She shrugged impatiently. "I was in a rush."

"I wasn't complaining."

Yorick shook his head slowly, clucking his tongue. "Messy, messy! What'll we do with them?"

"We could hook them up to the dream-machines," Chornoi suggested.

"No!" Roksa cried. The hostess's terror turned to horror.

"It won't be that bad." Mirane stepped out from behind Stroganoff. "I've been doing a little reprogramming on your computer."

Roksa and the hostess stared, white showing all around their eyes.

"I changed it to stop conditioning people," Mirane explained.

"But that's impossible!"

"Not at all; I just told it to insert new plot-alternatives that stress individuality and skepticism."

Roksa didn't exactly look reassured. "We'll wake up totally confused!"

"No, just curious. You'll question authority—and you'll keep questioning, until you find answers you can prove."

"But there won't be time to enjoy life!" the hostess wailed.

"Learning can be fun," Yorick assured her.

"Would you rather not have a life?" Chornoi watched her, taut and alert.

"I . . . think I'll take the dream," the young woman said slowly.

Rod nodded. "Very wise." He turned to Roksa. "You'll take it, too. The only question is whether or not you'll do it willingly."

Roksa stared at him.

Then his fist slammed into Rod's belly.

Rod doubled over in agony, and Roksa started to turn to the door, so he was at just the right angle as Yorick's fist crashed into his jaw. The manager folded, very neatly.

"Courage, husband." Gwen was beside him, massaging his back, soothing. "'Tis but pain, and 'twill pass."

Yeah, but so will I. Rod couldn't say it aloud, due to a temporary malfunction of the diaphragm. He fought to breathe in. Finally, air came in a long, shuddering gasp. He straightened slowly, turning to Mirane. "Can you make it a nightmare?"

"We don't stock any," the hostess said quickly.

Stroganoff gave her the jaundiced eye. "That makes me think I ought to check through your whole catalog."

"We don't have time," Mirane said quickly.

Rod nodded. "I'm afraid she's right. We've got to hook them up for the longest time the computer will manage, and get out of here." He turned to the hostess. "We need something that will handle a dozen men."

The hostess thought a moment. "How about *The Flying Dutchman?*"

Rod nodded. "The very thing. I hope Eaves hates Wagner."

They wrestled Eaves up onto one of the couches and set the helmet on his head. Mirane found one of the injectors, pressed it against his wrist, and squeezed. She turned to press the "start" button, but Rod held up a hand. "Just a sec. He should be very suggestible right now." He slapped Eaves' cheek gently. "Come on, wake up, old man! Debriefing time. Report!"

Eaves' eyes fluttered and opened, but they were glazed.

Rod stepped back out of sight. "So. You followed the Gallowglass party from Wolmar in your own ship, and intercepted them on the resort-planet Otranto. What measures did you take to secure them?"

Eaves nodded slowly. "They took refuge in a dreamhouse. I bribed and coerced the manager into giving them the zombie drug."

The rest of the company stared at Rod, amazed. He nodded, grim-faced. "Where did you leave your scoutship?"

Eaves frowned at the strangeness of the question, but answered, "In the Palazzo of Montressor."

"What password did you use?"

Eaves' frown deepened, but he answered,"Excelsior."

"Send out the St. Bernards," Whitey muttered.

Eaves' eyes closed, and a gentle smile curved his lips.

"When did you become a double agent?" Rod said softly. "When did you begin working for GRIPE?"

Eaves raised his eyebrows. "Never. I am loyal to VETO." Then his face smoothed out, and his breathing deepened.

"A Totalitarian," Rod muttered. "I might've known. They come in batches."

"What's VETO?" Whitey demanded.

"A secret society that works for PEST." Rod turned away to the litter of unconscious bodies. "Come on, let's get these bozos off to dreamland."

Whitey frowned, but he turned to help David heave a thug up onto a couch.

A few minutes later, the whole dozen were drugged and dreaming.

Rod turned to the hostess, and she shrank back at the look in his eye. "Any preferences?" he asked.

The girl just stared at him for a moment. Then, reassured, she gazed off into space, and a reverent look came over her face. "Jane Eyre," she murmured. "I always wanted to be Jane Eyre."

"With *him* as Rochester?"

The hostess' gaze focused again; she turned to look down at Roksa. Then she implored, "Can't you manage separate dreams?"

Rod and Gwen exchanged glances, and her thoughts said, *Grant what mercy thou canst, I prithee.*

Rod nodded. "Yeah, why not? You set up the couches and the dreams."

The hostess stared at him for a moment, then slowly smiled. She turned away to punch some buttons on the computer console. Mirane stepped over to watch her closely, and her eyes widened.

The hostess turned away with a bright smile. "I'm ready. Shall we try it?" And she stretched out on one of the couches, pulling the helmet on and pressing the injector against her arm. Then she tossed it aside, stretched luxuriously, and closed her eyes.

Rod gazed at her, chewing at the inside of his lip. "Well, the quality of *our* mercy sure isn't strained. Give me a hand with this hulk, will you, Yorick?"

As they left the dreamhouse a few minutes later, Rod asked Mirane, "What dream did she give him?"

"The Dunwich Horror."

"Hurry, will you?" Yorick demanded. "That dream will buy us time, but not a lot of it. We need to get off-planet, and fast! I don't think even Whitey, Stroganoff and Mirane will be welcome here after this number."

Whitey's face set. "No. I'm afraid you're right."

Stroganoff stared. "You don't mean it! What about *Dracula Rises Again?"*

"We'll send back orders for the company to finish it."

"But they'll destroy it!" Stroganoff wailed. "They'll ruin it! It won't even pull a decent box office!"

Mirane was pale. "That'd be money down the drain, Whitey, without you there—750,000 therms!"

"Graves are even more expensive," Whitey answered, "especially on Otranto. And for myself, I don't plan to go on working after I'm dead."

Mirane and Stroganoff paled, and followed.

Rod clenched his jaw. "It's all because of us. You wouldn't be in this bind, if we hadn't crashed your set. I'm sorry, Whitey—very."

"Don't worry about it," the poet growled. "I had a hunch you were worth it."

The tour guide held up a hand to stop them, and pointed

down a narrow, winding stair. "We're about to go down into the dungeons—and beyond them. You see, Palazzo Montressor was built on top of the catacombs."

"Which were built especially for Palazzo Montressor," Whitey muttered under his breath.

"Take note of the niter on the walls." The guide smiled cheerfully. "Farther on, you'll notice a pile of bones. We'll move a few of them aside, and you'll notice a brand-new brick wall. Fortunato's behind it, of course. All set? Here we go!"

He set off down the stairway, holding his torch high. The tourists followed him, single file, with the eight fugitives in their midst. The walls quickly dampened and darkened; patches of moss appeared here and there.

Whitey leaned forward and muttered into Rod's ear, "If only Poe could've collected the royalties while he was still alive!"

Rod nodded. "He would've lived longer."

Whitey frowned. "Yeah . . . Maybe it's just as well . . ."

They trooped down a long and winding stairway. The tourists began to mutter in excitement over the decrepitude of their surroundings, but Gwen pressed close to Rod, for which he was infinitely grateful. "My lord, 'tis eldritch."

"Yeah." Chornoi glanced up at the dripping walls. "This place gives me the creeps."

"That's what it's supposed to do," Stroganoff explained.

"You mean people *pay* to feel so lousy?"

They came out into a low stone hallway. The guide sauntered away ahead of them, carrying the torch and whistling. They followed the wavering flames, as masonry gave way to bedrock. They passed by a niche in the wall, with something in it that was wrapped in old, brittle cloth.

Gwen stared. "What is that?"

"A fake corpse, dear. We're in the 'catacombs.'"

The rest of the tour group oohed and aahed at the sight. One lady giggled.

Rod scowled. "Now, if I were Wirlin Eaves, where would

I have hidden my scoutship?"

The tunnel broadened out into an open space, about ten feet on a side. Three tunnels branched off from it. There was a pile of very realistic-looking skeletons stacked up to the ceiling against one wall.

One lady stared at it, her face a fascinating blend of disgust, loathing, and delight. "Is that . . ."

"Yes, ma'am." The guide gave her a solemn nod. "That's Fortunato's personal crypt."

Rod lifted his head, a gleam coming into his eye.

"What do you scent, O peerless leader?" Yorick whispered.

"Look," Rod said, "if you were Wirlin, you'd want your ship stashed out of sight, but in a place where you could get at it any time you wanted it, right?"

"They're moving on without us." Chornoi sounded nervous.

"Let 'em." Rod waved a hand. "I find this particular exhibit fascinating."

Yorick was running his hands over the wall by the pile of bones. "Here's the button."

Rod nodded. "Press it."

Machinery purred, and the whole wall-full of bones swung outward. The space behind it was huge and unlit.

"Got a match?" Rod said softly.

"Not since Shakespeare," Whitey grunted, but he lifted out a lighter, struck a flame, and held it aloft. "Sometimes it's handy, having vices."

The flickering glow revealed unused maintenance robots lined up against the walls, a pile of construction material—and the nose of a sleek spaceship, streamlined for atmospheric flight.

"Pay dirt," Rod breathed.

They stepped forward, awed by the bulk of the ship. It wasn't really all that big, but in an enclosed space, it seemed gigantic.

"Excelsior," Rod called softly.

Lights brightened around the craft. With a grunt of satisfaction, Whitey let his lighter snap closed and slipped it into a pocket.

"You are not Wirlin Eaves," stated a voice from the ship.

Rod nodded. "Eaves couldn't make it. In fact, he may not be able to get loose if we don't go get help."

Silence hung for a moment, then the ship said, "Ready to transmit."

Rod stared, strapped for a moment.

"Code," Chornoi suggested. "The renegades broke it."

Rod nodded, with a grin of relief. "That's right. We can't send word; it would be intercepted, and so would we. We have to get back to base to call for help."

The ship was silent.

"Excelsior," Rod said again. "Eaves told us that word. How else would we have known it?"

Slowly, an iris opened in the ship's side.

With a sigh of relief, Rod beckoned his people aboard.

PART III
TERRA

IF ANY DETECTORS noticed their takeoff, there was no sign of it. Still, Rod didn't relax until the ship had isomorphed with H-space. Then he sighed and hobbled back to the wardroom, weak-kneed.

As he came in, Gwen was shaking her head in dismay. "I do not understand. How can people become naught but numbers?"

"Not *become,*" Brother Joey corrected, "just described as. I can describe you with words, can't I? Then believe me, I can describe you even more faithfully with numbers."

Gwen sighed and shook her head. "I must needs accept the truth of what thou dost say, since I've not the knowledge to judge it for myself."

"I know." Brother Joey had a smug smile. "That's the secret of the clergy's success."

"But if this 'isomorpher' of which thou dost speak, doth make note of me as a mile-long string of numbers which it doth paint on the wall of eternity, which thou dost term 'H-space,' and then doth take those numbers off that wall to build them once again into myself—have I not died, and been reborn?"

Rod noted that she wasn't at all discomfitted by not having felt anything major as they isomorphed into H-space.

But Brother Joey was shaking his head. "No. You've simply changed form, nothing more."

Gwen threw up her hands in despair.

"Let's try something a little more relaxing." Rod held up a hand to forestall Brother Joey. "I know, I know—to you, this *is* relaxing. But the rest of us like a little help." He touched the base of an air filter, and its telltale glowed to life. "The smoking lamp is lit. Anyone who wants to pollute, come sit next to it, Whitey."

The poet grinned and slouched into the chair right under the filter. He pulled out a long, sinister-looking brown cigarette, then his lighter. "Just wine, if you don't mind."

Rod peered at the synthesizer's list. "Chablis, Liebfraumilch, or Reisling?"

"Reisling, if you please."

"It's all one set of buttons to me." Rod said, as he punched. "What'll it be, Chornoi?"

"Bourbon. Who made you bartender?"

"I watched Cholly. Yorick?"

A few minutes later, with spirits for everyone and Manischevitz for Brother Joey, Rod propped his feet up on the table with a sigh. "Safe at last—for the moment."

Chornoi shrugged. "We were safe enough, in the dream."

"Yeah, except that a bunch of thugs was getting ready to package and ship us."

"As long as we were dreaming, who cared?"

"All dreams must end." Yorick frowned. "I wonder how that one would have come out?"

"Oh, I think it was pretty well wound down." Whitey held his glass up to the light. "After all, boy had gotten girl."

Gwen was gazing at Mirane, but her eyes weren't quite focused.

"Would have been interesting to see what happened to the rest of them," Yorick sighed. "But how did Mirane's computer-pad get pulled into the story?"

"Oh, it was the dog, Deviz."

"I know *that,* of course." Yorick glared at Chornoi. "I meant, how did it get tied into the dream-computer?"

"Through Mirane." Gwen kept her gaze on the young

woman. "I think thou mayest have some trace of Power about thee, my dear."

"She's talking about psi power," Rod explained. "Oh, don't look so horrified! A lot of people have a touch of one power or another. You just happen to have enough to be useful, that's all."

Mirane shook her head. "How can you mind-read a computer?"

"Thine did say that it hath capacity for joining to thy mind," Gwen explained. "Is that not what 'interface' doth mean?"

"Well, yes, but I'd have to wear a transmitter-helmet."

Yorick shook his head. "Apparently you're capable of sending your thoughts without one. Projective telepathy—right, Major?"

Rod nodded. "A little bit of telepathy, period; the computer-pad said it was wireless, so it must be geared to transmit."

"The operative point," Brother Joey explained, "is that the pad has a built-in converter to transform its operating frequencies to human thought-frequencies. But don't take our word for it—ask it." He raised his voice. "How about it, Notem-Modem 409? Did we guess correctly?"

"Preliminary analysis of available data indicates 88 percent probability of validity," the computer-pad confirmed.

Mirane was pale, but she clutched the notepad to her.

"So." Yorick sat back, studying his glass as he spun the stem between finger and thumb."Mirane was Petty Pure, huh? I mean, she was the one who was closest to Deviz."

Mirane blushed, but she nodded.

"Thought so. I was Frank, of course."

Gwen frowned. "Why dost thou say, 'of course'?"

"Monster to monster, Lady Gallowglass. I was the easiest conversion."

Rod nodded. "The dream-computer did seem to match us up by personalities. But you're no monster."

"Tell it to your folklore, Major."

Gwen was frowning again. "Yet wherefore would it match myself with an old hag?"

"She was a witch," Rod explained, "or thought she was. But don't worry, dear, I didn't exactly find it flattering to be depicted as a klutz of a handyman, either."

"Nor I as a devil." Brother Joey was magenta.

Rod shrugged. "At least it had something to do with religion."

"More importantly," the friar said in a very low tone, "I was the voice of Authority."

Whitey snorted. "Well, if you don't like the idea of orthodoxy, Brother, you blasted well better decide that before you take your final vows. Me, I didn't exactly find it complementary to be depicted as an incompetent vampire."

"But you had a heart of gold," Rod pointed out. "Sweets to the sweet, poet."

"Fangs for nothing," Whitey snorted. He turned to Chornoi. "But you didn't *really* enjoy being a meanie, did you?"

"Oh, but I did." Chornoi nodded sadly. "And I wish I really was. Callous people seem to do so much better in this world."

"You've been hanging around a tyranny too long." Rod frowned. "Besides, I thought you'd already tried that way of life."

Chornoi looked down at her hands, lips tight. "And I couldn't take it. Right."

"Well," Rod sighed, "I guess you'll have to settle for being a good person, underneath it all."

"And that," Whitey said, "leaves only one role uncast." He directed a stare toward Stroganoff.

The producer shifted uncomfortably. "All right, so I was McChurch. So way down deep, all I want to do is lie around. Is that any crime?"

"Only when you really want to bleed for other people," Whitey said softly.

Mirane stiffened, glaring. "That's a wonderful quality!"

"It is, until he bleeds himself dry," Whitey reminded her. "But I think you two are avoiding a point."

Mirane and Stroganoff glanced at each other, then quickly glanced away."None of your business, Whitey," Stroganoff growled.

"Of course not. That's why I enjoy it so much." Whitey leaned back in his chair. "But the rest of us have bared our souls a bit, so it's your turn. Why was McChurch so totally hooked on Petty at first glance, Dave?"

"We were being controlled by a script," Stroganoff muttered.

"So were we all." Chornoi gave him a look of scorn. "Everybody else turned out to be quite capable of resisting it—except me; I *liked* it. And you two. You couldn't have cared less."

"How could I care, when I was in a coma? And besides . . ."

"Strog, cut it off and talk straight!" Whitey demanded. "Are you in love with the lady, or not?"

Mirane paled still further. So did Stroganoff, but he blustered, "That's none of your damn business, Whitey! And besides, I'm a fat ugly fool, and she's way too young."

"Why, thank you." Mirane looked up, some of her color coming back. "Especially because I'm not really all *that* young—I'm thirty-five. You would have noticed, if you'd ever bothered to look behind the lenses and kerchief. And *I* think you're handsome!"

Stroganoff stared at her, totally taken aback. Then he glanced about him quickly, and stood up, sliding her chair back a little. "Uh, would you step into my office over here, for a quick conference?"

Mirane stared at him, surprised. Then her chin lifted, and she stood up and walked in front of him, shoulders back, over to the far end of the wardroom. Stroganoff followed her, pantomimed closing a door, and leaned against the bulkhead, hands in his pockets, chatting. Mirane watched him closely.

Gwen's lips curved a smile that was both fond and amused.

Quit eavesdropping, Rod scolded silently. He turned to Yorick. "Well. We seem to be in moderately good shape at the moment."

Yorick grinned, but he swung with the change of topic. "Yeah. We're bound for Terra, and we didn't have to pay a dime."

"I like that last part," Whitey agreed.

"Unfortunately, word is probably traveling ahead of us," Rod sighed. "I expect PEST will be ready and waiting for us by the time we get there."

"How?" Brother Joey frowned. "Nothing can travel faster than an FTL ship."

"Nothing except a faster ship," Rod reminded him.

Brother Joey shook his head. "The time we spend in H-space isn't really transit time, Mr. Gallowglass . . ."

"Rod," Rod prompted.

"Rod. Thank you." Brother Joey nodded. "As I was saying, it isn't really transit time, it's more a matter of seeking and translating."

"Well, then, bigger ships search faster than small ones."

Brother Joey frowned. "I have to admit that the power input does have an effect . . ."

"And bigger ships go faster from breakout point to destination," Rod added. "Eaves is sure to have a courier after us as soon as he comes out of the coma."

Brother Joey relaxed. "We have lead enough."

"Yes, *if* some other agent wasn't shadowing us, and sending off a report of his own. Ah, for the dear old days of Morse code!" Rod sighed. "The days of yore, when people communicated from ship to shore by radio, which could be jammed."

"Yeah, I remember Morse code." Yorick grinned. "Would you believe I actually learned it once?"

Chornoi nodded. "So did I. Not that we ever used it, but it was part of basic training, anyway."

Rod slouched down in his chair, and started drumming his fingers.

"Courage, people," Whitey reassured them. "I know some people who're working on trying to invent FTL radio."

Brother Joey stared. "How do they think they can do *that?*"

Rod started tapping his toe against Yorick's. The caveman showed every sign of paying close attention to Brother Joey and Whitey.

Whitey shook his head. "Search me. But there's my granddaughter—she's a computer expert—and the kid she married; we traveled together for a while."

Think PEST might really know we're coming? Rod tapped out against Yorick's foot.

"They settled down on a big asteroid called 'Maxima,' where they found a lot of kindred souls who liked tinkering with computers and ignoring PEST."

Rod went rigid. Maxima was his family home.

Not a chance, Yorick tapped back. *If there were another agent, he would've tried to kill us.*

"So your granddaughter and her husband are trying to put the two together, by inventing FTL radio to use against PEST?" Brother Joey asked.

Whitey nodded. "They figure that's got to be the logical consequence. See, they figure that the main reason the Terran Sphere lapsed into dictatorship is because its territory grew so big that the governing representatives on Terra couldn't keep track of what was going on at home."

Then we shouldn't have any trouble getting through their security, should we? Rod tapped. *I mean, we* are *in one of their own ships.*

Good point . . .

"And not knowing about home, meant that they passed laws their constituents didn't like?"

Whitey nodded again. "So their constituents wanted to kick them out of office."

"Naturally," Brother Joey murmured.

Is there a time machine on Terra? Rod tapped.

"So the only way to keep power was to take it," Whitey said.

Brother Joey nodded. "Be done with all this nonsense about elections, eh?"

How many times do I have to tell you? Yorick tapped back. *If VETO didn't have a time machine in PEST headquarters, they couldn't be giving aid!*

"Ah, you know the symptoms. And, of course, they couldn't *make* the outer planets obey them, if they couldn't get their orders to them in time—so the sensible thing to do was to cut off the frontier."

"Keep only the planets they *can* rule," Brother Joey sighed. "Well, I'm afraid that does make *some* sense."

Whitey smiled. "So the whole problem boils down to the territory having grown too big for the speed of the communications."

And if VETO hasn't been helping PEST, Yorick tapped, *I'm a monkey's uncle!*

Thought it was the other way around, Rod tapped back.

Awright, Darwin. Just wait, and let's see what you *evolve into.*

"Wait a minute." Chornoi sat forward. "You mean your granddaughter figures that if she can develop faster-than-light radio, PEST will automatically collapse?"

"Well, not right away, and not all that easily, but that's the gist of it, yes," Whitey confirmed.

Brother Joey sat back, dazzled. "My heavens! What an audacious scheme!"

Whitey cocked his head to the side, watching him. "Kinda makes you want to join them, doesn't it?"

"It does, yes!"

Rod looked up, having caught the last bit of the conversation. "I expect we could drop you off there, on our way."

Brother Joey gazed off into space. "I do seem to be a better engineer than a missionary . . ."

"*We're* going to try to gate-crash Terra," Rod explained. "We ought to have a fairly good chance, in one of their own scoutships."

Chornoi frowned. "*If* PEST hasn't been told who's in this ship."

Rod shrugged. "Life is filled with these little uncertainties."

Whitey shook his head sadly. "'Fraid I can't come along, folks. On Terra, I'm a very wanted person."

"So are we," Rod agreed, "but we don't have much choice in the matter."

"But I do, and this time I'm going to play smart and use it," Whitey sighed. "Just let me off at Maxima, will you?" He looked up as Stroganoff and Mirane came up, holding hands and beaming. "How about you two? Want to get off at Maxima?"

Mirane paused halfway down to her seat. "That's where that cadre of engineers and physicists are building robots, isn't it?"

"The very place."

Mirane finished sitting. "I'd like to visit there, yes. I'm going to need to know everything I can about computers."

"Oh?" Whitey perked up. "Just what are you two planning to do?"

"Get married, first," Stroganoff said, with a smile at Mirane that could have seared paint. "Then we're going to make the Grand Tour from pleasure-planet to pleasure-planet."

"Oh?" Whitey lifted an eyebrow. "And what're you planning to use for money?"

"Oh, we're not going to *pay* for it," Mirane cried, scandalized. "The company will."

"Company? What company?"

"The epic company," Stroganoff explained. "I've banked

enough to start my own corporation, Whitey. We'll make three or four epics on each resort, then move on to the next one. Care to write us some scripts?"

"I just might, depending on what you're planning to do on each planet, besides making epics."

Mirane gazed at Stroganoff. "Well, we thought we'd try every dreamhouse, and have duo-dreams together."

"Just the three of you?"

Stroganoff nodded. "Me, Mirane, and Notem-Modem 409."

"So." Whitey leaned back, grinning. "You figured it out, too, huh?"

Mirane nodded. "PEST has every dreamhouse computer rigged to condition its users to obey authority, which means that, eventually, PEST will be able to rule the outer planets without having to worry about a navy."

"But we only experienced one dream in one computer," Brother Joey objected.

"True, Brother, but if they could do it to one, they've probably done it to all."

"Sure can't hurt to check," Stroganoff explained, "and if we find out PEST has, Mirane and Notem-Modem will reprogram that computer."

"I do wonder what Master Eaves' thoughts will be, when he doth waken," Gwen mused.

"Probably the same," Rod grunted. "I have a notion he linked up with PEST out of pure self-interest." He turned to Chornoi. "How about you? Want to get off at Maxima?"

Chornoi was pale as ivory, but she shook her head. "I'd be no safer there than anywhere else, which is to say that I won't be safe anywhere." She shrugged. "Why not try Terra? It's the last place PEST would think to look for me."

Rod shook his head. "Sorry I got you into this, folks."

"We're not." Stroganoff smiled as he gazed into Mirane's eyes.

Whitey grinned. "And I'm suddenly looking forward to

seeing Lona and Dar again. Might not have managed it ever, if it hadn't been for you. Talk about a surprise visit!"

"I've had a bit of a surprise, too." Brother Joey was gazing off into space. "I might have muddled along, wasting years without discovering my true vocation, but for this."

"Not cut out to make converts?" Rod sympathized.

"Oh, yes, but of a different sort. And on a much larger scale. . . ."

"All *that?"*

Chornoi nodded. "A hundred security satellites, Major, in a hundred different orbits. They're really there—and each one's armed with everything from lasers on up to a small tactical nuke."

"Well, our detectors say so, all right. But *why?* What're they afraid of?"

"Whatever shows up."

"From outside, or inside? Are those satellites supposed to keep invaders out, or the population in?"

"Yes."

Rod rolled his eyes up in exasperation.

"Wouldn't matter if we *could* get through the security net," Yorick pointed out. "Where could we land?"

Rod frowned at the blue-and-white globe floating in front of him on the viewscreen. "There must be some farmland, here and there—maybe even some parks!"

"The farms are run by robots," Chornoi said, "and every square foot of the parks is covered by a surveillance camera or two."

"Well, back to the original idea," Rod sighed. "Looks like we'll have to bluff it out."

That wasn't too hard, up till the actual landing. Whenever one of the satellites challenged the scoutship, it honestly and truthfully identified itself as an official government craft. It even handled spaceport clearance—being a spy ship, it could bypass Luna, where all commercial ships had to dock; shuttles took cargo and passengers down to Terra. It was a cumbersome system, but it did give PEST total control over who came to Terra, and who left.

Well, almost total. They really hadn't counted on enemies coming in on one of their own ships, and a spy ship at that. So the satellite net bucked the landing request to an actual human, a division head, and he gave the scoutship clearance to go directly to the spaceport PEST maintained on Terra for official use. It all went perfectly smoothly, even the landing—until they stepped out of the ship.

The little man in the gray tunic with the tan tabard stepped forward with a smile pasted on, holding out a hand—obviously a bureaucrat. "Welcome back, Agent Ea . . ." He stopped short, staring at the quartet stepping out of the scoutship.

Rod managed a sickly grin. "Uh, hi there."

The bureaucrat turned and snapped his fingers at a large man behind him. There were a half-dozen of them, all bulky, all with surly frowns on their faces, all in uniform. The one he'd indicated slipped a small, flat square out of a pocket and pointed it at the Gallowglasses.

The bureaucrat turned back to them, his face totally without expression."Where is the agent Wirlin Eaves?"

"Uh, afraid he couldn't make it." Rod swallowed. "Bit of a rough trip and all, you know. Vicious criminals on that planet Otranto, not to mention a couple of vampires and a wolfman, and a rampant dreamhouse computer . . ."

The bureaucrat turned to his henchman. "Do you have them? Good. Send for identification." He turned to the rest of the thugs and nodded at Rod. "Arrest them."

"Now, wait a minute!" Rod held up a hand. "You don't know anything about us! We're legitimate agents, all of us—except for my wife, maybe, and I didn't see any problem in bringing her along on a business trip. We just stumbled across this scoutship, and we needed a way to get home, and nobody else was using it, so . . ." He swallowed.

"Uh, it was really too bad about Eaves, but he just couldn't make it."

The man with the flat square pressed a button into his ear and gazed off into space for a moment, then nodded. "Confirmed. The crop-haired woman is a renegade agent marked for execution."

"Crop-haired!" Chornoi squalled. "I'll crop your head, you foul-mouthed chauvinist!"

The man ignored her. "The other woman and the talkative man are tied for first place as Public Enemies—and the burly man is a major foe."

Yorick stared. "Why me?"

"I do not know," the bureaucrat snapped, "but my superiors must have had excellent reasons for so designating you."

"Don't worry about it," Rod assured Yorick, "the excellent reasons just haven't happened yet."

The bureaucrat stared at him, at a loss for a moment. But only a moment, then his mouth tightened in contempt, and he snapped his fingers at another flunky, one wearing a portable control console strapped to his waist and shoulders. The man threw a key and thumbed a toggle, and the air around the quartet seemed to thicken. A faint moiré of colors, like the refractions on a soap bubble, swam about them in a sphere.

"A force field now surrounds you," the bureaucrat said. "My superiors have informed me that the four of you are very skilled at evading capture, but there is no method of escaping this globe of force."

Yorick took an experimental kick at the force field. His foot slowed and stopped, all within the space of an inch or three. Chornoi stared, then slammed a chop at the moiré, but her hand bounced right back, clipping her in the nose. She howled in anger.

"I gotta see this to believe it!" Rod aimed a jab at the moiré, straight from the shoulder. It felt as though his hand hit a mattress. The moiré roiled on, unperturbed.

The bureaucrat actually smiled. It was a bare twitch of the lips, but it was a smile.

Gwen tested the field with her fingers, feeling it with a thoughtful frown.

The bureaucrat turned away, beckoning to the man with the console. "Come."

The operator followed him.

The force field scooped the company off their feet as though it were a snow shovel and rolled them down the hall, shouting and squalling.

The bureaucrat smiled again.

Gwen scrambled to her feet, flushed with anger, and scurried to keep up with the force field, one hand touching the unseen wall, scowling in concentration.

Rod saw, and shuddered.

Gwen reached out and hauled Chornoi to her feet with deceptive ease. "How can that gleaming slab make an invisible wall like to this?"

"Well, I don't know the details," Chornoi panted, "but roughly, it's a sort of transmitter. It projects a small magnetic field that triggers a localized warping of the gravitational field. It wraps itself around the tiny globe of electromagnetic force, then expands according to how much power the operator feeds into the trigger field."

Gwen nodded, then glared at the back of the operator's head for a few minutes. Finally, she closed her eyes—and the moiré disappeared.

The operator jarred to a halt, fiddling frantically with sliders and pressure-pads. "My board died!"

The bureaucrat whirled about, staring, appalled. So did all his henchmen.

So did Rod. He knew he couldn't even dream of understanding that console—and here his wife, who hadn't even heard of an electron till a few weeks ago, had figured out a gadget that was so complicated, it was almost abstract.

At least, she'd figured it out well enough to turn it off from twenty feet away.

Gwen smiled gaily, snapped her fingers—and the moiré swirled about them again. Rod stared at it in disbelief, then reached out to probe. Yes, the wall of force was there again.

"Do not fash thyself," Gwen said to the bureaucrat, "we are once more enveloped."

The bureaucrat darted a glance at his operator, who was still stabbing at pressure-pads and jamming toggles. Sweat rolled down his brow; he shook his head.

The bureaucrat turned back to Gwen, staring in horror.

Gwen nodded. "This time, 'tis of my doing—and 'tis I who have the managing of it." She smiled brightly at Rod. "Come, husband, let us go." And she strode straight toward the bureaucrat.

Chornoi and Yorick yelped as the field scooped them off their feet again. They rebounded and scrambled back up, and joined Rod in a quick scurry to keep up with Gwen.

The bureaucrat jumped aside, shouting, "Stop them!"

His thugs instantly formed a line.

Gwen sailed into them.

They flew like tenpins and bounced off the walls. A couple of them rolled to the ground, unconscious, but the rest whipped out blasters and started firing.

Yorick frowned, feeling the unseen wall. "It's growing harder."

Gwen nodded, tight-lipped. "My field doth drink the flame of their weapons. I do feel it."

Rod's head whipped around, staring at her. "Be careful!"

In spite of the strain, she smiled and reached out for his arm. "Fear not, my lord. I can contain it."

The "my lord" helped. "Mind telling me how you did this little trick?"

Gwen beamed up at him. "I felt within that 'console,' as thou dost term it, with my mind. Thou hadst taught me long ago, husband, how to make the tiniest bits of matter speed their movement, or slow; so 'twas not totally strange to me, to sense the flow of bits so much tinier. I let my mind flow with their movement, and did discover how they streamed in patterns that did set up a small ball of force, which did summon up and mold a force much greater, from the earth itself."

Rod's mind reeled, also his ego. Just by feel, with only a little knowledge to guide her, she had figured out how to shape an electromagnetic field and use it to make a gravity wave extrude a bubble of force around them. He patted her hand and said, "I'm just glad you're on my side."

She smiled sweetly at him. "I, too."

"Just a little warm." Chornoi was feeling the force field with her fingers. "All that wild, pure energy going into it, and it's just a little bit warm."

"'T will grow hot soon enow, an we cannot find sanctuary." Gwen's brow was moist. "'Tis thou must now direct me."

"Sanctuary?" For a moment, Chornoi just stared, totally at a loss. Then inspiration struck, and she grinned. "Turn left at the end of this hallway!"

Yorick waved a hand to fan himself. "Give her every shortcut you know. It's getting hot in here!"

"The charges in those blasters just have to run down soon," Rod grumbled.

They turned a corner, and the hallway opened out into a broad concourse. People in drab coveralls were hurrying here and there all about, most of them carrying satchels.

Another half-dozen uniformed men came running, blasters waving, shouting.

"So much for the chance of their charges running down," Rod growled. "But they won't shoot when there're so many taxpayers around!"

"All personnel and passengers seek cover," an amplified voice boomed around them. *"Dangerous criminals are at large within the concourse. Security agents must fire to kill. All personnel and passengers seek cover!"*

"So much for the taxpayers," Rod grunted.

Heads jerked up all along the concourse. Then people dived for doorways or fled around corners, screaming.

"Down here! Quickly!" Chornoi pointed at a broad staircase.

Gwen swerved and stepped onto the escalator. Everyone managed to stay with her except Yorick, but he was back on his feet in a second.

Behind them, the uniformed men started yelling in panic.

"Oh! Steps that move!" Gwen cried in glee. "Then 'twas not a mere dream!"

"What? . . . Oh! The dreamhouse!" Chornoi wrinkled her nose. "Yeah, I hated that stairway. But keep walking, please, Miz Gallowglass. They'll try to head us off."

"Certes, an thou dost wish it!" Gwen tripped gleefully down the staircase. Rod tripped, period, but the field gave him a soft landing, and he caught Gwen's hand to steady himself as he came back onto his feet.

"Why do they shout so?" Gwen frowned back up at the security guards, who were just appearing at the head of the stairs.

"Because what we're doing is dangerous," Chornoi explained. "Here,we're at the bottom! See that clear wall, Miz Gallowglass? Just stroll over there, would you?"

Rod suddenly realized what they were doing. He paled.

"All the way," Chornoi directed. "Up against the doorway—that's right. Now, we wait."

Gwen turned to face the stairway. "Wherefore do we no longer flee?"

The armsmen thundered down the escalator, saw the company against the doorway in the clear plasticrete wall, and skidded to a halt, frozen in horror.

"This tunnel is a linear accelerator," Chornoi explained. "It's lined with ring-shaped electromagnets, and they turn on and off in sequence, so it's almost as though a magnetic field were moving down this tunnel."

Gwen's eyes had lost focus as she absorbed the concept.

She nodded. "Ingenious. Yet what purpose doth it serve?"

"They put, uh, 'carriages' inside the tunnel, Miz Gallowglass—tubular carriages, without wheels; they call them 'capsules.' They're fitted out with seats and carpets, and each one holds a hundred people."

Gwen frowned. "'Tis an odd mode of travel."

"Not really. You see, these capsules can shoot through these tubes at hundreds of miles per hour, and there's a huge network of tubes, so you can get to almost anyplace in the world through them. If we climbed into a capsule now, here underneath the island of Medeira, we could be in Puerto Rico, the nexus for the Americas, in four hours. That's thousands of miles away."

"'Tis incredible," Gwen breathed. Then her eyes focused, and she frowned. "How many folk are in such carriages at this moment?"

"Probably a million or so."

"And," Gwen said slowly, "What would happen if these men-at-arms so filled my field with flame, that I could no longer hold it in its form?"

"All that energy would be released in a single instant," Chornoi said softly. "It'd all cut loose in one huge explosion. It'd kill the four of us, of course, but it'd also wreck this station, and this section of tube."

Gwen nodded slowly. "Then the force would no longer flow."

"That's right," Chornoi said.

"And all the carriages with all those folk would come to a halt?"

"Yes. Slowly—but they would stop. And their lights would go out. Also the fans that blow cool air to them. The farther down you go, Miz Gallowglass, the hotter it gets."

"Would they all die, then?" Gwen said faintly.

"Not most of them—at least, not right away. But some of them would be hundreds of miles from the nearest station—even thousands, for the ones under the sea floor. So it'd take so long to get them out, that some of them might actually starve. More likely, they'd panic and trample each other. Or suffocate."

Gwen was trembling. "Whate'er the cost, I will not slay so many."

"You won't—*they* will. Only they won't take a chance on it, because they know what their bosses would do to them. They don't dare risk it, especially since some of the people in those tubes right now might be PEST officials. Or their wives and families."

Sure enough, the armsmen were holding a quick conference, darting glances at one another while they kept their blasters trained on the company.

"Shake 'em up a little," Chornoi advised. "Expand the field."

Gwen frowned, but the moiré moved away from them on all sides. It touched the clear wall, then went through it.

The armsmen went rigid, staring. Then one of them barked an order, and they began to retreat to the "up" escalator. Slowly, they disappeared from sight, one by one, backwards.

When the last was gone, Gwen released her breath in a huge sigh. "Tell me, sin that thou dost seem to know—how can I dissipate this bubble of force, without the explosion thou didst speak of?"

Chornoi frowned. "Think you can let all that energy go, slowly?"

"Aye, that I can. Yet where shall it go when I do release it?"

Chornoi expelled a sigh of relief. "Into the wall, Miz Gallowglass. *That's* no problem, thank Heaven. Just take us over next to one of the rock walls, and let the power discharge."

Gwen looked puzzled, but she moved slowly over to the nearest solid wall.

"That's it, so the bubble's just touching it," Chornoi prompted. "Now, as it gets smaller, move closer to the wall, so the bubble stays in contact. Okay, try letting go."

Gwen scowled in concentration, and sparks cracked like pistol shots, wherever the skin of the bubble touched the wall.

Rod watched in awe as the power grounded itself out, wondering how he'd ever be able to embrace Gwen again.

"It's bedrock," Chornoi explained as the bubble shrank. "The energy goes through the wall, on down into the bones of the very earth itself. It's big, Miz Gallowglass, very big. There's a lot of rock there to soak up power."

"Mayhap it soaks not swiftly enow," Gwen said, frowning. "The stone doth glow."

They looked and, sure enough, the rock wall had turned cherry red.

"I think the bedrock can take it." Chornoi frowned. "After all, the bubble's almost gone, and the stone's not softened yet."

Rod nodded. "As long as it's only red, we're probably okay."

"'Tis gone," Gwen sighed, as the last of the power jumped into the wall in one final pistol-shot spark. "Now whither do we go?"

"Why, into a tube-car, of course." Chornoi grinned. "Shall we?"

They waited by the door in the clear wall for five minutes or so. It was five minutes too long for Rod; he kept glancing back at the escalators with apprehension. But finally, a tube-car swooshed up to the door and hissed to a stop. The door rolled back, and a stream of people filed out.

"Let 'em go, let 'em go," Chornoi murmured. "The more of them who get off, the more room there is for us."

Finally, they could step aboard. There were only about twenty people in the car, so they were able to take four seats that faced each other, but were well away from anyone else.

Gwen glanced nervously at the door. "When will it start?"

"It already did." Chornoi smiled, amused. "Smooth ride, isn't it?"

"It is, indeed." Gwen's eyes were wide with astonishment. "Yet tell me—how is't we ride? Wherefore hath that little man's 'superiors' not halted all carriages near to us?"

"They can't," Chornoi explained. "They'd have to shut off power to this whole sector, and that would leave thousands of people trapped until they could find us. And I think they realize that if they leave us alone in the dark in a tunnel-complex like this, they might *never* find us."

Rod's face was wooden; he was filled with sullen resentment, hearing Chornoi explain the facts of the situation to Gwen. He glared around him, looking for an outlet for the emotion—surely it couldn't be jealousy?

There! That gleaming, modest, inch-wide circlet on the front wall. "Smile," he advised, "we're on somebody's screen."

The other three turned around, staring at the front of the car. But Rod's eyes narrowed as he glared at it, and the faintest whiff of smoke coiled out of the vent nearest it. Passengers in the front of the car began to sniff, frowning.

"Neatly done." Gwen sounded surprised. "Yet wherefore, husband? What harm was there in it?"

"It was an electronic eye," Rod explained, "and when we decide to get off this high-speed sausage, I'd rather the security people didn't know exactly where we did it."

"Ah! Well thought!" Gwen swept the rest of the car with a thoughtful gaze. "Nay—I sense no more of them . . ."

Rod stared. She could sense electromagnetic fields now, too?

Gwen shook her head with decision. "Nay, only the one."

"Makes sense," Chornoi snorted. "No doubt the Proletarian Eclectic State of Terra was too cheap to put more than one audio and one video pickup on each car."

Rod's mouth tightened, though he had a fleeting thought that Chornoi might have been trying to be tactful. Irritated, he directed a glare at the small grille in the ceiling in the center of the car, thinking searing thoughts. When smoke curled out of it, he relaxed. "Okay. Audio's out now, too."

Yorick nodded, satisfied. "No way they can tell where we get out now."

Rod frowned at a sudden thought. "But they don't have to, do they? They just have to detail a bunch of guards at *every* station." He turned to Chornoi. "How many do we have coming up?"

She had paled. "Only one—the Canary Islands. After that, the next stop is Puerto Rico."

"So." Rod leaned back, pursing his lips. "We've got one chance."

"Why bother?" Yorick settled back, grinning. "I always liked the Western Hemisphere."

Rod suffered a shy grin. "Well, actually, *any* place will do fine." The realization suddenly hit him like a bottleful of champagne. "Hey! We're *home!* This is *Terra*—the real, bona fide ancestral home of humanity! The planet where we evolved!"

Yorick cocked an eyebrow. "Never been here before?"

Rod shook his head. "Heard about it, though. Lots."

Gwen was looking from one to the other, totally lost.

"This is the planet people started out from, Miz Gallowglass," Chornoi explained. "Your ancestors spread out from here in starships, in all directions. They colonized the planets you live on now."

Awe filled Gwen's face.

"There's still the problem of getting off," Yorick reminded, "without getting arrested."

Chornoi's gaze roamed the car. "Most of these people have luggage, don't they?"

"They do?" Yorick sat up, looking here and there all about the car. "Son of a gun! I suppose those shoulder bags *could* be suitcases."

"Sure. You don't need much room to pack a weekend's clothes."

"I'll never get used to this compact clothing you folks use," Yorick sighed. "Personally, I always thought we should leave spider silk to the arachnids."

Chornoi smiled. "Okay, primitive. What backward planet did *you* come from?"

"You'd be surprised." The caveman looked wary. "But I gotta admit, it is handy having a suit that can fold as flat as a board."

Chornoi frowned. "What's a 'board'?"

Rod said quickly, "So they've all got luggage. You're not thinking what I think you're thinking, are you?"

"I think so." Chornoi nodded at a nearby passenger. "He's about your size, and he's got some clothes to spare."

"Of course, we would have to knock him out," Rod reminded her.

Chornoi nodded, scowling. "That's the part I don't like. But it won't do him any permanent damage—and when he wakes up, he'll never know it was you who robbed him."

"We'll leave cash." Yorick eased a flat wallet out of his pocket.

Rod stared. "You've got PEST credits?"

"Sure." Yorick shrugged. "What kind of a traveler would I be, if I left home without some of the cash of the country I was going to?"

A time-traveler, Rod thought, but he had to admit the sense of what Yorick said. A person who was going to travel chronologically, should naturally take the same precautions as a person who was going to travel geographically. It was just that he couldn't count on being able to exchange currency once he got to his destination. . . ."

"So why were we going through that whole elaborate routine at the casino?" Chornoi demanded. Then she frowned. "Oh, yeah, I forgot. Nobody on any of the frontier planets will accept PEST credits for anything anymore."

"Why—because they're free of PEST's tyranny?"

"No—because the PEST BTU isn't worth very much.

Legislation never was a very sound basis for a currency, Major."

"The price of thrift," Rod sighed. "I hate to point this out, but while we're stealing that guy's pajamas, won't the other passengers notice?"

Gwen sat very straight for a moment, gazing off into space. One by one, the other passengers began to snore. Finally, she relaxed with a bright smile and said, "Nay."

Chornoi stared about her, closed her eyes, shook her head, and looked again.

Yorick expelled a hissing breath and said, "Yes." Then he said, "Well." and, "Someday maybe I'll get used to what you can do, Lady Gallowglass."

Privately, Rod hoped *he* would, too.

Yorick pushed himself out of his seat. "Let's get on with it, shall we?"

A few minutes and quick trips to the powder room later, the four of them sat down again, leaving four suitcases a little lighter and a lot richer.

Gwen plucked at the flimsy gray fabric. "'Tis so light that I feel quite unclothed."

"I know what you mean," Chornoi agreed. "After my tights and jerkin, it feels really odd."

"You weren't kidding with that crack about pajamas, were you?" Rod asked.

"Not a bit," Yorick said sadly. "But on Terra, going outdoors is a job for specialists now, so why should anyone else bother wearing all that heavy, uncomfortable wool and buckram?"

"I'm just not used to common sense, I suppose." Rod looked down at his bland, gray pajamas. "How come they all wear the same thing?"

Yorick shrugged. "Standard government issue. This is the Proletarian Eclectic State of Terra, Major. . . . Hey! Don't take it so hard, Chornoi! How could *you* know what they were going to do?"

"By really thinking about what they were saying," she whispered, "instead of just latching onto the parts I liked."

They filed off the car with the other passengers, just four more gray-clad bodies. Rod was glad the pajamas had come with hoods; it gave them a fighting chance that no one would recognize their faces. They filed onto the escalator and glided up. Rod stared at the blank tan plasticrete wall, letting his thoughts go numb. Then he frowned. "This isn't plasticrete anymore."

"Right." Chornoi looked at him strangely. "Plasticrete is tan. This is red."

"It's stone!" Rod wanted to reach out and touch it, but the wall was four feet away from the escalator. "It's real, bona fide rock! But why so far away?" He looked down at the shallow stairs cut into the slope beside the escalator. "And why are there steps there?"

"Because that's the way the Spanish built them," Yorick answered.

"The Spanish?" Rod looked up, frowning. "I thought PEST was an international government."

"Yeah, but they're thrifty, remember? Why pay good money to build a new station, when you can just adapt an old one?"

Rod stared around him. "You mean . . ."

"Right." Chornoi nodded. "You're in Puerto Rico, Major, where the Spanish once had a colony. They fortified the island heavily. We're inside the castle El Morro, built in the seventeenth century."

"Fourteen hundred years ago!!?!"

Chornoi nodded. "And it's still standing. They built well, back then."

Daylight struck them like a spray of needles, and the moving stairs delivered them gently onto a moving belt. Gwen breathed deeply of the warm, fragrant air. "Why, 'tis Paradise!" Then she frowned out toward a low rock wall

Rod looked, then stared. "That, dear, is an ocean. Water. All of it."

Gwen gazed for a while, then said, "Rarely have I seen waters so blue. What sayest thou, husband?"

Rod was staring up at the other side.

"What seest thou?" Gwen turned to look, and gasped.

The red wall towered up, blotched here and there, but stern and sheer, tilting back away from them, curving away around the headland, and up, up, up.

"'Tis the abode of giants," Gwen whispered.

Rod glanced nervously around the terrace. It somehow seemed very narrow now. The wall was so huge that it made him feel like a fly clinging by his toes.

"*Men* built this?" Chornoi said softly.

Yorick nodded. "Lots of them. And they didn't have much choice about it."

The slidewalk delivered them to the base of another escalator. It carried them into a tunnel, rising up along a rampway. Rod stared around at the size of it. "Seventeenth century, you say?"

Chornoi nodded.

"What was this tunnel for? I mean, they didn't have escalators then."

"For cannon, Major. Huge cannon, ten feet long, made out of cast iron. They threw iron balls as big as your head, and they weighed like sin. Tons. You saw those six-foot notches in the seaward wall, down there on the battlements?"

Rod nodded.

"Well, that's what they were for—cannon. Only to get them there, they had to lower them down this ramp. And to get them back up, they had to use horses." Chornoi gazed around her, looking grim. As they neared the top of the rampway, she nodded toward a niche in the wall with a grille of iron bars covering it. "Torture dungeon. When some poor bastard of a soldier broke the rules, they locked him up there for a while. Not enough room to stand up straight, and not much in the way of sanitary facilities, either."

"Plus knowing all his mates were watching him suffer every time they came down here." Rod nodded. "Nice guys."

"Yeah." Chornoi looked at the red stone around her, and shuddered. "A soldier must have thought he was in Hell here, back then. This piece of rock was all there was for him—and the officers were his masters."

"Legalized slavery," Yorick said with a scowl.

They came out into the sun again, and found themselves in a wide courtyard, with a score of rooms cut into its walls. Two huge cylinders stood in its center.

Chornoi nodded toward them. "Cisterns. They were ready for a siege here."

"Siege, cannon..." Gwen frowned. "Why so much might?"

"Because Puerto Rico was the gate to the Caribbean, Miz Gallowglass, and to all the wealth of the countries that lie along its shores. That's the Atlantic Ocean over there, with Europe on its far side—but just around the curve of this shoreline, is the Caribbean. Other countries tried to take this island from the Spanish, and that wealth with it. The Dutch tried it first, then the English, so they built this castle to guard against those enemies."

Gwen gave a somber nod. "It must have guarded well."

"It did," Chornoi agreed. "It was built to ward off seventeenth-century caravels, but it'd be very effective against any rebel group that tried to take over the transatlantic tube, today."

Rod lifted his head slowly. "So that's why the trip ends here!"

Chornoi nodded. "It'd also be easy to lock out anybody trying to invade through the tube from Europe. All you'd have to do would be to lock those big gates over there, and shoot down from the battlements up there." She pointed up at the rooftops. They could just make out the shape of the gun-slits against the sky. It wasn't hard to see the uniformed armsmen walking their beats, though.

Rod shuddered and looked away. "Not an entirely happy

with a slice of blue between it and the sky. "What is that azure field?"

thought, under our circumstances."

"Don't worry about it." Elaborately casual, Chornoi strolled out the main gate. The others followed her, with sighs of relief. "Where're we going?" Rod asked.

"Over there." Chornoi pointed at the skyline.

Another fortress topped a rise before them.

Gwen shivered, then squared her shoulders. "We do what we must." She stepped onto the slidewalk.

"That was the *only* tube from Europe?" Rod asked.

They were coming in through another gate in a reddish stone wall, and they found themselves in another courtyard. Gwen gazed about her. "Why, 'tis like to the other, only far smaller."

Chornoi nodded. "Good way to put it. I mean, it makes sense, doesn't it? If it worked with El Morro, why not do it again? This is the fortress San Cristobal, Miz Gallowglass—and yes, Major, that El Morro tube is the only one from Europe."

"For the whole Western Hemisphere?"

Chornoi nodded. "Oh, it makes for traffic jams, right enough, but it sure lets PEST control who moves where."

"So why aren't they stopping us?" Yorick muttered.

Chornoi frowned. "I was wondering that, myself. They must have figured out that we're not in the Canaries."

"But they don't know we're wearing gray," Rod reminded her.

Chornoi shook her head. "They've got to have guardsmen out with our pictures by now. All we had was a change of clothes, not plastic surgery."

They rode the slidewalk through the courtyard of San Cristobal slowly, each mulling at the thought. Finally, Yorick said, "You don't suppose the local guardsmen might not be too happy about PEST telling them what to do, do you?"

The slidewalk shot them into another dark tunnel.

* * *

This one was low, and not very wide. Discreet, indirect lighting showed them when the slidewalk turned into an escalator.

"They didn't used to have lights in here," Yorick muttered.

Chornoi's gaze snapped to him, eyes narrowed.

"They had charges of gunpowder set at regular intervals. That's what the lines there are for." Yorick pointed at straight cracks, an inch wide, that ran up the walls and across the ceiling. "If they blew up the far end of the tunnel, the near end would still stand. So if any poor bastard of a soldier had to come down here at night, he wasn't allowed to carry a torch."

Rod looked around at the dark close walls, glanced forward and backward, and saw that all the daylight had been blocked off by the curve of the tunnel. He shuddered.

The slidewalk stopped, and they stepped through a low doorway into a small tunnel at right angles to the main one. Rod noticed that they passed another grille of iron bars, blocked open.

He found himself in a very long room, like a section of tunnel that had been closed off. Far away at the end, daylight glared through a small rectangle.

"We wait here," Chornoi explained. "When the next car comes, we'll go down that escalator to board it." She pointed at a plasticrete portal that obtruded in the side of the tunnel, hideous in its smooth blandness.

Rod was looking about him. He noticed a clear panel and stepped over to it. Behind it was a section of tunnel wall with five crudely-drawn ships colored in earth tones, and a scrawled word above them.

Yorick noticed his gaze. "A young officer did that. He led a mutiny, and they locked him in here for sixty days before they took him out to kill him."

Rod darted a quick glance around the chamber. For a moment, he could imagine what it must have been like to be locked up in this small space for so long a time—day after day, never knowing when he'd be taken out to be slain, with nothing to do except rant at his fate and curse himself for a fool. He shook his head, turning away from the thought. "What does the word say?"

"What would *you* say, if you were locked up in here for sixty days?"

Chornoi frowned up at Yorick. "How come you know so much about this place?"

But Yorick only shook his head, brows drawn so low they hid his eyes, and muttered something under his breath.

A green panel glowed to life by the stairway.

"Loading time," Chornoi said softly.

As they came into the Atlanta interchange, a 3DT tank burst into color with a picture of a group. "These persons are criminals," a resonant voice informed them. "They endanger the state and, therefore, every citizen."

Rod stared, appalled. "Wow! I never looked worse!"

"It's the harried, hunted look," Chornoi assured him, "and they *would* catch me without makeup."

Yorick nodded. "I look like a thug."

Gwen didn't say anything, but the expression on her face spoke volumes.

"If you see any or all of them," the voice went on, "report them immediately to the nearest Security Service officer."

"See the scoutship in the background?" Yorick pointed. "This must be the picture that the little viper with the loud mouth had his flunky take."

Rod nodded. "Wonder what took 'em so long to get it on the network?"

"Who says it did?" Yorick countered. "We could be looking at the hundredth replay."

"Yeah, we could." Rod frowned. "Either way, we'd better get gone. Gwen, let's go. Chornoi . . . Chornoi?"

But Chornoi was over against the wall, talking at a blank viewscreen. "Yeah, I just saw them!" She was speaking in a higher, more nasal voice than usual, and fairly danced with excitement. "I mean, I'm right here in Atlanta, human, and I . . . huh? . . . No, I don't know why you're not getting any picture. I don't have one of you either, y' know? Hey, what can I tell you? The way you guys keep up these public call booths . . . Oh, them? Yeah! I just got in on the tube from Florida! And back in Jacksonville, when I was getting on, they were getting off! . . . No, of course not! How could I call you any sooner? There weren't any call booths on that capsule! Besides, I didn't see your blurb about them until I got off here in Atlanta . . . What? . . . Oh, sure, sure! Glad to help! I always wanted to be a good citizen. . . . Yeah, 'bye, now."

"That," Yorick said, leveling a forefinger, "is a damn good idea." He jumped for another call booth, put his palm over the vision pickup, and said, "Security Service. Reporting."

But Rod was already at a booth of his own. "Huh? . . . Well, yeah, I'm in Atlanta now—but, I mean, I didn't see your blurb about 'em until I was waiting for my tube in Puerto Rico, and my capsule came right after that, and well, hell, you couldn't expect me to . . . Well, yeah! I saw them, yeah! Sicily, just before I got on the capsule there! . . . No, now, look, I know that was eight hours ago, but, yeah, I'm sure! . . . Yeah, I mean, you couldn't miss those clothes anywhere! What happened to that guy's jacket—did he get scrambled eggs on it?"

Gwen had her hand over another vision pickup, and was staring at the microphone inlay. Suddenly she smiled, and said, "Emergency," and began talking in a fast, nasal voice. "Hello? . . . Yeah, them! . . . No, no, the four in the tank! The ones with the weird . . . Yeah, sure I'm sure . . . Oh! Yeah, right here where I'm talking from . . . Where? Oh, I don't know. Someplace in Mexico . . . Whup! There comes my capsule!"

She disconnected and turned, to find Rod standing over her. "*What* did you do?"

She beamed up at him. "I traced the paths of the 'electrons' with my thoughts, and made each wait one second in an instrument a thousand miles away, then begin its course anew."

Rod stared. "You mean you figured out how to route that call through a terminal that far away in just a few seconds?"

"Nay—I've been learning of these things thou dost term 'electrons' sin that we were kidnapped."

"I noticed." Rod swallowed through a suddenly dry throat. "Uh . . . where does Security think that call came from?"

"I believe 'tis called 'Acapulco.'"

Rod turned away, just barely managing to restrain a gibber. "You, uh, seem to have developed a feel for the local dialect."

Gwen shrugged impatiently. "'Tis naught, for one who reads minds."

Fortunately, right then, Rod bumped into Yorick, who was trying to shoo them all into a tightly-knit group again. "All right, all right! That's enough with the phone calls, already! Let's get under cover, before somebody tracks the origins of these little bulletins of ours, and adds two and two together, and comes up with three! We need a hiding-place, don't we?"

"Right!" Rod looked about him, thinking fast. He pointed a finger. "There!"

Yorick turned, looked, and grinned. "The very place. Come on, folks, let's go." And he shooed them all toward a shop front replete with flashing letters, garish holos, and animated enticers. They sauntered into a huge mouth with incarnadined lips below a mustache that read, "GAMES ARCADE."

Where the upper teeth should have been was a sign that read,

"NO CALCULATORS OR
PERSONAL COMPUTERS ALLOWED!

They louse up our games."

As they stepped in, they were assaulted with a primal cacophony of whistles, squeaks, booms, shrieks, screeches, chimes, explosions, cackles, zooms, and rings. Gwen pressed her hands over her ears. "Aiee! Wherefore must they needs have such a deal of noise? And wherefore is there so much haze?"

The hall was filled with smoke, and dimly-lit by spotlights focused on each separate gaming machine.

"It's supposed to help their concentration," Rod called into her ear. "They won't be distracted by the other machines around them, because they can't see them clearly."

Gwen only shook her head, exasperated.

As they plowed on through the arcade, they were assailed by gunfire from a variety of periods: the booming of muskets, the sharp cracks of squirrel rifles, the continuous racket of repeating rifles, the rattle of machine guns, the sizzle of blasters. Names of famous battles flashed past them as they slogged doggedly ahead. Finally, gasping and panting, they reached an island of comparative quiet, where there were only a few rings of people sitting on the floor, chatting and laughing, and a man talking to a machine.

"Praise Heaven," Gwen gasped. "I feel as though I have just run the gaunt of the worst of Man's history."

Beside them, a calm voice asked, "What is the acceleration of a falling body on the planet Terra?"

"Thirty-two feet per second!" the player cried, and the machine chimed agreeably. A counter on its panel registered the number "20." "Excellent," the machine murmured. "What was the first English novel?"

"Richardson's *Pamela!*"

The machine chimed again. "Excellent. Why did Alexander's empire fail?"

Rod looked up at the name of the game. It read, "Universe-Class Trivia."

"Invalid." One of the people in the nearest ring held up a hand. "He can't be using a two-handed sword in pre-Roman Britain."

One of the other people frowned. "Why not?"

"Because it wasn't invented until the 1200s."

"So what did the British use?"

"Axes."

The young man shook his head with deliberation. "He's my character, and he's using a broadsword."

"No way-o, Wolfbay-o. This game sticks to historical accuracy. That's Rule Three."

"Says who?"

"I do—and you know Rule One."

The young man sighed and said, "Okay. 'Wolfbay unlimbered his twenty-pound war-ax . . .'"

"Hold it." The first man held up a hand again.

"Okay, O-kay! A two-pound ax!"

Gwen bent down and murmured something to one of the other players. The player answered her, and Gwen straightened, nodding, but still mystified.

"What was that all about?" Rod asked.

"I wished to know the source of the smaller man's authority." Gwen shrugged. "She told me 'tis because he is the . . . my lord, what is a 'diem'?"

"'Diem'?" Rod frowned. "I think it was a Latin word that meant 'day,' dear."

"Lost!" Beside them, Yorick gave a machine a slap. "Doggone it, this is too much! Three straight losses—in three moves each!"

A neatly-dressed man was at his elbow in a second. "I'm Alkin Larn, the manager. Do you have a problem with our games, citizen?"

"I sure do." Yorick nodded toward the machine. "You know how this thing gives you three tries on each game? Well, I never got past the first hurdle once! I think the joystick's broken!"

The manager stepped in front of the machine and slipped

a credit card into the slot. "Let me see . . ." He began to play.

"This is one hell of a welcome to Terra," Yorick snorted. "Here I am, just in from the outlying planets—you know, Wolmar, Otranto—and I met a guy in a bar who recommended this particular arcade, so I came in here to get a taste of Terran high life, and what happens? The machine beats me out!"

Rod was frantically making shushing motions.

The manager stilled, gazing at the screen. Then he looked up at Yorick with a polite smile. "You may have a point about this machine, sir. I'll certainly arrange a refund; your acquaintance's recommendation is exactly what I'm always hoping to hear. Would you like to step into the back room to try the really advanced games?"

"Fine." Yorick grinned. "Just take me to them."

Personally, Rod hadn't thought Yorick had exactly been piling up a sky-high score, even on the kiddie level.

But the manager slipped a "MALFUNCTIONING" sign out of his coverall, hung it on the machine, and turned away. Yorick turned with him.

Chornoi and Rod looked at each other in mingled panic and disbelief.

"We have trusted him thus far," Gwen reminded them. "Wherefore should we think him mistaken now?"

"A point," Rod sighed, "and I must admit we don't see any squadron of armsmen charging down on us. Come on."

They turned and followed Yorick and Larn.

"With the advanced games, I really must warn you," Larn was saying, "that the stakes are advanced, too."

"Oh, sure, I know these machines are really just low-level gambling." Yorick shrugged. "After all, the government has to have an income, doesn't it?"

"It certainly does," Larn said grimly, "sixty percent of all gambling profits."

Yorick nodded. "But you can make a living off the forty percent that's left over?"

"A good living." Larn opened the door to the back room. "But I don't have any assistants—only two night managers. You're just in from Otranto, and you stepped into a games arcade?"

"What can I tell you?" Yorick shrugged as he stepped through the door. "We got tired of the Gothic motif."

Rod stepped aside for the ladies, then followed them in, feeling as though he were walking into a trap. Larn closed the door behind him.

Gwen was staring around at the walls. "So many books!"

Chornoi gawked. "Why? Why not just keep them on cube?"

"Books are more convenient in a great number of ways." Larn walked around in front of them, gesturing to an easy chair and a table with a lamp. "But the main reason is atmosphere. You can hide away from the world in here—and about twenty percent of our customers do."

Rod was still looking around. "I don't see anything *but* books. Where's the gambling?"

"The gamble is whether or not we get caught," the manager answered. He moved past them, beckoning.

They followed, past six people sitting around a circular table. The oldest was saying, "All right, Gerry, but you're assuming that nice, fair political system Plato's proposing, is representing the whole population."

Gerry frowned. "But that's what he said, isn't it?"

"Yeah," another student answered, "but that's not what the real city was like, the one he was modeling this 'Republic' of his after."

Gerry frowned. "How?"

"There were a lot of slaves in the population," answered a third student, "and they *weren't* represented."

Larn escorted them into a six-by-six cubicle with transparent walls, a small table, and a single chair. He closed the door behind them and explained, "This is a study carrel—soundproof, so the student won't be distracted by the discussion groups."

"Those are *volunteers* out there?" Rod asked.

Larn nodded. "They got bored with the games. Sorry to have to put you through this." He pulled a small rectangle out of his pocket and passed it over Rod's body, head to toe, about six inches in front of him. "Turn around, please."

Resentment smoldered, but Rod complied. After all, he was the one asking for help.

"Okay. Thanks." Larn turned to Gwen. "If you don't mind, Miz?"

An angry refusal leaped to Rod's lips, but Gwen threw him a quick, imploring, determined glance, and he swallowed the words.

Larn scanned Gwen front and back, then Chornoi and Yorick. Finally, he nodded and slipped the rectangle back in his pocket. "All right, no bugs."

Gwen frowned.

"Listening devices," Chornoi explained. "Surveillance."

Gwen's lips formed an O.

"You ought to recognize the setup by now, Major," Yorick said, with a steady gaze.

Rod met that gaze, frowning. Then his eyes widened, and he spun to the manager. "Good grief! You're a Cholly Barman graduate!"

The manager nodded. "And our great and glorious masters of the Proletarian Eclectic State of Terra have decreed that no one is to learn more than basic reading, writing, and arithmetic. Oh, a very small number of very talented students will be allowed to go on through high school, and maybe even college—any society has to have at least a few people to keep the machinery running, and collect the taxes—but the vast majority will never be taught to read anything more than the directions on a food packet."

Yorick nodded. "And, strangely, the children of PEST officials are already almost all included in that small number of 'very talented' chosen to go on in school."

"Despite the fact that some of their parents are total idiots," Chornoi said through clenched teeth.

Rod gazed at the manager. "You're taking quite a risk."

Larn smiled. "I suppose a good lawyer could get me off. All those games out there are just machines. The customers may be learning, but nobody's teaching, right? And they don't learn very much, by the hour."

"Sure, but they spend so many hours at it, that they *do* learn!"

Larn nodded. "And will keep on learning, for the rest of their lives, I hope. Which is better than spending all their days without anything more than the primary education the law allows."

Rod frowned. "How many of them graduate from the games to the back room?"

"Only about twenty percent. Most of them are very satisfied with the games, which is why we have to keep thinking up more and more challenging ones. But between games, 3DT epics, and song cubes, I think we're getting a good, solid elementary education across to about a third of the population."

"'Tis remarkable, surely," Gwen said, "yet can you teach them no more than that?"

Larn shook his head. "Not with the techniques we've worked out so far, though I understand some drunken poet Cholly knows, has come up with some new approaches to epics that're conveying abstract concepts. But the real limitation is learning how to reason—and that takes a live teacher to guide you."

"Yet ere thou canst so guide them, thou must needs bring them to this place of study."

Larn nodded. "The few who do develop real intellectual curiosity are quietly ushered back here to the books, where tutors can guide their reading and develop their thinking abilities through discussions. Education always comes down to the live teacher, right there with the student. Nothing can really replace the human mind."

"And once they have started learning to think," Rod

inferred, "they're not too apt to turn you in?"

"No, not terribly." Larn smiled. "But if they do, there's always that lawyer."

"The lawyer can't get you off if the case never goes to court though," Chornoi said softly.

Larn nodded again. "There is that little problem. PEST intends to enforce the laws, even if they're not sure the person's guilty. And if they lock up one innocent man for every three guilty ones, who cares?"

"No one who counts," Rod growled.

"Which means no PEST officials," Chornoi added.

"Except." Yorick held up a forefinger. "Except that they're not going to lock 'em up—prisons cost too much. It's a lot cheaper to terminate them."

"Lends a wealth of new meaning to the term 'executive,' doesn't it?" Larn gave him a bleak smile. "However, there is hope, if you can call it that. There're still a lot of jobs that're cheaper to do by hand than by machine—as long as the worker doesn't have to be paid."

"Convict labor." Yorick nodded, lips thin. "Well, it beats execution, I suppose."

"Don't be too sure. For myself, I'd rather not find out the hard way. So let's get you folks helped and moved on, shall we? From the 3DT bulletins, I gather the armsmen are after you, and I don't relish having them as patrons."

"They are," Yorick confirmed. "But behind them are the PEST spies. They're trying to eliminate us."

"Join the club," Larn snorted.

"I did." Chornoi's face was frozen. "But I began to realize that their 'more efficient government' was going to end up being total oppression, so I quit."

Larn shook his head. "Only one way out of the Security Service."

Chornoi nodded. "That's what they're trying for."

Larn gazed at her. Then he gave a bleak smile. "Well, that explains it all nicely. Can't think what I can do to help, though; we can't hide you for more than a few hours—too risky. How about a quick makeup job?"

"That would help." Yorick nodded. "But what we really need, see, is to get into PEST's central headquarters."

"What!!?!"

"I know, I know." Yorick held up a hand. "But we're stranded time-travelers, see, and we think PEST might have a time machine hidden away somewhere in the bowels of its labyrinth."

Larn just stared at him for a minute, then shrugged his shoulders. "Why not? I believe the masses can be educated, don't I? But they've got an outer wall and an inner wall, folks, and all the gates are guarded by lasers that fire if you *don't* push the right button. The landing pad on top of the building has blasters all around it, and a dozen live guards day and night. I could go on, but I think you get the point; the only way into PEST HQ is to be carried in . . . as a prisoner."

Yorick looked at Rod. Rod looked at Gwen. They both looked at Chornoi. All four swallowed heavily, and nodded. "Okay," Yorick said. "How do we commit a crime?"

"We could have thought of this ourselves, you know," Chornoi growled as they walked down the concourse.

"But we didn't," Rod reminded her. "That shows we needed help."

Chornoi shook her head. "I still don't like it. Letting myself get caught goes against all my training."

"Yes, but this is a bright new innovation," Yorick pointed out. "This way, getting caught lets you *keep* control of the situation."

"Keep talking," Chornoi growled, "you may convince me."

Yorick shook his head. "No time. If we're gonna do it, we gotta do it *now.*" He dropped back and, before the other three could quite realize what he was doing, he was pointing at them and shouting, "There they go!"

Everyone walking on the concourse, in both directions, stopped and stared.

Rod felt the old sick sinking feeling in his stomach and the itch between his shoulder blades, where he just *knew* somebody was aiming a blaser. "Too late now," he growled. "Gotta go through with it! *Run!*"

They broke into a sprint.

Behind them, Yorick was shouting, "Get them! That's Public Enemy Number One—both of them! And Public Enemy Number Two! Haven't you seen them on 3DT?"

But the passersby only stared at him, then at the fleeing trio. Fear haunted their eyes.

"Oh, f' crying out softly!" Yorick growled. "If you want something done right . . ." And he ran after Rod and the ladies, howling, "Stop them! *Stop!*"

He'd managed to catch up to them before the Security Service finally showed up. Even then, not a bystander was doing anything but standing by—and most of them had just speeded up their walk a little, heads down, shoulders hunched.

But the Security Service finally did come swerving around a corner, and the ones in front dropped to one knee, aiming blasters.

"That's no good!" Rod yelped, and Gwen glared at the blasters long enough for her companions to charge.

The armsmen almost started to retreat, taken by surprise—but then reflex took over as Yorick slammed a fist into an armsman's belly, and Chornoi aimed a chop at another's collarbone. They blocked out of sheer reflex, and their mates joined in.

Gwen caught up and spun, back-to-back with Rod, as he furiously blocked and punched. She managed to stop every blow aimed at his back, and if a slender lady's forearm shouldn't have been able to stop a blaster swung by the barrel, who noticed?

Chornoi was chopping and kicking for all she was worth, and three guardsmen surrounded her at a respectful distance; but they were watching for an opening, and kept leaping in for a quick jab. Sometimes she caught them, but they were professionals, too.

Yorick grabbed an arm and a strap and threw an armsmen into one of his mates, but a third caught him with a forearm around the throat and yanked back. Yorick dropped to one knee and lurched back up, bowing, too fast for the armsman to counter. He sailed over Yorick's head, but another armsman slammed a haymaker into Yorick's face as he stood up.

Out of the corner of his eye, Rod saw Chornoi crumple. Apprehension gripped his belly as he thought, *This is it, dear. Remember, knock 'em out if they try to kill us—or if they even get fresh!*

Aye, my lord, her thought answered. She dropped her guard, closing her eyes, and started to fall just before the blow caught her. Then a sap cracked into Rod's skull, and searing pain heralded darkness.

He came to with a raging headache and a dry-sand thirst. He cracked his eyelids open in a squint, and looked around. All he saw was white tile, and the surface under him was cold, very cold. He rolled his head to the side, and saw Yorick and Chornoi strapped to steel slabs, wrists manacled up next to their heads. As he did, Chornoi blinked, squeezed her eyes shut, then strained them open. Beyond her, Yorick was watching him, looking surly.

Rod took a second while a huge burst of relief washed through him. Then he stared at Chornoi and raised one eyebrow in question. She squinted against pain, but she nodded. Beyond her, Yorick shrugged.

So. They were okay. *Now* the apprehension could claw loose. Where was Gwen? She was supposed to have stayed awake the whole time, faking unconsciousness.

He heard a soft moan behind him.

Rod turned his head quickly and winced at the pain, but opened his eyes wider.

He saw Gwen with her eyes closed. Frantically, he felt for her mind, and found it lulled, buffered, adrift on a sea of drugs.

Rage erupted in him, but he fought to hold it in. Not yet. Soon—but not yet. Not quite.

The anger abated a little, enough for him to notice a nearby voice saying, "But why didn't any of them use any of those tricks we've been hearing about?"

"They did," another voice snapped. "They froze the blasters."

"All right, so they did pull one. But just one! From what I've been hearing about this gang, they had a hundred gimmicks like that in their arsenal!"

"So they panicked," the second voice snarled. "Or maybe their tricks really *were* just a bunch of gadgets, no matter what superstitious claptrap you've been hearing!"

"Then where are they?"

"In a trash cycler, dodo! They ran out of power, and these yahoos threw them away! Now will you shut up and get busy finding out what they know about those gadgets?"

The other man grumbled and turned. He saw three out of four looking at him, and stopped short. "Bruno!"

Bruno turned. "What? Oh, they've come around! Well, isn't that cozy? Okay, folks, let me explain—you're going to tell us everything you know about those gadgets you used, especially that force-field generator and the invisibility field. And, of course, everything about this revolutionary underground you're working for. If you don't want to, you're going to go through an awful lot of pain, but you'll wind up telling us, don't doubt it."

"Wwwhy . . . why not use drugs?" Chornoi still squinted against a headache.

"Because it isn't as much fun." Bruno grinned. He looked up, and saw the direction of Rod's gaze. "No, don't go looking for any help from her! We got our doubts about her, so we did use drugs to knock her out. She won't wake up for another dozen hours." He fell silent, eyes narrowing as he stared at Rod. Then he nodded and moved forward. "We'll start with you—and the old-fashioned methods."

Rod felt hands undoing his manacles. Frantically, he retreated inside his own mind, remembering the analog-appearance his mind had given him for the inter-universal realm they'd traveled from Tir Chlis. He knew he only had a few seconds before the beating started, and with that kind of sensory stimulation, he'd never achieve a trance.

But he made it—awareness of his body faded out as it was being lifted upright. Through the limbo about him, he reached out for the feel of Gwen's mind. There it was, a fragile hull on waters of Nepenthe, slumbering, removed. Gently, he moved closer, merged, melded, and moved inside. *Waken,* he thought. *We're all done for if you don't. I might be able to handle them alone—but I might not.* It hurt him to say it, but he had to.

Dimly, he felt a stirring; but she lapsed.

They could kill us, he thought. *We might never waken.*

This time, there was response—the single thought, *Together.*

Rod hauled back on the reins of exasperation, reminding himself that women's romanticism wasn't completely incurable. If *that* basic drive could be met in oblivion, there was one that couldn't. Grimly, he conjured up a vision of Magnus hugging a weeping Cordelia to him, while a glum-looking Geoffrey sat by, holding a dry-eyed but fearful Gregory. *Alone, without us,* he thought. *Can you bear to leave them to strangers?*

He had the impression of a titan, roaring up from the waters to look around. Then it clambered up, rage building into an avalanche.

Rod got out, and got out fast. Limbo seemed very safe suddenly.

But Gwen would awaken, and fight those sadists alone.

He pulled himself back down, forced himself to become aware of his body . . .

And it hit. Pain. Every square inch of his body ached, and some of it seemed to burn. Instantly he was aware, seeing, as Bruno threw him back against the steel slab in disgust. "This is getting us nowhere! You'd swear the guy doesn't even have a mind! Go get the probes, Harry!"

Rage built, at two brutes who would so maltreat a helpless body—*Rod's* helpless body! And they meant to do it to his friends, too—and his wife! The rage rose, and Rod welcomed it, reaching down into it for the power he needed . . .

But beside him, manacles burst like grenades, and Gwen stepped away from her slab, fury fairly flaming from her.

Bruno and Harry slammed into the wall, their bodies actually seeming to grow thinner for a moment before they slid to the ground.

Gwen turned, glaring in wrath. "They have hurt thee!" she cried, and began to touch and probe Rod's body. Wherever she laid her hand, the pain abated as the neurons stopped firing. But even as she did it, howls of agony filled the air, then were still.

Chornoi stared in horror. "What the hell was *that?*"

"Folk who watched us, unseen," Gwen answered. "What thou dost hear came through a device they had, should they need to speak to those within this chamber. They sleep now, of course."

"Of course," Chornoi repeated, numbed.

"I would nurse thee a week, an I could," Gwen said gently, "yet I cannot, and thou must needs arise and aid me."

"Oh, no—Ow!—problem. No, now, I can stand." Rod removed her hand gently as he hefted himself up onto his feet, aching in every joint—but functional. He kept hold of her hand, though.

Gwen gazed at Chornoi's wrists, and her manacles exploded. She stared, then rubbed her joints to make sure they were untouched by all that force. As she did, two more explosions burst the cuffs at her ankles.

"Watch out for shrapnel," Yorick said softly.

"I did." Gwen looked up at him. "None struck thee, did it?"

"Not a bit," Yorick assured her.

Gwen nodded and glared at his handcuffs. They burst, then his ankle-cuffs, too.

He stood up, flexing his fists. "Shall we go?"

Gwen nodded and turned toward the chamber door. "What bearing, husband?"

Rod frowned, gazing off into space as he opened his mind to the myriad of thoughts that spun and twisted through the great complex around them. Down—it would be down low, for protection . . . There! He caught the thoughts of someone thinking about sending something ahead. He focused on the thoughts . . . yes, "ahead" meant "future"—3511, after Rod's own lifetime. He nodded, satisfied, and reached out to touch and meld with Gwen's mind, leading, showing her.

She nodded. "Aye, I see. Then let us go, husband."

The door blew out and away from them, its hinges and bolts shredded like raveled rope. Yorick and Chornoi stared, appalled.

"She's angry," Rod explained. "Catch up, folks."

They leaped to keep up with Gwen, and the familiar moiré sprang up around them. Just in time—four guards stationed outside looked up in alarm, then yelled as they leaped back, whipping out their blasters.

The blasters burst into flames in their hands.

They howled, throwing the torches from them, nursing their burns. Gwen ignored them and moved on. The other three had to hurry to keep up.

Chornoi was still staring back at the guards, then turned her head around to look up at Rod. "But she's the gentlest soul I've ever met!"

"I told you," Rod said impatiently, "she's angry."

An iron grille blocked their path. Gwen glared at it, and it burst into smithereens. She marched through the steel rain of its pieces, into an intersection. Blaster fire erupted from both sides. The bubble around them glowed briefly before the blasters exploded in the armsmen's hands. They screamed and whirled away. Gwen marched on.

"Uh, I hate to be indelicate," Yorick said, "but . . ."

"Because she loves me," Rod answered. "Besides, I've got some power myself, you know. I could survive long enough to get out of range."

They turned into a stairway. As they came out at the bottom, they saw a dozen men blocking their path with iron nets. Gwen narrowed her eyes, and the strands glowed white-hot. Flames licked out along them, and the guardsmen dropped them, cursing. Gwen surged forward, and the force field crashed into the dozen, bulldozing them out of the way. Some of them screamed as it squashed them against the wall, but Gwen paid no heed.

They turned a corner into a wide hallway. Twenty men were drawn up in front of a high double door in two ranks, one kneeling, one standing, all with blasters ready.

The blasters melted in their hands.

They threw them away with yowls of agony, just before the door behind them exploded into iron filings. The guards leaped aside, staring in terror. The iron filings filtered softly to the floor.

Gwen stepped through the door.

A lone technician stood by a wall full of keys, pressure-pads, and sliders, with an open-faced cubicle six feet wide set into it. At the sight of them, his mouth stretched in a grimace of horror, but he whirled and started slapping at keys and pads.

Gwen glared.

An invisible hand yanked the man off his feet, three feet into the air. Suddenly he slumped, unconscious, and the unseen hand dropped him in an untidy bundle.

"He sleeps," Gwen explained. The moiré around them disappeared.

Yorick leaped for the wall and started turning and punching.

Rod stood slack-limbed in reaction. Only once before had he ever seen Gwen in a real towering rage, and there hadn't been anywhere nearly as much power arrayed against her.

"Dost'a truly know how this device doth function?" Gwen demanded.

"No fear," Yorick snapped. "I know the standard settings by heart."

"But this isn't your brand," Rod protested.

"No," Yorick agreed, "it's a copy. Who do you think invented the damn thing, anyway?" He twisted a final key. "There! That's date!" He pushed a slider. "That's location!" He punched a sequence on a keypad. "That's the security code! And the instruction to forget!" He punched at a pressure-pad. "And that's the time-delay control! Everybody inside! It'll start up in one minute!"

A huge, hulking shape filled the shattered doorway.

"Laser cannon!" Chornoi yelped.

"Inside, quick!" Rod all but threw her into the six-foot cubicle. Yorick leaped in after her, and Gwen stepped up. Rod was right behind her. He turned just as the cannon rotated, its huge maw facing them. Rod stared into doom.

Doom was suddenly warped and twisted and shot through with the color-swirl of the moiré. Gwen clasped his hand with both of hers. "'Tis as thick a field as I can manage. Now, husband, lend me of thy strength!"

It took a moment. There had been so much power flying around loose during that march from the torture chamber—and she'd been learning so horribly much about electronics! But after that moment, Rod managed to remember the girl in the haystack, the mother with the baby in her arms, the gentle partner, and his thoughts flowed and melded with hers.

"Thirty seconds," Yorick groaned.

A stream of ruby light lit the force field.

The whole doorway filled with a sheet of flame. It raged and twisted in convolutions—not in a single blast, but in an endless roiling rage.

Sweat sprang out on Gwen's brow. Her hold tightened on Rod's hand.

Rod gave her all the energy he had, all there was of him.

She paled, trembling.

Concern flooded him, and washed into her—concern, tenderness, love.

Heat seared him, a Sahara noon, an oven, a flaming furnace. Chornoi gasped, and Yorick groaned, "Ten seconds."

It was ten seconds of eternity, ten seconds of agony, ten seconds of the sickening realization that, this time, they just might not make it, as the flames baked and raged—but it was ten seconds that were just long enough for their minds to meld completely, and for Rod to realize, in the midst of Hellfire, that she was still the same, loving partner, and that she was still his self-interest, as the flame wrapped them up . . .

The floor lurched, slamming them against each other, and air flooded in, blessedly cool. Dazed, Rod straightened, clinging to Gwen, gradually becoming aware that the flame was gone, that he was staring into a vast chamber filled with bench after bench full of electronic equipment, huge wardrobes, tall cabinets . . .

And, right in front of them, a short, spare man in a white lab coat, with a mane of white hair and an eagle's face, on a head that was too large. He glared up at them with a gaze that was so piercing Rod almost shuddered, even though he had borne that stare before.

But he pulled himself together, squared his shoulders and

took a deep breath, then stepped down out of the time machine carefully and said, "Dr. McAran, I presume."

They were sitting around a circular table, drinking restoratives (hundred proof). Around them, other tables filled the large room, with a variety of people clustered in discussion groups. Egyptian scribes rubbed elbows with ninth-century paladins; Sumerian peasants chatted with Ming Dynasty bureaucrats. The whole room was a glorious mélange of periods and styles, a meeting place of the centuries in a riot of colors, with a nonstop buzz of conversation in a pidgin English that Rod could just barely recognize as the ancestor of his own century's Anglic.

He frowned intently at McAran's last comment. "Well, sure. Of course I understand that Gramarye's pivotal. If it develops into a constitutional monarchy, it'll be able to provide the communications system the DDT will need to keep democracy alive."

"More than that," McAran said. "Your neighbors aren't going to be standoffish, Major. They're going to leave their home planet, lots of them, and they're going to fall in love and marry, wherever they go. A thousand years from now, about half the people in the Terran Sphere will be telepaths—because of your people."

Rod just stared. He felt Gwen's hand tighten on his, and squeezed back.

McAran waved his last earthquake away. "But that's really secondary. Gramarye's *real* contribution will be the wiping out of this artificial dichotomy we've developed between intuition and intellect, humanity and technology. Your local chapter of the Order of St. Vidicon is the cutting edge of that revolution, but it's simply formalizing something your whole people have been developing since they landed on Gramarye. Of course, they just view it as magic and mechanics—and they see absolutely no reason why one person can't be gifted in both."

Rod transferred his stare to Gwen.

She looked about her, confused, then back at him. "Milord?"

"Uh . . . nothing. We'll talk about it later." But he tucked her hand into his elbow and kept firm hold of it with the other hand, as he turned back to McAran. "Okay, so Gramarye is immensely important to the future of democracy, maybe even to the future of humanity, period. So what does that have to do with your coming eleven hundred years into your future, just to meet *me?*"

McAran looked a little uncomfortable. "Well, I really only came over to the time machine that was bringing you in. You're in the twentieth century right now, Major—technically."

Rod pushed his jaw back into place.

Yorick erased the problem. "Doesn't really matter, Major. This time-travel base could be located in any century. It is, in fact—just keeps going for a couple of thousand years, all the way through the Fourth Millennium. And it was just as easy to set the controls for this century, as for the one we were in. Easier, in fact—these are the ones I have memorized. Quicker to punch in, when you're in a rush."

Rod gave his head a shake. "Okay, if you say so. But . . ."

"Why did I want to meet you?" McAran wore his grim smile. "Well, I've heard so much about you, Major!"

"Great. Can I present *my* side of it?"

"No. Because if Gramarye is pivotal in the development of democracy, *you're* pivotal in the development of Gramarye."

Rod froze.

Gwen gazed at him, wide-eyed.

"Me?"

McAran nodded.

"Why not *her?"* Rod jabbed a finger at Gwen. "She's at least as powerful as I am! And she's done as much as I have toward putting Gramarye on the road to freedom!"

"Aye, yet I've espoused thy cause only for reason that

I've espoused thee," Gwen said softly, "and so would I continue to do, e'en—God forbid!—an thou wert ta'en from me. Yet had I never known thee, I ne'er would have so much as thought of it."

McAran nodded. "She was reared in a medieval monarchy, Major; she didn't have the vaguest notion of democracy. Nobody there did—except the future totalitarians and anarchists, who had come back in time to subvert Gramarye."

"And she wouldn't have learned advanced technology if those Futurians hadn't kidnapped the two of you back in time," Yorick said.

Gwen shook her head. "Thou canst not avoid it, my lord. Thou mayest not be the person who doth bring matters to fruition, but thou art the one who doth sow the seed." She flushed, smiling, and turned to McAran. "Which doth bring to mind that thou hast not spoken of the role our children are to play in this."

"Mighty," McAran assured her, "but only an extension of what you two are doing. An extension and an expansion, I should say, there are four of them, and each of them will grow up to be more powerful than either of you. Still, they'll only carry on what you've begun." His frosty smile etched itself on his face again. "Even if they don't quite realize it."

The exchange had given Rod a moment to recover. He took a deep breath. "But that still doesn't tell me what I'm doing here, talking to *you*."

"Do I have to lay it out for you?" McAran growled. "I want to make sure which side you're on."

"Why . . . democracy's."

McAran just regarded him, with a glittering eye.

"No," Rod said slowly, finally recognizing the transformation within himself. "Gramarye's."

McAran nodded.

"But democracy *is* in Gramarye's best interest!"

"If you're so sure about that," McAran grated, "you won't mind joining GRIPE."

Rod sat still for a minute, letting the shock pass. Then he said, "I'm already a SCENT agent. Doesn't that make me an affiliate member?"

McAran shook his head. "There's no official alliance between the two groups—just common interest. We don't even have a formal tie to the Decentralized Democratic Tribunal. In fact, neither of them knows we exist—and frankly, we like it that way. So, of course, one of the responsibilities of membership is maintaining that secrecy."

"Of course," Yorick added, "we do have overlapping membership. Other than you, I mean."

McAran nodded. "Some of our best agents are SCENT operatives. We even have a few DDT bureaucrats, and the odd tribune or two."

"Must be pretty odd, all right," Rod muttered.

"So how about you?" The eagle's eye was still on him. "Are you for us or not, Major?"

Rod met McAran's stare, and took a deep breath. "For you—but not part of you. Call me an associate member."

McAran sat still for a moment. Then he nodded. "As long as you're for us, and not against us." He stood, holding out his hand. Rod stood, and clasped it. He was amazed at how fragile and slender the scientist's hand seemed.

But McAran was nodding, and smiling again. "Good to have you, Major. Now, would you like to go back where you came from?"

"I would indeed," Gwen said instantly. "Eh, my little ones!"

Rod nodded, grinning. "Yeah. I think I've had my fill of high-tech society for another dozen years or so. Send me home."

McAran turned to Chornoi. "What do you want to do, O worm in the woodwork?"

"Worm?" She leaped to her feet. "Who the hell do you

think you are, throwing insults around like lava?"

"The volcano on whose slopes the tyrants live," Doc Angus snapped, glaring.

Chornoi's eyes narrowed. "I made a mistake. It was a bad one, and I helped hurt a lot of people. But I think I've kind of paid for some of that on this trip—even if Gwen and her husband did help me as much as I helped them."

McAran's smile was sarcastic. "Oh. You don't like dictators anymore, huh?"

"No," Chornoi snapped, "especially on the personal level."

"Prove it," McAran jibed. "Join GRIPE."

Chornoi stared, totally floored.

"He means it, Miz," Yorick said softly.

"But . . . but . . . how *can* you?" Chornoi exploded. "For all you know, I could be the worst PEST agent alive, trying to infiltrate your organization!"

McAran nodded. "Possible, very possible—but if you were, you wouldn't have been helping fight totalitarianism at every turn."

Chornoi frowned. "When did I do that?"

"When you helped avert a war on Wolmar," Yorick reminded her, "and when you helped us fight off Eaves and his buddies on Otranto. Listen, Miz, if you *were* really a PEST agent, you would have shoved a knife in Whitey the Wino's ribs at your first chance. He's at least as important to democracy as we are."

Rod nodded. "Charley Barman, too, and you never lifted a hand against him."

"But . . . but . . . I didn't know! I didn't know either of them were important to democracy!"

"Yeah, but you would have, if you were still a PEST agent. Besides, you helped get the Gallowglasses through."

"Only because I liked them—personally!"

Gwen's smile was radiant.

"Him, too!" Chornoi stabbed a finger at Yorick. "It's not just them, you know!"

"Yes, I know," McAran said grimly, "and I'll bet this is the first time in your life you've found people who liked you."

Chornoi stood very still.

"I'll take personal loyalty," McAran said. "I'll take it over loyalty to an idea, any time—even if it's loyalty to the group, and not to me."

"I might not like your other people as well as I like him," Chornoi said slowly.

"Then again, you might." The frosty smile was back. "Why don't you circulate a little, get to know them better?"

"Yeah—kick around for a while, Miz!" Yorick grinned. "I've got some buddies here I think you'd like."

"Buddies?" Her tone was frigid. "No women?"

"Of course." Yorick shrugged. "What do you want me to say, 'bosom buddies'?"

Chornoi's eyes narrowed. "Definitely not."

"Okay, then—friends. A person's a person. So I've got friends, all right? And I think they'd like you. Okay? So why don't you come and meet them?"

"Yes," Chornoi said slowly. "Yes," she said, nodding. "Yes, I think I will."

Yorick grinned, and held out an elbow.

Chornoi hooked her hand through it, and turned to Rod and Gwen. "Major—Milady—a pleasure meeting you." She actually inclined her head, smiling.

Rod grinned, lifting a hand. "See you in the time zones."

Chornoi smiled, tossing her head proudly, and whisked away on Yorick's arm. They stopped two tables away, where Yorick introduced her to a small troupe of Mongolian barbarians. She pressed palms.

McAran watched her go with a victorious smile. Then he turned back to Rod and Gwen, leading them away. "That's the basis of our organization here—misfits. None of my people ever had any friends, never felt they belonged—until they found us." He cocked his head to the side. "Doesn't apply to the two of you, of course."

"Oh, I wouldn't say that," Rod mused.

"Thou hast never been a Gramarye witch or warlock," Gwen agreed.

"Could be." The frosty smile turned into amusement. "Could very well be."

They came up to a thirty-by-thirty area, lined with time machines. One of them had a large sign over the portal, which said in Gothic lettering,

GRAMARYE

Rod's eyebrows lifted. "We rate a machine all to ourselves?"

McAran nodded. "I told you Gramarye's important to us. It's locked onto real-time there, dating from . . ." he coughed into his fist. ". . . from that little incident we had, with those Neanderthals."

"Yeah." Rod frowned. "I've been meaning to ask you about that."

"Some other time, okay?" McAran said quickly. "Right now, there're some people who've been waiting to see you for a couple of weeks."

"Aye—we must needs be gone to them, right quickly!" Gwen leaped into the time machine's cubicle. "Send us to them at once, doctor, an it please thee!"

"Oh, I could send you quicker than that." McAran peered closely at the date. "I could set it back a couple of weeks, and return you to the same night you were kidnapped."

Gwen's eyes lit, but Rod frowned. "How long would it take?"

"Only a minute, to reset the machine," McAran answered, "but the trip itself would take a couple of hours, because the time-matrix would have to readjust itself into a different configuration."

"I cannot wait so long." Gwen clasped Rod's arm. "I doubt me not an they have been well tended in our absence—and I burn to see them once again!"

Rod shrugged. "It'll probably have done them good to be without us for a while, especially since their baby-sitters have probably been indulging them horribly."

"Oh!" Gwen clasped her hand over her mouth, eyes wide. "Robin will be wroth with us, to have been so long away!"

"Yeah, but think how glad he'll be to see us come back!"

"There's some truth to that." Gwen turned back to McAran. "Send us now, doctor, I beg of thee!"

McAran shrugged. "As the customer orders." He reached out and pressed a button.

Rod and Gwen felt a twisting lurch, and were just fighting down nausea when they realized they were staring around at twilit woodlands, and the calm sheen of a pond.

Rod blinked, staring around him in surprise. "Well! Right back at the pretty little woodland pool I told you about!"

"An thou'lt pardon it, I'd liefer not stay to contemplate it," Gwen said, "especially an I doubt the virtue of that crone who told thee of it."

Gwen threw her arms around his neck. "Eh, husband! We are home!"

"Yeah!" Rod hugged her to him with massive relief.

Then he remembered the power he'd seen her wield, and that reminded him how much she'd learned about electronics; and he felt the cold fear seeping through him, at the thought of grappling a woman who could wreak such mayhem—especially since it was his own *kind* of mayhem. And wreaked at least as well as he could, himself.

She felt the change. "Husband? My lord?"

He held her off at arm's length. "We're not exactly the same people who left here, are we?"

"Wherefore not?" Gwen stared, startled and hurt. "We are still ourselves, my lord. Who else could we be?"

"Well, all right, still us," Rod growled, "but we've changed. And you, shall we say, have learned a lot in the process?"

"Yet it hath not changed who I am, nor the way I do feel toward thee," Gwen protested. "Nay, my lord. Do not think—

ever!—that only because I learn more, or gain more skill or power, that I shall ever love thee less!"

"Yeah, but it's not just your kind of learning." Rod hooked his hands in frustration at trying to find the right words. "It's that you're learning my kind of knowledge!"

Gwen stilled, staring up at him. Then she said, "Ah, then. So that is the way of it."

"Yes," Rod admitted. "The skills and knowledge I had, that you lacked, were all that were keeping me thinking I was good enough for you."

"Oh, how poorly thou dost know thyself, Rod Gallowglass!" She threw her arms about his neck and pulled his head down to hers. "Thy goodness and thy greatness have so little to do with thy knowledge or skill, or even thy power! 'Tis thy gentle, caring self that drew me into love of thee, and the strength of thy resolve that doth shelter me and mine! 'Tis thee I love—not thine attributes!" She drew back a little, cocking her head to the side. "And, in fairness, thou must needs own that thou hast learned my skills and knowledge, even as I've but now learned thine."

"Well, yes," Rod admitted, "but that's different."

"Only in that I rejoice at such joining, where thou dost seem to dread it," Gwen returned. "Yet thou hast no need of such trepidation, for 'tis thee I love, that inexplicable, unwordable, indescribable essence that is Rod Gallowglass—and only that! Not thy power or knowledge!"

Then she frowned as a new thought came. "Or dost thou love me less, because I know summat of *thy* magicks?"

Rod stared at her, horrified. Then, slowly, he smiled. "*Love* you less, no—but I do feel threatened by it. I'm sure I'll get over that, though." He caught her hands. "After all, if you've managed to adapt magic to advanced technology, *I've* learned to adapt technology to magic!"

Gwen threw her head back with a silvery laugh, and kept her lips parted as she swayed back up against him. He buried himself in her kiss.

Finally, he had to give up and gasp, though he did wish

he'd seen the kiss coming in time to hyperventilate a little. He hooked an arm about her waist and pointed at the path that wound away through the trees. "We do have to get back to the children, you know. Besides, we have a bed in the house."

She beamed up at him. "I think 'twill be an early slumbering for them this night, my lord."

And, arm in arm, they strolled away through the trees, hand in hand, mind in mind, pausing only occasionally to scan for mental traces of ambushers.

They came in the door with a word of cheery greeting—but it died on their lips. Rod stared, aghast. The table and chairs had been pushed back against the walls. A giant of a man, at least eight feet tall, took up most of the living room floor, with two people of standard size beside him, one wearing a robe and pointed hat of dark blue, sprinkled with signs of the zodiac, and the other a pretty lass in her twenties with her hair bound in a kerchief. The three of them were so tightly wrapped in hempen rope that they looked like candidates for a joint sarcophagus.

Geoffrey stood over the giant with a cudgel in his hand; Cordelia sat at the woman's feet, singing lightly and embroidering a handkerchief; Magnus stood over the wizard, arms akimbo, as though he were daring the man to try a spell; and Gregory sat cross-legged on the mantelpiece, contemplating the whole mess.

By the hearth sat a very worried-looking Puck. At the sound of Rod's voice, his head snapped up; he took one look at Rod and Gwen, moaned, leaped into the fireplace, and darted up the chimney with a howl of despair.

Gwen stared, appalled.

Then she took a deep breath.

But Rod beat her to it. "And just what do you think *you've* been doing!?!"

MORE SCIENCE FICTION ADVENTURE!

☐ 87310-3	**THE WARLOCK OF RHADA,** Robert Cham Gilman	$2.95
☐ 01685-5	**ALIEN ART & ARCTURUS LANDING,** Gordon R. Dickson	$2.75
☐ 73296-8	**ROCANNON'S WORLD,** Ursula K. Le Guin	$2.50
☐ 65317-0	**THE PATCHWORK GIRL,** Larry Niven	$2.75
☐ 78435-6	**THE STARS ARE OURS!,** Andre Norton	$2.50
☐ 87305-7	**THE WARLOCK IN SPITE OF HIMSELF,** Christopher Stasheff	$3.50
☐ 80698-8	**THIS IMMORTAL,** Roger Zelazny	$2.75
☐ 89854-8	**THE WITCHES OF KARRES,** James Schmitz	$2.95
☐ 78039-3	**STAR COLONY,** Keith Laumer	$3.50

Prices may be slightly higher in Canada.

Available at your local bookstore or return this form to:

ACE
THE BERKLEY PUBLISHING GROUP, Dept. B
390 Murray Hill Parkway, East Rutherford, NJ 07073

Please send me the titles checked above. I enclose ______ Include $1.00 for postage and handling if one book is ordered; 25¢ per book for two or more not to exceed $1.75. California, Illinois, New Jersey and Tennessee residents please add sales tax. Prices subject to change without notice and may be higher in Canada.

NAME____________________

ADDRESS____________________

CITY____________________ STATE/ZIP____________________

(Allow six weeks for delivery.)